W9-CCE-506

EREBOS

EREBOS

IT'S A GAME.
IT WATCHES YOU.

URSULA POZNANSKI

Translated by Judith Pattinson

 annick press
toronto + new york + vancouver

Title of the original German edition: *Erebos*
© 2010 Loewe Verlag GmbH, Bindlach
English translation © 2012 Judith Pattinson
Third printing, November 2013

Copyedited by Linda Pruessen
Designed by Monica Charny
Cover adapted from the design by Christian Keller

Annick Press Ltd.

Cataloging in Publication

Poznanski, Ursula
    Erebos : it's a game : it watches you / Ursula Poznanski ; translated by Judith Pattinson.

Translation of German book with same title.
ISBN 978-1-55451-373-4 (bound).—ISBN 978-1-55451-372-7 (pbk.)

    I. Pattinson, Judith II. Title.

PZ7.P7578Er 2012   j833'.92   C2011-907622-5

Published in the U.S.A. by   *Distributed in Canada by*   *Distributed in the U.S.A. by*
Annick Press (U.S.) Ltd.   *Firefly Books Ltd.*   *Firefly Books (U.S.) Inc.*
                        50 Staples Avenue, Unit 1   *P.O. Box 1338*
                        Richmond Hill, ON   *Ellicott Station*
                        L4B 1H1   *Buffalo, NY 14205*

Printed in Canada

Also available in e-book format. Please visit www.annickpress.com/ebooks for more details.
Or scan

Visit us at: www.annickpress.com

FOR LEON ~ U.P.
TO S, T & J ~ J.P.

It always begins at night. At night I feed my plans on darkness. If there is one thing I command in abundance, it is darkness. Darkness is the ground that will nurture what I desire to grow.

I would always have chosen night over day and the basement over the garden, given the chance. It's only after sunset that the deformed creatures of my mind dare to venture from their bunkers to breathe icy air. They are waiting for me to lend their misshapen bodies a grotesque beauty. After all, a lure must be attractive so the prey only becomes aware of the hook when it sits deep in the flesh. My prey. I almost want to embrace it, without knowing it. In a way, I will do that. We will be one, in my spirit.

I have no need to seek out the darkness; it is always around me. I release it like my breath. Like the transpiration of my body. Nowadays people shun me; that is fine. They all creep around me, whispering, uneasy, fearful. They think it's the stench that keeps them at bay, but I know it's the darkness.

ONE

Ten past three already, and still no sign of Colin. Nick pounded the basketball on the asphalt, dribbling first with his right hand, then his left, then his right again, making a short, singing drone with each ground contact. He tried to keep up the rhythm. Twenty more times—if Colin hadn't arrived by then, he'd go to practice by himself.

Five, six. It wasn't like Colin not to show without an explanation. He knew perfectly well how quick their coach was to kick someone off his team. Colin's cell wasn't on either; it was a sure bet he'd forgotten to charge the battery. Ten, eleven. But forgetting about basketball too, and his friends and his team? Eighteen. Nineteen. Twenty. No Colin. Nick sighed and shoved the ball under his arm. Well, that was okay—today, *he'd* finally score the most baskets.

Practice was brutal, and after two hours Nick was soaked in sweat. He hobbled into the shower on aching legs, stood under the stream of hot water, and closed his eyes. Colin still hadn't turned up, and Frank Bethune had gone crazy, as expected. The coach had taken all his anger out on Nick, as if it was his fault that Colin had been absent.

Nick put shampoo on his head and washed his long hair (way too long, in Bethune's opinion), then tied it back into a ponytail with a worn-out rubber band. He was the last to leave the gymnasium. It was already getting dark outside. On the way down the escalator to the Underground, he got his cell out of his bag and hit the speed dial for Colin's number. The voice mail picked up after the second ring, and Nick hung up without leaving a message.

Mom was lying on the couch, reading one of her hairdressing magazines and watching television. "There's only hot dogs tonight," she said, almost before Nick had closed the door behind him. "I'm completely worn out. Can you get me an aspirin from the kitchen?"

Nick dumped his gear in the corner, limped to the kitchen, and tossed an aspirin–vitamin C tablet in a glass of water. *Hot dogs. Great.* He was starving to death.

"Isn't Dad home?"

"No, he's going to be late. It's a colleague's birthday."

Nick scanned the fridge on the off chance that there was something more desirable than hot dogs—maybe the leftovers from yesterday's pizza—but no luck.

"What do you think about that business with Sam Lawrence?" Mom called from the living room. "Can you believe it?"

Sam Lawrence? The name sounded familiar, but he couldn't put a face to it. When he was exhausted, like today, his mother's coded messages really got on his nerves. He served up the anti-headache cocktail she'd ordered and thought about popping a tablet himself.

"Were you there when they came to get him? Vera Gillinger told me the story today while I was doing her highlights. She works at the same company as Sam's mother."

"Help me out here. Does Sam Lawrence go to my school?"

Mom eyed him with disapproval. "Of course he does. He's only two years behind you. Now he's been suspended. Didn't you hear about the whole drama?"

4

No, Nick hadn't, but his mother was happy to fill him in.

"They found weapons in his locker! Weapons! Apparently there was a gun and two switchblades. Where does a fifteen-year-old get a gun from, can you tell me that?"

"No," said Nick truthfully. He hadn't heard a thing about the drama, as his mother called it. He thought about the massacres that sometimes occurred at American schools and gave an involuntary shiver. Were there really such sick people in London? At his school? His fingers itched to ring Colin. He might know more about it. But Colin wasn't answering, the lazy bum. Just as well, maybe, because Mom was probably exaggerating again. This Sam Lawrence had probably only had a water gun and a pocketknife on him.

"It's terrible, all the things that can go wrong as children grow up," his mother said, and gave him a look that meant *my precious bunny, my little one, my baby, you wouldn't do such a thing, would you?* It was an expression that always made Nick wish he really could move in with his brother.

"Were you sick yesterday? You should have heard Bethune swearing!"

"No. I'm fine." Colin's red-rimmed eyes were fixed on the wall of the school corridor next to Nick's head.

"Are you sure? You look awful."

"Positive. I just didn't get much sleep last night." Colin glanced briefly at Nick's face before he went back to staring doggedly at the wall. Nick stifled a snort. Since when had lack of sleep mattered to Colin?

"Were you out somewhere?"

Colin shook his head and his dreadlocks swung back and forth.

"Fine. But if it's your dad again, and he's—".

"It's not my dad, okay?" Colin pushed past Nick and walked into the classroom, but he didn't sit down at his desk. Instead, he strolled over to Dan and Alex, who were standing by the window, totally absorbed in their conversation.

Dan and Alex? Nick blinked in disbelief. The two of them were so uncool that Colin called them The Freaks. Freak One, Dan, was distinctly on the short side, and you got the impression he was trying to make up for it with his exceptionally fat behind, which he loved to scratch. Freak Two, Alex, had a face that changed from couch-potato white to stop-sign red at record speed every time someone spoke to him. Every time.

Was Colin intending to audition for the role of Freak Three?

"I don't get it," Nick muttered.

"Talking to yourself?" Jamie had come up behind him, slapped him on the back, and sent his shabby bag skidding right across the classroom. He grinned at Nick, revealing the most crooked set of teeth in the entire school.

"Talking to yourself is a bad sign—one of the first symptoms of schizophrenia. Are you hearing voices as well?"

"Oh, shut up!" Nick gave Jamie a friendly shove. "It's just that Colin's getting friendly with the Freaks."

He glanced over again, and did a double take. Hang on. That wasn't getting friendly—that was groveling. Colin's face wore a pleading expression Nick had never seen before. Instinctively, he moved a couple of steps closer.

"I don't see what the problem is if you give me a few tips," he heard his friend say.

"I can't do that. Stop making a fuss—you know that perfectly well," said Dan as he crossed his arms over his flabby belly. He had a bit of egg yolk stuck on his school tie from breakfast.

"Come on, it's no big deal. And it's not like I'm going to tell anyone."

Alex was looking over at Dan uncertainly, but it was clear from Dan's face how much he was enjoying the situation.

"Forget it. You're always so full of it—you'll have to figure your way out of this yourself."

"At least—"

"No! Just shut your trap, Colin!"

Any second now. Any second, Colin would take Dan by the shoulders and send him flying across the aisle. Any second.

But Colin just lowered his head and gazed at the tips of his shoes.

Something was fishy. Nick strolled over to the window and joined the threesome.

"So, what's going on?"

"Did you want something?" Dan asked belligerently.

Nick looked back and forth from him to the other two. "Not from you," he replied. "Only from Colin."

"Are you blind? He's busy right now."

Now Nick really was speechless. Just who did this guy think he was?

"Is that so, Dan?" he said slowly. "What would he have to talk to you about? Your stamp collection maybe?"

Colin threw him a quick look, but didn't say a word. If his friend's skin hadn't been so dark, Nick would have sworn he was going red.

This couldn't be happening. Did Colin have some terrible secret that only Dan knew about? Was he blackmailing him?

"Colin," Nick said out loud, "Jamie and I are meeting some people after school at Camden Lock. Are you in?"

It was a long time before Colin answered.

"Don't know yet," he said, his gaze fixed resolutely out the window. "You should probably count me out."

Dan and Alex exchanged a meaningful look. It gave Nick an uneasy feeling in his gut.

"What's all this about?" He took his friend by the shoulder. "Colin? What's going on?"

It was that pathetic moron Dan who took Nick's hand off Colin's shoulder. "Nothing that concerns you. Nothing you would even know the first thing about."

At half past five it was standing room only on the Northern Line. On the way to the movie theater, Nick and Jamie were jammed in between tired, sweaty people. At least Nick towered over the masses and got unused air, but Jamie was hopelessly wedged in between a suit and a large-bosomed woman.

"I'm telling you, something's wrong," Nick insisted. "Dan was treating Colin like his lackey, and he treated me like a little kid. Next time I'll …" Nick paused. What would he do the next time? Thump Dan? "Next time I'll straighten him out," he finished his sentence.

Jamie shrugged one shoulder; there wasn't space to do more. "I think you're talking yourself into something," he said calmly. "Maybe Colin is hoping Dan will help him with his Spanish. He tutors lots of people."

"No. That wasn't it. You should've heard them!"

"Then perhaps he's plotting something." Jamie's grin widened, reaching right to his back teeth. "He's messing with them both, don't you get it? Like the time he convinced Alex that Michelle really liked him. That joke lasted for weeks."

Nick had to laugh despite himself. Colin had been so convincing that Alex had practically stalked the shy Michelle. Of course it all came out, and for a couple of days Alex's face stayed a bright shade of red.

"That was two years ago, when we were only just fourteen," said Nick. "And it was infantile."

The doors slid open and a few people got out, but far more

pushed in. A young woman in high heels stepped on Nick's foot with all her weight, and the pain banished all thought of Colin's strange behavior for a short while.

It was only later, when they were sitting in the dark theater and the commercials were showing on the giant screen, that the image of Colin alongside the two freaks appeared before Nick's eyes. Alex's face glowing with zeal, Dan's superior grin, Colin's embarrassment. There was no way it was about tutoring. No way.

Nick didn't see or hear from his friend for the whole weekend, and on Monday Colin only spoke to him when he had to. He always seemed to be on the go. At one recess Colin saw him pass something to Jerome. Something slim and made out of shiny plastic. Jerome looked mildly interested while Colin went on at him, gesticulating madly, before he took off again.

"Hey, Jerome." Nick went over to him, deliberately upbeat. "Tell me, what did Colin just give you?"

Jerome shrugged. "Nothing much."

"So let me see it."

For a brief moment it looked as though Jerome was going to reach into his jacket pocket, but then he changed his mind.

"Why are you so interested?"

"No reason. Just curious."

"It's nothing. Anyway, go ask Colin." With that, Jerome turned away and went over to join a few people who were discussing the latest soccer results.

Nick fetched his English books out of his locker and strolled into class, where, as always, Emily caught his eye first. She was drawing with great concentration, her head lowered. Her dark hair hung down to the paper.

He tore his eyes away and headed for Colin's desk. Freak Alex was in residence. He and Colin had their heads together, whispering.

"You can go shove it," Nick muttered grimly.

Colin wasn't at school the next day.

"They could be up to just about anything. Hey, I'm normally more suspicious than you!" Jamie slammed the door of his locker for emphasis. "Has it occurred to you that maybe Colin's got a crush on someone? That's when most people start acting crazy." Jamie rolled his eyes. "Maybe it's Gloria. Who knows? Or Brynne. No, she pines only for you, Nick, you old charmer."

Nick was only half listening, because two boys from sixth grade were standing a bit farther down the corridor, outside the toilets. Dennis and ... a boy whose name Nick just couldn't recall. At any rate, Dennis was doing some fast talking at the other boy as he shoved something under his nose: a narrow, square package. It looked very familiar. The other boy grinned and discreetly tucked the thing into his bag.

"Perhaps Colin's madly in love with sweet Emily Carver?" Jamie was still speculating. "He'd be up against it with her; that would explain his bad mood. Or maybe it's everybody's favorite—Helen!" Jamie nudged the plump girl just as she was trying to get past him into class.

Helen spun around and gave him a shove that sent him halfway across the corridor. "Get your hands off me, you jerk," she hissed. Jamie recovered quickly after the initial shock. "But of course— although with your looks it's a real struggle. I'm just crazy about pimples and blubber."

"Leave her alone," said Nick. Jamie looked astonished.

"What's with you? Have you just joined Greenpeace or something? Save the walruses and stuff?"

Nick didn't answer. Jamie's jokes at Helen's expense always left him feeling like someone was shooting firecrackers at cans of gasoline.

The Simpsons were on the television. Nick sat on the couch in his track pants and spooned lukewarm ravioli out of a can. Mom wasn't home yet. She must have been in a rush to leave and done a sloppy job with her packing again, since half the contents of her "toolkit" were lying around the living room floor. Nick had stepped on a hair roller as he'd come in and nearly fallen flat on his face. Chaotic Mom strikes again.

Dad was snoring in the bedroom and had hung his "Do not disturb—sleeping in progress" sign on the door.

The ravioli can was empty and Homer had just driven his car into a tree. Nick yawned. He'd already seen the episode, and anyway he had to go to basketball practice now. He got his things together without much enthusiasm. At least Colin might show up today, since he'd missed the last session. It wouldn't hurt to ring him and remind him. Nick tried three times, but he only got the voice mail, which Colin was well known for checking about once in a blue moon.

"Anybody who's not serious about the game shouldn't be on the team." Bethune's bellow easily filled the gym. The members of the noticeably shrunken team looked down sheepishly at their shoes. Bethune was yelling at the wrong people. After all, they'd come to practice. But there were only eight of them instead of the usual seventeen. You couldn't even make two teams with eight players, let alone think about substitutions. Colin hadn't come, of course, but Jerome was also missing. Curious.

"What's the matter with those losers? Are they all sick? Has everyone around here suddenly gone soft in the head?" Nick hoped Bethune would be hoarse soon.

"Since he's always in such a foul mood lately, I might as well stay home next time too," he muttered, and was rewarded with twenty-five push-ups.

On the way home Nick rang Colin twice, but there was no answer. Damn it.

Why was he so upset, actually? Just because Colin was acting stupid? No, he decided after thinking it over a bit. Stupid would have been okay. But by the look of it, Colin had cut Nick out of his life completely, and he done so overnight. That meant he owed Nick an explanation, at least.

When he arrived home Nick bolted into his room and flung himself into the wonky swivel chair at his desk. He booted up the computer and opened his e-mail.

From: Nick Dunmore <nick1803@aon.co.uk>
To: Colin Harris <colin.harris@hotmail.com>
Subject: You okay?
Hey dude! Are you sick? Is something wrong? Did I offend you or something? If so, I didn't mean to. And by the way, what's up with you and Dan? The guy is really weird. I thought we both agreed about that …
Are you going to be at school tomorrow? If there's a problem, we should talk about it.
CU
Nick

He clicked Send, then opened his browser and entered the basketball team chat room. But no one was there, so he surfed over to deviantART. To Emily. He looked to see whether she'd put a new manga or a poem on her site. She was incredibly talented.

He found two new sketches today, which he saved on his hard disk, and a short blog entry. He hesitated before reading it. He had to overcome an invisible barrier each time he logged on to Emily's site, because he knew the contents weren't meant for him. Emily had gone to a lot of trouble to stay anonymous, but she had friends who talked.

He shook off the thought. Here, on this page, he was close to her. As if he were touching her in the dark.

Emily wrote in her blog that her head felt empty. She wished she could move to the country, away from the giant beast that was London. Her words felt like stabs to Nick. It was unthinkable that Emily would leave his city and his life. He read the entry three times before he closed the page.

Another check for e-mails: not a word from Colin. No new tweets either, not for days now. Nick sighed, thumped the mouse down on the desk somewhat harder than necessary, and shut down the machine.

Chemistry was a punishment from the gods. Nick pored over his book with increasing desperation and tried to understand the problem Mrs. Ganter had saddled them with for this lesson. If only getting a C at the end of the year would do. But if he got less than a B he could forget it—and what he really needed was an A. Medical schools didn't take chemistry duds.

He looked up. Emily was sitting in front of him, with her dark braid falling down her back. It wasn't one of those narrow, elfin backs; you could tell she was a swimmer. Her legs were long and muscular too, and—he shook his head as if to force his thoughts back to the right place. Damn it. How many moles did 19 grams of CH_4 have again?

All too soon, the bell rang for the end of the lesson. Nick was one of the last to hand in his work, and he was convinced that Mrs. Ganter wouldn't be pleased. Emily had already gone. Nick automatically looked around for her and spotted her a little farther down the hallway. She was talking to Rashid, whose enormous nose cast a beak-like shadow on the wall. Nick sauntered a few paces closer, pretending to look for something in his backpack.

"You're not allowed to tell anyone, got it?"

Rashid was holding something out to Emily—a flat package wrapped in newspaper. Square again. "It's really important. You'll be amazed—it's the coolest thing."

The skepticism in Emily's voice spoke volumes. "I don't have time for this stuff."

Nick stood off to one side, earnestly studying the chess club notice board.

"No time? Whatever! Here, just try it!"

A sidelong glance told Nick that Rashid was holding out his newspaper package to Emily, but she wasn't taking it. She took a step backward, shook her head, and walked away. "Give it to someone else," she called over her shoulder to Rashid.

Yes, give it to me, Nick thought. What on earth was going on? How come no one was talking about these packages that were being passed round? And why the hell didn't he have one yet? It wasn't like him to be left out.

Nick watched Rashid, who had stuffed the package in his jacket pocket and was now shuffling down the corridor. He was homing in on Brynne, who was just saying good-bye to a friend. He started to speak to her, pulled the package out of his pocket—

"What are you gazing at, dreamy?" Someone slapped Nick hard on the back. Jamie. "How was the gruesome chemistry class?"

"Gruesome," Nick muttered. "What did you expect?"

"I just wanted to hear it firsthand."

A few people had stopped in the middle of the hallway and were blocking Brynne and Rashid from sight. Nick went closer, but the transaction was already over. Rashid was walking away with his typical dragging gait, and Brynne had disappeared around the corner.

"Damn it," Nick swore.

"What?"

"Something's going on. The other day Colin passed something to Jerome and they were making a big mystery about it. Now Rashid's just tried the same thing with Emily, but she told him to get lost, so he started chatting up Brynne." He ran his hand over his tied-back hair. "I missed the rest. I'd really like to know what it's about."

"CDs," Jamie said matter-of-factly. "Pirate copies of something, I'd say. Twice today I've seen someone dragging someone else into a corner and palming a CD off on them. It's no big deal, is it?"

CDs—that would explain the format of Rashid's parcel. A pirate copy going from hand to hand—maybe banned music. Then it would hardly be surprising that Emily didn't want to have anything to do with it. Yes, that was possible. The thought appeased Nick's curiosity a bit, but … if it *was* a CD, why wasn't anyone talking about it? The last time a banned movie had done the rounds it had been the number-one topic. All the people who'd seen it held forth with wild descriptions, and everyone else listened enviously.

This was different. As if it was a game of Telephone, as if a secret password was going around. The insiders were keeping quiet, whispering, staying apart.

Nick was pensive as he made his way to his English class. The lesson that followed was pretty boring. He dwelt on his own thoughts, and a full twenty minutes passed before he noticed that not only was Colin missing today, but Jerome too.

Warm autumn light fell on Nick's desk through his bedroom window, turning the chaos of books, notepads, and crumpled work sheets golden. The English essay Nick had been brooding over for the last half hour was only three sentences long; the margin, on the other hand, was strewn with doodled lightning, curls, and wavy lines. Damn, he just couldn't concentrate. His thoughts kept straying.

In the kitchen he heard Mom clattering around and changing the radio station. Whitney Houston was singing "I Will Always Love You." Really, what had he done to deserve that?

He chucked his pen down on the desk, jumped up, and slammed the door. It couldn't go on like this—somehow, he had to get one of those CDs. How come he didn't have one? And how come no one was telling him anything about them? He tried ringing Colin yet again, but there was still no answer—what a surprise. Nick left a few rude words on his voice mail, scrolled down till he got to Jerome's number, and pressed Dial. It rang once, twice, three times, and then the call was disconnected.

Damn it all. Nick took a deep breath. This was ridiculous. He was all set to hurl his cell into his backpack, but paused suddenly. An idea was teasing him, light as a feather. He had Emily's number saved on there as well.

Before he could think of too many reasons why he shouldn't do it, he had already dialed. Again he heard the phone ring once, twice—

"Hello?"

"Emily? Um, it's me, Nick. I just wanted to ask you something … It's about today … at school …" He shut his eyes tight, took a breath.

"About the chemistry test?"

"No. Uh … I happened to see Rashid trying to give you something. Can you tell me what it was?"

A few seconds passed before Emily answered. "Why?"

"Well, I … it's because … A few people have been acting strange lately. Lots of people have been away from school, too. Have you noticed?" Amazing—he was finally managing to speak in whole sentences. "And I think it has something to do with these things that have been going around … That's why … you know … I'd like to find out what it's all about."

"I don't know either."

"Didn't Rashid tell you anything about it?"

"No, he was interrogating me. He wanted to know stuff about my family that's none of his business—whether they give me lots of freedom, that sort of thing." She gave a short, joyless laugh. "And whether I've got my own computer."

"Aha." Nick was trying in vain to make heads or tails of this information. "Did he say *why* you needed the computer?"

"No. He just said he was going to give me something unbelievable—better than anything I'd ever seen before, and that I had to look at it *alone*." Emily's tone of voice made it obvious what she thought of this. "He was pretty pushy and frantic. But of course you saw that yourself."

The last sentence sounded snippy. Nick could feel himself going red.

"Yes, I did." There was a pause.

"What do *you* think it is?" Emily asked finally.

"No idea. I'll ask Colin when he comes back to school. Or … I mean, maybe you have a better idea?" There was silence down the phone line.

Then Emily said, "No. To be honest, I hadn't really thought that much about it."

Before his next sentence, Nick took a deep breath. "Would you like to know if I find out something? Only if it's interesting, obviously."

"Yes, sure," Emily said. "Of course. But I have to go now. I have stuff to do."

The conversation made Nick's day. Colin could go screw himself. He had made a connection with Emily, and he had an excuse for getting in touch with her again soon. As soon as he knew more.

Colin was back. He leaned against his locker as if nothing had happened, flashed Nick a grin, and tossed his dreadlocks back over his shoulder. "I had the worst sore throat of my life," he said, and gestured at his scarf. "Couldn't even talk on the phone. I was totally hoarse."

Nick tried to figure out from Colin's face whether he was lying, but he couldn't. "Bethune really went ballistic. I've never seen him that mad," he said. "Why didn't you tell him you were sick?"

"Oh, I felt really lousy. The old man shouldn't go on about it."

Nick chose his next words with care. "What you had must be really infectious. The day before yesterday there were only eight of us at practice. That's an absolute all-time low."

If Colin was surprised, he didn't show it. "So? It can happen."

"Jerome was away too."

Only the tiniest twitch of his eyelids betrayed Colin's sudden interest. Straightaway, Nick dug deeper.

"Speaking of Jerome, tell me, what was it you gave him recently?"

Colin's answer came like a shot. "The new Linkin Park album. Sorry, I know I should copy it for you too. I'll get it to you tomorrow, okay?" And with that he slammed his locker door shut, shoved his math books under his arm, and looked questioningly at Nick. "So, can we go?"

With a start Nick shook off the daze Colin's explanation had put him in. Linkin Park! Had he just been imagining all that conspiracy stuff? What if his imagination was playing tricks on him, and a flu outbreak was the real reason for the missing students? On closer consideration, there weren't really that many. Nick did a quick head count as he went into class just ahead of the bell. Freak Two was missing, as well as Jerome, Helen, and the quiet kid, Greg. The others were lolling about, half asleep, in their seats.

Okay, thought Nick. So I've just been imagining it all. There's no big secret—only Linkin Park. He grinned at himself, and turned to Colin to describe Bethune's rant. But Colin wasn't paying attention to him. He was staring intently at Dan, who was standing in his usual place by the window. Dan held up four fingers, half concealed by his belly. Colin raised his eyebrows in acknowledgment and stuck out three fingers.

Nick's gaze darted back and forth between the two, but before he had a chance to ask Colin what was behind the hand signals, Mr. Fornary entered the classroom. For an hour he bombarded them with such hideous math problems that Nick had no time to think about such basic things as three or four outstretched fingers.

TWO

Some money and an unbelievably long shopping list were lying on the kitchen table. Mom was conducting a large-scale perming operation; it seemed autumn had awakened a desire for freshly curled hair among the women of London. Nick studied the list with a frown. Endless frozen pizza, plus lasagna, fish fingers, and instant noodles. It didn't look as though Mom was planning to do any cooking in the next little while. He sighed, grabbed three of the big shopping bags, and set off for the supermarket. On the way he started thinking about Dan's hand signals again, and Colin's silent response to them. Was he seeing things? Jamie certainly thought so. "You're bored, man," had been his diagnosis. "You need a hobby or a girlfriend. Should I fix you a date with Emily?"

Nick bagged a shopping trolley, shaking off thoughts of school. Jamie was right; it was better to worry about real problems. For example, the question of how on earth he was supposed to lug home the twenty bottles of water on Mom's shopping list.

When Nick walked into school the next day, the air was buzzing with excitement. Lots more students were gathered in the entrance hall than usual. They were mostly standing around in small groups, whispering, murmuring. Their conversations were all blending into a tapestry of sound; Nick couldn't make out any individual words.

Everyone's attention was focused on two policemen who were heading purposefully for the corridor leading to the principal's office.

Nick spotted Jamie in a corner not far from the stairs, caught up in an intense conversation with Freak Alex, Rashid, and a boy whose name Nick couldn't quite think of. Oh yes, his name was Adrian. He was thirteen and didn't usually hang out with older students. But Nick recognized him because his family story had done the rounds when he'd come to the school two years ago. Apparently Adrian's father had hanged himself.

"Hey!" Jamie beckoned Nick over with a sweeping gesture. "It's all happening today!"

"What are the cops doing here?"

Jamie showed his teeth. "There are criminals among us, no-good scoundrels and thieves. Nine computers have been stolen—brand-new laptops that were all bought for IT lessons. They're checking the computer room for evidence."

Adrian nodded. "It was actually locked," he put in shyly. "Mr. Garth told the policeman that, I heard exac—"

"Shut your trap, kid," Alex droned. His pimples were glowing—probably the excitement, Nick surmised.

He felt an urgent need to thump this idiot. He turned to Adrian so he didn't have to look at him anymore. "Did they break the door open?"

"No, that's the thing," he said eagerly. "Someone unlocked it. The key must have been stolen, but Mr. Garth said that's impossible; all three are where they belong. He even carries one of them around with him—"

"Nick?" A soft voice interrupted Adrian's flood of words, and a hand with clear-varnished fingernails came to rest lightly on Nick's shoulder. Emily, Nick thought for a split second, but corrected himself immediately. Emily didn't wear three rings on each finger, and she didn't smell so ... oriental.

He turned his head and looked into Brynne's light-blue eyes. Like puddles of water. "Nicky, can you ... I mean, could we just quickly—in private ..."

Alex smirked and licked his lips, making Nick want to clench his fists.

"Okay," he said to Brynne. "But only a few minutes."

The irritated tone of his voice obviously didn't worry her—or if it did she hid it well. She was pretty, admittedly, but basically she talked too much and he found her empty-headed. Now she was prancing along ahead of him, swaying her hips and steering him to the staircase that led down to the gym. There wasn't a soul there at that time of day.

"So, Nick," she whispered. "I'd really like to give you something. It's incredibly awesome, honest." She reached into her tote bag, paused a moment, and drew her hand out again.

Nick was staring at the bag. He had an inkling what this was going to be about, and he almost smiled at Brynne.

"But first I still need to ask you something." She pushed a strand of hair off her forehead, slowly and deliberately.

If you want to do yourself a favor, don't ask me what I think of you.

"Go for it."

"Have you got a computer? That's important. In your room."

Finally, this was it! "Yes, I do."

She nodded her satisfaction.

"Um, and do your parents go poking around in your stuff a lot?"

"My parents aren't weird."

"Oh. Good." She thought for a moment, her forehead creasing with the effort. "Hang on, there was something else. Exactly." She came another step closer and lifted her face to him. Her bubblegum breath and the musky perfume made a bizarre combination. "You're not allowed to show it to anyone. Otherwise it won't work. You have to put it away right now, and don't tell anyone that I gave it to you. Promise?"

Well, that was stupid. He pulled a face. "Why?"

"They're the rules," Brynne said insistently. "If you don't promise, I can't give it to you."

Nick sighed loudly. "Whatever. I promise."

"But don't forget, okay? Otherwise I'll be in trouble." She held her hand out to him; he took it. Felt how hot it was. Hot and slightly damp.

"Good," Brynne whispered. "I'm relying on you." She sent him a look that Nick feared was supposed to be seductive, and then she pulled a slim, square plastic case out of her bag and thrust it into his hand.

"Have fun," she breathed, and left.

He didn't watch her go. All his attention was focused on the object in his hand: a plain DVD in an unlabeled case. Nick opened it, full of curiosity.

Linkin Park—yeah, right.

It was pretty dim on the staircase, and he shifted the DVD into the light to get a better look at what was written on it in Brynne's playful script.

It was just a single word, a word that was completely unknown to Nick: Erebos.

For the rest of the day Jamie teased him about Brynne—that was typical Jamie and not a problem. The real problem was fighting the temptation to get the DVD out of his jacket pocket and show his friend. But he decided against it every time. He'd take a look at it himself first—see what it was, and why everyone was acting so mysterious. But there was no way he was going to take part in all the cloak-and-dagger stuff that had gotten on his own nerves so much.

The school day dragged on agonizingly. Nick barely managed to concentrate—his attention kept drifting back to the insignificant-looking object in his jacket. He could feel it through three layers of clothing. Its weight, its edges.

"Are you feeling sick?" Jamie asked him just before the bell rang for the last class.

"No, why?"

"Because you're making a weird face."

"I'm just thinking about something."

The corners of Jamie's mouth twisted mockingly. "Let me guess. Brynne. Did you ask her out?"

Nick would never be able to understand how Jamie could think he liked someone like Brynne. But today he couldn't be bothered arguing.

"What if I did?" he retorted, and ignored Jamie's I-just-knew-it expression.

"Then hopefully I'll hear all about it tomorrow."

"Yeah. I mean, I don't know. Maybe."

THREE

The apartment was empty and freezing cold when Nick got home. Mom must have been in a hurry again and forgotten to close the windows. He kept his jacket on, closed all the windows, and turned the radiator up in his room as far as it would go. Only then did he fish the case out of his jacket and open it: Erebos.

Nick grimaced. Erebos. Wasn't there some Greek god named Eros? Maybe it was a matchmaking program? That would be just like Brynne. Well, she could get that right out of her head.

He turned on the computer, and while the thing was booting up he fetched himself a blanket from the living room, which he draped around his shoulders.

He had at least four uninterrupted hours in front of him. Out of habit—and to heighten the suspense even more—he retrieved his e-mails first (three ads, four bits of spam, and an embittered message from Bethune, threatening dire consequences to anyone who skipped one more practice).

Just when he was about to open his Facebook page, Finn instant-messaged him.

"Hey, little bro. How's it going?"

Nick couldn't help but smile.

"Fine."

"How's Mom?"

"Busy, but okay. How about you?"

"Ditto. Business is doing nicely."

Nick refrained from inquiring more closely.

"Nicky, listen. The shirt I promised you ... You know the one?"

And how Nick knew. A shirt from Hell Froze Over, the best band in the world, according to Finn.

"What about it?"

"I can't get your size—not in the next four weeks. You're just too tall, baby brother. The Fan shop people have ordered it, but it's going to take time. Okay?"

For a moment Nick couldn't figure out why he was so disappointed—probably because he had a picture in his mind of him and Finn at the concert in two weeks' time, both in the HFO shirt with the ice-blue devil's skull, bellowing out "Down the Line."

"Not a big deal," Nick typed.

"I'll keep on it, promise. Are you going to drop round again?"

"Of course."

"Did you know I miss you, baby brother?"

"Yeah, I miss you too." And how. But he wasn't going to rub Finn's nose in it—otherwise he'd start feeling guilty.

After the chat with his brother Nick looked in on Emily's drawings, but nothing on deviantART had changed since yesterday. That figures, he thought, feeling a bit ashamed, and went off-line again.

An inner voice was telling him it would be better to write his English essay before he devoted himself to Erebos. It didn't stand a chance. Nick's curiosity was too strong. He opened the case, made a face at the sight of Brynne's handwriting, and pushed the DVD into the drive. It took a few seconds before a window opened.

It wasn't a movie or music. It was a game. The Install window showed a grim picture. A ruined tower could be seen in the

26

background, surrounded by scorched countryside. In front of the tower a sword was planted in the bare earth, a piece of red cloth tied to its handle. It fluttered in the wind, like a last memento of life in a dead world. Above that, the word Erebos arched, also all in red.

There were butterflies in Nick's stomach. He turned the volume up, but there was no music, just a deep rumbling like an approaching storm. Nick hovered the cursor over the Install button with the vague feeling he had forgotten something … of course, the virus scan. He checked out the files on the DVD with two different programs and breathed a sigh of relief when both gave the all-clear.

The blue Install bar inched forward in agonizing slow motion. In tiny tiny steps. Several times it seemed as though the computer had crashed—nothing was happening. Nick tried moving the mouse back and forth—at least the cursor still responded, but only slowly, jerkily. Nick shifted around on his chair impatiently. Twenty-five percent—oh, come on. He might as well go to the kitchen and get himself something to drink.

When he came back some minutes later, the install was at 31 percent. He dropped onto the chair, cursing, and rubbed his eyes. What a pain.

After what felt like an hour 100 percent was finally done. Nick was already inwardly rejoicing when the screen went black. Stayed black.

Nothing helped. Not banging on the case, not all his key sequences or his angry outburst. The screen displayed nothing but unrelenting darkness.

Just as Nick was about to give up and press the Reset button, though, something did actually happen. Red letters were emerging out of the dark, words that pulsed as if a concealed heart were supplying them with blood and life.

Enter.

Or turn back.

This is Erebos.

Finally! Tingling with anticipation, Nick chose "Enter."

The screen went black again—what else was new?—for several seconds. Nick leaned back in his chair. Hopefully the game wouldn't stay so slow. His computer couldn't be at fault—it was pretty much state of the art. His processor and graphics card were lightning fast and all the games he had ran without a problem.

Gradually the screen lightened up, revealing a very realistic-looking forest clearing, with the moon above. A figure was standing in the middle in a ragged shirt and threadbare pants. No weapon, just a stick in his hand. Presumably that was supposed to be his game character. As a test Nick clicked a spot to the right; the figure leapt up and moved to exactly the spot he'd selected. Okay, the controls were idiot-proof, and he would have the rest figured out before long. It wasn't exactly his first game.

Right then. But—which way should he go? There was no path, no indication. A map, maybe? Nick tried to call up an inventory or a game menu, but there was nothing. No indication of quests or goals, no other characters in sight. Just a red bar for the life meter and a blue one underneath. Presumably it indicated stamina. Nick tried various key sequences that had worked in other games, but they didn't do anything here.

The thing was probably rotten with programming errors, he thought grumpily. Just to test, he clicked directly on his shabbily equipped character. The word "Nameless" appeared over his head.

"Even better," muttered Nick. "The mysterious Nameless." He got his ragged character to walk straight ahead for a bit first, then left, and finally right. There wasn't even a hint as to which way to turn. Every direction seemed to be wrong, and there was no one around he could ask.

"It's incredibly awesome," he mimicked Brynne's voice in his thoughts. On the other hand … Colin seemed to be keen on the game too. And Colin was no fool.

Nick decided to make his character walk straight ahead. He figured that was what he would do if he were lost. Keep on going in one direction. He'd eventually come across something or other, and every forest had to end somewhere. He focused his attention on Nameless, who was skilfully dodging trees and pushing aside the branches in his path with his stick. You could clearly hear each step the game character took: the undergrowth snapped, dead leaves rustled. When the character climbed over a rocky outcrop, small pebbles came loose and rolled down.

On the far side of the outcrop the ground was wetter. Nameless wasn't making such good progress anymore, since his feet kept sinking up to his ankles. Nick was impressed. It was all extremely realistic—when he was wading through the mud it even made a sucking noise.

As Nameless struggled on, he began to pant. The blue bar had shrunk to one third of its length, so Nick allowed him a rest at the next rock. His character rested his hands on his thighs and bent his head down, obviously trying to get his breath back again.

There must be a stream somewhere around. Nick heard it gurgling and cut short the rest stop. He sent Nameless a short distance to the right, where he did in fact find a small watercourse. His character stopped short of it, still panting.

"Come on, drink." He pressed the down arrow on his keyboard and was delighted when Nameless actually bent down, cupped his hand, and drank water from the stream.

After that he made better headway. The ground was no longer damp, and the trees weren't as dense either. But he still didn't have any points of reference, and gradually Nick began to worry that his go-straight-ahead strategy was a dead loss. If only he had an overview—maybe a map or ...

Overview! Nick grinned. Let's see ... maybe his virtual self could not only bend down, but climb as well! He chose a massive tree with low-hanging branches, positioned the figure in front of it and pressed the up arrow.

Nameless carefully put his stick aside and pulled himself up on the branches. He stopped as soon as Nick released the arrow key, and started climbing when it was pressed again. Nick sent him up as high as possible—until the branches became too weak and he nearly slipped. Only when the figure had a secure foothold did Nick venture a look around. The view was fantastic.

The full moon was high in the sky and shone its light on a seemingly endless greenish-silver sea of trees. To the left the foothills of a mountain chain could be made out; the plains stretched out to the right. The landscape straight ahead was hilly; dots the size of pinpricks on a few of the hills revealed settlements.

See, Nick thought triumphantly. Straight ahead *is* the right way. He had his finger over the down arrow when a gleam of warm yellow light between the trees caught his eye. That looked promising. If he corrected his route a bit to the left, he would come across the source of the light within a few minutes. Maybe it was a house? Impatiently he sent his figure back down to the ground, where it took up its stick again and walked on. Nick chewed on his bottom lip, hoping he had fixed the direction correctly in his memory.

It wasn't long before he thought he could make out the first weak glimmers of light between the tree trunks. Almost at the same moment he struck an obstacle: a crevice that was much too wide for his character to jump over. Damn! The crevice stretched a long way in both directions and disappeared somewhere in the darkness between the trees. To go around it would cost Nameless a lot of time—and possibly his bearings.

Nick discovered the fallen tree only after he'd spent some time cursing. If he could get it into the right position ... The space bar was the key to success. Nick's game character dragged, pulled, and pushed the trunk in every direction the cursor specified. By the time the tree was lying across the crevice, Nameless was gasping for breath and the red life meter wasn't looking so good.

With the greatest care Nick made his screen hero balance on top of the tree trunk, which turned out to be a very precarious bridge. On his fifth step it rolled slightly to the right, and Nick only just got his figure to safety with a daring jump.

The beam of light was stronger now than before, and it was flickering. Straight in front of Nick was a tiny forest clearing, in the middle of which a fire was burning. A solitary man sat before it and stared into the flames. Nick released the mouse button, and Nameless immediately stood still.

The man by the fire didn't move. He wasn't carrying any weapons Nick could see, but that didn't mean anything. His long black cloak indicated that he might be a mage. Perhaps clicking on the character would reveal more. Nick's cursor had hardly touched the man when he lifted his head, revealing a narrow face with a very small mouth. A dialogue box opened at the same time at the bottom of the screen.

"Greetings, Nameless One." The silver-gray letters stood out against the black background. "You were quick."

Nick walked his figure closer, but the man didn't react; he only pushed the pieces of burning wood in his campfire together with

31

a long branch. Nick was disappointed. He'd finally encountered someone in this forsaken forest, and all he'd come out with was a meager greeting.

It was only when Nick spotted the blinking cursor on the next line in the window that he understood he was expected to answer.

"And greetings to you too," he typed.

The man in the black cloak nodded. "It was a good idea to climb up the tree. Not many nameless travelers have been so resourceful. You are a great hope for Erebos."

"Thanks," Nick typed in.

"Do you think you would like to proceed?" The man's small mouth twisted into an expectant smile.

Nick wanted to type in "Sure!" but his counterpart wasn't finished yet.

"Only if you ally yourself with Erebos will you be any match for this game. That is something you should know."

"All right," Nick answered.

The man lowered his head and poked his stick deep in the embers of his campfire. Sparks flew up. That looks real, Nick thought; it looks so real.

He waited, but the man didn't make any move to continue the conversation. Presumably he'd already reeled off all the text assigned to him.

Curious to see whether he would react if addressed, Nick typed "p#434<3xxq0jolk-<fi0e8r" into the text field. That seemed to amuse his virtual companion. He raised his head briefly and smiled at Nick.

He's looking me straight in the eye, Nick thought, and tried to suppress his disquiet. He's looking at me as if he can see right through the screen.

32

Finally the man turned back to his fire.

Only now did Nick notice that music had started to play softly—an intricate but insistent melody that was oddly moving.

"Who are you?" he typed.

Naturally, there was no answer. The man simply put his head to one side, as if he needed to think. However, a few seconds later, to Nick's stupefaction, words appeared in the dialogue window.

"I am a dead man." Again the character looked at Nick, as if he wanted to test the effect of his words. "Just a dead man. You, on the other hand, are alive. Nameless, admittedly, but not for much longer. Soon you will be able to choose a name, a vocation, and a new life."

Nick's fingers slipped from the keyboard. That was unusual—no, it was scary. The game had given a meaningful answer to a random question.

Maybe it was a coincidence.

"Dead people don't usually talk," he typed, and leaned back in his chair. It wasn't a question as much as an objection. The man by the fire wouldn't have any appropriate response programmed in for that.

"You're right. That's the power of Erebos." The man held the stick into the flames and drew it out again, alight.

Even though he didn't want to admit it, Nick felt a bit alarmed. He checked whether his computer really was off-line, or whether someone was playing a joke on him. No. There was no Internet connection. The branch in the dead man's hands was blazing fiercely, and the reflections danced in his eyes.

Nick's fingers typed the next sentence almost by themselves. "What is it like to be dead?"

The man laughed—a gasping, panting laugh. "You are the first Nameless One to ask me that!" He threw the rest of his stick into the fire.

"Lonely. Or full of ghosts. Who can say?" He brushed his hand across his forehead. "If I asked you what it's like to be alive, how would you answer? Just as everyone lives his own life, so too everyone has his own death." As if wanting to underline his words, the dead man pulled the hood of his cloak over his head, throwing a shadow over his eyes and nose—only his small mouth remained visible. "No doubt you will find out one day."

No doubt. Nick wiped his damp palms on his pants. He wasn't feeling comfortable with this subject anymore.

"How must I proceed?" he typed, and realized to his own amusement that he was expecting a meaningful answer.

"Do you really want to proceed? I'm warning you: it's not a good idea."

"Of course I want to."

"Then turn to the left and follow the stream until you come to a ravine. Walk through it. After that ... you will take it from there." The dead man withdrew deeper into his cloak.

"And watch out for the messenger with the yellow eyes."

FOUR

Along the stream, always keeping its throaty gurgle on the left, at an easy trot that didn't strain the stamina meter too much. Stamina, Nick was discovering, wasn't his nameless character's strong suit. After the smallest climb he started gasping and had to take a rest and wait until the bar on the bottom right-hand edge of the screen started glowing blue again. Then he could go on. Clambering over stones, jumping over obstacles, keeping an eye out for the ravine. Nowhere was there a messenger with yellow eyes to be seen.

The land to the right and left of the stream was gradually rising, and the dark forest floor was giving way to stony ground. Again and again the loose rock slowed down Nameless's progress; more than once it caused him to fall. It was only when the terrain on both sides was twice as high as his figure that Nick realized he was already in the middle of the gorge. Moreover, he noticed that he was not alone. There was rustling in the dry undergrowth to the right and left of the path, and then—as if at an inaudible command—small toad-like creatures leaped out and fell upon him. Their feet were equipped not just with webbing but also with claws, with which they did considerable damage to Nick's Nameless. A few awful seconds passed before he remembered the staff his figure was holding in his hands and began to defend himself.

Two of the toads took flight. One died at Nameless's feet from a well-aimed blow with the stick.

"Strike," Nick murmured.

But there was one last toad clinging to Nameless's left leg and a bloodstain was spreading beneath its claws. Alarmed, Nick noticed that the red life meter was only a bit over half full. He struck at the space bar, which made Nameless jump but didn't impress the toad.

Finally, the Escape key achieved the desired result. Nameless executed a lightning-quick turn, shook the toad creature off, and, at Nick's command, finished him off with the stick.

In the meantime, however, Nameless's life meter had plummeted to way under half. Nick made sure there were no more attackers in sight, then moused over the toad's carcass, whereupon the information "4 meat units" appeared.

"That's something at least," he grumbled. He put his exhausted figure back on its feet and got it to collect the meat before he continued on through the gorge. He was on his guard, and had his stick at the ready to clobber any clawed toad that turned up. But no further adversaries appeared. Instead, a noise became audible in the background, rhythmic and rebounding off the gorge walls. Hoofbeats.

He made Nameless slow down and creep very cautiously around the next curve, but it concealed nothing more than further precipitous rock walls and even more gravel. A few moments later the hoofbeats broke off. Nick sent Nameless skirting along the rock wall, past thorny bushes as tall as a man. On further, until another rock wall rose up in front of him. Halfway up the wall—but still way above Nameless's head—a wide overhang jutted into the gorge. At the back was the narrow mouth of a cave, and in front of it, on a giant armored horse, sat a gaunt figure in a gray tunic, beckoning to both Nick and Nameless. Nick noticed the figure's bald, pointy head and excessively long, bony fingers only in passing. All his attention was focused on the man's pale-yellow eyes.

"You have been very skillful."

"Thank you."

"However, your life force isn't looking too good."

"I know."

"You need to be mindful of that in the future."

The messenger's businesslike way of speaking stood in bizarre contrast to his gruesome appearance.

"It is time for you to be named," he continued. "Time for the first rite." With an unhurried gesture he indicated the cave behind him. "I wish you luck, and the right decisions. We will meet again." He turned his horse around and charged off.

Nick waited until the hoofbeats had faded away before he took his figure over to the rock face. Steep steps, cut into the stone, led to the plateau. "Time for the first rite." Why were his hands damp again? He left-clicked on the darkness of the cave entrance. Nameless marched up to it and disappeared. The next moment the screen went black.

Darkness. Silence. Nick shifted around on his chair. Why was it taking so long? He hammered at the keyboard a bit just in case, which achieved precisely nothing.

"Oh, come on," he said, and banged the computer case. "Don't flake out."

The darkness continued and Nick's nervousness increased. He could take the DVD out of the drive and put it in again, or he could press the Reset button, but that was risky. That might mean he'd have to start again right from the beginning. Or the game mightn't start again at all.

Suddenly there was a sound. *Tap tap.* A knocking sound,

like a heartbeat. Nick opened the top drawer of his desk, got out headphones, and plugged them into his computer. Now he heard the noise more clearly, and he thought he could make out something else in the background too. Horns that were playing a succession of short notes. It reminded him of a hunting call. It sounded full of promise. As if, in the background, the game were in full swing without him. He turned the volume up, feeling annoyed that he hadn't thought of the headphones earlier. Perhaps he had missed important information— warnings or hints. Perhaps he hadn't caught the one crucial tip about how to keep the game running!

More from impatience than in the hope that it would speed things up, Nick hammered on the Enter key.

The tapping stopped, and the red letters once again started to emerge out of the black background.

"This is Erebos. Who are you?"

Nick made a quick decision. He would choose the same name he had already used in a few other computer games.

"I am Gargoyle."

"Tell me your name."

"Gargoyle!"

"Your real name."

Nick was stunned. What on earth for? Fine. He would supply a first name and a last name so he could finally move on.

"Simon White."

The name was there, red on black, and for a few seconds nothing happened. The cursor just blinked.

"I said—your real name."

Nick stared at the screen in disbelief. Once more he had the feeling that someone was staring back. He took a deep breath and had another go.

"Thomas Martinson."

There was no response for a moment, and then the game answered. "Thomas Martinson is incorrect. If you wish to play, tell me your name."

There was no sensible explanation for this. Maybe it was a software glitch and the game wouldn't accept any name whatsoever. The writing disappeared; just the blinking red cursor remained. Suddenly, Nick worried the program might have crashed, or shut down at the third incorrect answer, like a cell after three incorrect PIN entries.

"Nick Dunmore," he typed, half expecting that the truth would be rejected as well.

Instead, the program whispered his own name in his ear. "Nick Dunmore. NickDunmore. Nick. Dunmore." Over and over again, the words were passed around like a chant from one whispering being to another—the welcome greeting of an invisible community. The feeling of being watched was scary, and Nick groped for the headphones to take them out of his ears. But the writing was disappearing already, just like the voices, and an enticing melody had begun to play—a promise of mystery and adventure.

"Welcome, Nick. Welcome to the world of *Erebos*. Before you start playing, acquaint yourself with the rules. If you don't like them, you can end the game at any time. Okay?"

Nick stared at the screen. The game had caught him lying. Knew what his real name was. Now it seemed it was impatiently awaiting an answer—the cursor was blinking faster and faster.

"Yes," Nick typed, with the vague feeling that everything would go dark again if he took too long. He would think it over later. Later.

"Good. Here is the first rule. You have only one chance to play *Erebos*. If you waste it, it's over. If your character dies, it's over. If you break the rules, it's over. Okay?"

"Okay."

"The second rule. When you play, make sure you are alone. Never mention your real name in the game. Never mention the name of your player character outside the game."

How come? Nick wondered. Then he remembered that even Brynne, who had never been troubled by self-restraint, hadn't blabbed anything about *Erebos* to him. "It's incredibly awesome"—that had been it.

"Okay."

"Good. The third rule. The content of the game is secret. Do not speak to anyone about it, especially not to people who are not registered. You can converse with players around the fires while you are playing. Don't pass information on to your friends or your family. Don't post information on the Internet."

As if you'd ever find out, thought Nick, and typed "Okay."

"The fourth rule. Keep the DVD somewhere safe. You need it to start the game. Don't copy it under any circumstances, unless the messenger asks that you do so."

"Okay."

Nick had hardly pressed the Enter key when the sun rose. Or at least it felt like that. The blackness of the screen yielded to a delicate red, which soon changed to tones of yellow and gold. Nick's Nameless appeared as a shadow slowly taking shape, just like his surroundings—a forest clearing flooded in sunlight, in which long grass was growing and through which a beaten track wound its way. The track led to a mossy tower with a door that was hanging by just one hinge. On a rocky outcrop a little to the left sat Nameless, with his eyes closed and his face turned to the sun. Nick felt a twinge of envy, as if he was looking at really nice holiday pics. For a brief moment he thought he could smell the resin of the forest trees and the flowering herbs all around the tower. Crickets chirped, and the wind moved gently through the grass.

The crooked door of the tower banged loudly against the wall and the figure, still in ragged clothes, stretched and stood up. Put a hand up to his face and removed it like a mask. Behind it was nothing but smooth skin, bare as an eggshell.

Another gust of wind unfurled the flag that was mounted at the top of the tower. It showed a faded number one.

This was the way to the first level, Nick assumed, and steered his figure, whose missing face unsettled him more than he wanted to admit, to the tower.

Inside everything is quiet, even the wind is silent, the gate is no longer banging. Among straw and scattered bones stand wooden chests with rusty clasps. Copper tablets on the wall gleam; there are words carved into them. The first word is always the same: Choose.

He inspects the tablets in order.

"Choose a gender," the first demands.

Without hesitating he chooses the man. Only after his decision does it occur to him that playing as a woman could have a certain appeal. Doesn't matter—it's too late.

"Choose a race," he reads on the tablet.

Here he pauses longer. Rejects the barbarian and the vampire, although he slips their bodies on to try them out; at the sight of the barbarian's shoulder muscles, gleaming with oil, he grimaces. He considers the lizard man for a few minutes—his body scales shimmer so seductively, changing color in different lights. The human is an option too, but it's not worth considering. Too everyday. Too weak. Dwarf, werewolf, cat-person, or dark elf—these last four options are all tempting. He tries the dwarf body on: small, gnarled, and strong.

Not bad. The small stature appeals to him; the crooked legs and the pinched facial expression less so.

In the end he decides on the dark elf. Medium height at most, but agile, elegant, and mysterious. His decision is acknowledged.

"Choose your appearance," the third copper tablet demands.

He wants to resemble his real self as little as possible. So: short blond hair that sticks up from his head in spikes, a pointy nose, and narrow gray eyes. He contemplates his newly created character, who no longer bears any resemblance to Nameless. Carefully he chooses clothing: a gold-green doublet, dark pants, bucket-top boots. A leather cap that will be better protection than nothing, although he would have preferred a helmet. Unfortunately, they're not available to dark elves.

He does some more work on his facial features—enlarges the eyes and the distance between the mouth and nose. Raises the eyebrows. Makes the cheekbones more pronounced and thinks that now he looks like a king's lost son.

"Choose a vocation," it says on the fourth tablet.

Assassin, bard, mage, hunter, scout, guard, knight, thief. Ample choice. The advantages of each and every class are explained to him. He learns that werewolves make particularly good mages, whereas vampires have a talent as assassins, and also as thieves. Dark elves, too, make good thieves.

He hesitates. And jumps when the hinges of the door suddenly creak. It swings open and someone enters the tower. A deformed shadow. A gnome with a hunched back and crooked legs, a red, bulbous nose, and a dark-blue growth on his neck. He hobbles closer, sits astride one of the chests, and licks his lips.

"Another dark elf, well, well. A popular species, so it seems."

"Really?" That doesn't please the new-fledged dark elf. He doesn't want to be one of many.

"Indeed. Have you already decided on a profession?"

He looks at the list. "Maybe a thief or a guard. Or possibly a knight."

"How about the mage? They're powerful, they've got the gift of magic."

He mulls over this possibility briefly before he rules it out. He's not in the mood for witchcraft; he's in the mood for sword fighting.

"No, not a mage. A knight."

"Are you sure?"

Yes, he is. Knight sounds noble, almost like a prince. "Knight," he affirms.

"Choose your abilities," the fifth tablet demands. Underneath, there is an overwhelmingly long list of characteristics. He chooses far sight. Strength, stamina, and the ability to blend into the surroundings. Lighting fires. Speed. Jumping power.

He is cautious because he doesn't know how many skills he is entitled to in total. Even now every decision means that other options are lost to him. When he selects "slight healing power," the "death curse" option ceases to exist. For "shield of strength," "ironskin" disappears.

After ten choices it's suddenly over. The writing dissolves into nothing, right when he's convinced himself he can keep going forever.

"You will soon miss some of the things you have spurned," says the gnome, and smiles.

"Maybe."

He wonders what this ugly fellow is doing here—he would actually prefer to be alone. The sixth tablet is waiting.

"Choose your weapons." A massive chest opens underneath the tablet. Swords, spears, shields, several morningstars of various sizes. A few hideous-looking barbed blades, whips armed with claws, spiked clubs.

"Would you like some advice?" the gnome asks.

So you can put one over on me?

"No thank you."

He wants to find the right things himself. Carefully draws one sword after the other out of the box and lines them up along the wall. Tests how well he can lift each of them, how quickly he can swing them. Finally, his choice falls on a longsword with a narrow blade and a handle swathed in dark red. It buzzes seductively when he swings it through the air.

The shields are all made of wood and don't inspire much confidence. Besides, the bigger they are, the heavier—they'll slow him down. So he chooses the smallest shield he can find: round, with a bronze boss and blue serpentine patterns painted on the wood.

"You can strap it onto your back," the gnome advises him and swings his crooked legs energetically, as if the chest is a horse he wants to spur on.

The dark elf doesn't deign to answer. He approaches the seventh and final tablet.

"Choose your name."

Nick is somewhat surprised to remember that not so long ago he intended to call himself Gargoyle. Suddenly that doesn't suit him at all. He looks around to see whether another chest might not open, containing scrolls with suggested names. No. He's on his own.

Almost, anyway, since the gnome has his own idea of helpful advice.

"Elfintail, Elfinsnail, Darklingdithersmall! Pointy-Ear, Weaselfear! Or more classical? Momos, Eris, Ker, or Ponos, not forgetting Moros! Something there you like?"

Briefly he toys with the idea of taking his sword and doing away with the gnome. It can't be all that hard, and then he would have some peace in which to think. But the thought of shrill gnomish death cries and pools of blood on the tower floor deter him.

Classical, he thinks, is a good cue. Something classically Roman. Marius. No, Sarius.

He doesn't hesitate—the name is exactly what he was looking for. He enters it.

"Sarius, Ssssarius, Sa-ri-us," the name is murmured through the tower. "Welcome, Sarius."

"Sarius? How boring! The boring ones die quickly. Did you know that, Sarius?"

The gnome hops off the chest and as a parting gesture pokes his pointy green tongue out. It reaches down to his belly.

Sarius follows him out of the tower, out into the sun-drenched meadow. Only when he sees the gnome limp off into the forest and disappear does he strap the shield to his back.

FIVE

They're glowing red like small round rubies between the furry leaves. Sarius has reached the forest's edge and he's spotted berries growing in the shade of the trees. Can he pick them? He can. To his delight he notices that he now has an inventory he can use, in which everything belonging to him is stored. In it he finds the toad meat he captured when he was still Nameless. Apart from that the inventory is empty, so he has enough room for berries.

He straightens up when he hears a rustling. Are there snakes in the bushes? A quick look around—no, there's nothing there. No one. Sarius turns his attention back to the berries. Surely they must be growing here just so he can stock up on food supplies.

The attack comes so suddenly that it's all over by the time Sarius gets scared. Two men have jumped on him from behind and are holding him down on the ground. One pushes his knee into Sarius's back, bends his arms back, and ties them up. The other one holds a dagger under his chin; the weapon has dried blood and hair stuck to it.

Sarius can't defend himself. He tries but only manages to thrash about. He can't stop the bigger of the two men from picking him up and throwing him over his shoulder like a sack. So this was it, then. Sarius, dark elf and knight, is caught by surprise while picking berries and kidnapped. If he's unlucky, the man with the dagger will do him in. Then the adventure will be over. Damn it, damn it, damn it! It's typical. He's probably the only one stupid enough to have been caught by surprise like that.

They march through the forest and the bloke who's carrying Sarius keeps adjusting his load on his shoulder. Presumably he doesn't want to inadvertently lose him. But then he does after all. At the edge of an embankment he stops dead, throws Sarius off, and dispatches him down the slope with a kick.

Sarius goes head over heels twice before he comes to rest on level ground.

There are three figures waiting for him down here, all of whom bear a strong resemblance to his kidnappers: torn clothing, skin covered in dirt, scars. One is missing an eye; another has a hunched back. Only their weapons look well cared for.

"Where did you find this one?" the hunchback asks.

"Crawling around on the ground near the tower. Caught him easier than a little dove."

The hunchback takes Sarius by the collar and sits him upright against a tree trunk.

"Do you think he'll be any use as a robber? Should we keep him?"

The one-eyed character cocks his head to the side, as if he could examine Sarius better that way.

"No," he declares. "This one's not suitable. He doesn't fit in with us, you can tell just by his clothing. He's one of those who are moving against Ortolan."

"Then we'll slit his throat!" the hunchback says enthusiastically.

Sarius would really like to say something in reply—for example, that he doesn't know anyone called Ortolan and would gladly join a robber band any time, if it means he's allowed to live. But he can't. Before, with the gnome, he could speak, but now he's mute. Things are happening around him, as if he's in a movie.

The third man, whose face is hidden in the shadow of a big hat, hasn't said anything yet. Now he takes a step closer.

"No. We won't kill him. This one isn't like the others."

He bends down and reaches into Sarius's pockets.

"Take a look. No poisons, no ransom letters. No gold. We can let this one go again."

"Just like that?" The hunchback is disappointed. "Where's the sense in that? It's no fun!"

The man with the broad-brimmed hat silences him with a gesture.

"I wish someone like him was going to win in the end. The thing is though, Sarius, I'm afraid it's mostly the little ones who lose. Like you. But I'm not going to lay a hand on any of them."

He chases off the hunchback, who's just trying to get at the contents of Sarius's pockets.

"I'll give you a piece of advice instead. Do you know what would be best for you?"

No, Sarius would like to say, if he could. But his opposite number isn't expecting an answer. He grabs Sarius by the arms and unties him.

"You should leave Erebos. Go and never come back. Pretend you've never been here. Forget this world. Will you do that?"

Of course not, Sarius thinks. He tries to make out a face under the man's hat brim, but he can't even see eyes.

"If you want to leave Erebos, then run away. Run back to the tower. Now."

Is this a chance to escape, or a trap? Will *Erebos* lock him out if he takes the opportunity to escape from his kidnappers? He stands there undecided. The robber takes that for an answer.

"I thought as much," he sighs. "Then listen to me carefully. No one here is your friend—even if it looks that way to you. No one will help you, because everyone wants to get into the Inner Circle and only a very few make it."

Sarius doesn't understand a word. What Inner Circle?

"At the end only a few will be left—those who have been chosen for the battle against Ortolan. Killing the monster, finding the treasure—it's not something everyone is cut out for."

It's hard to tell whether the robber is joking or not, and Sarius can't inquire.

"Don't divulge any of what I'm telling you to the others. Don't rob yourself of your advantage—it's small enough. See to it that you find wish crystals. They will make your life easier. Your life, do you understand?"

"Don't tell him anything about wish crystals," the hunchback interjects.

"Why not? He will need them. You know what, Sarius? Wish crystals are one of Erebos's biggest secrets. They serve you. They make the impossible possible. They make your dreams come true."

"If the messenger finds out all the stuff you've been whispering in the lad's ear, he'll make you shorter by a head," the hunchback snarls.

"He'll do that in any case, if he gets his hands on me."

The man with the big hat—he's the leader, he must be the leader, Sarius thinks—turns his back and walks away slowly through the undergrowth. The others follow him; the one-eyed character hurriedly spits in Sarius's face before he goes. Apart from that, no one's harmed a hair on his head. But then no one's let on what he's supposed to do now, either.

He climbs back up the embankment and tries to get his bearings. The tower would have to be to the left, and he doesn't want to go back there. He looks around, searching for a reference point. Suddenly, he can hear a faint clanking sound coming from the direction where the forest is darkest.

Sarius follows the sound, which is becoming clearer with every step. Iron striking iron, and wood, and stone. Mixed with a dull roar and something like cries of pain. A battle. He keeps following the noise with a hot feeling inside that could be curiosity or fear, or both, until he's suddenly faced with an obstacle. He slows his pace and stares nonplussed at a black wall that runs right across the countryside and towers high above the trees. The black shines like tar.

Climbing over the wall is out of the question—he needs to find a way through. Or find the far end of this giant obstacle. He turns to the left—the battle sounds are coming from that direction—and runs till his stamina is used up. No gateway. Enraged, he strikes at the wall with his sword. Black splinters off. Underneath, two letters become visible: er.

Convinced that a message is hidden under the shiny coating, he keeps working away at the wall with his sword, hoping he won't break the weapon in the process. But it works. The sword holds up, and a few minutes later Sarius has exposed a whole sentence. An ambiguous sentence: Enter the net. He hears himself laugh.

I'm a good catch, he thinks, and opens a connection to the Internet.

At that moment a part of the wall collapses, revealing a battle scene. Two barbarians, a cat-woman, a werewolf, several dwarves, three vampires, and two dark elves are doing battle with four incredibly ugly trolls. One of them already has three arrows sticking out of his throat. They must be from the cat-woman—she's the only one with a bow. Another troll swings a lump of rock and hurls it at the werewolf, who takes a giant leap to safety. Two of the dwarves are working with their axes on the third troll's legs, aided by the larger of the two barbarians, who is flailing the troll's back with his cudgel.

A bluish oval floats above them all. It sparkles like a giant polished sapphire, turning slowly on its own axis. Is it a wish crystal, Sarius wonders? If so, it would be too big to take with him. And besides, the others—the fighters—are completely ignoring the thing. They're far too busy.

Sarius feels for the sword at his belt. It suddenly appears so harmless and small. He should probably hurl himself into the fray, but he doesn't dare. One of the dwarves has blood dripping from under his helmet, running into his beard, and pooling there. And yet he is fighting like a madman.

Sarius takes a deep breath. No injury he suffers here can cause him real pain, no matter how genuine it looks. He takes a step forward, and then immediately reverses it to work out his tactics. The fourth troll is free now. He has a vampire woman cornered; she's trying to keep him and his morningstar at bay with her long, narrow blade. He hasn't noticed Sarius yet.

So, the troll it will be. Sarius pulls his shield off his back in a rapid motion, raises his weapon, and throws himself into the battle—briefly embarrassed that he actually has to summon the courage to do it.

His sword bounces off the troll's skin the same as it did off the wall, only this time it doesn't make the slightest impact. The troll bellows derisively. He grabs the vampire with one hand and flings her into the air. She flails her arms, loses her sword, and hits the ground with an ugly sound. The red sash she's wearing around her waist goes dark gray—only a tiny bit of flashing red remains. The life meter, Sarius realizes. It's only now he notices that all those fighting have something red on their outfits—mostly a chest harness or a belt like his own.

The vampire must be aware of the danger she's in. She crawls into the bushes. Her left leg is twisted out, and she's dragging it behind her like a dead weight.

The troll, however, has lost interest in her; he turns around.

Measures Sarius with dull eyes. Stringy saliva is hanging from his jaws. Sarius shrinks back instinctively. He hasn't forgotten the rule: "You have only one chance to play *Erebos*." It can't be over this soon, no way.

The troll is plodding toward him—Sarius circles him lightning fast. He has to hit a sensitive spot, and quickly. He aims for the tendons on the lizard-like legs. Strikes.

The troll bellows again, this time in pain. Dark red blood, thick as syrup, wells up out of a wound. Stunned, Sarius stares at the broad trickle and notices too late that his opponent's morningstar is spinning above him. He sees it whistling down and instinctively dives to the side.

The spiky ball scrapes his shoulder. An ear-splitting squealing rings out, stabbing his brain like a red-hot poker.

He falls. The troll is looming above, looking down at him with stone-gray eyes. Raising his weapon again. Sarius thinks he hears the sound of thunder through the painful buzzing and squealing. The troll staggers, revealing the larger of the two barbarians, who has appeared from nowhere and is trying to smash the troll's backbone with his cudgel.

The blow hits home, and Sarius's monstrous opponent rears up. Another blow and the troll sinks to his knees. He isn't bellowing anymore, just moaning. One last blow to the back of his neck and he lies still.

Sarius wants to sit up, but with every attempt the horrible droning in his head grows louder. It's better if he moves slowly. He glances down and sees that his belt is still about one-quarter red. Will it recover if he stays still? He lies flat on the grass. What he's seen is enough to reassure him for now. The battle is almost over. Two trolls are already lying on the ground, defeated. A third has fled. The fourth is still upright, but the two barbarians are really laying into him, and now everyone who can still walk is joining in the bloodbath. The troll stands no chance against these numbers. He sways, lashes out again, and falls toward the ground, a dwarf ax buried deep between his shoulder blades.

"Victory," breathes a disembodied voice.

The next moment, the messenger with yellow eyes appears at the forest's edge and reins in his horse.

"You have conquered the oval," he says, and touches the shimmering blue disk still hovering above the battlefield with his bony fingers. "You shall be rewarded. BloodWork!"

BloodWork? Sarius doesn't get it, until the large barbarian steps forward and bows before the messenger.

"You made the most valuable contribution in the battle. Your reward is a helmet with a strength of twenty-seven. It will protect you against poison, lightning strikes, and fever spells."

The messenger hands BloodWork a golden helmet with rams' horns.

The barbarian hurriedly removes his simple steel cap from his head and pulls on the gleaming head armor, which makes him look even bigger.

"Keskorian," the messenger continues, and the somewhat shorter barbarian steps forward.

"You gave your best, but you hesitate too often. Nevertheless you have earned your reward. Take BloodWork's old helmet—it is better than yours."

Keskorian does what is asked of him.

"Sarius!" the messenger calls.

Already? This astonishes him. After all, he had joined the battle late, and hadn't exactly covered himself in glory. It's an incredible effort to get to his feet. Every movement makes the excruciating hum louder. His shoulder is bleeding again, and he sees that a tiny bit more of his belt is turning black.

"It was your first battle, and you showed courage instead of contenting yourself with the role of observer. I value courage. Therefore you will receive what you need most: healing. Take this potion. It will restore your health and increase your resistance. To your health, friend."

Sarius sees the glowing sunshine-yellow bottle floating before him. He reaches for it and opens it. Drinks.

The traces of blood on his shoulder dissolve into nothing; his belt gleams with fresh new red. And what a relief: the buzzing that started when he was injured disappears, replaced by the music he had heard in the tower. The melody promises everything. Everything he has ever wanted.

"Sapujapu, you held out until the end for the first time. For you I have a new ax."

The dwarf steps forward, takes the ax, and quickly withdraws. There's a pause. The messenger eyes them, one after the other, as if he needs to think.

"Golor!" He calls up a vampire and rewards him with twenty-five minutes of invisibility. The second vampire—LaCor—is granted fifty gold coins.

Nurax, the werewolf, receives praise and a breastplate; the cat-woman, Samira, receives a twice-hardened sword. The messenger dispenses gifts, small and large, to all: a shield with rune spells to the second dwarf; a poison dagger to Vulcanos, the dark elf. Another dark elf and the wounded vampire lying in the grass next to Sarius are the only ones remaining.

"Lelant, you stayed on the sidelines. You were cowardly, and only struck three ineffectual blows with your sword. You will receive no reward. I am considering depriving you of a level." Lelant, the dark elf with the black hair, is standing on the edge of the clearing, half concealed by the trees among which he took refuge during the battle.

Sarius feels a curious satisfaction. He wasn't especially good, he knows that, but someone else was worse.

"I caution you, Lelant. Fear does not pay. In the next battle I will expect your resolution, your strength, your whole heart."

Finally, the messenger turns to the vampire woman. "Jaquina. You are as good as dead. If I leave you here, you will die in a few moments. If that is what you want, lie down to die. If not, follow me."

The vampire struggles to her knees. The blood flowing from her wounds is black. She crawls toward the messenger. As soon as she's near enough, he lifts her onto his horse.

"You have permission to light a fire," he says, then pulls his mount around hard and gallops away into the darkness.

Sapujapu is the quickest. All it takes is three pieces of wood and a red spark that shoots from his fingers, and a campfire is blazing in the middle of the clearing. Everyone immediately gathers around it.

"What do you think he wants from Jaquina?" Nurax asks.

"The usual," Keskorian says. "Who cares? When she comes back, she'll be Level Four."

"*If* she comes back," Sapujapu replies.

One after another they sit down. Sarius feels out of place, uncomfortable, even though it's quite possible that he knows some of the people here, maybe all of them.

"We've got a newbie. Sarius," Samira declares.

"Yeah, another stupid dark elf," jeers BloodWork, who's been silent till now. "They're like flies."

"At least they're better-looking than barbarians," Lelant chimes in.

"Just shut your mouth, loser," BloodWork growls. Lelant really does stop talking, and BloodWork turns his attention back to Sarius. "Why a dark elf? Didn't they tell you we've already got too many?"

"What's it to you anyway?"

"I bet you're a scout as well." The barbarian keeps griping at him. "Like your whole clan."

"I'm a knight. Do you mind if I call you Bloody?"

The vampire LaCor finds that marvelously funny. "A knight! You're going to bite the dust faster than you can blink. Especially if you come up with nicknames for BloodWork."

What's wrong with a knight? Sarius would like to ask, but doesn't want to show himself up any further. Maybe the gnome would have told him, if Sarius had been able to bring himself to ask his advice.

"Where is the messenger taking Jaquina?" he inquires instead.

"You'll find that out yourself later." Sapujapu gives him the brush-off.

"Why don't you just tell me?"

"Not allowed. You're Level One."

Level One—of course. He's only just started and the others must be dying to see him fall flat on his face. Or bite the dust, as LaCor put it with such relish. He takes a closer look at Sapujapu and Samira, but can't find any indication of their levels. How does everyone know that he's a beginner?

Meanwhile, another topic is being discussed. "Does anyone know where Drizzel is today?"

"No idea. Perhaps he's running with another group."

"Or he's got a solo quest."

"I think he has to do stuff outside right now."

Interest in Sarius has evaporated. He's pleased about that, wonders who Drizzel is, and what it means to have stuff to do "outside." Even if he doesn't understand everything people are talking about, he is gradually sinking into the embrace of the beguiling music, which flows languorously through him like honey. It makes him heavy and contented, as if the next victorious battle already lay behind him.

Even in this state, he notices that Samira has been standing near him the whole time. He keeps getting the impression that she wants to talk to him, but doesn't know how to go about it.

"Blood's old helmet is crap," Keskorian gripes. "I would have preferred a decent sword."

"Well, you should have really gone for it just now then," Nurax says.

"Yeah, yeah. Great, go ahead and enjoy your breastplate. But I'm telling you, it's crap too. How many defense points does it have? Fourteen? You might as well just fold yourself a paper one."

"As if," Nurax splutters. "Fourteen is definitely going to repel orc arrows—which nearly cost me all my life energy yesterday!"

Sarius is keeping out of the discussion. He's just realized that his doublet might be a problem. Only five points of defense. Hopefully there aren't any orcs nearby.

"Take a look at Blood's harness! How many points of strength does it have?"

BloodWork takes his time to answer.

"Fifty-two."

"I really don't want to know what he had to do for that," Sapujapu says.

"And it's none of your bloody business," declares the giant barbarian.

"Careful! The messenger already cautioned someone about swearing. A dwarf. I was there."

As Nurax speaks, a new figure comes up to the fire—a dark

she-elf with a longbow hanging over her shoulder. The black, tightly woven plait reminds Sarius of Emily. He calls up her name: Arwen's Child.

"Hi, AC," Nurax greets her. "Wow, you're a Three now! Congratulations!"

"Thanks. It wasn't a big deal. No battle today?"

"We're just finished," Keskorian informs her. "Four trolls—it was no joke. Do you know everyone here? You know BloodWork at any rate, don't you?"

"Yes, we searched for a stone changeling together. Hi, Blood."

The barbarian doesn't answer, just stands unmoving, staring into the fire.

"But I don't know LaCor—or Sapujapu or Samira or Sarius either. Are names starting with 'Sa' in right now?"

"Better than being nicked from *Lord of the Rings*," Sarius responds and earns applause from Samira.

Arwen's Child takes a few steps toward Sarius. "You're a One," she states.

"Yes."

"Any more Ones here?"

"I've already seen four of them today," Lelant says. Sarius has almost forgotten about the quiet dark elf, possibly due to the fact that Lelant has taken the "dark" bit very literally. His clothing is all black, and his hair as well. His face is the color of coffee with hardly any milk. Nick can't help wondering whether Colin might be concealed behind the figure.

"There are more and more Ones. Including Sarius, there have been two dark elves, a werewolf, and a human today."

"Humans are totally rare," Sapujapu states.

"And unnecessary," BloodWork adds.

Sarius would really like to ask a few questions during the ensuing lull in the conversation. Like whether the spinning oval stone above them is a wish crystal. And what he should do in order to survive the next battle without any decent equipment. Or how he can get to the next level quickly. Because by the look of it, he's nothing as a One.

"Have you got any good tips you can give me?" he finally asks.

"Yes. Try to stay alive," Nurax says. "It's best to stay close to a very strong character while you're still so weak yourself."

"But keep away from me," BloodWork says. "Bloody elves."

"How come you're giving the newbie tips?" Keskorian grumbles. "We're opponents, remember? Do you want to get the final reward yourself, or have him get it? For all I care, all the newbies can snuff it. There's too many of us already anyway."

"That's right," says BloodWork.

"Too many for what?" Sarius enquires.

Nurax stays silent following such a sharp reprimand, but Sapujapu ignores the barbarian's objections.

"Too many for the last fight—the big battle against Ortolan. Only five or six people can be in on it, and then they're going to win ... a sort of jackpot. You wouldn't believe how keen BloodWork is to do it."

The barbarian in question swings his fist and knocks Sapujapu to the ground with one blow. Part of the dwarf's belt goes black.

"Shut your faces, you idiots. You haven't got a clue."

With this, BloodWork moves away from the fire. He goes and stands at the forest's edge, and Keskorian follows him the way a dog follows its master.

"Can he do that? Is that allowed?" Nurax asks agitatedly as Sapujapu struggles to his feet again.

"Apparently. Otherwise one of the messenger's gnomes would have turned up long since and cautioned him. They're always here straightaway if there's the teensiest breach of the rules," Arwen's Child declares.

At exactly that moment something hops out of the bushes. A gnome with orange-colored skin. Apart from that, he looks just like the one from the tower.

Ah, Sarius thinks. Trouble for the muscleman.

But the gnome doesn't say a word about BloodWork's roughness.

"A message from your master. Grave robbers are looting the sacred sites. Kill them and their loot is yours. Get started! Separate, spread out, speed up!"

He extinguishes the fire with a wave of his hand and disappears into the bushes.

What do we do now? Sarius wants to ask, but now the fire is gone, and with it the opportunity to converse. Do the others know where the sacred sites are located? Obviously not, since they are running in various directions. BloodWork is bashing his way through the thicket to the left with Keskorian following close behind. LaCor and Arwen's Child run to the right; Nurax, Golor, and Lelant have also dashed off after the barbarians.

Sarius sticks by Sapujapu's side so he won't be left behind on his own. The dwarf is not exactly nimble, and at least speed is one of the attributes Sarius chose for himself. The way ahead leads into the forest, where they are greeted by darkness and threatening noises. Sarius manages to stay close to Sapujapu, but his stamina is dwindling with every step. Is it because he's a One? Sapujapu is trotting along slowly but steadily. If Sarius needs to rest, the dwarf won't wait. Why would he?

The stamina bar is getting shorter and shorter. Sarius is gasping, breathing fast, and beginning to stumble. If he could just take a quick breather … but Sapujapu is pulling away from him like a steam engine, and Sarius doesn't want to stay behind by himself. So he runs, always keeping an eye on the blue bar. Then there's a climb—it's not long or steep, but it's too much. He simply falls to the ground. His chest rises and falls in rapid, desperate breaths as Sapujapu disappears through the undergrowth.

The sound of fighting can already be heard some distance away. Well, well—BloodWork had been on the right track, and now he was probably living up to his name. Sarius gets slowly to his feet. He's swaying, and weary to the bone. At least he knows the direction now, and he can follow the battle sounds. If some grave robbers are left for him, that's fine. If not, it can't be helped.

Sarius continues on cautiously, bent on conserving his energy. It's not long before the black wall appears on his left again. He stops for a rest and taps around on the shiny stones with his sword, hoping to once again uncover a bit of text that will help him along.

The black crumbles, but behind it there's just more black. Sarius follows the wall a short distance into the forest and tries again. Black stone, nothing more. In frustration he hacks away at a tree for a change, whereupon something flies up out of the treetop and takes off with a muffled beat of its wings.

The bird is evidently not the only creature he has startled. Something's rustling in the thick bushes only a few paces away. And sparkling.

Sarius still has his sword in his hand. He runs up to the thicket and strikes at it blindly. There's a scream and a tinkling sound, and the next minute, a goblin-like creature jumps out, with skin as yellow and creased as parchment. He's bleeding heavily from his shoulder, but still won't let go of the sparkling things clutched tightly in his arms. It's a grave robber, for sure. The knowledge spurs Sarius on. He runs after the creature, lunges at it with the sword, but misses.

The goblin loses something that looks like a silver bowl, and runs on. With the next thrust of his sword Sarius inflicts a deep wound in the grave robber's leg. He cries out and falls, without letting go of his loot. Sarius doesn't hesitate. Twice he thrusts at the goblin, until he's not—

"Nick?"

—moving anymore. His arms slide to his side, a helmet rolls to the ground, a short dagger, an—

"Nick? What's that you're playing?"

"Tell you later."

—an amulet, and something that looks like leg armor. Hurriedly, Sarius gathers up everything, but there was something else too, there was—

"Is it new? Where did you get it?"

"Hang on, okay? Give me another minute!"

Exactly. The bowl that the robber lost. Where's it gone? Rolled away. Blast it. It has to be somewhere. He pokes around in the bushes.

"Have you eaten already?"

"Can't you just leave me in peace for just one minute, for god's sake?"

There's the bowl. It's rolled against a tree trunk. A sudden noise behind him is shockingly loud. He spins around.

But it was just his mother slamming the door.

SIX

Out in the kitchen water was bubbling away in a large pot. Mom had her elbows propped on the counter and was leafing through a women's magazine. She'd almost drained her glass of red wine.

"Sorry about before." Nick inspected his mother from behind. She'd had two orange streaks put in her black hair. They were new, and he didn't like them.

"There's pasta with sauce from a jar," she said without looking up. "That's all I can manage today." She yawned. "What was that I interrupted so terribly?"

"Oh, nothing. Sorry, I behaved like an idiot."

"Yes, you did." Mom turned around and smiled. "I guess it was just getting exciting?"

"Yeah." He felt obliged to explain a bit more. "I just got it today. It's an adventure game. Not bad at all."

His mother tipped the pasta into the boiling water. "I hope you've done some stuff for school as well."

"Of course," said Nick, and hid his bad conscience behind a smile.

Eleven p.m. The buzzing of the light bulb over the desk. A car parking on a nearby street. And exhausted quiet in an apartment that smelled of tomato sauce with garlic powder.

After dinner Nick had managed to quickly scrawl his English

essay. Now he switched the computer on and started up *Erebos*. For several minutes he waited tensely for the black of the screen to vanish and the red writing to appear. He only noticed that he'd been holding his breath when the game started and he breathed a sigh of relief.

The nighttime landscape is unfamiliar to him. This isn't the forest where he slayed the grave robber, nor the place where he battled the troll. It's heathland, and slightly hilly. There are trees here and there.

The grave robber! It occurs to Sarius that he hasn't yet checked whether he's retained all his captured treasure. He takes a look in his baggage and breathes a sigh of relief. The bowl is there, the helmet, the dagger, the amulet. He wants to put the helmet on straightaway, but annoyingly it doesn't work.

He walks a bit farther through the rustling heath grasses, once more without a destination in mind. He longs for the music, or the sound of voices, but there is only the night wind's light breeze, and ... a distant rushing sound. This time he doesn't hesitate to follow the sound and it's not long before he comes upon a river that glows a completely unnatural light-blue in the night landscape. Sarius looks out for a fire. Without a fire there's no conversation, and without conversation there's no information. He could kindle one himself— after all, he has the ability. Perhaps the fire would attract someone, and they could talk. Sarius is almost bursting with unspoken questions. Then he remembers that Sapujapu only lit his fire after the messenger with the yellow eyes granted permission. Better not to break any rules.

He walks for a long time, until he thinks he sees a gleam of light some distance away. His initial delight is mingled with trepidation. Alone in the forest, Sarius feels very vulnerable to attack. He draws his sword but immediately feels ridiculous and puts it away again. Each step seems to betray him with its loudness.

When the fire finally comes into view, he sighs with relief. The scene appears peaceful. There are only two figures standing in the flickering light: a dark elf and a vampire. He doesn't know either one.

"Is there room for one more?"

The dark elf, whose name is Xohoo, shifts aside.

"Of course. Even for a One. What's your name—Sarius? Shit, that reminds me of Latin."

"Don't mention the world outside Erebos," the vampire, whose name is Drizzel, warns him. "Otherwise you'll get your knuckles rapped so hard by the messenger that you won't be able to hold a sword anymore."

Drizzel. Sarius has come across the name before, he just can't recall where. He looks at the glowing blue river thoughtfully.

"Can I ask you guys something?"

Drizzel bares his fangs.

"Sure. And then we'll think about whether we give you an answer."

Sarius considers carefully before he voices his question.

"How come you can see that I'm a One, but I can't see your level?"

It's Xohoo who answers.

"Because we're more advanced than you. You only ever see the levels of those weaker than you."

"So when I'm a Two, I'll be able to recognize the Ones?"

"Exactly."

Finally—some useful information. Feeling pleased, Sarius follows up with his next question.

"How do I become a Two? I can't see my points anywhere, or a progress bar."

"That's not how it works. You have to wait until he thinks that you're ready."

"He?"

No further answer is forthcoming from Xohoo, which pleases Drizzel.

"Good, you're finally shutting up. You know perfectly well that we're not supposed to blab so much."

"But I haven't given any secrets away," Xohoo defends himself.

Steps can be heard in the background, and a barbarian joins the small group. She's much taller than Sarius, but her tiny skirt is ludicrously short over her muscle-packed thighs. She carries an enormous ax over her shoulder. Sarius checks out her name: Tyrania. That's very telling.

"It's dead boring around here," she states in greeting. "Don't we have a quest?"

"No. Can't you tell?" Xohoo answers.

"Okay, anyone feel like a duel?" Tyrania takes the ax off her shoulder and whips it around in a semicircle, barely missing Sarius's chest.

Drizzel has nothing but scorn for her suggestion.

"Are you stupid? We're not in the city here, let alone in the Arena! Anyway—me fight a duel with a barbarian? I'd have to be as thick in the head as you guys. Go start a fight with one of those other muscle-bound idiots. One of these days you'll figure out that life energy doesn't grow on—"

The attack comes without any warning, from the water. Even worse, it's the water itself that attacks. The glowing blue torrents make towering waves and form themselves into gigantic female figures that leap onto the riverbank with one bound and submerge everything in surreal blue light.

Sarius tugs his sword out of its sheath, although he really feels like running away. It's water, he thinks, just water.

Unfortunately, his blows go through his attackers' bodies as if through water too. There are seven of them, and they outnumber Tyrania, Drizzel, and him terrifyingly. Xohoo must have slipped away; he's nowhere to be seen.

Sarius tackles the smallest of the water women. He swings his sword against her body, searching for a vulnerable spot, but there's nothing there. His weapon just glides through her leg, stomach, and chest with a soft smacking sound. For the life of him he can't reach any higher.

Well, at least we're not hurting each other, he thinks. Not I her, nor she me.

The next moment the woman takes a big step toward Sarius— no, *onto Sarius*—and stays there. Her leg imprisons him like a shining blue column of water.

The agonizing buzzing in his ears is there again, drilling into his brain. He sees the life draining from him and realizes he is drowning.

A step to the side, another. The giant follows him effortlessly. He's trapped in her and can't get out, no matter how wildly he thrashes with his sword. Tyrania is in trouble too, though Drizzel has reached the safety of the trees. Sarius sees him disappear in the darkness, wants to follow him, but can't. The five attackers who haven't found opponents glide back into the torrents. He just manages to take that in as the tone in his head reaches an unbearable level.

The fire spell, thinks Sarius. Fire against water. He has to figure out how it's done; he's never lit a fire before. It will have to be quick though—his belt is almost completely black. Quickly!

There's a sizzle, and steam rises. The water giant gives him up with a sound like storm-tossed waves, flows apart, and reunites with the river. A few moments later the same thing happens with Tyrania. She copied my trick, Sarius thinks, a bit miffed.

To his annoyance she's in much better shape than he is; she's barely lost half her energy. As for himself, Sarius sees only now how little life is left in him. He hardly dares to move. In any case, he's paralyzed by the high tone that set in with his injury, just like last time. He's probably going to croak when the last bit of red disappears from his belt. But that mustn't happen, it can't. So he's not going to take any risks now. Sarius stands motionless. Who knows: even stumbling might be enough to send him to the hereafter.

But it seems that he's not going to be granted any time to recuperate. Someone is approaching—Sarius can hear hoofbeats. Is it just one person, or several? Now he does move, drawing his sword and walking slowly to the forest's edge. Drizzel had vanished in there just moments before, and Sarius plans to follow suit. He can't afford courage anymore. Damn! Why couldn't he have been more careful? He's already standing in the shadow of the trees when he recognizes the messenger's armored horse. He hears a whispering voice.

"Sarius. Come out."

The messenger brings his mount to a halt right on the spot where the fire had been. The yellow eyes under the hood look directly at Sarius's hiding place.

He steps out reluctantly from the protection of the trees.

"The water sisters inflicted considerable damage on you both," the messenger states.

"Yes."

"You faced them on your own, you and Tyrania?"

"Yes."

"Were there no other fighters nearby?"

Sarius says nothing, but Tyrania is eager to inform him.

"Drizzel and Xohoo were here, but they took off."

"Indeed?" The messenger looks toward the forest into which the two had escaped. Then he reaches into his cloak and removes a small pouch.

"For you, Tyrania. There are forty-four gold coins. Use them to buy better equipment from the next trader. If you hike downriver from here you will soon come to a small settlement. Don't be concerned about the lateness of the hour. Wake the trader and inform him that I have sent you. Seek the red-leaved herbs on the riverbank for your health."

Tyrania hurriedly grabs the bag of gold and sets off.

"Sarius?" The messenger bends down from the saddle and reaches out a bony hand. "It's looking bad for you. You should come with me."

The messenger's gesture fills Sarius with disquiet. Somehow it looks … greedy.

"Are you going to help me?" he asks, and regrets his words immediately. They sound childish and silly.

"We will help each other," the messenger replies and reaches his hand out a little farther still.

Since he doesn't have a choice, and since this time around the messenger is obviously not planning to just hand over a bottle of healing potion, Sarius grasps the proffered bony fingers. The messenger pulls him onto the horse, which snorts, turns on its hindquarters, and dashes away.

Sarius is already feeling better. The noise has disappeared and the beautiful music is playing again. It tells him that everything is going to be fine. Nothing can happen to him. He is the hero in this epic tale. Everything here revolves around him. He is glad that he faced up to the battle with the seven water giants, and didn't run away like Drizzel and Xohoo.

The messenger's horse is swift. They gallop along a forest path that slowly climbs upward. On the right, large rocks, dark as dirty water, soon replace the trees. The messenger guides his animal away from the path, toward the rocks. As they approach, Sarius spots symbols carved into the rock—messages he cannot decipher. They stop in front of a cave and dismount. The messenger points to the mouth of the cave, and Sarius enters. The anxiety that he had to overcome when mounting the armored horse is gone, and doesn't return, even when he steps into the cave, which is as big as a cathedral, and in which every step echoes over and over.

"You fought well," the messenger says.

"Thank you. I certainly tried to."

"It is a great pity that you were wounded so seriously. You won't survive a further battle."

It's not as if Sarius doesn't know that. But the way the messenger says it makes it sound as though nothing can be done. As if Sarius is doomed. He hesitates with his response, and in the end decides to couch it as a question.

"I thought we were going to help each other?"

"Yes. That was my suggestion. I would say you're no longer a rank beginner. You should be ready for the second rite."

That's more than Sarius was expecting. After the second rite he'll be a Two, he assumes.

"I will therefore heal you and give you more strength, more stamina, and better equipment," the messenger continues. "Is that what you would wish?"

"Of course," Sarius replies.

The moment has come for the messenger's demand—the price he will have to pay for all of this. But the messenger remains silent, interlacing his overlong fingers. Waits.

"And what can I do for you?" Sarius asks, when the silence seems to last too long.

The messenger's yellow eyes light up.

"It's just a trifle, but it's important. It's an errand."

Sarius, who's been expecting to have to vanquish a monster or fight a dragon, doesn't know whether to be pleased or sorry.

"I'd be happy to do it."

"I'm glad. These are your instructions: Go to St. Andrew's Church in Totteridge tomorrow morning. An ancient yew stands there. Very close by you will find a box with the word 'Galaris' on it. It is sealed. You will not open it; instead, you will put it in the bag that you have brought with you. You will make your way with it to the Dollis Brook Viaduct, where it crosses over Dollis Road. You will place the box in the bushes under one of the arches near the road. Conceal it so that it is not visible to outsiders. Then go, without turning round. Did you understand everything?"

Sarius stares at the messenger, speechless. No, he doesn't understand anything at all. Totteridge and Dollis Road? They're located in London, not in the world of Erebos. Or are they? He hesitates, thinks it over, and finally double checks, just to make sure.

"That means I have to carry out your instructions in London? In reality?"

"That is exactly what it means. Whatever 'reality' may be."

The messenger is looking expectant but Sarius doesn't have a quick answer ready. This is all just nonsense. He's not going to find a box at St. Andrew's—how would that work? On the other hand, there's nothing to stop him from claiming all sorts of things, is there? For example, that he has followed the instructions exactly as described.

"Fine, I'll do it."

"I am glad. Don't wait too long. We will see each other tomorrow, before noon. By then your task must be carried out. If you disappoint me ..."

For the first time since Sarius met him, a smile steals over the messenger's features. As if he knows what is at the back of Sarius's mind.

"... if you disappoint me, this will be our last meeting in friendly circumstances."

With a parting wave the messenger turns and goes, and the mouth of the cave closes behind him. As the gap disappears, so does the light. Blackness. So impenetrable that Sarius no longer knows if he is a part of this darkness, or if he has ceased to exist.

We all die in the end. It's strange that most people make such a fuss about whether it happens sooner or later. Time flows like water and we float along with it, however much we may try to swim against the current.

How agreeable it is to give that up. To let the days and nights fly past, not to see or hear or feel the goings-on of the world anymore. To live in one's own world, where one's own rules apply. Not to pursue countless goals, but only the one, steadily and resolutely.

Oh yes, resolutely. I am not much anymore, but I am resolute. What I am creating is good. It is so much better than I am. One of the few things in life that still has meaning for me is creating something that grows far beyond one's own self. And it is growing. And growing.

I realize now. I was dishonest when I said it was a matter of indifference to me how long the lives of people around me last. That is not true. But it's not extending them that's important to me. On the contrary. I sit here and hone the tool with which I will cut short that which needs to be cut short.

SEVEN

Every single key sequence was futile. Nick pressed the Reset button with a sigh, and to his relief the computer restarted and began booting up. The time it took till his desktop image appeared and everything was operational seemed interminable. He tapped his foot and glanced at his watch: 1:48 a.m. Thank goodness tomorrow was Saturday. He could safely play a bit longer—if he got *Erebos* running again. But it was going to work out. If necessary he could still set up a second character—that was a good idea anyway. Maybe a barbarian or a vampire this time. Barbarians were incredibly robust.

He searched on the desktop for the *Erebos* icon, a simple red E, and clicked it. For a fraction of a second the cursor turned into an hourglass, then it resumed its usual arrow form. That was it. Nick double-clicked again on the E, took the DVD out of the drive, put it in again—nothing.

After two more restarts he gave up. All the other programs were running without a problem. It was just *Erebos* that wasn't responding. Damn it all.

Nick was far too agitated to go to bed. While he was sitting around idly, epic battles were certain to be raging at the blue river or the black wall. And even if they weren't, you could still stand by the fire and chat with the others.

But by the look of it, his copy of the game had a serious bug.

All of a sudden he could picture Colin again, asking Dan for tips, groveling and still not getting them. Had the game crashed terminally on him as well?

Morosely Nick opened *Minesweeper*, blew himself up three times in a row, and swore absurdly loudly. Well, he'd just go to bed then.

Or maybe pay a quick visit to Emily's page?

No, he wasn't in the mood for that. Not relaxed enough. Not romantic enough.

Not curious enough.

Contrary to his usual habits, Nick woke up at seven in the morning, a bundle of nerves—as if he was about to face an exam. His eyes felt sticky, and they stung. The thought of getting up made him tired again immediately. On the other hand, he didn't actually have to get up. At least not yet. Not at all, really. He buried his head deep in the pillow and tried not to think of anything, but soon caught himself going over the keyboard shortcuts he'd discovered in *Erebos* yesterday. Ctrl+F to light fires, B to block, Space to jump, Escape to shake off. He wondered whether Colin was playing right now. No way; he was asleep. Colin, alias…?—Nick had a suspicion it was that dark elf. What was his name again? He'd slunk away into the background in the battle against the trolls. Lelant, that's right. He'd stood to one side at the battle the way Colin was in the habit of doing when he thought a basketball game was lost. He just kept out of it then, wouldn't lift another finger.

Okay, he would put down Colin as Lelant on his mental list. Of more interest, however, was who was concealed behind BloodWork. Probably one of those thugs who were always hanging round by the garbage bins in the schoolyard scaring the eleven-year-olds. He knew hardly any of them by name.

Dan? Dan was certain to be a fat dwarf like Sapujapu. Or he'd have made himself extra thin and beautiful—as a vampire, for example. Or he was one of the dark elves who were so common, much to Nick's chagrin. In any case, he would be able to recognize Dan immediately from his stupid sayings and his smugness, and then he'd clobber him with his sword.

Nick sighed. How was he ever going to get back to sleep with the game going round and round in his head? He stretched, sat up, and swung his legs over the edge of the bed.

Totteridge wasn't far. The Northern Line was right near home. He might as well quickly go to St. Andrew's Church, just to go through the motions. Even though the game wouldn't start up anymore.

Just to test it, Nick sat down at the computer and tried once more. He got the same result as before he went to bed. *Erebos* wouldn't open.

Fortunately the Internet was working. Nick found the location of St. Andrew's Church on Google Maps within a few minutes—and even a picture of the yew, which was supposed to be two thousand years old and thus the oldest living thing in London. Wow. Its branches started so low that it looked like an enormous bush in the photo.

Dad had already gone to work an hour ago, and Mom would sleep in till at least ten. Nick brushed his hair, tied it back, and dragged on yesterday's clothes. He decided to take the opportunity to bring breakfast back with him. Chocolate chip muffins—Mom would love him for that. He grabbed an old grocery bag, stuffed it in his jacket pocket, and left his mother a note on the kitchen table: Taking something round to Colin. Back soon.

He closed the door behind him, so quietly that he could barely hear it himself. Mom wouldn't ring Colin to check Nick's statement. And even if she did, Colin hadn't answered the phone for days.

Nick got out at Totteridge & Whetstone Tube station and had

to wait ten minutes for the bus that took him along Totteridge Lane to the church.

You couldn't miss the yew. Unfortunately, however, its location wasn't as secluded as Nick had imagined from the photo on the Internet. There were people strolling around the churchyard: an elderly couple, two women with strollers, a gardener. Admittedly they weren't paying any attention to Nick, but he was going to feel pretty silly looking for something at the foot of this mighty tree—especially something that probably wasn't there.

Suddenly he became aware of how absurd the situation was. Why was he here? Because a character in a computer game had instructed him to look for something under a tree? God, that was ridiculous.

At least no one knew about it. He could just go home again and forget the whole thing, have breakfast with Mom, and then go out somewhere with Jamie later. Or settle down and play on the computer.

Except that the game wouldn't start anymore. The bloody crap game.

To keep himself occupied and give his morning outing some purpose, Nick walked once around the St. Andrew's churchyard. Took a look at the red-brick building with its square white tower and came to a decision. It would be stupid to go home without at least taking a quick look at the yew.

Ancient crooked gravestones stood in the shadow of the tree. Great atmosphere, thought Nick. He touched the mighty trunk almost reverently. Would it take four people to reach all the way around the tree? Or even five? It wouldn't be at all difficult to hide things inside the trunk, either. But there was nothing there, at least not at first glance. Nick reached his hand into a wide crevice in the wood and felt earth that had collected in there. He lowered his gaze to the ground. There wasn't anything there either—how could there be?

He walked on, ducked under the low-lying branches, got to the rear of the giant tree. Bent down.

There was something square and light brown peeping out from between the plants that grew in bunches close to the cracked bark of the tree. Nick pushed the stalks aside.

The box was about the size of a thick book, and its edges were sealed with wide black duct tape. Nick picked it up incredulously, registering fleetingly that it was heavy. He wiped off the earth that was still sticking to it.

"Galaris" was written on the wood in sweeping script, and there was a date underneath: 18/03. Nick struggled with a sense of unreality.

The 18th of March was his birthday.

Nick stared out of the train window, the bag containing the light-brown box resting on his knee. One part of him was concentrating on not missing the right stop. Another, and considerably larger, part was trying to make sense of it all. It had been almost two in the morning when the messenger had given him the order to look for the box. Had it already been lying under the tree at that point? And even more important: how had it gotten there? Why was his date of birth on it? What did the word "Galaris" mean?

More than ever he wished he could talk his questions over with Colin. He was bound to know a lot more about *Erebos*. Had he also been sent to the old yew?

Nick got out at West Finchley. He had a good fifteen-minute hike in front of him, but at least it would be through the countryside. He knew the area; he'd often gone for walks around there. It was a paradise for joggers and dog owners. As Nick was crossing a small bridge over the Dollis Brook, he got his cell out of his pants pocket and dialed. Colin answered before the second ring. Nick was so surprised that he forgot for a moment why he'd even called.

"Listen, I've got stuff to do," said Colin. "If you just want to chat, we can do that at school. Okay?"

"Wait a sec! I wanted to ask you something about *Erebos*. It's ... I got such a weird task, I had to—"

"Shut your mouth, will you?" Colin interrupted him. "You've read the rules, haven't you? Don't pass on any information, not even to your friends. Don't talk about the contents of the game. Are you stupid or what?"

For a second Nick was speechless.

"But ... but ... are you taking it that seriously?"

"It is serious. Keep your stuff to yourself, or you'll get kicked out before you can count to three."

Nick said nothing. There was something very unpleasant about the thought of being kicked out. Humiliating.

"I ... I just thought. Forget it," he said.

When Colin answered, his tone was noticeably friendlier. "Those are the rules, man. And believe me, it's worth obeying them. The game is wicked. And it just keeps getting better."

The bag with the mysterious box weighed heavily in Nick's hand. "Great," he said. "Well then ..."

"You haven't been there for that long." Now Colin sounded eager. "But you'll soon see. Just stick to the rules. And one of the rules is that you don't go round blabbing."

Nick took advantage of his friend's change of mood and asked one last question. "Has the game ever actually crashed on you?"

Now Colin laughed. "Crashed? No. But I know what you mean." He lowered his voice, as though he feared someone might be listening in. "Sometimes ... it just doesn't want to work. It waits. It tests you. Know what, Nick? Sometimes I think it's alive."

⊗ ⊗ ⊗

Nick had left the colorful community gardens on either side of the path behind. Dollis Brook flowed sedately along next to him, almost without making a sound.

"Sometimes I think it's alive." Very funny, Colin.

The sun came out from behind the clouds just as the path took Nick into the forest. He stopped and turned his face to the warming rays. If he found himself a nice quiet place in the forest where he could loosen the tape off the box ever so carefully ... Just for one look? Just to find out what was so heavy?

Nick let three joggers pass him and looked around. Nobody was looking at him now. He could see a woman who was walking a dog, but she was still far enough away.

The back of his neck tingled as he drew the box out of the bag. It was as big as a cigar box at most, but the contents certainly didn't have anything to do with cigars. Nick held the box at an angle, and whatever was in there slid to the left.

It was probably made of metal, and not especially big. Based on the time it took to slide from one edge of the box to the other, it didn't even fill half of the container.

Nick stuck an exploratory fingernail under the edge of the adhesive tape. It was awfully well-sealed. Trying to get it off would take ages, and leave telltale signs. Not a good idea.

Furious yapping interrupted Nick's thoughts. A Labrador and a light-brown hunting dog had encountered each other a short distance behind him and obviously didn't like each other's looks. The owners of the dogs in question were yanking at the leashes in order to separate the animals.

Nick slipped the box into his bag and entered the forest, accompanied by the howls of one of the dogs.

It wasn't difficult to find the Dollis Brook Viaduct—it rose high above the forest and the road, carrying the track for the Northern Line. An underground line that ran sixty feet above the ground, in the bright sunshine. Underneath the viaduct, however, it was shady and damp.

One of the arches near the road, the messenger had said. But "near" was a relative term. Nick decided on the second of the massive arched columns and submerged the box in the grass, which was particularly rampant right at the foot of the brick pillar. Someone would be able to find it there, but no one would stumble on it accidentally.

All done then. Nick stood there, looking around, until he remembered the messenger's words: "Leave without looking back," he had said.

Because *what* would happen otherwise? If you thought about it logically, absolutely nothing. The game couldn't know if and how he had followed the instructions. On the other hand, it had known his name. And the hiding place of the box and the inscription, Galaris.

A train thundered above Nick's head on the way to Mill Hill East. He wasn't supposed to turn around now. Actually, there wasn't the slightest reason to do so. Apart from a persecution complex, maybe, and Nick certainly didn't suffer from one of those.

He folded the bag up into a small bundle and stuck it under his jacket. Then he left, without once looking back.

It was getting very close to midday by the time Nick got back home, carrying a paper bag with the four muffins he'd just bought. Mom was on her second coffee.

"We got talking," Nick murmured as he arranged the muffins on a plate. He was dying of hunger.

"Want a coffee?"

"Love one. If it's quick."

His mother set to work on the espresso machine, although she kept sending covetous glances toward the plate of muffins. "Are they the ones with the chocolate chips?"

"Yes, the two dark ones. Keep your mitts off the coconut ones—they're mine."

Mom put a jumbo-sized cappuccino with frothy milk under his nose.

Nick devoured his first muffin, feeling as though he'd barely escaped death by starvation, and chased it down with half his coffee.

"I'm going over to your Uncle Harry's this afternoon. He's renovating. It would be nice if you came too. Dad has to fill in for a colleague, so you're the only one who can reach the ceiling without a ladder—and someone has to paint it."

Nick's mouth was full, which gained him valuable seconds. "I'd really like to," he said, and put as much regret in his voice as possible. "But the thing is, I've got to hand in a really difficult chemistry assignment in a few days—and I'll feel terrible if I don't keep on working on it. I thought I'd do that today ..."

The look his mother gave him was amused and searching at the same time. "You want to study chemistry? Not go to the movies?"

"No, I swear. There's no way I'm going to the movies today." Nick smiled at his mother, his conscience as pure as the driven snow. His last sentence was true, word for word.

EIGHT

Turn the computer on. Insert the DVD. Put the headphones on. Wait. Tense seconds till the program starts.

"Sarius," whispers a ghostly voice.

He is in the cave where he met with the messenger last night. But unlike yesterday, light is radiating from the walls, which are bright and polished, like crystal. *Wish crystal?*

Sarius is bending down for something that looks like a gold coin when the cave entrance opens and the messenger enters. He studies Sarius with his yellow eyes.

"You carried out my instructions," he says.

"Yes."

"Just out of interest: What was written on the box, other than 'Galaris'?"

"Numbers. 18/03."

"Very good. There is new equipment for you here. A breastplate, a helmet, and a decent sword. I am satisfied with you, Sarius." He points to a rock that resembles a table, up against the crystal wall.

Curiosity drives Sarius over toward it at once. The helmet gleams in copper tones and is ornamented with the engraved head of a wolf baring its teeth. Sarius is happy—wolves are among his favorite animals. He dons the harness—nine points of strength!—and reaches for the sword, which is longer and made from darker metal than his current one. He looks completely different, right away. To crown it all, he puts the wolf helmet on.

"Are you satisfied?" the messenger asks.

Sarius gives his wholehearted approval. He is a Two, and he looks cool.

"There's more to come."

The messenger draws his cloak tighter around his lean body.

"This is Erebos. You will see that loyal service is rewarded. Tell Nick Dunmore he should ensure that no outsider can intrude, then he should make his way to the inside courtyard of the block next door. The grating on one of the ventilation shafts is loose. If he removes it and reaches into the shaft, he will find something."

Find something? Sarius doesn't actually want any interruptions right now—he wants to get started and try out his new sword.

"Right now?" he asks.

"Of course. I'll be waiting."

The messenger leans back against the crystal wall and folds his arms across his chest.

Delays and more delays. Nick took off the headphones. To be on the safe side he would have to lock the door to his room. But if Mom noticed she would ask questions. He had to walk past her too, and if she asked where he was going, he couldn't give her a sensible explanation. He'd better just get it over with quickly.

He snuck out, turned the key very very quietly, and listened for sounds in the apartment. He could hear Mom's voice in the kitchen—she was talking on the phone. That was a stroke of luck. Nick crept to the front door, slipped his running shoes on quickly, and grabbed his jacket. He was outside.

The inside courtyard of the block next door exuded benign

neglect. Years before, someone had attempted to grow flowers in the tiny open space, but most of them had withered up. Anything that had survived was growing wild.

There were three ventilation grates, all mounted at knee height. The first one was rock solid. Nick jiggled it a bit, but nothing moved. He peeked through the square holes in the grating—there was only darkness and the whiff of damp basement.

The second grating seemed more promising. It sat in the wall loosely and barely offered any resistance when Nick pulled it out.

Only now did he wonder what was waiting for him in the gap behind it. Another box with his date of birth on it? Another task? Or would it be the reward that the messenger had hinted at?

Chocolate, Nick thought. A supply of gummi bears for long *Erebos* nights. He felt around in the square opening and drew his hand out again immediately.

Coward, he berated himself. What's the problem? Afraid of rats? Pull yourself together—this is the real world.

But he still got goose bumps when he pushed his hand back into the gap. At first there was nothing at all except dirt, but then he felt plastic. He grabbed it and pulled out a yellow shopping bag with something soft inside. The first thing Nick thought of was some sort of *Erebos* uniform that all players were allowed to wear from Level Two on—that was ridiculous, of course, but it still made more sense than what he actually pulled out of the bag.

"Hell Froze Over" was printed in blue on the black shirt, with the icy devil's skull grinning underneath.

For a few seconds everything stood still. Because that just wasn't possible. HFO was something between him and his brother. The only people who knew about the shirt were Finn and himself. Nick was absolutely certain that he hadn't breathed a word to the messenger, or to anyone else for that matter. He glanced at the size on the label: XXL. So it was in stock after all.

He would ring Finn. There would be an explanation, of course: it was probably Finn himself who had hidden the shirt there. Nick held it to his nose. Did it smell of stale smoke, of Finn's place? No, only of laundry detergent and a trace of damp basement.

Was it possible that Finn played *Erebos*? Sure—why not? The craziest coincidences happened sometimes.

"Where were you?" Mom asked when he burst into the apartment. Just as well he'd thought to hide the shirt under his jacket.

"Just around the corner. I got myself some chewing gum from the kiosk."

He even had an opened packet in his pocket, but Mom didn't want to see it.

Back in his room he hurriedly checked that the messenger was still there before he grabbed his cell from the bedside table and rang Finn.

"Hey kid! Good to hear from you. What's new?"

"Finn, did you get the HFO T-shirt after all?"

Short pause.

"No, I wrote and told you that, remember? You just can't get them at the moment, but I'll have a good crack at it, okay? I had no idea it was so important to you."

"No, don't worry—it's fine. Don't stress about it."

Finn wasn't lying—of course not. Why would he?

"Nicky, don't be mad but I've got to get back to it. The shop is full of people."

"Okay. Hang on, one thing: Have you been playing on the computer a lot lately? Adventure games?"

"Not at all. I just don't have any time—that's life when you're a businessman!" Finn laughed and hung up, leaving Nick even more at a loss than he had been before the conversation.

The messenger doesn't appear impatient—rather the opposite. No sooner does Nick move again than he leans off the wall—slowly, as if he has all the time in the world.

"Did you find your reward?"

"Yes. Thank you."

"I hope you liked it. Are you pleased?"

"Sure. Very pleased, actually. Can I ask something?"

It seems as though the messenger hesitates briefly.

"Of course. Ask your question."

"How do you know what I would like? You couldn't possibly know that."

"That is the power of Erebos. Be grateful it is on your side."

The messenger puts his head to one side, and a smile contorts his gaunt features.

"Do not disappoint us and it will remain so. Now, tell me what you feel like doing. You can help destroy an orc village—there's heaps of gold up for grabs. Or search for the secret portal to the White City. Arena fights will take place there tomorrow. It's a good chance to make a Two into a Three. Or even a Four."

"That's possible?"

"It certainly is. In the Arena you can see what a fighter is really made of. You can win everything there—and lose everything. It's better to win, of course: wish crystals, weapons, levels. Last time, a vampire named Drizzel took three levels away from another vampire named Blackspell. In a single fight."

"That's possible?" Sarius repeats, thrilled by the opportunities that are suddenly opening up.

"Of course."

Sarius's decision is made. To hell with the orc village.

"I will look for the city."

"Good choice. I only hope that you find it in good time. Registrations for the fights close tomorrow when the tower clock strikes three. Good luck."

The messenger dismisses him with a wave of his bony fingers and Sarius steps out of the cave into a sun-drenched meadow full of flowers. Once again he is left to fend for himself.

Flowering trees, flowering bushes. He turns all around, but there's not the slightest sign anywhere of a white city. Rather than just stand still, he walks straight ahead. That worked out once already.

The chirping of the birds is getting on his nerves. It's creating a holiday atmosphere instead of a mood of adventure. And there's no secret portal in sight either. Not even a molehill.

Although ... there is something lying up ahead in the grass. Could be a piece of material, or maybe a flag. He goes closer, bends down, freezes. Lifts up a blood-soaked piece of cloth. Still dripping. A shirt.

In the distance he hears a noise like muted growling. Sarius drops the shirt and begins to run—away from the growling that doesn't sound like an animal or a human, but rather a hideous mixture of both. His stamina is better now, he's pleased to find as he runs over a slight mound.

It's pure chance that he slows down just in time, before he plunges into a crater that opens up unexpectedly on the crest of the hill. Sarius glances down into the depths, which look fissured, precipitous, and not at all inviting. Behind him the growling is getting louder. However curious he may be, he doesn't want to find out who or what is making this noise. A few steps farther to the right, he discovers a rusty ladder that doesn't inspire any confidence whatsoever, but nevertheless seems to present an attractive opportunity to escape from the growling creature. He thinks about the blood-soaked shirt and puts a foot cautiously on the first rung. There's a grinding sound, but at the same time the wonderful music starts again, strengthening Sarius's conviction that he's on the right track. He can do nothing wrong. Without further hesitation he climbs down the ladder, borne by the melody and happily anticipating what is awaiting him below. With every rung he descends it gets darker. By the time he reaches the bottom, he can make out only what the torches on the wall are bathing in flickering light: roughly hewn rock faces, paths, passageways, turnoffs. He has landed in a labyrinth. He sets off blindly, and loses his bearings within seconds.

There's nothing in his inventory that would be suitable for marking the walls. No chalk, no thread. The only thing he could try is making scratches in the rock, but there's no way he's going to do that. Not with the new sword.

A glance upward reveals to him that the cleft he descended through is already a long way behind him. The daylight doesn't reach all the way in here, but torches have been mounted on the walls at irregular intervals. Every shade of darkness prevails in between.

Sarius walks on, his footsteps echoing over and over. Are they just his? He stops, and the echo dies away.

The music encourages him to continue on his way. He tries his luck with the first turnoff to the left, and regrets it at once because the next torch is an awfully long way away. He hurries to reach the light, but stops just before it. Something is glittering on the rock face. A wish crystal? Sarius fumbles for it eagerly, but under his touch the sparkling something dissolves, flowing down the wall in a slimy trail. He turns away, revolted. Finally—the next torch. Beyond it yet another turnoff awaits. To the right or to the left?

It's lighter to the left. He creeps cautiously around the corner, keeping a firm hold on his sword. Every step echoes; if there are monsters down here, they'll have heard him long since.

Once again Sarius reaches a fork. Something like anxiety is stirring in him. He still has plenty of time to register for the Arena fights, sure … but everything looks the same here. Dark rocks, torches, puddles of water. And nothing else. Not another fighter anywhere to be seen, he's thinking, just as he stumbles over a body immediately past the turnoff. The shock turns Sarius's legs to jelly. He jumps back onto his feet as quickly as he can and points his sword at the obstacle that tripped him up.

A cat woman. Sarius checks her name: Aurora. There's only a tiny trace of red left on her belt—the rest is black as coal. She's not quite dead yet. When he touches her, she moves her hand weakly. It takes Sarius a moment to figure out what she wants. He lights a fire.

"Thank you. I've just about had it. Can you help me?"

"What did this to you?"

"A giant scorpion. There are three or four running around here. Damned bugs—if they sting you, you're done for."

"Giant scorpion" doesn't sound appealing to Sarius.

"Are we the only ones down here?"

"Of course not; there are heaps of people here. Listen, do you happen to be able to heal?"

Sarius has to think fast. She's taken so much punishment that the injury tone must be almost unbearable.

"I can. But I've never done it."

"Damn. I can't do it, and I don't even know how it works."

It will be like lighting a fire, Sarius reasons, and has a bit of a go.

It's not long before there's a red flash. Aurora's belt regains some color. Sarius's life force sinks considerably in return. He wasn't expecting that—he needs every scrap of energy not to perish down here.

"You could have told me that," he snarls at Aurora.

"What?" The cat woman is sufficiently recovered to struggle to her feet and draw her weapon. A cat-o'-nine-tails—how appropriate.

"That healing you reduces my own life span!"

"Keep your shirt on. It will regenerate again. Not like real injuries."

Still furious, Sarius stares at his belt. Something on there is moving, in fact. The gray is turning red again, bit by tiny bit.

"Are you on the city quest too?" Aurora asks.

"Yes. I didn't feel like having a fistfight with orcs."

"Me neither. Although they'd probably be nicer than the scorpions. That gave me the creeps like you wouldn't believe."

Sarius can't help wondering whether he knows Aurora. Outside of Erebos.

"Did you hear the growling just now? Up top, I mean. On the hill."

"Of course," she says.

"Do you know what sort of animals they were?"

"They weren't animals, they were zombies. I had to bump two of them off before I made it onto the ladder. It made me want to throw up—they just crumble away when you whack them."

Sarius is secretly glad that he didn't see any zombies. It was definitely the right thing to head downward, if only because of the quest. Although now he thinks he can hear something. Many legs scuttling on the hard, stony ground.

"You're only a Two, hmm?"

"Yes. So? What are you?"

There's a rumbling above them, like an approaching storm.

"I can't say. You know the rules."

The scuttling is coming closer. Can't Aurora hear it? Or doesn't it mean anything?

"Can you at least tell me who's down here apart from us?"

"You'll find out soon enough. A few people I don't know, and a few who are always around. I saw Nodhaggr and Duke and Nurax before, as well as someone called Samira I've never met before, and some vampire or other."

"I know Samira," Sarius says eagerly.

"So? In any case, she cleared off when—"

The black scorpion that comes flying around the corner behind Aurora is gigantic. The clacking of its legs is unmistakable now. Sarius dodges sideways from the up-curved stinger and raises his sword. He could try to hack off one of the creature's claws if it comes closer. But it doesn't; it stops at Aurora, who sees it far too late, then gets itself into position and attacks. Aurora falls to the ground. Is there still some red on her belt? Sarius has no time to look, and no desire to waste life energy on the cat woman again. He thinks he hears another scorpion approaching from the other side. It would block his path, and then he'd have to turn around ...

Sarius doesn't think twice. He swings his sword and hacks at the left claw. It sounds like metal striking metal. The scorpion draws back a bit. Sarius aims for its tiny head; the animal thrashes at him with its claws and cranes its stinger up into the air again. Something is dripping from the tip onto the ground—blood, poison, or both—making a steaming puddle on the stony ground.

Now Sarius takes aim at the stinger, which is swinging back and forth not far above his head. He hits it on the second attempt. The scorpion recoils, does an about-face, and runs off. It disappears in one of the labyrinth's dark shafts.

Sarius takes one last look at the motionless Aurora and makes off. *I helped her once; that will have to do.* He keeps a watchful eye on his surroundings. Why didn't Aurora hear the scorpion? He has a vague hunch. She was injured and wanted to spare herself the painful squealing in her head. *Big mistake.*

He listens all the more intently now for any sound. He's not going to be caught by surprise. He's not going to die a Two.

A scorpion is behind him; Sarius can feel it. And hear it, of course. It's unnerving, but he's not going to make the same mistake as Aurora and forego one of his senses. Apart from that decision, he doesn't have a strategy for getting out of the labyrinth in one piece.

When he's got some distance behind him, he stops for the space of a second and listens. No sounds of fighting. And he can't hear the running sounds of the scorpion pursuing him anymore. It worries him. Sarius walks on slowly. He follows the passage to the right and is faced with a fork in the path. Could he starve to death in this labyrinth?

He obeys his instinct and goes to the left—and sees a scorpion clinging to the wall like a spider, its black back plates reflecting the light of the torches. It's even larger than the last one. The creature swings its stinger as if it's trying to hypnotize Sarius. Before he can think about it, he's raised his sword above his head. He doesn't swing it, he just stabs, aiming somewhere around the middle of the armored body, the bit where the back plates meet …

There's an ugly grinding noise and the sword disappears deep into the body of the creature, which is now frantically trying to strike Sarius with its stinger. But it can't move—the sword has it pinned down. Sarius's arms are shaking—hanging on to the scorpion is more arduous than running up a mountainside. He doesn't want to think about what will happen when his stamina runs out.

Die, he thinks; will you just die.

At some stage—it seems to Sarius as if hours have passed—the creature's movements cease. It goes limp; its stinger-wielding tail falls to the side. Finally he can pull out his weapon. What he hasn't reckoned with is that dead scorpions aren't in any state to cling to walls. By the time he realizes this, it's almost too late—he only just manages to leap aside so the creature doesn't bury him under it when it falls. It lies still, with only the occasional twitch of one of its legs.

Sarius sits down with his back to the wall and stares at the dead scorpion. He listens for the approach of any more of its kind, strains his ears but can't hear any scuttling. Instead, slowly and almost imperceptibly, music starts playing again. It is new but at the same time familiar, and it convinces Sarius that he is not in danger at present. He can take his time to study his defeated adversary more closely, and he discovers that he can dissect it without much trouble. Remove the claws, for example. Sarius stashes them away, and a portion of the back plate as well. He hesitates over the poison stinger. Who knows—maybe just touching it will do him harm. He could really do without the nerve-racking injury tone right now.

He touches the stinger very cautiously, just at the wide end. Nothing happens. With the greatest care, he removes it and packs it in his inventory.

When he gets to his feet again, a dark elf is standing only a few steps away from him. Sarius recognizes him at first glance. It's Lelant. He's evidently earned himself some new equipment since the last time they met. He's swinging a morningstar with alarmingly long spikes.

The two scrutinize each other briefly. Neither lights a fire. As far as Sarius is concerned, he doesn't want to make the first move. He still feels like a newbie—he's only a Two. Anyway, there's only one thing he would like to find out from Lelant: whether he's Colin. No, that he *is* Colin. And Lelant would never give that away to him, even if he lit ten fires.

The scorpion looks disgusting in its half-dissected state. Sarius doesn't want to touch its moistly gleaming grayish-pink flesh. He takes a couple of steps toward Lelant, who is standing against the wall like a motionless shadow.

What is he waiting for? Does he want to continue on together? That wouldn't be bad, because there's another fight in progress somewhere nearby. The sounds of jangling, crashing, and metallic blows echo through the passageways of the labyrinth.

Sarius checks on his life energy. Looks okay. Most of what it cost him to heal Aurora has been restored. He's survived the fight against the scorpion pretty much unscathed. Right—time to go find the next battle. He takes one last look at Lelant, who has moved away from the wall and is strolling toward the dead animal. He's welcome to stock up on disgusting rations if he wants. The scorpion yields seven meat units, but Sarius doesn't want a single one.

The sound of fighting is claiming all his attention. He follows the noise, finds an alarmingly low passage that's pitch black, then reaches a wider passage with sides that look furry, as though they're covered in dark blue mold. At the next fork he turns right and finds himself in a dead end again. Bloody labyrinth. He suppresses his annoyance and turns right again at the next opportunity. There's not even a single torch lighting this corridor. If there's a scorpion lurking, Sarius will only find out about it when there's a stinger sticking out of his back.

But there's a lot to suggest that this fork is the right one. He can hear the fight more clearly than before. And the click-click-click of scorpion legs. He takes a step into the darkness, senses a pervasive threat. He raises his sword and turns on the spot. Is there something near him, behind him? No.

There's no choice—if he wants to get further, he has to go

through here. He holds his shield close to him and his sword at the ready, then he feels his way step by step into the darkness.

The walls seem to be getting closer together the farther he advances into the passageway. A long way ahead he makes out a tiny glimmer of light. That's where he must go. Feeling happy that he's nearly made it, he quickens his step—and falls. Panicking, he thrusts his sword into nothing, expecting an attack at any moment, an injury, the excruciating tone, but none of that happens. He gets to his feet again. What light there is tells him he's alone here. Apart from the something that he stumbled over.

He bends down. Makes out bones, a few tufts of red hair, a longbow, and two broken arrows. The skull that belongs to the body has rolled a bit farther and is lying up against the rock face.

Is it one of us? Who cares; he has to get out of here. He takes a last uneasy look at the skeleton before he continues on. To where it's brighter and louder. There's a fight up ahead— it's better than uncertainty, and much better than solitary darkness.

Where did the light disappear to? He can't have gone the wrong way; how come he's facing a wall again? He turns around—*I'll never get out of here again.* He can't help thinking of the blood-soaked shirt he found in the grass. If he'd stayed up there he would have been fighting zombies, but in daylight, at least.

Now there's something flickering again, throwing a shadow on the wall. He only realizes the shadow is his own when he strikes at it with his sword. The echo of his blow fades away in the dark passages.

The sounds of fighting are so near—the others must be right behind the next wall. He gropes his way along the wall, his harness squealing as it scrapes against the rock. Suddenly the wall disappears. Sarius stumbles into a recess where—at last—he sees a door. Closed, of course. He investigates, finds a latch, pushes it up. Braces himself against the wood with all his strength and manages to create a chink that lets in loads of light. The sound of fighting is louder than ever. Legs in leather-trimmed boots come into view, and straight after them come clicking black scorpion legs.

A part of him—a large part—wants to shut the door and wait until everything is over. Nobody has seen him, have they? Apart from the messenger, perhaps, who sees everything, knows everything ...

The thought of those yellow eyes is enough. Sarius pushes the door open and dashes forward. He sees three scorpions and six, no, seven fighters. Does he know anyone? No time to have a closer look. One of the scorpions is turning away from his adversary and running toward Sarius.

He draws back and makes sure that his sword is pointing in the direction of the attacker. Its stinger is raised right up, swinging backward and forward, searching for a target. Sarius lunges, hits the body of the scorpion from the side. There's a grinding sound. He directs his second thrust at the poison stinger. That drove the first scorpion away—but unfortunately not this one. Perhaps Sarius's aim was poor; at any rate, his adversary only draws back briefly before attacking again at twice the speed.

Sarius leaps to the right and the stinger misses him. He seizes his opportunity and strikes the stinger again with his sword. Finally the creature is swaying a little. With a bit of luck Sarius can run it through like the specimen on the wall. One of the sharp claws whooshes past, alarmingly close. He cowers in anticipation of the terrible tone, but the scorpion has missed him. One thrust with his weapon, and the armor gives way. The animal buckles over to the right and Sarius pursues it, stabbing at its unprotected belly. Bull's-eye. Suddenly there's someone next to him, slashing at the scorpion with a halberd.

96

However much Sarius wished for company a short while ago, at this moment it's most unwelcome. Some stupid dark she-elf is getting under his feet—now, after he's managed the hard part, and the rest is a walk in the park. His fellow fighter won't be pushed aside. Her weapon must be stronger than his—after only three blows the scorpion is lying motionless on the ground.

Deep down inside, Sarius feels hot. His sword is smeared with gray slime, to which he'd like to add the blood of the dark she-elf who just pushed in and took over the easy part. As if he needed her help. As if he wouldn't have managed it by himself.

He checks her name. Feniel. Stupid cow. What's she doing now? Throwing herself on the dead scorpion and making mincemeat of it. She doesn't have her eye on the stinger or the claws, as Sarius did just before. Instead, she's literally rummaging through the carcass. Sick.

"Victory," a voice breathes in Sarius's ear. He looks around. The battle is fought, but the other Erebos fighters are still fully occupied. Like Feniel, they are dissecting the dead scorpions into the tiniest pieces, and Sarius is getting the feeling that maybe he's missed something.

When he hears the hoofbeats, he knows what's coming. The next moment, the messenger's armored horse trots up. Its rider raises his hand in greeting.

"You have done a good job and will once more be rewarded. I think I will start with Drizzel."

The vampire, who still has both his arms deep in the stomach cavity of one of the scorpions, stands up. Sarius is trying not to think about what's actually stuck to Drizzel's hands.

"You have fought well, albeit not outstandingly. I will give you a new shield. It is also good. Not outstanding."

Drizzel takes the shield in his sticky hands and throws his previous one away. It lands on the labyrinth floor with a clang.

"Feniel."

The dark she-elf pushes past Sarius.

"It gives me pleasure to see that you don't show any misplaced consideration, and that you take for yourself what you wish to have. It follows that you should also do that with your equipment. Here are fifty gold pieces for you. Decide for yourself what you will buy with it."

It takes all Sarius's self-control not to clobber Feniel with his sword. She pushed him away and gets rewarded for it? What a joke.

"Sarius."

He steps forward. *I was fantastic. Come on, admit it. Seriously good for a Two, man.*

"You emerged unhurt from the battle. Congratulations. However, you arrived late in the piece and didn't kill the scorpion yourself. Nevertheless I would like to reward you. I will increase your healing magic. You will now be able to give others more of your strength."

There's a bit of a hiss, and that's it. That's it? Sarius stares at the messenger incredulously. What sort of reward is that supposed to be? If he heals someone, he harms himself—and now he'll harm himself even more? There's no way he's going to use this idiotic magic again—he's not that stupid.

The messenger calls the next name. "Blackspell."

A vampire whose praises he sings, and whom he presents with a sword that is deep red, and translucent like dark wine. Sarius would like one too. But oh no, he just got a new one today—and, of course, this wonderful increase in healing magic. How amazing.

Why is he really so mad? He's mad at Nurax too, the werewolf to whom the messenger is just giving a special pair of endurance boots—and at Grotok, the first human he's encountered in Erebos, who receives some sort of scrolls.

The next to be rewarded is someone who, like Nurax, is known to Sarius: Arwen's Child. She's been slightly injured, and is supplied with healing potion and ten gold coins. All of that is better than the garbage Sarius got.

"Gagnar!" the messenger calls.

A ragged, seriously wounded lizard creature crawls out from behind one of the dead scorpions.

"That was close, Gagnar. If you remain here, you will die. Come with me."

Gagnar tries to get up. Sarius can clearly make out the number one on his torn doublet and also on the stained cap. It's seared on the material like a brand. He can't take his eyes off Gagnar. Finally— someone who has even less of a clue than he has. The lizard man allows himself to be helped onto the horse.

"You have permission to light a fire," the messenger announces, and then rides off.

Sarius's fire is burning before any of the others react. Arwen's Child and Blackspell approach slowly. The others have turned back to the carcasses and are grubbing around in them.

"What are they actually looking for?" Sarius opens the conversation.

Blackspell says nothing, but Arwen's Child answers readily.

"Wish crystals, of course."

"In the dead scorpions?"

Sarius is dumbstruck. That's the last place he would have looked. At least it explains the effort Drizzel and his lot are putting in. Sarius is almost tempted to join them.

"Have you found one yet?" he asks the dark she-elf.

"Not yet. They're really rare—and the most valuable thing you can get here. I was there once when BloodWork got one out of a giant spider. It was a blue one. No idea what Blood did with it."

Sarius looks pensively at the flames licking up from the campfire.

When did the music start playing again? He hadn't noticed, but now it's there, giving him strength. He could already face another battle—that's how strong he feels. And this time, he wouldn't let himself be driven off by Feniel.

"Do you know what you can do with the crystals, exactly?"

Arwen's Child takes her time to answer.

"They say they can fulfill your greatest desires. Except for waking people from the dead maybe. And they won't get you into the Inner Circle either."

"What is this Inner Circle?" Sarius asks. His ignorance doesn't even trouble him. That's the effect of the music—it makes him feel like a king. *I am the most important person here—the others are just extras.*

Despite that, he still doesn't get an answer, because now Blackspell barges in on the conversation. "Find out for yourself—we all had to."

"Never mind. I was only asking."

Drizzel and Nurax have given up. They abandon the scorpion bodies and come over to the fire.

"You could at least get cleaned up; you look bloody disgusting," Arwen's Child says, and moves away from them.

Drizzel ignores her. "Well, well, Sarius. I though you were done for. So those giant blue females at the river didn't finish you off after all?"

"Obviously not."

"And was it a total massacre?"

"If you hadn't snuck off, you would know."

"You've really got a big mouth for a Two."

Sarius doesn't respond. The others can see his level, but he can't see theirs. Suddenly he feels naked.

"Leave him in peace. Otherwise I'll tell him a few things I know about you," Arwen's Child puts in.

"Go for it. You know how much the messenger loves big mouths," Drizzel retorts.

At this moment Lelant comes round the corner. He stops abruptly and in a flash pulls his morningstar from his belt.

"Oh shit, it's an elf invasion." Blackspell groans.

"Shut your face," Sarius responds. Lelant is one of the people he's most pleased to see here. *I know who you are, man.* He moves over and gestures an invitation so Lelant will come and join him. But he doesn't seem to want to. He's keeping a distance from the fire. Then he sees Feniel and Grotok, who are still busy with the dead scorpions, takes a step toward them—and changes his mind. Finally, he comes over to the fire, but stays as far away from Sarius as possible.

"Hi, Lelant," Sarius greets him.

"Are the two over there looking for wish crystals?" Lelant asks in place of a greeting.

"Yeah," Blackspell says. "But they're not having any luck. The critters haven't got anything in them."

"Oh, that's too bad. Because I did quite well." Lelant reaches into his bag and draws out a crystal that gives off a green light. "Wicked, isn't it?"

"Where did you get it?" Arwen's Child asks.

"None of your business."

Sarius stares at the glowing stone and gets a hot feeling inside. He doesn't have to ask where the crystal is from. It was *his* scorpion, his prize that he left Lelant with, and the other dark elf has taken advantage. That's just plain mean.

"I guess you realize that the stone really belongs to me?"

"And why would that be?"

"Because I finished off the scorpion by myself, that's why. If you're fair, you'll hand the thing over."

"Dream on. I'm not that bloody stupid."

Sarius draws his sword before he's even had time to think. Now he stands there, at a loss. He doesn't actually want to attack Lelant; he just wants the crystal that he's entitled to. *If you knew who I was, you would just give it to me.*

"Hey, no duels outside the cities," Drizzel yells.

"Oooh, I'm so scared. The Two wants to have a go at me," Lelant sneers. "One stroke with the sword and the messenger will come and take you away. Go for it. Do me a favor."

As a matter of form, Sarius keeps his sword pointing at Lelant's chest for a few more seconds before he puts it away again, secretly happy to have gotten out of it without a fight.

"You know perfectly well you have no claim to the stone."

"Why not? Can I help it if you just sneak off and only take the stinger and the claws with you? Guys, you should have seen it! Cuts the claws off the brute and stuffs his inventory full with them. What are you going to do with them? Play dress up?"

Sarius stares at Lelant. The dark brown skin, the stubbly black hair, the gleaming dark eyes. *I'll get you back for this, you bastard.*

"Then keep it. You're a bloody coward."

"Yeah, a bloody coward with a wish crystal. Does anyone know what direction the city is?"

"Why don't you ask your wish crystal?" Sarius snipes. "Or do something for yourself for a change."

He doesn't wait for Lelant to respond. Instead, he turns his back on the fire and marches into the first passageway he comes across. He would rather continue on by himself than hang around with idiots like them.

He was so close to finding a wish crystal—so close. It's still dark in the passages, but the thought of that damned Lelant propels him on. If a scorpion gets in his way right now, he'll make mincemeat out of it. He keeps going, and going. He still has plenty of time to reach his destination, and he tells himself that the others will soon be eating his dust.

Unfortunately, all the passages here look the same again. There's nothing that hints at the White City. He wanders on, meets no one, no one attacks him. After what seems like forever he halts. His anger has shrunk to a small glowing kernel inside him.

What now? He could kick himself for his impulsiveness. Why didn't he at least ask Arwen's Child to come with him? She was on his side—there was no need to leave her behind with the others. If she were with him, he'd be able to light a fire. If she were with him, he wouldn't be all alone.

He has one more go at getting his bearings. There must be some sign. Perhaps white pebbles at the correct turnoffs, or a bell pealing on the hour. He strains his ears. Peers in every direction. Listens intently at every fork. And then, at the third crossroads he hears something—not bells, but a rushing sound. It's only very soft, but it's a sign. Something he can go after.

The rushing sound gets clearer the longer Sarius follows it. He has abandoned his caution—something tells him that no danger is threatening. He pauses for a moment to figure out why he feels so safe. It's the music, he realizes. Gently, imperceptibly, its character has changed. It makes him confident, leaves him in no doubt that he is on the right path.

A few minutes later Sarius discovers the source of the rushing sound: an underground river. In the meager light of the torches its waters appear almost black, but as he gets closer they prove to be blood-red.

In spite of himself horrible pictures start crowding into his mind. Battlefields, corpses stacked up in great piles, sacrificial rites. After all, the blood has to come from somewhere.

If it's blood! He can't quite tell. The color of the water could be due to the stones on the riverbed, or ... It doesn't really matter. There's no way Sarius is going to drink it, even if he could do with some refreshment right now.

He walks over and stands at the stone edge, right by the water. It flows evenly, straight as an arrow, like a channel. Cities are often built on rivers, so he'll take his direction from this one. But upriver or down? He examines his surroundings for clues, finds none, and resolves to go upriver.

After only a short while the passageway gets brighter—braziers at the river's edge illuminate the path at regular intervals. Suddenly it's child's play. Sarius runs, runs faster when he discovers a broad staircase that leads upward, but has to stop shortly before it because he hasn't been paying attention to his stamina. He regains his breath and begins the ascent. Jubilant music surrounds him, daylight streams toward him.

The view that greets him when he finally reaches the top is magnificent. Walls, towers, and archways of white marble sparkle in the sunlight. Even the road that leads to the city gleams like ivory.

Sarius isn't in a hurry anymore. The city seems to be waiting only for him. He soaks in the sight of it and slowly approaches.

On his arrival the four guards at the gate lower their lances in greeting. A fanfare sounds, and the potbellied herald high above on the city wall announces the latest news. "Sarius has arrived. Sarius, knight, of the race of dark elves, is entering the White City."

NINE

"Would you like some more rice?" Mom was brandishing the heaped-up ladle enthusiastically over Nick's plate.

"No thanks."

"Don't you like it? You're just poking around at the meat."

Nick was finding it hard to concentrate on his mother's words. Sarius had just taken a room in an inn in the White City, and the innkeeper there had prescribed three hours of rest. Wham—a black screen yet again.

"Nick! Your mother asked you something!"

"Yes, Dad. Sorry. No, it's really tasty. I'm just a bit tired."

His father took a sip of his beer and frowned.

"You didn't even have school today!"

"No, he was studying chemistry," Mom put in helpfully. "Just be glad that he's taking school seriously. I was talking to Melanie Falkner yesterday. Her son is never at home anymore, and apparently all he does at school is make trouble ..."

Nick's thoughts were drifting again. He wasn't registered for the Arena battles yet. He didn't even know where he needed to go to register. What if he didn't find the right place, or there were still tasks he had to complete before that? Then he mightn't make it. Still, it was only a bit less than an hour to go before the end of the rest period. Mom would doze off in front of the TV, and maybe Dad would disappear off to the pub for a third beer. It would have been better if Sarius could have taken his break later—after midnight, when Nick would have been tired anyway. He wondered whether the others had found the red river in the meantime, or whether they were still wandering through the labyrinth.

He rubbed his burning eyes. The innkeeper had eyed Sarius's armor and told him about the brilliant armorers in the White City. But Sarius didn't have any gold or a wish crystal. He didn't even know how he was supposed to pay for his room at the inn, but he had to take one. By written order of the messenger.

That damned Lelant. Come Monday Nick was really going to have a go at Colin, the bastard.

"... by next week?"

The sudden silence that followed this question led Nick to suspect it had been directed at him.

"Er, sorry—can you repeat that?"

"I said, is your chemistry assignment already due next week? For god's sake, Nick, what's the matter with you?"

Dad's impressive belly bumped into the edge of the table as he leaned forward angrily.

"It's just not acceptable, the way you're opting out of this conversation. It is about you, after all."

"Yes, I'm sorry." *Please don't start with the whys and what-fors.* "I'm supposed to hand it in next week, but I think I've got it under control. How was work today?"

Asking Dad about his work was a safe bet. There was always something to talk about. Today it was a patient who'd slipped Nick's dad some cash so his trusty nurse would go and get him fish and chips from the shop round the corner.

"What's more, his cholesterol was about as high as Mount

Everest," Dad informed them, and helped himself to some more chicken casserole. "You'd imagine the fact that they've already eaten their way into hospital would give these people something to think about, but no."

Nick gave a mechanical smile and wished he were back in the White City. "Can I leave the table?"

"Of course," Mom said.

"But help your mother with the dishes," Dad mumbled between bites.

Nick cleared the table briskly, hurriedly stuck the plates and glasses into the dishwasher, and ran up the stairs to his room. He tried to start the game even though he knew better. It didn't work, of course.

That left forty-five minutes he could use for chemistry. The thought had no appeal whatsoever. Come on, he urged himself. At least look at a few formulas.

Just when he'd opened the book and was trying to fight the wave of glumness that engulfed him, Dad burst into his room.

"I completely forgot to ask you about tomorrow. Are you ... Hey, you really are working!"

"Uh, yeah."

"Is it hard?"

"You can say that again."

Dad came over behind him and peered at the book, full of well-meaning interest that dissipated within seconds, to be replaced by paternal helplessness.

"My goodness. I really can't be much help with that anymore, Nick."

"It's fine, Dad. You don't have to, I can manage all right."

His father put a hand on his shoulder.

"Sorry I interrupted you. I'm really proud of you, did you know that? At least something will become of *one* of my boys."

Nick suppressed the desire to shake his father's hand off, and bit his lip. After a moment he felt the weight lift off his shoulder.

"I'm just going to the pub. Don't work too long, Nick."

The door closed behind him.

Still forty-three minutes to go. He rubbed his face with both hands before he bent back over his book and stared at the formulas. If he found at least a couple of sentences for his assignment, that would do for today. Nick shut his eyes and repeated what he had just read. It was a shame that there were no wish crystals in real life—he could really use them for chemistry. He was never going to get an A, never.

He took a piece of paper and wrote the title on it: "The Identification of Amino Acids by the Use of Thin Layer Chromatography."

There, he'd made a start. Now he needed an introduction. Really though, working this way wasn't worth it. If he was going to write, he might as well do it properly. Take lots of time, preferably tomorrow, after breakfast. Then there would be no scorpions crawling through his brain, and his anger at Colin would have blown over.

Nick took one last look at his book, then turned on the computer. Surfed over to Emily's page on deviantART, out of habit. Nothing new though. Disappointment flared up in him briefly; then he had an idea. Why hadn't he thought of it sooner? He opened Google and typed "Erebos" in the search bar. There'd have to be a page for the company that had developed it, a forum, maybe even updates to download. Tips, cheats, the whole lot.

Nick found a Wikipedia entry at the top of the search results. There you go, the game was famous. He clicked on the link and read.

In Greek mythology Erebos (Ἔρεβος from the Greek ἔρεβος, "dark") is the god of darkness and shadow, and its embodiment. According to the poet Hesiod he was created from Chaos at the same time as Gaia, Nyx, Tartaros, and Eros. As Hesiod describes it, first there was Chaos (the gaping, hollow space), out of which the lightless darkness of the deep, Erebos, sprang. From the union of Nyx and Erebos sprang not only sleep and dreams but the evils of the world: doom, old age, death, discord, anger, misery, and denial, Nemesis, the Moiræ, and the Hesperides, which appear here as threatening aspects of the moon goddess, but also joy, friendship (Philotes), and pity. According to later legends, Erebos was part of the underworld. It was the place that the dead had to pass through immediately after their death. Erebos was also often used as a synonym for Hades, the Greek god of the underworld.

Nick read through the text twice, and clicked it shut again. That might be quite interesting if you were interested in Greek gods, but it was of no value to him. Not a tip in sight.

He kept looking. Just links to Greek mythology, and a few to a death metal band. It was the very last entry on the page that drew a subdued whoop of triumph from Nick: It said "Erebos, the game." Nothing else. Nick clicked expectantly on the link. It took a moment before the page loaded. Red writing on a black background:

Not a good idea, Sarius.

Why not, he was tempted to ask for a second, then the enormity of the situation dawned on him and he closed the window, closed the browser as if he wanted to lock someone out. That wasn't real; he had imagined it. It wasn't possible. The Internet couldn't talk to him. Perhaps he should call the page up again and make sure that he had made a mistake. It was bound to be—

His cell rang, and Nick's heart nearly stood still. Perhaps he shouldn't have closed the page? He read "Jamie" on the lit-up display and breathed a sigh of relief.

"Hi! Did I interrupt something? You sound so rushed."

"No. It's fine."

"Good. Listen, do you feel like going for a bike ride into the country tomorrow? We haven't done that for ages, and the weather is supposed to be good."

Nick needed a moment to think up a suitable excuse.

"That's a really great idea, but I'm just working away at my chemistry assignment. I've absolutely got to produce something decent, and I don't want to take any chances."

"Oh." Jamie sounded disappointed. "You know what? I'll help you. Just come over tomorrow and we'll do some research on the Internet. Then you're bound to be done really quickly!"

Shit.

"We'll see. But I can probably concentrate better by myself. And that's … kind of, uh, important."

Nick squeezed his eyes shut. God that sounded fake. And stupid as well. There was an astonished silence at the other end of the line. Nick could hear the TV squawking in the background.

"Are you serious?" Jamie asked after an unusually long pause. "That's not what you used to say. After all, we … Oh!" Jamie burst out laughing. "Nick, my boy, why didn't you tell me right away? You've got a date, and you're worried that Uncle Jamie won't stop teasing you if you admit it."

"Don't be stupid."

"Oh, come on, it's fine. Have fun, and tell me every little detail on Monday. By next weekend I'll finally make a move on Darleen too, then maybe the four of us can go out somewhere?"

"Darleen?" Nick asked, interested despite himself.

"Yes, the cute blonde from school orchestra. A year below us, plays the clarinet and wears her skirt really short. Darleen. Ring a bell?"

"Sort of. Listen, I have to go. Mom's calling me." The lie came readily to Nick. The clock on his computer said five minutes to nine. He'd be able to start the game again soon.

The room is bare, and has only a tiny window that doesn't open. The bed makes creaking noises every time Sarius moves—he's afraid it's going to collapse any minute and the innkeeper will put it on his bill.

He's pleased to find that his stamina and health are everything he could hope for. The rest did him good. It's only when he moves toward the door that he notices he's not alone in the room. A gnome, the same dirty white color as the walls, is sitting on a small stool, his arms around his drawn-up knees.

"Hey ho, Sarius!" he screeches, and grins. "I have news for you. From the messenger. I am the messenger's messenger, so to speak."

Sarius looks down at his visitor, whose crooked-nosed face is almost glowing with friendliness. Nevertheless, Sarius doesn't have a good feeling about this.

"My master is not edified by your curiosity," the gnome begins. "I believe you know what I'm talking about. Naturally he understands that you want to know more about *Erebos*, but he doesn't appreciate the fact that you have been making inquiries behind his back."

He pokes around between his teeth with a long fingernail, finds something greenish, and examines it exhaustively.

"He is, on the other hand, prepared to answer your questions. And guess what—he has his own questions to put to you too!"

Sarius watches in some disgust as his companion sticks the greenish lump back into his mouth and chews on it.

"What questions?"

"Oh, easy ones. For example, does Nick Dunmore know someone by the name of Rashid Saleh?"

Sarius is taken aback. What's that got to do with anything? Then again, he can probably count himself lucky if all the messenger's questions are so easy.

"Yes, Nick knows him."

"Good. Does Nick know what Rashid really likes doing?"

That was easy.

"He likes skateboarding, he listens to hip hop, and he's a Stephen King fan."

The gnome nods his satisfaction, still chewing.

"Nick is well-informed. Does he perhaps also know what Rashid Saleh is afraid of?"

No. How would he know that? Although actually, there is one thing he's noticed. Rashid is afraid of heights. One time the whole class had gone to the London Eye, the Ferris wheel right on the Thames, and Rashid went up as well, but he turned as white as a sheet. Nearly threw up afterward.

"He doesn't like heights. He avoids lookout towers and things like that."

The gnome clicks his tongue. "That matches what we've already found out. Thanks, Sarius. My master will be inclined to forgive you your excessive thirst for knowledge. Now I will divulge something to you in turn."

He leans forward and winks at Sarius confidingly. "You will find the list of competitors for the Arena fights in Atropos's tavern. Give the old woman my regards."

He hops off the stool, bows with exaggerated politeness, and leaves.

Sarius puts on his helmet and hangs his shield on his back. It's only when he's on the way to the door that something occurs to him. The white gnome didn't answer any questions, and Sarius didn't ask any.

The streets of the city are more than busy, despite the lateness of the hour. Sarius keeps to the wide thoroughfares and avoids dark side alleys that remind him of the passages in the labyrinth. Here, braziers on every corner color the cream-rendered walls golden. Now and then Sarius meets other warriors; he knows a few of them. For example Sapujapu and LaCor. He'd really like to know whether Drizzel, Blackspell, and Lelant have found their way here. Presumably they have. They can't have taken that long to find the red river. But maybe another horde of giant scorpions had dispatched them. He likes that idea.

It's a pity he didn't get the chance to ask the gnome the way to Atropos's tavern; he hasn't spotted it on his walk down the main streets. He needs someone who can give him some information. He soon finds out that the braziers don't compare with the campfires in the wilderness. They provide lighting but don't allow conversation.

It only dawns on him that he could go into one of the numerous shops to the right and the left of the thoroughfare when he sees a dwarf who is struggling to open a heavy wooden door. "Butcher's Shop" is written in big letters on the wooden sign nailed above it.

A few minutes later Sarius walks into a junk shop. Its shelves are overflowing with curiosities. His gaze is caught by a vampire skull: its fangs have spools of thread skewered on them. He's in the right place. It must be possible to mount spools on scorpion stingers as well.

A gray-bearded man shuffles out from the darkest corner of the shop.

"Buying or selling?" he asks without a word of greeting.

"Selling," Sarius answers. He opens his inventory and places both of the claws, the back plates, and the stinger onto the counter. The anger boils up in him again. He could already be the owner of a wish crystal.

"Ah. Critter bits," the dealer declares. "You won't get much for them. Apart from the stinger, if it's still got poison on it."

He examines the curved black spike with a magnifying glass.

"How much will I get for that?" Sarius asks. "I'd be interested in a wish crystal, for example."

The dealer looks up.

"You can't buy wish crystals. Have to find 'em. Or get them as gifts. I'll give you three gold pieces for the stinger, another two for the rest."

That doesn't sound like much. Tyrania got forty gold coins after the battle with the water women, Sarius recalls.

"That's not enough," he says, acting on a sudden inspiration. "I want ten gold pieces or I'll take my stuff and leave."

The dealer looks from the scorpion parts to Sarius and back again. "Six at the most."

They agree on seven and Sarius leaves the shop feeling elated at how well he's done. That feeling wears off immediately when he sees a scorpion stinger being offered for fifty-five gold pieces in a neighbouring shop. And besides, he'd gotten so caught up in the bargaining that he forgot to ask the way to the tavern.

The next shopkeeper—a shoemaker selling boots that repel poison, boots equipped with blades, and some that even throw lightning bolts—answers his questions readily.

Following his advice, Sarius takes the third turn to the left and finds himself facing a crooked door with its varnish cracking off. The sign above it shows open scissors and, underneath, the lettering "The Final Cut."

Inside, it's almost darker than the nighttime street. The small lanterns just barely throw light onto the tables and the hands of those sitting at them. The faces remain hidden in the dark.

Sarius goes and stands at the bar; the ancient woman behind it ignores him. She's tracing the lines in the wood with her crooked index finger and muttering quietly to herself.

"I would like to register for the Arena fights," Sarius says.

The old woman looks up briefly but doesn't answer.

"Where will I find the list where I can register my name for the Arena fights?" he tries again. "You are Atropos, aren't you?"

At the mention of her name the old innkeeper seems to wake up.

"Yes, I am. You will find the list in the cellar."

She examines Sarius from top to toe. "Do you really want to compete in the fights?"

"Yes."

"As a Two? That's not very clever. But go right ahead. It's got nothing to do with me."

She turns back to the wood grain on the bench.

Sarius finds a staircase that leads down. There's more light in the cellar than upstairs; an open fire illuminates the vaulted ceiling. The list is impossible to miss: it's affixed to the wall and guarded by a soldier. As Sarius approaches, the man addresses him.

"Have you come here to register?"

"Yes."

"What is your name?"

"Sarius."

He peers past the soldier, trying to get a glimpse of the list. He knows some of the names recorded on it: BloodWork, Xohoo, Keskorian, Sapujapu, Tyrania. There's no Lelant, as far as he can tell, nor anyone else who was with him in the labyrinth.

"What weapon do you wish to compete with?"

"A sword."

The soldier notes something down in a book.

"You're still a Two, I see."

Sarius is sick of having that thrown in his face constantly.

"Yes. So? I haven't been here that long. That's why I want to take part in the fights—so I can catch up."

Something is stirring at the back of the vaulted cellar. A tall man with long black hair gets up from his chair and stands in the light from the open fire.

"If you are in such a hurry to catch up, why don't you compete against me? We'll fight a duel."

The sight of his challenger gives Sarius a weird feeling: there's something about him that's not right. Who does he remind him of? A shiver runs down his spine as the realization finally dawns: the unknown warrior looks like Nick Dunmore in ten years' time. The same straight dark hair, the narrow eyes, the dimple in his chin—his features exactly, just more mature and with a touch of stubble. The name of the fighter is LordNick. There's no way that's a coincidence.

"So, what's it to be? Duel or no duel?"

"If it's permitted ..."

It's too bad that he doesn't know LordNick's level. What if he's a Seven or an Eight? But perhaps he's only a Three; then maybe Sarius would have a chance. He thinks about how he did away with the scorpion and feels a surge of confidence.

"Duels in the tavern are permitted," the soldier declares; he's even leaving his list unguarded at the prospect of a fight. "However, the weaker one must challenge the stronger. In this case it means the challenge must come from Sarius."

Sarius is not sure if that's really what he wants. Until now he's fought only against monsters, not comrades. On the other hand, if he wants to compete in the Arena, it can't hurt to have a practice round under his belt.

"Fine. I challenge LordNick to a duel."

"Terrific!" his opponent yells.

It's all very well for him, Sarius thinks. After all, he can see that I'm only a Two. He draws back from LordNick, who's already lining him up in his sights.

"What shall we fight for? I like your wolf helmet—what about that? I'll wager my shield on it; it's got thirty points of defense."

"There's no way I'm risking my helmet."

Not even if you tell me who you are and why you look like me.

"Well, what then?"

Sarius runs quickly through what he owns. "Four pieces of gold."

"What? That's not even worth the trouble." The figure that seems so unpleasantly familiar to Sarius turns back to his table.

"I'd say it's definitely worthwhile," the soldier puts in. "Every successful battle gains you experience and power—you shouldn't undervalue that."

LordNick, who is just about to sit down again, pauses. "Oh, all right then. Four pieces of gold."

They take up a position in front of the fireplace. Sarius can't take his eyes off LordNick's face; it's as though he has to fight against himself. It's no surprise that his opponent's first blow scores a hit. Sarius lifts his shield far too late; LordNick's sword wounds him in the side. The screeching sound starts up immediately.

There's no time to look at his belt and check his meter; Sarius has to trust in the fact that he'll survive another hit. He throws himself on his adversary and lands a blow on his helmet, a second one on his thigh. There! A bit of black is showing on LordNick's belt.

But Sarius's triumph is short-lived. His opponent shoves his shield at Sarius's chest and lunges at him with his sword, gets him in the stomach. Sarius falls to the ground. The injury tone is hurting, hurting, hurting.

"Stop!"

A shadow steps between them. The soldier.

"Sarius is badly injured. He must decide whether he will keep fighting or admit defeat."

It's not really much of a decision. Sarius can barely stand up. The tone is like a circular saw in his head; he'd really like to switch it off but doesn't dare—then he might miss a warning. A hint, something important.

"I give up."

LordNick stands over him triumphantly. "Then pay up the four pieces of gold."

Sarius opens his inventory, carefully avoiding any movement that could make his injuries worse. He hands over the required amount. Now he has only three coins remaining. He ought to quickly sell off the objects that he took from the grave robber. Provided that he even gets the chance. The last remnant of red on his belt is ridiculously thin.

He looks to the side, where a few tables and chairs stand in the half-light. LordNick has moved back there again. A figure rises from one of the other tables in a single flowing motion. Under the hood that casts a shadow over the face, Nick sees the familiar yellow eyes.

"Lesson one," the messenger lectures. "Do not challenge an opponent about whom you know absolutely nothing. Stick with those you have seen fighting."

He kneels down by Sarius and puts a hand on his head. The circular saw tone becomes quieter.

"Lesson two. Only fight for worthwhile things. Gold coins are laughable. Now stand up."

He extends his bony hand; the fingers remind Sarius of scorpions' legs, but he grasps them nonetheless.

"There is something we must discuss. Come with me."

The messenger leads him into the small room next door, where there is a round table in the middle with a single candle on it. They sit down.

"Once again you are in need of healing," the messenger says. "I'm sure you remember the rules that apply in this world? You have only one life, one single life. It seems to me that you are not taking especially good care of it."

Sarius can't think of a fitting response, so he says nothing. It doesn't seem to be easy to please the messenger. He rebukes those who take things easy, and also those who go all out.

"Don't misunderstand me—I value your courage," the messenger says, as though he had heard Sarius's thoughts. "That is why I am here. To help you."

He places a small bottle of sunshine-yellow liquid on the table. Sarius recognizes the healing potion he received after the battle with the trolls.

"I would really like to give this to you. As you know, the Arena fights will take place tomorrow. They don't happen every day—whoever wants to make progress should be there."

"I intend to be," Sarius answers.

"Good."

The messenger leans forward, as though he wants to tell Sarius something confidential and prevent anyone else from hearing it. "The fights begin at midday. Whoever has registered must be at the

Arena at this time. So make sure that you don't miss the beginning, otherwise you will not be admitted!"

"All right," Sarius responds, and reaches his hand out for the little bottle.

"One moment."

The messenger's pale-yellow eyes flicker. He places his hand on Sarius's arm, and suddenly the injury tone becomes louder again.

"I said I would like to *give* this to you, not that you should help yourself to it."

Sarius obediently draws his hand back. It's a little while before the messenger speaks again.

"I think it would be better if you competed in the fights as a Three, not as a Two."

"As a Three? Yes, that would be great."

"Well, then let us pretend that this is the third rite. I will give you an order, Sarius."

The long bony hands play with the healing potion.

"I am sure you have kept the silver disk that opened Erebos to you?"

It takes Sarius a moment to grasp what the messenger means.

"Yes. Of course."

"Good. My orders are as follows: Recruit a new warrior for us—a male or a female. Copy the silver disk and give it to the person whom you consider worthy. But observe the rules!"

A reddish something mingles with the messenger's yellow gaze.

"Do not divulge anything about Erebos. Nothing at all. Tell the novice that you are giving him a great gift. That is what you are doing, in fact—after all, you are giving him a world. Assure yourself of his silence. Explain to him that he may not show this gift to anyone. Explain it to him in such a way that he believes it. You must also make it clear to him that he may only enter Erebos alone, and without witnesses. Just as you do. And take care that he, or she, arrives here soon."

The messenger gently swings the little bottle with the potion.

"Until the new fighter arrives, you will not be admitted either. And you do not want to miss the beginning of the Arena games, after all."

Sarius swallows.

"But it's the middle of the night now, and tomorrow is Sunday! How can I possibly do it so—"

"That is not my responsibility. You are a cunning warrior—and wish to reach Level Three. Should it take longer, so be it; the fights will take place without you."

Sarius is dumbstruck. How will he manage to do it so quickly? He doesn't want to miss the fights for anything. If he becomes a Three now, and does well in the Arena, he could be a Four by tomorrow!

"Do you already have someone in mind?" the messenger inquires.

"Well, yes."

"Who is it?

"A friend of mine. Jamie Cox. I don't think he's here yet."

"Aha. Jamie Cox. Good. And if not him, then who?"

Emily, Sarius thinks. There's no one I'd rather share a secret with than Emily.

"There's a girl I could ask as well," he says.

"What is her name?"

He doesn't want to say the name. He really doesn't.

"Is it Emily Carver?" the messenger asks, more casually than curiously.

Sarius stares at him in disbelief.

"Because if it is, I can only wish you luck, and more success than the other three who have tried so far."

The nerve-racking tone, the messenger's inexplicable knowledge, the sudden time pressure—that all makes it impossible to think clearly. Sarius tries to push everything else aside, to concentrate on what is important: the completion of the task for the third rite.

Jamie, Emily ... Who else could there be? Dan and Alex have long since been infected, Brynne as well. Colin, Rashid, Jerome ...

His best chance is probably one of the girls. He could maybe ask Michelle, or possibly Aisha or Karen. Otherwise he'll have to aim for the lower years ...

"Adrian McVay would be another possibility," he informs the messenger. "I don't think he's in yet, and I'm sure he'd like *Erebos*."

The yellow-eyed man shakes his head almost imperceptibly. "He will not accept either."

There's a pause; the messenger doesn't take his eyes off Sarius. Silently he turns the little bottle in his hand; the sunshine-yellow of the potion, the pus-yellow of his eyes, and the whitish-yellow candle flame are the only bright spots in the room.

"I would still like to try Adrian; I reckon he's curious about the game."

"Then try. So: Jamie Cox, Emily Carver, and Adrian McVay. Good. I will expect one of them. If you should decide on someone else, let me know."

He sets the flask down in front of Sarius and waits until its contents are consumed. Only then does he leave the back room. Sarius barely registers that his belt is regaining its color and the injury tone is disappearing before the door slams shut and the darkness becomes absolute.

TEN

A glance at the computer clock told Nick that it was 12:43 a.m., far too late to ring Jamie. Jamie had a computer for his own use—that was a good start. He didn't use it very often, but Nick would manage to convince him that he couldn't possibly miss out on *Erebos*.

The idea of doing chemistry now was ridiculous, but nevertheless it crossed Nick's mind briefly. The Arena fights could last a long time, so it would be reassuring to get a head start with the writing. But it was more important, far more important, to copy the game first. Nick rummaged through his desk drawers. He still had blank DVDs, he was certain. But where?

It took a little while before he found one, still in its original packaging, under a pile of papers and books. He just hoped that the weight had not ruined the silver disk.

The copying process took longer than Nick had expected. The bar on the progress window jerked forward slowly ... very slowly. Nick stared at it, as if that would speed it up. On the other hand, what difference would it make if it did go faster? He had to wait till morning, had to sleep—although he couldn't imagine even closing his eyes. His mind was just bursting with questions.

First of all, who'd had the idea of giving his player character, LordNick, Nick's appearance? Why would someone do such a thing? He still vividly recalled the situation in the ruined tower, and what he had thought about while creating Sarius. He hadn't wanted to make him resemble anybody, not for a second. Especially not someone he was acquainted with.

It has to be someone who knows me. Someone I know. The thought was exciting and unpleasant at the same time. Was it a friend? Colin? Was *he* disguised as LordNick, and not Lelant after all?

The blue progress bar hadn't even crawled halfway. Nick's train of thought felt similarly sluggish.

All the other players who knew him would believe that he was LordNick. They would be convinced that they had identified at least one of their fellow fighters. Or one of their opponents, depending on how you looked at it. No one would put forward the equation Sarius = Nick. He wasn't quite sure whether that pleased him or bothered him.

His computer copied, copied, and copied.

Hmm, what name would Jamie choose for himself? And which race? The dwarves came spontaneously to mind, but straightaway Nick decided that was unfair. Jamie wasn't short—he was average height. Anyway, what mattered most was how Jamie *wanted* to be. Dark and mysterious, like a vampire? Elegant, like a dark elf? Massive and threatening, like a barbarian?

None of them really suited him that well. He was just himself. Full stop. But whatever he decided on, Nick was sure he'd be able to recognize Jamie in any get-up—even as Alditha the lizard lady or something. He grinned. Maybe he really should try to ring him? He would understand, and the cell wouldn't wake anyone else.

Hopefully.

Or a text message. But what to write?

Have 2 meet u, urgent, preferably right away, otherwise 2morrow @ 7am?

No, that was impossible. Nick knew how much Jamie loved

sleeping in on Sundays. He wouldn't be up and about before nine o'clock. Nine o'clock! That was horribly late—because who said Jamie would start playing immediately?

The DVD had finally finished burning. Nick got it out of the drive, wrote "Erebos" on the upper side with a waterproof marker, and put it back carefully in its case.

Get to bed, he told himself. But his thoughts wouldn't stop going round and round: as he was brushing his teeth, in the bathroom, and finally under the bedcovers, which smelled of fabric softener.

What would happen if he didn't manage it in time? He'd miss the Arena games—so what?

But he *did* care. It was finally a chance to make progress. The messenger was on his side; Nick could feel it. After all, he'd already given Nick some tips, and he'd been right. It was smarter to pick only those opponents he'd already seen in action. LordNick wasn't one of them, and BloodWork certainly wasn't. But he'd give Lelant a good thrashing if he got his hands on him, and Feniel as well. Provided they both even found their way into the city.

Nick bored his head deep into the pillow. He'd go over to Jamie's first thing in the morning and get him out of bed at nine by ringing the doorbell. That way he wouldn't lose any time, and Jamie could make a start at once. Perfect. Nick knew his friend would be beside himself with enthusiasm.

"You're not serious." Two half-opened eyes looked out through the half-opened door. Jamie was wearing a weird striped robe and two odd socks. He must have thrown something on in a hurry in order to answer the door.

"Oh well, come in. But be quiet, my parents are still asleep."

Nick's bad conscience cast only a light gray shadow on his elation.

He'd handled it all perfectly. Woken Jamie with the cell instead of the doorbell, so that Mr. and Mrs. Cox wouldn't be sitting bolt upright in bed as well. He tried all the harder now not to make a noise; the last thing he wanted was to endanger the success of the mission. He slipped his shoes off and followed Jamie into the kitchen, where there was a delicate aroma of stale fat. A frying pan was sitting on the stove; someone had tried in vain to scrape the burnt hamburger out of it.

Jamie got himself a glass of water and sat down opposite Nick at the kitchen table. Judging by the look of him, he wasn't quite all there yet.

"What time is it actually?" he murmured.

"Just on eight o'clock."

"You are completely off your rocker," Jamie said, and drank the water in one gulp.

"If I remember rightly," he went on, "I suggested yesterday that we should meet, but you decided you didn't have any time. That's fine. But why ... why on earth are you standing at my door at the crack of dawn?"

Nick hoped his expression looked mysterious and promising at the same time.

"I've got something for you," he said, and pulled the DVD out of his jacket pocket. "But before I can give it to you, we need to agree on a few things."

"What is it?" Still half asleep, Jamie wiped his hand over his eyes and reached for the case.

Nick pulled it back with a rapid movement. "Just a moment. There are a few things we need to sort out first."

"Huh? What the hell is this?" Jamie furrowed his brow angrily. "Are you messing with me? First you wake me up, supposedly because it's something important, and then you start playing some cat-and-mouse game?"

Nick realized he'd gone about things the wrong way. Why did he have to be the one unlucky enough to get the recruiting task on the weekend? On a normal school day everything would have been far more straightforward.

"Okay, once more from the beginning. I'd like to give you something that's really fantastic—in the truest sense of the word. You'll love it, but you have to listen to me for a second."

His friend's face showed neither curiosity nor enthusiasm. "It's that CD that's been doing the rounds for weeks, isn't it? That pirate copy?"

"Uh, well, sort of ..."

"Who says I'm interested in it?"

"You will be, believe me! It's really cool. I wouldn't have thought it at first either, but it's incredibly awesome." He noticed he was using almost exactly the same words as Brynne had a few days before, and backed off.

"Uh-huh." Jamie yawned. "And what is it exactly?"

"I can't tell you that."

"Why not?"

"Because it's not possible!" Nick desperately searched for the right words, words that wouldn't give away too much on the one hand, but would arouse Jamie's curiosity on the other.

"That's just how it works. I'm not allowed to tell you anything, and you're not allowed to tell anybody else. I'll give you the ... uh, the DVD, but only if you don't show anyone." Even before Nick had finished speaking, he knew that this talk was going wrong. The furrows on Jamie's forehead had turned into full-blown craters.

"You're not allowed to tell me anything—who says so?"

Nick shook his head to get rid of the image of the yellow eyes. It was enough to drive him up the wall. Even if he were to disregard the messenger's instructions, he still wouldn't be able to give Jamie the whole picture. He couldn't *explain* what made *Erebos* so unique. Jamie had to experience it himself.

Apart from that, he didn't dare break the messenger's rules, as he reluctantly admitted to himself. The messenger would take note of his infringement. The messenger had even guessed that he was thinking about Emily Carver.

"It doesn't matter who says so. I can't tell you anything; that's part of the rules."

"What rules? Listen, Nick, I'm beginning to get a funny feeling about this. I mean—you know me. You know that I'm curious and I'd really like to find out the story with these mysterious DVDs, but all this beating around the bush is totally ludicrous. Either you give me the DVD, just like that, or you forget it. I think conditions are stupid."

"Well, yes, but—" Nick searched for words. It had been so easy with him. Brynne hadn't taken three minutes to lure him. "But the others are sticking to it too—it's no skin off their nose."

"Ouch." Jamie stood up, filled his glass with water again, and drank it in one gulp. "You're acting completely unlike yourself, you know that? The *others*! You never used to care about them."

He sat down at the table again; his eyes were distinctly more alert now.

"Know what? Give me the thing. Now I really want to know what the story is."

"You're going to stick to the rules? Not talk to anyone about it? Not show it to anyone?"

Jamie shrugged his shoulders, looking amused. "Maybe. That depends."

"In that case, I can't give it to you."

"Fine. Forget it. Then I can go back to bed again."

"You're an idiot, d'you know that?" The words slipped out of Nick's mouth before he could consider them. His disappointment over the fact that his superb plan was going to be thwarted by Jamie's stubbornness had overwhelmed him for a moment. But it was really enough to make you scream. Why didn't he at least want to try it? Why was he letting him down like this? And above all, how was Nick going to get everything done on time?

The word "idiot" had an immediate effect on Jamie's expression. No more creased forehead; it was smooth as glass.

"You know, Nick," he said, "I think Mr. Watson is right. He suspects there's something dangerous doing the rounds at our school, and as from now I've started believing that too. I probably should have taken your DVD from you. Then I'd finally know what it's actually about."

What garbage, Nick wanted to say, but he bit his tongue. Anger was still choking him, and Jamie's self-important tirade made him want to puke. "Something dangerous," for goodness' sake.

"The interesting thing is," Jamie went on, "that people are obviously all keeping to these ... rules, as you call them. Nobody is talking. But a few bits of information are beginning to trickle through, Mr. Watson says. He's heard it's a game called *Erebos*."

"Oh yeah?" Nick snapped at him. "And what if I tell you that's complete bullshit?"

"Well, then tell me that," Jamie retorted. "Whatever. I'm keeping out of it completely. And incidentally, so are a few others who've noticed the same things I have."

Jamie's mischievous grin flashed for a moment. "Nick, you goof, just forget it, huh? It's just been hyped up; it won't last. But I've got the feeling that the people who get involved are very quickly going to be in way over their heads."

"Thanks for the warning, Uncle Jamie," Nick mocked, and saw with great satisfaction that he'd wiped the smile from his friend's face. "Little Nicky will be very careful. Man, you have no idea what a fool you're making of yourself."

He stood up and walked to the door, this time without being particularly quiet. What was he supposed to do now? Plan B was to ring Emily. The thought made Nick's stomach feel as if it was shrinking to the size of a walnut. Maybe he should try Adrian first after all. He didn't have his number, damn it—how come he hadn't thought of that yesterday?

"When you're fed up with this bullshit, give me a call," said Jamie, before he shut the door behind Nick.

He was never going to speak another word to Jamie. What a jerk. Didn't know what he was missing, and felt obliged to patronize Nick instead of just being pleased.

Now he was going to have to give his gift to someone else. Nervously he fumbled his cell out of his jacket pocket.

Hello, Emily, he would say. Or acting cool: Hey, Emily. Nick here. Can you spare me a moment? Can I drop in?

Just the thought of it made his hands sweat. He already knew Emily had turned down three others—he'd even been there to witness Rashid's attempt. *But I'm going to do it differently.* Suddenly he knew what he would say. It was obvious, and it didn't break the rules.

"Hello?" Emily's voice sounded rough—either with sleep or a cold. Nick hadn't even thought about what time it was—shit, shit, shit. His first instinct was to hang up again, but that would look even dumber.

"Hi, Emily." He cleared his throat. "Sorry to disturb you so early, but I need to talk to you briefly."

130

"Now?" That didn't sound very enthusiastic.

"Well, yes, now would be ... good."

"So what is it about?"

Nick prepared to launch into his explanation, which was to culminate in the sentence *I want to give you a world*, but Emily was already speaking again.

"Oh, I know—it's about these wretched CDs, is it? Did you find out any more details? Yesterday someone tried to palm one of them off on me for the third time. And they all make such an incredibly big mystery out of it."

Nick's laboriously constructed speech fell apart within the space of one breath. Now he had absolutely no idea what he should say.

"Nick? Are you still there?"

"Yes. Er ... why did you actually say no every time?"

"The same reason as you, I assume. I don't like the whole business. Besides, the guys who approach me about it are always a bit creepy, and I don't want any of them giving me anything."

Nick shut his eyes. He'd been a hair's breadth away from qualifying as a creepy guy.

"So?" Emily went on. "What did you find out?"

"Nothing. I'm sorry. There was something else I wanted to ..."

"Aha. What was it?"

Nick's brain felt completely empty. Desperately, he snatched at the first thing he could think of.

"It's about ... Adrian. Adrian McVay. Do you happen to have his phone number?"

The silence at the other end of the line sounded like complete bewilderment. Nick hated himself for his stupidity.

"Do you mean the thin blond one who always looks a bit frightened? The one whose father took his own life?"

131

Nick was speechless for a moment. "Took his own life"? Since when did Emily express herself like that?

"I only barely know Adrian by sight. What makes you think that I would have his number?"

Yes, what did? Nick rested his forehead against the nearest wall, strongly tempted to bang his head against it very hard.

"No reason. I thought you knew each other. I was probably wrong about that. I'm sorry."

He'd be able to end the conversation in a sec, which would be a great relief in one way. In another way it wouldn't be, since it hadn't been a good conversation. He made another attempt to rescue it. "Anyway, how have you been? Have you finished your chemistry assignment?"

Silence. Probably Emily had identified the sudden change of subject as exactly what it was—a clumsy conversation filler.

"Come on, Nick, tell me what you really want."

To give you Erebos. *Or at least to hear your voice.*

"I told you, Adrian's number." Yikes, had that just sounded snotty? "I'm sorry, I thought you had tutored him once, but I must have been wrong."

"Yes." Emily sounded as though she believed him. He was in luck. Now he could hear noises in the background; there was a rustling as though she was covering the microphone of her cell. Then she was back again. "Listen, Nick, I have to go. Dad's coming to pick me up in half an hour, and I have to help my mother with something before then."

"Oh. Yes, of course. Well, enjoy your Sunday."

He hadn't gotten anywhere at all. He had to be at the Arena by midday, and it was nearly nine already. Adrian, he had to get in touch with Adrian.

He opened the address book on his cell and went through it name by name—maybe one of his friends had some connection to Adrian.

He stopped at Henry Scott. Henry played basketball too, and he was in Adrian's class. Bingo.

Henry picked up after two rings.

"Hi. Listen, can you give me Adrian McVay's phone number?"

"Sure. Wait a minute."

Henry read out a landline number to Nick, which wasn't ideal. But never mind.

"What do you want from Adrian?"

Since Henry had been so obliging, Nick couldn't exactly tell him to take his curiosity and stick it somewhere.

"Oh, I've got something I'd like to give him."

He could actually sense the sudden attentiveness at the other end.

"Is it something you could give me too?"

Hello. Nick had to grin.

"Well, yes. In theory."

"Is it square on the outside, and round and silver on the inside?"

Now Nick laughed out loud.

"It certainly is."

"Then it's better off with me. Adrian has already said no once. You'll be wasting your time."

So the messenger had been right again. Was it really possible that all the candidates Nick had picked out disapproved of *Erebos*? Why, when they didn't even know the game?

"All right, if you say so. I'll just give it to you then. Where do you live?"

"Gillingham Road. But we could meet halfway!" Henry sounded exceptionally keen.

"All right. Let's meet at Golders Green station; that's near you, isn't it?

Half an hour later Nick's *Erebos* copy had changed hands. Henry had been willing to agree to everything: total silence, secrecy, and discretion. No questions, no doubts, only eager nodding. He had his own laptop and was dying to get started. Nick had formed the distinct impression that Henry already had a rough idea what it was about, but he hadn't asked. He didn't actually care. The main thing was that he had got himself a novice. Henry would have his fun, and every time Nick came across a One, he would wonder whether it was *his* One.

ELEVEN

"Have you carried out your orders?"

It's exactly eleven o'clock by the time Sarius is standing in the back room of Atropos's inn once more. The messenger is sitting at the table, scratching bits of wax off the tabletop with his bony fingers.

"Yes, I have," Sarius says. "But I didn't pass *Erebos* on to any of the three people I named yesterday; I passed it on to someone else."

The messenger's fingers cease scratching. Sarius thinks he can discern disapproval in the yellow eyes.

"To whom?"

"His name is Henry Scott, and he's fourteen years old. Goes to my school."

"Tell me more about him."

More? He doesn't know any more. Only some trivial things.

"He has blond hair and he's fairly tall for his age. He plays basketball as well. He lives in Gillingham Road. He was pretty keen on *Erebos*; I think he already knew what it was about."

The messenger doesn't answer for a moment. He makes a little pile out of the wax he's scratched off the tabletop.

"All right. We will consider your task to be completed. Tell me, nevertheless, why you didn't bring me one of the others? Jamie Cox? Emily Carver? Adrian McVay?"

Why is the messenger holding him up? Sarius needs to find the

Arena; who knows where it is? There'll be another labyrinth on the way if he's unlucky, or trolls will hold him up. Anything's possible. Besides, he's secretly hoping for new equipment, which was what he received on his last advancement. Now, so close to the fights, it would really come in handy.

"Jamie and Emily weren't interested, and I didn't speak to Adrian because I'd already been able to sort things out with Henry," he explains.

The messenger's eyes glimmer like embers fanned by a gust of wind. "Why did Jamie Cox refuse?"

Does that really matter? Sarius wants to get going again. He wants to see the list of all the registered fighters, wants to think about who he might have a chance against. He doesn't want to talk about Jamie.

"He didn't like the whole secrecy thing."

"Did he say anything else?" the messenger insists.

Oh, for goodness' sake! Was he expected to take notes on the whole conversation?

"Yes, he said that he reckons all the sneaking around is stupid, that he thinks I'm behaving like an idiot, and that a few of our teachers think something dangerous is being circulated."

The messenger leans forward attentively and rests his chin on his hand.

"What teachers?"

Sarius hesitates. Why would this interest the messenger? He's itching to ask the question, but he doesn't want to prolong the conversation unnecessarily. Besides, it doesn't matter, because there's no way Mr. Watson is interested in *Erebos*—being denied entry isn't going to bother him.

"Actually, it's only one teacher. His name is Watson, and we have him for English."

The messenger nods to acknowledge the information.

"What was the reason in Emily Carver's case?"

The memory of the conversation stung Nick.

"She's already said no a few times and ... didn't want to accept any gifts."

"... didn't want to accept any gifts," the messenger repeats thoughtfully.

Is that it? Sarius would like to ask. He really hopes so. It's late, he has to hurry, and the messenger's face is disturbing him more than usual today. He wants to get away.

"Good. Let us hope that Henry Scott isn't a long time coming. Let us hope that you have brought us a worthy novice."

The messenger stands up without letting Sarius out of his sight.

"It is your first fight against your peers, isn't it?"

"Yes," Sarius says, eager for good tips.

"I am keen to see how you will acquit yourself. How you will choose your opponent. Some of the best fighters are here, and all five from the Inner Circle."

It's about time for the messenger to answer one of his questions for a change.

"What is the Inner Circle?"

The messenger smiles. Whenever he does that, Sarius feels chilled.

"The Inner Circle? They are the best of the best. These fighters will contest the last and greatest quest on their own. If they triumph, they will be richly rewarded."

Sarius doesn't need to ask how to make it into the Inner Circle; he knows already. By being more cunning than the others, stronger. Gaining victories, finding wish crystals. It's perfectly clear to him that he is still nowhere near.

The door leading to the taproom room opens, and light penetrates. Grains of dust dance in the bright-yellow beam.

Sarius turns around one last time to face the messenger. "Don't I get any new equipment?"

"You would have gotten it for Jamie Cox," the messenger answers, still smiling. "Good luck at the tournament. I am very keen to see what happens—did I say that already?"

There are noticeably more people milling around in front of the inn than last night. Sarius follows a group of heavily armed barbarians who are obviously on their way to the Arena. A few minutes later two lizard people, three vampires, three dark elves, and a dwarf have joined them. The dwarf is an old acquaintance: Sapujapu. He's armed himself with a giant halberd and a shield he can hide behind entirely. Sarius can't see his level—so it must be higher than three. But there's a Two walking along with the vampires, and even a One among the dark elves. Sarius smiles indulgently.

"Hi, Sarius!" Sapujapu greets him.

"Hello," Sarius returns his greeting, amazed. "I didn't know we could talk here without a fire."

The dwarf shifts his halberd onto the other shoulder.

"There are different rules in the cities than in the open countryside. Are you going to the Arena fights too?"

Sapujapu's talkative mood is an unexpected gift. Sarius grasps it with both hands.

"Yes. This is the right way, isn't it?"

"It is. I already went there last night and had a look around. The Arena is gigantic. It's an amazing sight—you'll see."

"Is this your first tournament?" Sarius inquires.

"What? No, of course not! I've been to the Arena at the King's Tomb twice already. Haven't you?"

It's smarter to tell the truth if he wants to find out more.

"No, this is my first time. I'm really keen to see how it works."

Xohoo runs past them, then Nurax, who bares his werewolf's fangs. In greeting or threat, who knows? Well, well, Sarius thinks. They made it this far too.

"How it works? Well, you can challenge others or be challenged, and then there's a fight. It's incredibly loud all around you, everyone is yelling and screaming, they stamp their ..."

BloodWork stomps up with giant strides and barges into Sapujapu, who immediately loses his train of thought. He and Sarius stare after the giant barbarian, who carries an enormous executioner's sword on his back. His dark braid dangles down over it.

Now, where were they? Sarius still has to coax the most important information out of the dwarf.

"What can you win? And how?"

"That's agreed on beforehand. You decide that together with your opponent: my sword for your sword, my wish crystal for one or two of your levels. That sort of thing. I'm feeling all jittery this time. My halberd isn't great. I have to wield it in two hands, and that means I can't use the shield."

Sapujapu's weapon must be seriously heavy. Just the long handle itself looks extremely unwieldy; the sharpened blade at its tip shines like polished steel.

"But if you hit someone, you're bound to do some wicked damage," Sarius comforts him.

"Yes. *If* I hit someone."

They turn a corner and Sarius sees the Arena at the end of a long avenue. It is circular, snow white, and broken up by high arches, like the Roman Colosseum. He feels awe at the sight ... Or is it from the music that surrounds him? It must have started up again a little while ago. He never notices when it begins, only suddenly realizes that it's back, staying with him like a fortifying spell. Or calling him, as it does now. It explains everything, without words. It's suddenly completely clear to him that the Arena is his destiny, for better or worse.

A colossal copper tablet right at the entrance to the Arena lists all the registered fighters. Sarius finds himself between someone called Nodhaggr and an old acquaintance—Tyrania, his partner in the fight against the water women. While a green-skinned gnome records his presence, Sarius skims over the list, looking for other familiar names. He quickly finds Keskorian, Nurax, Sapujapu, and Xohoo. Samira and LordNick are also registered—and the fighters from the labyrinth: Arwen's Child, Blackspell, Drizzel, Feniel, and Lelant. How annoying. So they've found their way to the White City after all, instead of ending up as scorpion food.

"Sarius is registered. Sarius should make his way to the dark elves' rooms and wait for the start of the fights," the gnome squawks.

Fortunately, the inside of the Arena is peppered with signposts. The dark elves' preparation rooms are situated right next to those of the cat people. For the first time, Sarius sets eyes on the males of the species: heavy and sleek like tigers.

As expected, the small room where the dark elves wait for the games to begin is overcrowded. Sarius finds some space over by the wall and listens to the conversation between a red-haired elf with particularly long ears and a Two with sandy hair. A Two!

"What happens if I lose?" the Two asks.

"Then give up quickly—otherwise you might get finished off by your opponent. I've seen that happen."

"What then? Am I out then?"

"Of course you are. Don't tell me you've forgotten the rules?"

"Nah. Got it."

Sarius pushes on through the crowd. He's spotted Xohoo

at the other end of the room—of all the dark elves Sarius knows, Xohoo is his favorite. Along the way he keeps catching scraps of conversation.

"... heard that BloodWork wants to give it a try today."

"Yeah, well, he's crazy. Yes, okay, he's strong, but still ..."

The crowd is getting denser by the minute.

"... any more chances; that's why I absolutely have to win a wish crystal today."

"I want to go up two levels. You just wouldn't believe how heavy my instructions were at the last rite. I don't want to go through that again."

Sarius has almost reached his goal. Xohoo is standing alone in a corner, adjusting his helmet.

"Hi, Xohoo."

"Hello, Sarius."

"Nervous?"

"Yes. Kind of. You?"

"Me too. This is my first tournament."

"Oh. Yeah, well, you'll see. The Arena's really something."

Sarius looks up toward the vaulted ceiling of the room. He can hear noise coming from up there—the sounds of voices, laughter, and stamping. It's the crowd, Sarius realizes, his nerves throbbing. It would have been better to have a look at the fights first instead of leaping in straightaway without having a clue. What should he do if LordNick challenges him again? Or if he has to compete against BloodWork? Then he might as well give up now.

"Who did you fight against last time?" he asks Xohoo.

"Against Duke first—I beat him. Then against Drizzel. That was really dumb of me. He's totally devious."

"Aha. So that means you can choose your opponents?"

"Mostly, but not always. Hey ... I think it's starting."

Bam bam bam! Above their heads a rhythmic pounding is starting up. The crowd is stamping out its impatience. A few voices can be heard, then more join them. A chorus of many voices is chanting the same word, over and over: "Blood—Blood—Blood."

"Fighters into the Arena!" a voice bellows outside. Jubilation breaks out.

Sarius stands mute in the corner; he's happy to let the others go first. But the others are hesitating as well. No one wants to be the first to go.

"Move it, you heroes!" screams the giant soldier on guard. He has buffalo horns growing out either side of his helmet; his whip cracks once, twice. "You registered yourselves—now it's time to show what you're made of!" He pushes the first fighter through the archway; the others follow hesitantly.

Outside they're bellowing. "Blood—Blood—Blood."

I'm not made to be a hero, Sarius thinks. I'm made to be a spectator. I'd much rather be sitting up there in the crowd, shouting and stomping.

The others push and pull him to the exit. They run along a passageway, a dark maw that releases them into the light and noise at the end, into a gigantic circle.

"The dark elves!" the crowd shouts. The applause fires up. Sarius looks around and wishes he could sink into the sand of the Arena.

Thousands upon thousands of spectators fill the tiers of the round building, which seems to reach into the sky. The crowd is made up of all shapes and sizes imaginable, including some Sarius has never seen before. In one of the lower tiers, a bit to the right of him, there's a man with a spider's head. The eight legs that grow out of his skull in place of ears are wriggling with anticipation. Sarius turns away, looks a snake creature in the face. It is darting its tongue in and out mockingly. Two seats farther on, he discovers a woman with an eye sticking out of her forehead on a stalk. All around them is a throng of dwarves, elves, vampires, and some translucent creatures that look as though their skin is covering nothing but air. For a moment Sarius struggles for breath; the high circular rows of seating seem like a noose of sound and bodies that will tighten as soon he steps into the middle of the Arena.

In order to distract himself he turns his attention to the other two groups of bold fighters who are already in the Arena: cat people and lizard people. In comparison with the dark elves, there aren't many of them.

"The dwarves!" the crowd bellows, and now a whole bunch of the small, muscular, short-armed characters stumble out of another exit. Five stewards in black cloaks make sure that they go and stand in their allocated place.

Sarius spots Sapujapu, who's holding his halberd in front of him as though it is a talisman against the ugly faces around him. Sarius spies three dwarf women as well. They scarcely differ from their male counterparts—only the beards are missing.

The vampires are loudly announced and step into the shadiest part of the Arena. Their group is big; their numbers are almost approaching those of the dark elves. Drizzel and Blackspell are standing right out in front, as though they can hardly wait for the fighting. Sarius gets the impression that Blackspell is looking in his direction. *Surely he won't want to challenge me?*

It seems to Sarius that everyone here is stronger, more agile, and more experienced than he is. I'm going to die, he thinks. All this will go on without me and I will never find out what this great task is that awaits us, because no one will tell me. Probably these are my last minutes in Erebos. Unless the messenger is here ... unless he saves me again.

He looks around, searching for the gaunt figure that is so familiar to him in all its eeriness, but his gaze gets lost in the masses of spectators. And besides, now the humans are stepping into the Arena. There are only three, and of them LordNick is the only one Sarius knows. The barbarians follow after them to a deafening roar; they are cheered like no one before them.

What do you know? thinks Sarius. The victors are coming. Why are we even bothering?

They look gigantic as they march across the sunlit stadium to reach their allocated place. Their weapons are massive; Sarius doubts he could so much as lift one of them, let alone fight with it. The ax Keskorian is carrying is about as big as Sarius himself.

The barbarians have taken up position and a drum roll starts.

Soon it will start and then I'll be dead. Soon it will start and then I'll be dead.

But the excited whisper that's rippling over the rows of spectators isn't to do with the start of the fights. A new gate opens, bigger than the others. Four Titans the size of trees, with golden skin, carry in a circular golden platform, on which five fighters are standing. Two barbarians, a dark she-elf, a human, and a cat man. The spectators' cheering swallows all sound except for the music, which wordlessly recounts heroic deeds, secrets, things that normal warriors cannot even imagine. The bearers come to a halt in the center of the Arena. All that gold shines in the bright daylight like another sun.

"Welcome the warriors of the Inner Circle," says a voice that seems to come from all directions at once. "They are the best among you, the strongest, the boldest. Until they are defeated by one of you. Do not forget when you go into battle that each of you can be counted among the Inner Circle, if you show yourself worthy."

Seldom has anything seemed more desirable to Sarius. The five chosen ones on the platform appear invulnerable. He would change places with any of them instantly—and there's a dark elf among them after all, not just barbarians. He could stand a chance. He could be standing up there. But certainly not as a Three.

The platform is given pride of place at the edge of the Arena. The members of the Inner Circle sit down, and all at once it goes quiet. There's just whispering, impatient rustling, and quiet, furtive music that quickens Sarius's heartbeat.

Then a man steps forward from nowhere. He is naked except for a loincloth; his skin is as brown as old leather, his physique muscular. He holds a long staff in his hand that he strikes twice rapidly on the ground, like a master of ceremonies at court. Sarius's attention is caught by curious details: long—no, very long—pointy ears that would put those of a dark elf to shame. Tufts of hair like gray balls of wool over said ears and right on the brow, and a mustache that stands out horizontally to the sides. That's all disconcerting enough; but what throws him most are the goggle eyes, light-colored and spherical. Big white marbles that threaten to fall out of his head at any moment.

The man looks around with these bulging eyes. It seems as though everyone is shrinking from his gaze. *There's something weird about him.* Sarius studies the master of ceremonies more closely and discovers further peculiarities. The feet! Human feet with the claws of a bird of prey. But that's still not it. The revolting spider man Sarius is trying not to look at also has strange traits, but despite the disgusting twitching legs on his head, he seems to be in harmony. As if he belongs here. Big Goggle-Eyes, on the other hand, looks out of place, as if someone had accidentally abandoned him in the world of Erebos.

When the man speaks, there's a rushing sound like water in his voice.

"The rules are known. I call upon the fighters. No one may choose a partner who is less advanced than the challenger himself. I will make a start with the dwarves. Bahanior!"

It takes a few seconds before the dwarf summoned steps into the middle. Sarius cannot spot a number branded anywhere on his clothing, so Bahanior must be at least a Three.

"Choose your opponent," Goggle-Eyes demands.

Now Bahanior is really hesitating. He turns on the spot once, twice. Stares into the horde of dark elves.

If he chooses me, he must be a Three as well, Sarius concludes, otherwise my level would be too low for him. That wouldn't be bad. I can cope with a dwarf who's a Three.

But Bahanior keeps turning, lingers on the cat people, then on the vampires. The master of ceremonies raps his staff on the sand impatiently.

"Make a decision."

Several more seconds pass. The crowd begins to become restless, cries of "Weakling! Midget! Chicken!" begin to ring out. Sarius thanks his stars that he's not in Bahanior's place.

"I challenge Blackspell," the dwarf finally decides.

Sarius can tell from the brisk tempo at which Blackspell emerges from the ranks of the vampires and positions himself opposite Bahanior that the challenger hasn't made a good call. The vampire is probably at least two or three levels above him and is already looking forward to carving Bahanior into little pieces. Fleetingly Sarius recalls what the robber with the big hat had told him at the beginning: that Blackspell had been beaten by Drizzel at some stage and had to give up three levels. He's sure to have made them up again in the meantime. In any event, Drizzel must be gruesomely strong. There is no way Sarius is going to challenge him.

Blackspell draws the sword that Sarius so envies him for—the one that looks as though it were cast from red glass. Meanwhile, Bahanior gives the impression that he would like nothing better than to flee by leaping wildly over the rows of spectators. His sword looks like a butterknife next to that of his opponent.

"What will you fight for?"

Bahanior shifts indecisively from one leg to the other.

"If I win, I will receive one level and ... twenty pieces of gold from Blackspell."

"That's too little," the vampire counters. "Two levels and thirty pieces of gold."

Bahanior doesn't answer. It's obvious from looking at him that he is already deeply regretting his choice of opponent.

"Do you agree?" the master of ceremonies inquires.

"I have only twenty-five pieces of gold," Bahanior confesses.

They agree on that. Two levels, twenty-five pieces of gold. Sarius is convinced it's more than Bahanior can afford.

"Fight!" calls Goggle-Eyes.

Bahanior immediately shrinks back three steps. Blackspell pursues him, his shield turned casually aside, as if he wants to provoke the dwarf into an attack.

Knock knock knock! A sound from another world. "Nick?"

Shit, not now! No, please!

Without taking the headphones from his ears, Nick leaped up from the chair and watched over his shoulder as the doorknob turned. That was his father—why couldn't he leave him in peace?

Nick tried to conceal the monitor with his body, realizing at the same time how that must look. On a sudden inspiration he switched the monitor off and opened his chemistry book, at random, any place. The clanking of swords echoed in his ears.

"Your mother and I want to go to the movies. We can just make it to the afternoon show before my night shift. Want to come? We haven't all been out together for ages."

Groans of pain were coming through the headphones. That was bound to be Bahanior. A hissing sound and a blow followed.

"I asked you something, young man! Kindly take those things out of your ears. Or do you think I'm going to buy the idea that you're studying when you're blasting your ears full of music?" His father's face was taking on a more colorful hue.

Damn, damn, damn. Nick took the headphones off.

"That's better. So, about the movies—yes or no?"

"I don't think so, Dad. I've still got some more studying to do; it's harder than I thought."

William Dunmore shook his head in disbelief. "And you can't take a break just for two hours? You didn't even ask what film we're seeing."

The fight was probably over by now. Blackspell had probably won, but he couldn't be certain. And what if big Goggle-Eyes called up Sarius as the next challenger and he just stood there among everyone without moving? What would happen then? Nick would have liked nothing better than to shoot his father into space.

"Doesn't make any difference what the film is, Dad. I'm staying home, okay?"

His father's suspicious gaze ran over the desk, the computer, the book.

"Guess you feel too grown up to go to the pictures with your parents, hmm?"

The next sentence would be: *But we're still allowed to pay for everything. Keep coughing up more and more, and never get anything in return.* Dad occasionally got into this mood, but why today? Why did it have to be today?

148

Nick smiled, which took an enormous effort.

"Believe me, I would just love to go and see a film with you—I'd much rather do that than torture myself with this shitty chemistry assignment. But the topic is bloody difficult. And I slept atrociously last night." *Nothing but the truth.*

Perhaps it was the strong language that made Dad believe him. He always said that a liar doesn't swear. Too bad he was mistaken.

"Hmm. Well, if it's as serious as all that ... I must say I'm a bit taken aback. Hopefully all that effort will show in your results."

Very unlikely, unfortunately. "I hope so too."

"Well then, Professor. Have fun."

Bahanior has disappeared out of the Arena, and there's no trace of Blackspell either. But one of them must have won, mustn't they? Now a dark elf is fighting a lizard woman; Sarius doesn't know either of them. He is still standing in the same place, next to Xohoo, and would really like to ask him what he's missed. He tries, but it doesn't work. No conversations in the Arena, it seems. It's probably better that way. If no one has noticed his absence, no one can complain about it.

The lizard woman fights without weapons; instead she hurls lightning bolts at her elfin adversary. Is she a magician? The dark elf manages to dodge twice, and now the lizard is retreating too; she has no strength left, needs a rest. It doesn't take long for the elf to figure that out and attack her with his spear. But by then the lizard woman has already gathered enough magic for another bolt of lightning, which flattens her opponent.

"The victor is Dragoness. She will receive one level and fifteen pieces of gold from Zajquor."

There's a brief rushing sound and suddenly Sarius sees a Two appear on Zajquor's armor. Nothing about Dragoness changes, at least nothing Sarius can discern. The chosen ones on the platform are sure to see something. A Four that turns into a Five, for example.

"Xohoo!" big Goggle-Eyes calls.

A shudder runs through the dark elf next to Sarius. He hesitates only a moment before he grasps his sword and his shield more tightly and starts off. The others let him past, and Xohoo positions himself in the middle of the Arena.

Good luck, Sarius thinks.

"Choose your opponent."

Obviously Xohoo has already been thinking about his strategy, because he immediately turns toward the small group of humans.

"I challenge LordNick."

What on earth for, you idiot? You'll never beat him! On the other hand—who knows? His instinct could be wrong; he doesn't know Xohoo's level. So why is he so tense?

Is it possible that the person concealed behind Xohoo is someone acquainted with Nick? Who may know that Nick Dunmore hasn't been hanging out in the world of *Erebos* all that long, and who has now used his brilliant deductive powers to conclude that LordNick's level can't be all that high?

LordNick lets his gaze rest briefly on Xohoo before he steps forward. The same uneasy feeling stirs in Sarius as the previous night. The sight of the fighter unsettles him. As familiar as his reflection, except that he has no control over it.

Who are you, hmm? Once again it's clear to Sarius that all the fighters who've ever encountered him outside Erebos will be convinced when they look at LordNick that they're dealing with Nick Dunmore. In their minds, every time this self-proclaimed Lord screws up, it will be down to him. You asshole, he thinks. Who said you could?

"What will you fight for?"

"One level and twenty pieces of gold," Xohoo says.

"Too little."

By now, Xohoo should really be smelling a rat.

The elf seems unsure, waits for a counteroffer from his opponent. None is forthcoming, so he makes the next suggestion himself. "One level and twenty-five pieces of gold?"

"Certainly not," LordNick declares. "Two levels and ... let's say twenty-five pieces of gold. But definitely two levels."

"That's too much for me."

"Bad luck. Shouldn't have challenged me then. If you can surrender two levels without dying, you must accept. And you can."

If only LordNick wasn't such an arrogant bastard, Sarius thinks. Or if I could announce at school that he's nothing to do with me. But even that's against the rules.

Big Goggle-Eyes has raised his staff.

"Fight!"

In a flash LordNick has hurled himself at Xohoo, who obviously wasn't expecting such a swift attack. The human warrior's long sword strikes him on the hip. Blood gushes out and immediately the spectators take up their cry of "Blood—Blood—Blood" again.

Shut your faces and give him a chance, Sarius would like to bellow at them, but he's condemned to silence—and anyway, there's no point.

The lunge that Xohoo is trying now is doomed before it begins. He's dragging one leg, and his belt is already more than half black.

Wave bye-bye to your levels, Sarius thinks in heartfelt commiseration. If I didn't know better, I would challenge LordJerk as well, and smash his stolen face in for him.

Xohoo is growing weaker with every step. He's bleeding from

several wounds, and only half-heartedly parrying LordNick's attacks. In the end, a shove with the shield is enough to fell the dark elf.

"The victor is LordNick," Goggle-Eyes announces. "He will receive two levels and twenty-five pieces of gold."

The Roman numeral for two appears on Xohoo's armor. As if the shock has given him new strength, he struggles to his feet again and stabs LordNick in the leg with his sword. The victim of the attack, who was no longer expecting it, jumps back, leaving a wide trail of blood in the sand. After a brief moment of astonishment, he takes a wide swing with his weapon and hits Xohoo in the belly with the broadside. Two blows, and there's not a trace of red left to be seen on the dark elf's belt. He collapses motionless on the sand of the Arena. A deafening roar from the spectators. LordNick takes a step back, his chest rising and falling in heavy breaths.

Xohoo can't really be dead. A chill is spreading over Sarius. Surely, surely there must still be one last shred of color on Xohoo's belt—enough for the messenger to walk up to him and take him away to heal him. It won't be long.

"You have only one chance to play *Erebos*," someone breathes in Sarius's ear. Did he really hear that? Are his senses playing tricks on him?

Whatever. Xohoo is no longer moving, not even when the master of ceremonies prods him with his staff, gently at first, and then vigorously. A grin spreads over the man's face. He looks into the crowd and draws his left hand across his throat in a beheading gesture.

But where has the messenger gotten to? He's not sitting in the rows behind the barbarians, he's not near the lizards ... But what if he's seated himself right behind the dark elves? Sarius turns his head, scouring the rows, rebounds at the sight of the spider man, and quickly turns around again. Suddenly he sees him. The familiar, gaunt figure is sitting in the third row, between a woman with snake hair and a man with three eyes. His face is concealed by the shadow of a hood, but the yellow eyes shine out like thin, flickering candles on a grave. The messenger isn't lifting a finger for Xohoo.

They take him away. Two guards take a leg each and drag the corpse out through the sand, out of the Arena, leaving a wide, blood-splattered drag mark behind them.

Sarius looks after them, distraught. *It is all so real. So damned real.* The fear that he won't leave the Arena alive returns with redoubled force, and when the master of ceremonies steps back into the center, Sarius almost prays not to be called up. His wish is fulfilled. As Goggle-Eyes calls out the next fighter's name, the mass intake of breath is almost audible.

"BloodWork."

He's carrying an ax, a sword, and a shield across his back. For one crazy moment, Sarius thinks about what he would do if the barbarian chose him, but that's not possible. He's only a Three, and BloodWork is probably a damned Ninety-five or so.

The barbarian and the half-naked master of ceremonies are almost the same height. BloodWork is really steaming with energy; he can't stand still for a second. The weapons in his hands are twitching as if they were alive.

"Choose your opponent."

BloodWork doesn't hesitate for a moment. "I challenge Beroxar. I lay claim to his place in the Inner Circle."

The Arena holds its breath like a giant ring-shaped animal. You could hear a pin drop if not for all the sand. On the golden platform, one of the two barbarians rises.

That doesn't make sense, Sarius thinks. In his place, I would have chosen the cat man or the dark she-elf.

The adversaries are almost the same height. Beroxar is carrying a curved sword and a shield the size of a tabletop. His helmet resembles the head of a shark and reaches to his shoulders; it even protects part of his back.

"What do you demand of BloodWork, if he should be defeated?"

"Two weeks of slavery and six of his achievement levels."

Six! But if BloodWork is impressed, he doesn't show it. He quickly nods and gets himself into position. Beroxar splits the air in front of him experimentally with a stroke of his sword; it makes a buzzing sound like a swarm of bees.

Over the next few minutes, Sarius isn't capable of lucid thought. The fight makes him forget everything, including his own fear. At no time does either of the barbarians appear to show any weakness. They circle each other, execute short, lightning-fast attacks, and defend themselves with equal skill. Beroxar's scimitar is painting silver patterns all around his opponent; BloodWork's ax circles around his head while he searches with his sword for Beroxar's weaknesses. Which don't seem to exist. The fight is like a dance where the lead changes continuously. Till BloodWork suddenly twists round and turns his back on Beroxar. The scimitar hums and shoots toward BloodWork's shoulders, where the force of the blow drives it deep into the wood of the shield that BloodWork wears buckled on. A quick turn and the captured sword is torn from Beroxar's hand.

Without a weapon he has no chance. An ax blow to his leg and a sword thrust in his side lay him out on the ground.

"The victor is BloodWork."

The barbarian flings his arms up and turns around in a circle, accompanied by the cheering of the crowd, which has suddenly shaken off its daze. They clap and stomp, and call BloodWork's name over and over again.

Big Goggle-Eyes steps into the middle and silences the masses with a hand movement. He bends over the recumbent fighter and takes his neck adornment from him. An iron chain with a ruby-red ring as big as a bottle base dangling from the end. The inner side has a tip that resembles a rose thorn or a curved V and points toward the middle of the ring. The master of ceremonies places the ornament around BloodWork's neck and jubilation breaks out again. It doesn't even subside when Beroxar struggles to his feet and, at the direction of the master of ceremonies, takes his place among the assembled barbarians.

Sarius can't say how the messenger got into the center of the Arena, but now he's standing there, holding his bony hand out to BloodWork.

"Welcome to the Inner Circle. We all hope you will show yourself to be worthy of the honor."

BloodWork bows, and walks to the golden platform, where he seats himself in Beroxar's place. The red circle on his chest glows like a fresh brand.

The messenger turns to face the barbarians.

"Beroxar is still bound by his vow. On no account should he forget that. Traitors die quickly. Of course, he is free to win back his place in the Inner Circle at the appropriate opportunity. As any of you"—his sweeping gesture includes the entire Arena—"is free to fight for a place in the Inner Circle."

The very next warrior takes this encouragement literally and challenges Wyrdana, the dark she-elf of the Inner Circle. She doesn't so much defeat him as dispose of him. Her hail of fireballs, lightning discharges, and well-aimed spear throws doesn't last longer than it takes to blow your nose hard. It leaves the challenger lying in the sand; he departs the Arena a sad and sorry One.

Dark elves are no good? Yeah, right. Show me someone who can beat that for a start. Sarius feels something like pride rising in him. *No wonder Blood preferred to stick to one of the other muscleheads.*

The next three fights are so unspectacular that Sarius's thoughts wander. He sits up briefly and takes notice when a wish crystal is at stake for the first time. Neither LaCor, the vampire, nor Maimai, the cat woman, possesses one, but they both really want to. Goggle-Eyes conjures one up and offers it as a reward. The cat woman cleans up and LaCor loses a level. Who to? No one. Just because.

"Feniel!"

Sarius hasn't seen her so far in the mass of elves, but now she struts past him. Too bad the scorpions didn't get her, with her idiotic snub-nosed doll face. Sarius watches how she positions herself in the center of the Arena; he hopes she makes a really bad choice. Maybe Drizzel, or one of the others who'll absolutely thrash the levels out of her.

"Choose your opponent."

A heartbeat before the answer comes, he knows what it will be.

"I challenge Sarius."

Straightaway the fear is back, and the image of Xohoo, dead, being dragged out of the Arena. He can't see Feniel's level, and she can't see his either, or she wouldn't be allowed to challenge him. So she's a Three. That ought to be doable.

The crowd's impatient grumbling makes him realize that he's still standing thunderstruck among the other dark elves. *Go go go!*

Feniel can't know that he's a Three. So how come she chose him? Because she managed to oust him so effortlessly in the fight with the scorpion? Probably.

He pushes his way through the other elves without looking to the right or left. He needs tactics to use against Feniel's halberd. She'll keep him at a distance with it, no doubt. Sarius can already see himself poking around uselessly in the air with his sword while his opponent thrusts the tip of her weapon between his ribs.

"What will you fight for?"

Feniel doesn't take long to think about it. "One level and twenty pieces of gold."

Everyone has gold except him. But he does still have the grave robber's bowls and plates that he hasn't sold—that he'd forgotten about. How come it only occurs to him now, when the thought just gets in the way?

"I don't have any gold, and I'd rather fight for a wish crystal," he says, not very hopefully.

Close up, Goggle-Eyes' ugliness is really hard to take. His earthy brown skin shows cracks and rips as though paint had cracked off an old canvas. The feeling that the master of ceremonies doesn't belong here grows to a certainty in Sarius's mind.

"A wish crystal is not one of the choices," the man declares. "You will fight for a level. That will have to suffice." He raises his muscular arm as a sign that they may begin.

The trick will be to get past Feniel's lance. Sarius dances back and forth. Mustn't be too slow. Mustn't be an easy target. Unfortunately all his hopping around doesn't make Feniel even the slightest bit nervous. She looks as if she has all the time in the world, stands there calmly holding the halberd in both hands with the tip pointed—naturally—at him. Sarius tries a lunge, just feigning, and leaps back out of range again immediately. Nothing happens, the tip of the halberd merely twitches briefly in his direction, and that's it. It's only when he lowers his sword a little—more at a loss than exhausted—that Feniel really explodes. Two leaps and she's beside him, the tip of her weapon pointed directly at his chest. He yanks his shield up, but it's too late. She wounds him, and the screeching tone starts. He knocks her halberd aside with his sword.

Chalk on a blackboard, a fork on china. A saw right on the auditory nerve. This time, the tone arouses nothing but rage in Sarius. Without a thought to his own defense, he strikes at the halberd once again with his sword, hard, as hard as he can. He lets his shield drop and grabs the long handle, pushes it away from himself.

"Sarius—Sarius—Sarius!"

Are they cheering for him? It's more a whisper than a shout, from many ghostly voices. Are they hypnotizing him?

He steps on his discarded shield and almost stumbles, but he's not going to let go of Feniel's weapon, not for anything. Her body is unprotected. He'd be an idiot to hesitate now. Then she'll land a blow, the tone will pierce his hearing like glass ...

He thrusts his weapon into Feniel's chest, pulls it out, thrusts it into her belly. Blood is streaming from both wounds, her hands slip from the halberd; Feniel topples over. Sarius pursues her. Her belt is almost bereft of color. One more blow, one thrust and ...

"Sarius is the victor."

The voice tears him out of his fighting frenzy. Feniel is no longer moving, not at all. He lowers his sword, and at that moment the injury tone falls silent and music swells up. Magnificent music, like in the movies when the hero has won the decisive battle. That's how it was with BloodWork too, but I couldn't hear his victory music. Why? Because only the victor can hear it. Because it's part of the victor's reward. Like the Four that will be on my armor now, and the Two that suddenly appears on Feniel's leather vest.

His opponent is carried off—not dragged by the legs like Xohoo, but carefully, and quickly. So it's very likely that she's alive and that she has an in-depth discussion with the messenger to look forward to.

Whereas he is a Four. A victorious, unscathed Four. Sarius returns to the dark elves' corner. He looks around—now he can clearly recognize the Threes, and there are loads of them. The female werewolf, for example, whom the master of ceremonies is just calling up.

"Galaris!"

Hold on. Galaris—Sarius knows the name. The wooden box. Totteridge. The Dollis Brook Viaduct. Was it Galaris who hid the sinister box under the yew?

He can't ask her; right now she's busy choosing an opponent. Moreover, Sarius has a hunch that his curiosity wouldn't be taken kindly by the messenger and his gnomes. Galaris, whose dark-brown hair shimmers in the sunlight like melted chocolate, decides on a female barbarian called Rahall-LA. Courageous. Or dumb. In the end it's worth it, because she's fighting with a bow and arrow and Rahall-LA—also a Three—doesn't even get close to her.

After that a few of the higher-ups fight against each other; the fights last a long time and are carried on with enormous ferocity. Sarius attempts to remember the names and make out the adversaries' possible weaknesses, but he soon gives up. Interest is waning all around. A few of those who already have an Arena victory in the bag withdraw. Sarius follows them inside after he's witnessed the fight between Drizzel and Keskorian, in which the barbarian loses three levels. Drizzel is totally devious, Sarius remembers.

He finds Lelant and Arwen's Child in the dark elves' lounge.

" ... must have been an idiot to have another go after he'd already lost," Lelant says.

"I liked Xohoo," Arwen's Child declares after a brief pause. "It's sad that he's dead. I think he deserved another chance."

Sarius feels the same way. Xohoo, of all people—he at least was nice. Why couldn't it have been Lelant who copped it, that coward with his big mouth?

"Aren't you fighting at all?" Sarius asks him.

"Is that any of your business?" Lelant snarls.

"He never fights in the duels; he waits for the big battle at the end instead. It's not as risky and you can pick up more," Arwen's Child answers for him.

"Hey, do you always have to tell everyone everything?" Lelant complains.

He's still carrying the same weapons as in the labyrinth, no recent acquisitions as far as Sarius can tell. Does he still have the wish crystal? Would Sarius be allowed to jump him and search his inventory? Probably not.

"Battle at the end?" he asks instead, and pointedly turns his back on Lelant.

"Man, you really have no idea," the latter snipes before Arwen's Child answers.

"Yes, at the end of each tournament there's a big battle, a round robin. It's pretty dangerous, because then the higher levels can thrash you as well. But you can win their most valuable possessions from them."

"Wish crystals?" Sarius asks with a sideways look at Lelant.

"I suppose, if someone is lugging one around. That's not very likely though."

If he's honest, a big battle wouldn't actually suit him right now. He's only just won a level; it could be gone again all too soon. On the other hand, what's to say there aren't two or three more in the offing, right here and now?

"Wicked how Xohoo bit the dust." Lelant changes the subject.

The idiot just doesn't give up. Just wait, Colin.

"He was a stupid blabbermouth. Always bragging. He'd never have made the final cut; he might just as well have given the whole thing a miss. He was a wimp—just like you, Sarius. I reckon I'll finish you off as soon as the battle starts out there. Might as well say bye to Arwen."

"My name is Arwen's Child, you idiot."

"Like anyone cares."

It's as if everyone's waiting for the signal so they can start a race in different directions, and in a way that's true. Big Goggle-Eyes has positioned himself at the edge of the Arena and is holding his staff up. Sarius lets his gaze skim over the throng for the umpteenth time. There's a Two not far away, a vampire; he would be easy game, but LordNick is lurking close by, and Sarius needs to avoid him. The master of ceremonies explained it exactly: Someone who's already fighting cannot be attacked by anyone else.

That means quickly finding a worthwhile victim, an easy victim, before some Nine gets the idea that Sarius himself could be a good target.

The vampire Two is ideal, and very close. Goggle-Eyes lowers his staff and Sarius starts running, but straightaway Lelant enters his field of vision from the right. He has put the visor on his shimmering green helmet down, and now resembles a steel frog on two legs. The tip of Lelant's sword is pointed at Sarius, but his aim is poor because he's running. The blow doesn't hit home; it only scrapes Sarius on the arm. The hit doesn't trigger anything more than quiet creaking, like a badly oiled garden gate. But it makes anger rise up in Sarius like a hot red sun.

If that's what Lelant wants, then that's what he'll get. Sarius's shield bashes against Lelant's ribs like a battering ram. His sword strikes first his helmet and then his armor. The main thing is to make sure he has no time to recover his balance.

This time Sarius doesn't need any uplifting music in order to feel like a victorious general. It's enough to see how Lelant retreats, parries clumsily, stumbles, loses his shield. How he falls down and lies there, holding his sword up as if it were a bee stinger and Lelant was hoping Sarius would step on it.

After two hefty blows the sword is gone as well. Sarius sees the blood on Lelant's shoulder and chest with satisfaction. His injuries should suffice for a really nasty tone.

He puts his sword up to Lelant's neck, right on the edge of the armor, and resists the temptation simply to plunge it in. But what now?

Once again, a gnome provides the solution. A broad grin spreads over his bluish face. "Look at that. Sarius actually won," he squawks, and opens Lelant's inventory.

"Free choice to the victor."

The first thing Sarius looks for is *his* wish crystal. But it's not there anymore, naturally. Who knows what Lelant used it for?

Who knows what it's for at all?

But still, Lelant has 130 pieces of gold stashed away. Magnificent. Sarius starts helping himself and is promptly restrained by the gnome.

"Not more than half."

That's fine. Sixty-five pieces of gold are a decent sum. In addition, Sarius finds a pair of emerald-encrusted boots, a dagger, and a bottle of healing potion. He takes all of it for himself and the gnome doesn't protest. He only pipes up again once Sarius has stowed his acquisitions safely away.

"Rather greedy, the young master. It goes without saying that he may not help himself freely to levels. He can have two, if he leaves the defeated fighter his armor."

Naturally Sarius would rather take the levels than Lelant's armor and weapons. To his enormous satisfaction the Roman numeral five appears on the armor of the defeated fighter.

So he was a Seven and I was easy prey for him as a Four. Or maybe not. Tough luck, Lelant, you idiot. But now he's shown Lelant—the idiot—what's what.

162

He watches as Lelant slowly gets to his feet and hobbles off, just as a few other defeated fighters are also taking themselves off. As a Six, Sarius can finally see the bigger picture; now he can recognize the level of about a third of those present. Unfortunately there aren't many familiar faces among them. Blackspell, LordNick, Keskorian, and Arwen's Child are still superior to him, or at least Sixes like him. That's a pity. But Sapujapu turns out to be a Five, as does Nurax. Both of them are still caught up in their own fights. At the other end of the Arena, Sarius spots Drizzel, who's trying to drag BloodWork from the platform of the Inner Circle.

"Are you ready for another fight?" the blue-skinned gnome inquires.

Is he? He's not really sure. It would be very tempting to win another few levels, but he doesn't want to push his luck. Starting the day as a Three and finishing it as a Six really isn't bad going.

"No. That's enough for today."

"Then leave the Arena."

He does. He goes out the same gate he entered through, casts a glance into the dark elves' room—there's no one in there, no one at all—and marches toward the exit. When was the last time he felt so good? He doesn't know. Must be a while ago, a year perhaps, or two. With his pockets full of money, he walks boldly out onto the street. Time to see what else the White City has to offer.

TWELVE

It was dark outside the window. The evening news was droning on in the living room. Nick massaged his aching temples.

Sarius had traded all his remaining treasures for gold, including Lelant's dagger, which had brought a surprisingly large amount. After that he'd gone to The Final Cut, where Atropos had unceremoniously thrown him out. He didn't know why, and she wasn't prepared to explain. Night had slowly fallen over the White City; torches and braziers had been lit all around. Night was a promising time in the world of *Erebos*. Night was the messenger's time. But he hadn't put in an appearance anywhere. Nick's eyes were burning as though he'd been swimming in chlorinated water for hours. They were probably as red as the rubies on Lelant's dagger.

A break seemed like a good idea. Food seemed like a good idea. He would stand up, go out, and make a quick trip to the kitchen. No doubt Mom was already cooking something. He stared at the screen, at the streets of the city, his elfin self. Couldn't tear himself away. Something told him that, any minute, something was going to happen. An orc attack, orders from the messenger, a quest, a puzzle. Something he would miss if he disconnected now.

Maybe an hour? An hour to eat, exchange a few friendly words with Mom and Dad, and ... go to the bathroom. Only now did he notice how urgently he needed to go, and how much he'd twisted himself round on his chair to ease the pressure on his bladder.

Come on, move it. But first he had to exit the program. Nick ran the cursor over the screen. Where did he save the game and exit? He realized he'd never done that before. The game had chucked him out or made him take a break; he'd never left it voluntarily. It probably wasn't even provided for.

Nick weighed up his options. He could just power down the computer, but that was risky. If the messenger didn't like it, he might just take Sarius's hard-won levels back. Or he'd think of something even worse.

Another possibility was to leave the computer running and just turn off the screen. Then Sarius would be standing on the street as if he was rooted to the spot, and any One who just happened along could relieve him of his possessions. That wasn't a great idea either.

Nick's bladder felt as if it was about to burst. He had to go to the bathroom, there was nothing for it. First, though, he needed to get Sarius to safety quickly. But where to go?

The idea came out of the blue—he'd rented a room, hadn't he? He made his elf run through the nighttime streets of the White City as if big Goggle-Eyes himself was after him. Was this the right way? He remembered some narrow stairs leading up, next to a bakery—he had to go along there and take the next right. But where were the blasted steps?

He made Sarius run and run and run. The blue bar on the stamina meter got shorter and shorter—despite the fact that he was a Six. If he didn't find his way soon, he would just leave Sarius somewhere and go have a pee. But not here, on this dark corner, where dubious characters were hanging around.

Bakery. Steps. Finally. He rushed Sarius over the threshold of the inn, up the creaky steps to his little room. Closed the door. Turned the screen off. And now quickly, pleeease, quickly ...

Nick leaped up, ran out of the room as if wild dogs were chasing him, and sprinted to the bathroom. Just made it.

"Nick?" his father yelled from the living room. "If you slam doors like that again, you'll get what for!"

There was vegetarian lasagna with tofu instead of meat, but this time Nick didn't complain. He could hardly taste what he was eating. His parents were discussing the film they'd just seen at the theater, and were satisfied with the occasional "Mmm" or "Oh" he put in. They did wonder at the quantity of food Nick shoveled in, though. He was pretty astonished himself, until he realized he hadn't eaten anything since breakfast.

He was still in a hurry. He had left Sarius alone in the inn, unprotected and online. What if there was a fire? Or a raid? What if Lelant had tracked him down?

I should have cut the Internet connection, Nick thought. Except I haven't got the faintest idea what happens then. Will the gnomes get huffy with me and report it to the messenger?

He was already standing up as he pushed the last morsel onto his fork.

"Thanks, it was really good!" He smiled at his mother and she smiled back. Everything was fine, except that his father was making a face again.

"Don't tell me you're going off to study again. I'm really not buying that."

"No, I've done enough for today," Nick said, and yawned demonstratively. "I'm going to read a bit, and then go to sleep; I'm totally exhausted."

"The last time you went to bed at this time, you were eight."

"I just told you, I want to read a bit first!" Nick retorted, more fiercely than he'd intended. "Sorry about that. Chemistry makes me a bit tense."

His father mumbled something or other into his plate. Nick didn't inquire. He had to go and look after Sarius.

The moon that's shining through the window of the tavern is in exactly the same waning phase as the moon over London. But London is a long way away.

Sarius is lying on his bed, his hands clasped behind his head and his gaze directed at the ceiling. At some stage someone must have dropped a letter off; there's a yellow wax seal on it in the shape of an eye. Before he opens it he checks on his possessions and is reassured to find they're all still there. The gold, the healing potions.

He opens the letter, which is brief and not encouraging:

> *The others have gone. You were needed and refused your assistance. We are disappointed, Sarius. Your negligence cannot remain unpunished—do you understand?*

The letter is signed with a yellow eye-shaped mark—that's all that's needed. Sarius has screwed up.

The moment he puts the letter aside the candlestick on his table extinguishes; the next moment the moon extinguishes. The world of Erebos becomes dark and mute. Sarius is locked out; for a few frightful seconds he thinks: this time it will be forever. But that's ridiculous, of course—he fought so awesomely today. The messenger said he was looking for the best of the best. Sarius could be one of them. He knows it. He feels it.

The vegetarian lasagna was sticking in Nick's throat. *If I'd eaten less, if I'd eaten faster, I wouldn't have missed the quest.* It was enough to make him scream. Seriously. Nick stared at the black screen. It was so unfair. But as always the blackness remained relentless, and resistant to computer restarts, pleas, and curses.

Nick wondered where the others were right now. Was Lelant with them? Would he overtake him again tonight? Damn, damn, damn. And all because he hadn't known how to pause the game properly.

Listlessly he checked his e-mail, but didn't find anything that improved his mood. More from habit than from genuine need he loaded Emily's deviantART page and found a new poem.

Night

In my bed I keep guard
behind a palisade
of cushions and blankets.
With wide-open eyes
I watch for whispering creatures
who shrink from the daylight,
the dark twins of my thoughts.
With outstretched arms
I feel for familiar things
and cannot even find myself.
Only the prayer mill in my head clatters
steadily, incomprehensibly, insanely,
and I pray for a cease-fire
between day and night,
for sleep in my eyes
and the first light of morning
that's pale as you.

There was something in the poem that distracted Nick briefly from his frustration. It made him think that maybe he should talk to Emily some time. Ask her if she was actually okay, for example, or whether she was having problems. He thought about it briefly and dismissed the idea again straightaway. They didn't know each other well enough, and he'd only make a fool of himself.

Hi, Emily. I just wanted to quickly ask you whether you're okay. Or ... er ... you're having problems.

No, I'm not. Why?

I just thought, because I read this poem of yours ...

Oh yeah? Where?

On deviantART.

Well, well. How do you know my nickname?

Oh, I once heard you talking to Michelle about it. I'm sorry. Honest.

Not as sorry as me. Keep away from me, Nick. On the Internet and in real life.

Yep, that's definitely how it would go. Probably the poem was just art and didn't have the slightest thing to do with Emily's emotional life.

Nick gave the mouse a shove that sent it sliding right across the desk, and pushed his hair over his shoulder. He could at least have another go at getting *Erebos* running again. A good ten minutes had passed; possibly the messenger would think that was enough punishment. Maybe he only wanted to see how tenacious Nick was in his attempts to get back in.

It didn't work the first time, or the second, or the fifth. Shit, that really wasn't fair. The evening was ruined; the only bright spot was Nick's father's astonished face when he glanced into the room and actually found his son reading.

It was 9:34 according to the illuminated red numbers on the

clock radio. Ten minutes ago Nick had decided to go to bed early. He wanted to stock up on sleep; if he managed things better tomorrow, he could play right through the night and catch up on everything he was missing now.

Second possibility: look sick and stay home from school. He bet that was what Colin had done. Just like Helen, Jerome, Alex, and—well, probably everyone else.

But Nick knew that he wasn't going to skip school, not tomorrow anyway. It would be his first school day since Brynne had given him the DVD. Tomorrow he'd look at everyone in the school with new eyes: his flesh-and-blood opponents. He wanted to talk to Colin; they could get together and discuss who was behind which character. He wanted to find out who LordNick was.

Who knows what they're doing right now? Perhaps the best quest ever is happening. Without me. Screw it.

Nick turned onto his right side, then his left, but sleep wouldn't come. He'd hardly closed his eyes before he saw all the fights of the past day in his mind's eye: Big Goggle-Eyes swinging his staff and approaching him threateningly, Xohoo being dragged out of the Arena by his legs, over the bloodstained sand ...

With a deep sigh Nick clasped his hands behind his head. The clock said 10:13. That was almost approaching the time he usually went to bed, but he felt more awake than ever. He wondered how Xohoo would cope with being eliminated. Whether he'd recognize him in the morning. Assuming, that is, that he went to the same school as Nick. Not all the *Erebos* fighters would go to his school, obviously. Of course not; what a dumb idea. He closed his eyes again.

How many had there been in the Arena today? About forty or fifty dark elves, thirty vampires, and twenty dwarves. Barbarians? Also twenty at a rough estimate. Slightly fewer werewolves—fifteen?

170

That could be about right. The number of cat and lizard creatures had been of about the same order. And then there had been the three humans. Okay, so all in all that made … 160 or 170 fighters. Quite a lot, but small potatoes, of course, if you compared it to the player figures for other online role-playing games. Not all *Erebos* players had been gathered in the Arena, obviously—but definitely a large proportion. And that ominous Inner Circle. The champions. Had Drizzel managed to drag one of them down from their golden pedestal? Nick had to grin. Probably not. Probably Drizzel had just gotten a hefty thwhack on the head. Served him right.

Ten twenty-one. What if he tried again? Maybe the ban had been lifted. He wasn't going to be able to get to sleep anyway, if he didn't give it at least one more try.

He switched his bedside light on, went over to the computer, and turned it on with a cramped feeling in his chest. *Don't be nervous, you idiot.*

Double click on the red E. Nothing. Again. Nothing again. Without pausing to think, Nick surfed over to Google. If he found out more about the game, he was sure to find a way to make the software start running again. Except that the messenger had found out about Nick's first attempt—who knew how. A second attempt would possibly annoy him.

Acting on a sudden inspiration, Nick brought up Amazon. His game was a pirate copy, but there must be an original. He typed "Erebos" in the search bar and pressed Enter, half expecting another warning that would glow red in his nighttime room: *Not a good idea, Sarius. A dumb idea, to be precise. A fatal idea.*

However, Amazon listed a series of opera CDs, *Orpheus and Eurydice* in various recordings. Why? Aha, it was because of an aria with the title "Chi mai dell'Erebo," whatever that meant. Unfortunately this knowledge didn't help him in the slightest. There was no game with the title *Erebos*. Not even a pre-announcement. So how could there be a copy of it? And who on earth had the original?

Nick studied the various illustrations on the covers of the opera CDs. They were mostly details of paintings, and they reminded Nick of something. He took a few minutes to figure it out. They reminded him of big Goggle-Eyes.

Ten fifty-seven. Back to bed again—Nick had really had enough now. If he couldn't play, then at least he wanted to sleep; he felt hollow.

A game you can't buy. A game that talks to you. A game that watches you, that rewards you, threatens you, gives you tasks.

"Sometimes I think it's alive," Colin had said. Colin was never going to win a Nobel Prize, but he wasn't naive either. No, of course this game wasn't alive. But it was remarkable. Very remarkable.

Sarius is lying on the ground; LordNick is standing over him and grinning with that horribly familiar face.

"I was here first," he says. "You're just a pathetic little shit." He holds out a pouch to Sarius that contains heads: Jamie's, Emily's, Dan's, and Finn's. "Choose yourself one—or do you want to run around forever with that ugly elf mug?"

Sarius hates LordNick; he wants to leap up and draw his sword, but he can't move, and besides, it's dark as the grave.

"We could fight ... what do you think?" he manages to stammer.

"We'll fight for two levels. But you have to let me stand up."

"For levels? Not a chance, Sarius. We'll fight for years. Ten years of your life. What do you think?"

Sarius realizes that he's actually hearing the voice of one of his opponents for the first time. Why? And why years of his life? He can't be serious. That's just not possible. The thought makes him afraid.

"I don't want to, that's not a good bet." He hears his own voice too; it's tearful and high.

"Fine, then," LordNick says, and casts the pouch with the heads aside. "Then you're eliminated." He takes his sword in both hands, raises it, and stabs. He pins Sarius to the ground like a butterfly, and Sarius screams, he bellows, he doesn't want to die ...

It was his own whimpering that woke Nick. His heart was pumping as fast as if he'd been running. The darkness of his dream still surrounded him—perhaps he hadn't really woken up.

There was his clock radio, thank goodness. Three twenty-four. Nick fell back into his pillow and took a deep breath. His own scream was still ringing in his ears—hopefully he'd only let it out in his dream, otherwise it would have woken the whole house.

But all remained quiet in the apartment; neither Mom nor Dad was popping in to find out why their son was screaming his head off. He was in luck.

He shut his eyes, and opened them again straightaway. The thought of sleep was still too disturbing. It was quite conceivable that LordNick was standing by for another dream incursion, equipped with the pouch of heads and his sword.

It was a better idea to go have a pee. He dragged himself to the bathroom, being careful not to wake his parents. He tried to recall LordNick's voice, but somehow it had just been any voice, nothing he could place.

Why can't we chat live during the game? Talk to each other properly, like in other online role-playing games?

The answer was obvious, even at this late hour: because the players weren't supposed to recognize each other. Because they weren't supposed to know who they were really dealing with. But was everyone really keeping their mouths shut?

Nick snuck back into his room. He wasn't at all tired anymore. Not a bit. He really could just have one more go at starting *Erebos*. If it worked, he would go to school in a few hours feeling good.

In the complete silence of the night the noises of the computer starting up seemed hideously loud. Just the droning of the hard disk and the whooshing of the fan were bound to wake his parents.

He clicked on the red E, torn between pessimism on the one hand and hope on the other. Both yielded to astonished disbelief when the world really did open to him again.

Sarius is not in his room at the hostel; he's standing in the middle of the forest. It's almost like at the beginning, when he was still nameless. The forest is dark, and Sarius is alone. A hint of music floats in the air, buzzing as though to herald approaching disaster.

A narrow track snakes its way through the trees; it's almost impossible to make out in the gloom. Sarius doesn't have to grope his way through the darkness for long, though. After a short time the path leads him into a clearing.

He sees at a glance what it is. A graveyard, enclosed by a high wrought-iron fence. The gravestones shine brightly in the moonlight; some are leaning over, some are overgrown with ivy. They look as if they're waiting.

Even though he would really like to turn back, Sarius steps into the clearing. A tawny owl screeches; at the same time the music changes. A woman's voice is raised in a wordless, melancholy lament.

It is always courage that the messenger rewards, Sarius thinks, and takes two more steps. It's possible that the others are nearby. Or that I will get a task all to myself. Perhaps a secret is concealed in this graveyard.

He approaches the first gravestone and reads the inscription:

Aurora, cat person,
died from insufficient attention.

Aurora? It takes only a few seconds for Sarius to see the image in his mind's eye: the injured cat woman in the labyrinth, the scorpion looming up behind her with its stinger raised high. But she doesn't see it, she doesn't hear it. Sarius drives it off, but it has already stung her. *I didn't know she would die. I really thought that the messenger ...*

"Insufficient attention"—does that refer to her lack of vigilance or his lack of consideration? That's not written on the gravestone. He shakes off his bad conscience and goes on.

Rabelar, dark elf,
died from talkativeness.

Sarius has never come across the name Rabelar before. But talkativeness seems to be a common cause of death. Charmalia—vampire—and Vhahox—barbarian—both fell victim to it.

The dirges are becoming more and more oppressive. The image of a woman appears in Sarius's mind's eye. She's kneeling on the ground with her hands thrown up over her face, rocking backward and forward. Her face is hidden behind a black veil and she is singing ...

He shakes off the thought and goes on. He's looking for one gravestone in particular. He stops again at the one after the next.

Kaskaar, vampire,
died a traitor.

The stone is one of those that are leaning over. Someone has smeared a hideous gloating face on it.

The grass rustles under Sarius's footsteps. He moves on.

Ogalfur, dwarf,
died from laziness.

Berenalis, dark she-elf,
died from talkativeness.

Julano, human,
died from disobedience.

Trojobas, vampire,
died from inattention.

And then, although he was hoping not to find it:

Xohoo, dark elf,
died from lack of self-control.

So Xohoo is really dead. That's ... a pity. A great pity.

The darkness and the sobbing woman's voice, the fact that no one apart from him is upset about Xohoo—suddenly it's all hard to take.

Sarius drags himself away from the sight of the gravestone and goes on.

Airdee, dark she-elf,
died from curiosity.

A cause of death that could be dangerous for me, Sarius thinks bitterly. He quickens his pace involuntarily as he walks farther along the rows.

"Jostaban, werewolf, inattention."

"Grunalfia, dwarf, curiosity."

"Ruggor, dwarf, laziness."

"Grotok, human, disobedience."

Sarius has had enough. There are no adventures to be had here, and no quest to solve. The graveyard feels creepy. Any second he's expecting that dead hands will poke through the loose earth and snatch at his legs. He wants to leave this place.

He doesn't finish reading the rest of the inscriptions on the graves, doesn't care that there may be familiar names among them. Although it would be worth the trouble to find Drizzel and LordNick.

Wanting to leave and being able to leave are two different things, however. He can see the wrought-iron arches of a gate gleaming in the moonlight behind the rows of graves, true, but there's only forest beyond it. Some random forest. Probably far away from the White City.

The wind freshens and stirs up new noises; the swaying tree branches are beckoning to Sarius. Or are they scaring him off? He doesn't know; he really wants to cower down and bury his face in his arms, but someone is bound to be watching him.

Died of cowardice, of stone-cold fear. Okay, this won't do. He's going to pull himself together now, he's not going to get freaked out by the darkness or the despairing song, and he's going to find a way out. The gate is a good start.

He walks toward it, past more graves. Many of the inscriptions are grown over, or so weathered that he can't decipher them. Doesn't matter. He has to get out of here.

The singing gets softer as soon as he walks out of the gate. Thank god. But where to now? He doesn't dare to leave Erebos just like that. Who knows where he will find himself next time? Or if there will be a next time.

Then he hears something. A pounding, a knocking. Like sounds from a mine. He draws his sword. In the night forest the noise is alarmingly loud, as is each of his footsteps. The closer Sarius comes, the more loudly and clearly the knocking rings out. It's soon accompanied, to his relief, by a gleam of light.

It's another of those gnomes, of course—one of the messenger's minions. He's sitting with his back to Sarius in a wooden shed, a stone tablet in front of him on which he's working with a hammer and chisel. So now Sarius knows where the gravestones come from.

If I stand behind him and look over his shoulder, he'll probably be hammering my name into the stone, just to frighten me.

Sarius sneaks closer and looks over the gnome's shoulder. Wrong. The stone bears another name. Shiyzo. And even better, Sarius doesn't know him. Now, when he's standing right behind him, the gnome turns his ugly face toward him.

"Unusual hour for a visit, Sarius."

"I know. I actually don't want to be here either."

The gnome gives a screeching laugh.

"Who does?"

"Can you tell me how I get back?"

"Get back where?"

Yes, where? Sarius chooses his words carefully.

"I would like to leave Erebos briefly, but I don't want to suffer for it."

The gnome hammers at his stone, and appears to be thinking about it.

"It's not that simple."

If it were, I wouldn't need you, would I? Sarius takes care not to say that out loud. He waits patiently while the gnome scratches himself behind one ragged ear.

"All right then, go. We will expect you back tomorrow afternoon. It is in your interest not to disappoint us."

"Yes. Of course," Sarius says with relief.

"And give Nick Dunmore the following message: He should not forget the rules; we would find out. And he should keep his eyes open."

"Yes. Sure. After all, I don't want you to have to make me one of those," Sarius says, pointing at the piece of work in front of the gnome.

"Oh, but I've made one already. A long time ago. For all of you. Most of you will need one after all, won't you?"

The gnome is still grinning when the screen starts going dark.

Four forty-two. Too early to get up, and too late to crash again properly. Although he probably wasn't going to be able to sleep, Nick lay down again, pulled the bedcovers up over his ears, and closed his eyes. Tried to breathe steadily, but gravestones were dancing around in his thoughts.

Would the others still be on the move? He would ask Colin in a few hours. No, he wouldn't; it wasn't allowed. Damn. But at least he was sure to see on Colin's face how frustrated he was at being thrashed as Lelant in the Arena. With this comforting thought, Nick finally fell asleep.

THIRTEEN

The broken night's sleep, complete with graveyard visit, had left its mark. On the way to school Nick was already feeling a slight pressure in his temples, like the start of a cold. The feeling stayed with him the whole day, even if it occasionally got pushed into the background by other things. For example, by the sight of Jamie, Emily, and Eric Wu standing at the school gate, huddled together.

Eric. He was leaning toward Emily, talking forcefully to her. She wasn't flinching; in fact, she was smiling. Jamie was standing there with his arms crossed and nodding. Nick pretended he was looking for something in his bag and studied the trio out of the corner of his eye. Eric must have just said something witty, because all three were laughing, which made Nick realize how seldom he saw Emily laugh, and how much he wished that he was the reason for it, and not Eric.

Did Eric have to be such a pompous idiot?, Nick thought, and nearly forgot to keep rummaging in his bag. Was that the sort of man Emily went for? Lanky, half-Asian, with a pageboy haircut and brainiac glasses? A book club weirdo? He wasn't creepy, oh no; if he gave her something she'd definitely accept it. For heaven's sake.

Nick would have given two ... no, one of his levels to hear what they were talking about. If he hadn't gotten into a fight with Jamie yesterday, he could have simply joined them.

"Dunmore, stop standing in the way like a complete idiot."

Jerome barged into him on the way past, and Nick nearly dropped his bag.

"Get lost!" Nick bellowed after him. He wanted to run after him, grab him by the collar, and punch his lights out—because now, of course, Emily, Eric, and Jamie had noticed Nick. Jamie threw him a quick glance and turned away again, Emily lifted her hand in a half-hearted greeting. Eric—of all people—looked the friendliest.

Nick turned away and went into the school building. Where did this rage come from? Must have been the half-sleepless night he'd just gone through.

It was peaceful in math class for a Monday morning, but Brynne intercepted Nick right at the door.

"Well?" she whispered. "Well?"

He put a finger to his lips. How convenient it was that talking about the game was forbidden.

The expression on Brynne's face changed from beaming to knowingly conspiratorial. "I knew you would love it," she said.

"Yeah." Nick forced a smile.

Brynne looked exhausted too, he saw, but she'd taken great pains to cover her fatigue with makeup.

An attempt that wouldn't have served any purpose at all in Helen's case. Her appearance had never been pleasant, but today it outdid anything that had come before. Her hair was uncombed, her eyes half closed, and her mouth slightly open. She'd probably start dribbling any minute. Jerome and Colin weren't taking their eyes off her; they were imitating her expression and nearly laughing themselves silly.

Helen wasn't taking in any of it. She was staring at nothing, and now she was even starting to sway slightly. Something like pity glimmered in Nick. *Maybe she was one of those in the graveyard. Maybe she was Aurora, and I left her lying in the labyrinth.*

He went up to her. "Helen?"

She hardly registered him, just frowned slightly. Colin and Jerome killed themselves laughing.

"Helen? Are you okay?"

Now she looked up. There were dark-brown shadows under her eyes.

"What?"

"Are you all right? You look ..."—dreadful, he'd been going to say, but he bit his lip— "... sick."

A scratchy laugh emerged from Helen's throat. "Mind your own bloody business, Dunmore."

"Fine. Keep right on dribbling on yourself and making yourself a laughingstock." He pointed in Colin's and Jerome's direction. "At least they're enjoying it."

Why did he have to go and play Mr. Nice Guy to Helen, of all people? *You know exactly why,* a nasty little voice inside him said. *She could have told you something. About last night, for example. Or about how she passed away. Then you would have asked her for her name, wouldn't you? So you'd be able to tick off one of the many unknowns.*

He rubbed his face with both hands. God was he exhausted today. But at least he had succeeded in getting Helen to look a bit more normal. She was sitting upright in her seat, with her mouth shut and her fists clenched.

"Nick, you moron," Colin greeted him. "What did you want from Helen?"

"Shut your trap, Colin. She looked really done for—that's why I went over to her. Stop behaving as if you were twelve."

"Fine. What else? Any news?"

"No." Nick eyed Colin up and down. He didn't look pale, but his skin had an unhealthy gray tone that was new.

"Wicked day yesterday," Colin said.

"You can say that again. And what a cool night!" He could just pretend, couldn't he? As if he'd been there, and hadn't nearly wet his pants in the graveyard.

"Yeah, what a night," Colin mused. "That was ace. I wouldn't have thought it would turn out like that. Would you?"

"Nope. Me neither." Oh, come on, a few details, please!

"And that was just the beginning," Colin said. "You can bet your life."

"Yes. Of course. Can't wait to see what's next. What do you reckon?"

Colin raised his arms. "Do I look psychic?"

There was no point. Nick was never going to get anything more than vague hints out of his friend. But maybe he wouldn't object to just taking a few guesses?

"I would really love to know what name Helen is using," he murmured, so quietly that no one except Colin could hear.

"Yeah, well, that would be interesting. Not everyone gets around with their own face. I wouldn't do it either, if I were Helen."

Nick caught the reference and opened his mouth, but shut it again quickly. Colin grinned.

"Don't worry about it. I know it's not you. He's been there for much longer. But I don't think most people are onto it." He broke off when Jerome strolled over.

"Insider talk?" Jerome asked.

"Are you nuts?" Colin retorted. "Think I don't know the rules?"

"Anything's possible." Jerome walked off again, smirking. Helen's cloudy gaze followed him.

"He's right," said Colin. "Time to shut up. But Jerome was chatting himself, before. He can't talk." He grinned. "Besides, I won't get chucked out anyway."

When the bell rang for the first period Nick did a head count. Alex was there, Dan was missing. Aisha was there, Michelle was missing. On closer examination, Aisha did look a bit tired; her headscarf was a mess, and she kept blinking all the time.

Jamie was there, of course, and Emily. Gloria was there. Greg, the quiet one, was there, and obviously doing the same as Nick: scanning the rows and making mental notes. Then Mr. Fornary's math class started and put an abrupt end to Nick's research project.

The coffee vending machine was his last hope, but even from a distance Nick could see the giant queue that had formed in front of it. Damn. He desperately needed something to help him survive the next three periods.

Jerome was standing at the window and crushing an empty can of Red Bull in one hand. Smart guy, that Jerome. Tomorrow Nick would bring a supply of energy drinks too. Yawning, he collapsed onto one of the benches in the atrium. It occurred to him that this was the first time in ages that he was spending a recess completely on his own. Jamie was chatting with Eric Wu again; at least Emily wasn't with them this time. Colin was aiming to be conspicuous by his silence and was now doing surveillance around the corridors. The last time Nick had seen him, a girl from one of the lower years had been the object of his attention. Her name was Laura, unless Nick was mistaken. And she had been carrying a small package.

He looked at the clock. Still five minutes before the next class, just enough time to go to the toilet.

The bathrooms were the scene of a heated discussion. Nick, who'd already grabbed hold of the door handle, took a step back.

" ... not allowed—you know that. Leave me in peace."

"But it doesn't make sense! Just copy it for me again and I can at least try. I won't tell anybody."

"I said no."

"Whoa, you're nasty. It's no big deal, and you know it!"

"No, I don't. Why should I break the rules for your sake? You know he'll find out. He always finds out."

The door flew open and a boy whose name Nick didn't know stormed out. One of the younger students, Martin Garibaldi, followed right behind, his face bright red and his glasses sitting crooked.

"Wait!"

Nick watched as the two pushed their way past the students in the yard. It was quite easy to pick who was a gamer and who wasn't. The non-gamers looked astonished; the gamers grinned and shrugged their shoulders. When Nick turned away he found Adrian McVay standing next to him, waiting to be noticed.

"Hi, Adrian." He always found the sight of the boy oddly touching. Life had dealt him a hard knock, and it showed. He was missing a protective layer, a cool facade. Something in Nick made him want to stand in front of Adrian with his arms outstretched protectively, every time.

"Can I ask you something, Nick?"

"Of course."

"What's on the DVDs that you're all swapping back and forth?"

Nick said the first thing that occurred to him. "We're not swapping back and forth."

Very true. We're copying and passing round. That's quite different, right?

"Yes, okay. But people are slipping DVDs to each other. Can you tell me what's on them?"

"Why are you asking me, of all people?"

"I don't really know." The corners of Adrian's mouth lifted in a small smile. "To be honest, you're not the first person I've asked."

"But the others wouldn't give you an answer?"

He shook his head. "And you aren't going to give me one either, huh?"

"I can't, I'm afraid. I'm really sorry."

Colin marched past and waved, his eyebrows raised inquiringly. No, Nick thought, I'm not telling tales out of school. For god's sake, was Colin checking up on him? Every time he conducted a conversation now, was someone going to assume he was breaking the rules?

Adrian studied his own hands pensively.

"You all say that you can't. Is that true? Or is it that you just don't want to?"

"I heard that someone already offered you the DVD. Why didn't you take it, if you're so curious?"

The question wiped the smile from Adrian's face. "Because it's not possible in my case. That's just how it is."

"Even though you don't even know what's on it? Sorry, but now you've lost me."

It was a few seconds before Adrian answered. His voice was low.

"I'm afraid I can't explain it to you. I know it's stupid. I can't accept the DVD, but it's really important for me to know what's on it."

The bell rang for the next period. Luckily. The conversation had gotten more unpleasant with every word, and Nick was glad to be able to get away with a smile and a few empty words.

He dozed his way through physics and psychology.

"What did little McVay want from you?" Colin asked him just before English.

"Nothing much," Nick lied, once again feeling that inexplicable impulse to protect Adrian. Oh, and of course himself. "He just wanted to chat."

Colin was satisfied with that—he raised his eyebrows skeptically again, but so what. Nick certainly wasn't accountable to him, especially if he'd decided to appoint himself the guardian of the rules, the silly fool.

At the mention of the name McVay, Emily had turned around briefly and looked at Nick searchingly. Almost scornfully. Now what was that about?

All at once he understood. Of course. Jamie must have told her that Nick now possessed one of the sinister DVDs too. So she could work out for herself why he'd rung her, and that it hadn't had anything to do with Adrian's phone number. Shit. Why couldn't Jamie just keep his mouth shut?

Mr. Watson walked into the classroom with a pile of books under his arm. His gaze was searching too, and Nick thought he saw him nod knowingly as he counted up the empty seats.

"How are you?" he asked, and didn't settle for the general indistinct murmur for an answer.

"Six students are missing, if I'm not mistaken. Do you know why? There's an unusually large number of students away sick from the other classes too, but according to the school doctor there's no flu or gastro going around."

"No idea," Jerome said.

"But you were sick one day last week, weren't you? What did you have?"

Caught unawares, Jerome didn't answer right away. After thinking for a moment he said, "A headache."

" A headache, I see. And has it cleared up in the meantime?"

"Sure."

"Then get your books out. I hope you've read Sonnet 18 as discussed. 'Shall I compare thee to a summer's day' …"

They rummaged in their bags. Of course Nick had forgotten

to take a look at the poem, and hoped that Watson wouldn't call on him. He wouldn't be able to deliver an instant interpretation today, with his woolly head.

The scream ripped through him like an electric shock, and not just him—the whole class flinched as if a whip had been cracked.

Aisha held her trembling hands in front of her mouth; her face was completely white, as if she was about to keel over.

"What happened?" Mr. Watson, who was as shocked as everyone else, hurried over to her, which instantly caused Aisha to awaken from her paralysis. She hurriedly pulled something from between the pages of her book and crumpled it up in her hand.

"It's nothing," she said quickly. "I thought I saw a spider. But everything is fine." Her shaking voice and the tears she quickly wiped out of the corners of her eyes gave the lie to her words.

"Can you show me what you've got in your hand?" Undeterred, Mr. Watson kept walking toward her.

She shook her head silently. Now her tears were flowing freely.

"Please, Aisha. I would like to help you."

"But it was nothing. I just got a fright. Really."

"Show it to me."

"I can't."

Mr. Watson held out his hand. "It won't go any further than you and me. I promise."

But Aisha stuck to her "no."

Mr. Watson changed tack; he left Aisha in peace and turned to the class.

"Aisha doesn't want to talk about the thing that's upsetting her so much, but perhaps one of you could? You would be helping her, if she is bound to silence for reasons that I am not aware of." He looked at every single one of them. "We are a community. If one of us has a problem, we shouldn't be indifferent to it."

At first no one answered. The class had rarely been so silent. Only Aisha sniffed audibly. Greg passed her a tissue, and she took it without looking at him.

"Maybe she's just getting her period," Rashid said.

There was the odd laugh here and there.

Rashid grinned. "Well, she could be."

Mr. Watson looked at him for a long time without saying anything, until Rashid lowered his gaze. Suddenly Nick understood why quite a few of the girls redid their lip gloss before English class.

"It was foolish of me to ask you," the teacher observed. "But in fairness to you, I want you to know that I will go to great lengths to find out why Aisha is so distraught. I very much hope that none of you has anything to do with it."

He sat down behind his desk and opened his book. "Rashid, please read Sonnet 18 and then give us your interpretation of what you have read. Given your analytical prowess just now, I can hardly wait to hear more."

After the end of the period, Jamie waylaid Nick at the classroom door.

"Do you have any idea what was up with Aisha?"

"No, how would I? I didn't see what scared her any more than you did."

"I didn't mean that. I meant the bigger picture. It's something to do with the DVD, isn't it? With that game?"

"No idea," Nick murmured, and tried to push past. But Jamie held him by the sleeve.

"There's actually something really rotten going on," he said. "Come on, Nick. Can't we talk to each other normally? Aisha isn't the only one I've seen howling today. Something similar happened to a girl in Year Seven. Found something in her bag that completely shattered her. But she didn't want to talk about it or show it to anyone, not for anything."

"Yeah, so?" He pulled his sleeve out of Jamie's grasp but kept standing there. Colin and Rashid weren't around, the noise level in the classroom was high; no one could eavesdrop on Jamie and him.

"You don't seriously believe Aisha is telling the truth?" Jamie's face reflected more amusement than dismay. "A spider—fat chance. You saw it as well as I did: she had a note hidden in her hand."

"Maybe it was a picture of a spider," Nick joked. He immediately felt stupid and waved his remark off. "Yeah, okay, I saw the note too. But I don't know what the story is with it. Maybe her boyfriend broke up with her by letter."

Jamie gave him a lenient smile. "Honestly, stop acting dumb. For the last ten days or so, everything's been different around here. Since the game's been going around. You must have noticed that."

"You really are paranoid."

Jamie looked at him thoughtfully.

"It's a shame," he said. "I should have accepted your offer yesterday and got my hands on this DVD. Then I'd have something I could go to Mr. Watson with."

"Oh well, too bad. But you know what? You've got completely the wrong idea," Nick said. *Because the game is much smarter than you, Jamie Cox, and it would have easily outwitted you.*

The cafeteria was crowded, despite all the students who were away sick. Thanks to his height and since he wasn't feeling particularly polite today, Nick had nevertheless managed to nab a plate of salad and a bowl of unidentifiable pasta. But what now? Normally he would have sat down with Jamie or Colin, but neither of them was an option right now.

He looked around and reeled a bit, his tray along with him, when he spotted Emily at one of the smaller tables. She was waving, and he nearly dropped everything in order to wave back, but that would have been a waste. Because she wasn't waving at him. She was waving at Eric, who immediately steered a course toward her table. Within seconds they were engrossed in a conversation, as if they'd only been briefly interrupted.

Nick's hunger was history. He banged his tray down somewhere there happened to be space and stared at the food. School slops. He should have tipped the stuff over Eric's head.

"Is someone sitting here?"

The universe hated Nick Dunmore—that much was obvious. Smiling coyly, Brynne placed her bowl of salad on the table and put a glass of water next to it.

"Oh, spaghetti!" she said, as if she'd never seen any before. "Enjoy your meal!"

Now the food came in handy after all. Nick could use it to stuff his mouth full and hence avoid having to answer her drivel.

"Didn't Aisha make a big fuss! Could you see what was in her hand?"

Nick shook his head and twirled more pasta onto his fork. The white sauce it was swimming in tasted vaguely of mushrooms.

"Doesn't matter anyway. I would never put on a performance like that, that's for sure." She was waiting for his agreement, but Nick was concentrating solely on his salad, which was positively bathed in vinegar.

Why couldn't he be like Colin? He would have said, "Beat it, sister," and gotten some peace. But Nick dreaded the wounded expression he would see on Brynne's face, and his own bad conscience.

"Hello! Anybody home?" Her hand was making windscreen wiper motions in front of his eyes.

"Yes. Sorry. What did you say?" *I'm a bloody wimp.*

"I asked you a question," she said, with emphasis on the last word.

"Ah. Sorry. I'm quite tired. What did you ask?"

"If there's something that you're supposed to say to me."

Pardon? That he was supposed to say to her?

"You mean I'm supposed to say thank you? For the thing? Okay, thanks very much. Satisfied?"

Brynne's smile faded. She shook her hair back and pressed her lips together tightly.

What was wrong now? He'd stayed polite, hadn't he?

"I was wondering what was up with you and Jamie," Brynne began after a few seconds of silence.

"What do you think is up? Nothing at all."

She put on a knowing look. "Yeah, right. You two got into it about ... you know, about the *thing*. Didn't you?"

Nick didn't answer, and Brynne took that as agreement. "Don't even worry about it. You've got heaps of friends; you don't need him. He's not exactly one of the cool people, anyway. Did you see the shoes he's wearing today?"

She actually giggled. And she was actually trying to embroil him in a conversation about his best friend's bad taste in clothes. Nick threw the fork onto the rubbery pasta and pushed his chair back.

"I think I've had enough. And the next time you feel like bad-mouthing Jamie, choose someone else."

"Hey, it was just ..."

He didn't hear any more. He was already on the way out, although he still had to walk past Emily, who took no notice of him at all. She was listening to Eric, with her chin resting in her hands and her head tilted slightly to one side, and he was talking nonstop.

I need to go home, Nick thought. Beat opponents up until the hard drive starts smoking.

Except that he still had two periods to go. Couldn't he skip off for the rest of the day? He felt dizzy when he thought of the head start all those people who were missing from school today were getting.

But if he stuck it out now, maybe he could afford a fake sick day tomorrow. No, damn it, he had to hand in the chemistry assignment. It was due tomorrow!

Fine, well at least that settled how he was going to spend his lunchtime. He took his bag and looked for a quiet window seat in the library.

He fetched two books off the shelf and began copying out of them, changing the sentences as much as possible as he wrote. There! It wasn't all that bad after all. He'd already managed half a page. There was a graphic too that he could incorporate to give the assignment a professional look.

He copied and then kept writing, and managed two pages. They certainly weren't good, but they *existed*. Satisfied, Nick looked out of the window onto the rainy schoolyard below, as if there was some chance that he would find inspiration there for two more pages. But all he saw was Dan, who was supposed to be absent today. And yet he was standing down there, all by himself. Why wasn't Freak One sitting at his computer?

Nick watched Dan as he ducked behind the hedge that separated the schoolyard from the parking lot. He was holding something in his hand. Binoculars? No, a camera.

Nick squinted so he could see better. Dan was photographing something that was in the parking lot. Unfortunately, Nick couldn't tell what it was; the right wing of the school building was in the way.

After a short time Dan lowered his camera and looked around. He strolled into the middle of the courtyard and did a reconnaissance of the classroom windows at ground level. He stopped at one of the windows and took a few more pictures before entering the building and disappearing out of Nick's field of vision.

Nick would have really liked to leap up and sprint down the stairs so he could intercept Dan and ask him what he'd been doing there. Except Dan would never come out with it.

But it wouldn't be a problem to grab the camera and take a look at the last few pictures. No, he wasn't going to do that. No.

Instead, Nick turned over the sheet he'd just been intending to keep working on.

He wrote DAN on the right side and drew an equals sign after it. A quarter of an hour later he had created an astonishing number of equations. Not exactly textbook algebra but undoubtedly more interesting.

DAN = Sapujapu? No, he's too nice. Drizzel? Possible. Or perhaps Blackspell.

ALEX = no idea. A lizard perhaps? Gagnar? Or a dark elf: Vulcanos? Could be anyone. Could be everyone.

COLIN = Lelant. But he was too cheerful for that today. Feels invincible. But who knows what happened during the night. Maybe BloodWork, after all? Or Nurax?

HELEN = Aurora? If so, she's dead. Tyrania. A possibility. Arwen's Child? I'd laugh my head off.

JEROME = LordNick? But why?

BRYNNE = Feniel, probably, because disagreeable cow. Or Arwen's Child? Or Tyrania?

AISHA = probably dead, explains why so shattered. Aurora?

RASHID = Drizzel? BloodWork? Blackspell? Xohoo?

Defeated, Nick threw the pencil on the table. There was a question mark after each of his guesses. Not a single game character was a definite match. And it was equally possible that he hadn't even encountered Colin yet in the course of the game—like so many people from the graveyard, like the members of the Inner Circle. For example, who were Beroxar and Wyrdana?

No, there was no point. He would stop racking his brains about it. It was better to work a bit now and immerse himself in *Erebos* again later, with an easy conscience.

Nick took a new sheet of paper and kept writing, without really understanding what he was writing about. He had three-and-a-half pages finished when the bell rang for the start of class. That wasn't so bad; he would manage the rest this evening and then quickly type everything into the computer. It would work out. Somehow.

With every day that passes my reality loses more of its value. It's loud, disordered, unpredictable, and arduous.

Reality—what can it do? Make you hungry, thirsty, dissatisfied. It causes pain, strikes you down with disease, obeys laughable laws. But above all it is finite. It always leads to death.

It is other things that count, that are powerful: ideas, passions, even madness. Everything that elevates itself above reason.

I withdraw my consent from reality. I deny it my assistance. I dedicate myself to the temptations of escapism, and throw myself wholeheartedly into the endlessness of unreality.

FOURTEEN

"I have been expecting you."

The messenger is sitting on a chair in Sarius's room at the tavern when he arrives later in the afternoon. The sun is low, casting honey-colored rays through the windowpanes.

"I hear it has been an interesting day so far. Tell me about it, Sarius. Did anything unusual happen?"

The messenger wasn't going to accept no for an answer, that much was obvious.

"A girl called Aisha had a sort of nervous breakdown."

"Do you know why?"

"Not exactly. She found something in her English book and got a fright. I couldn't see what it was."

The answer seemed to satisfy the messenger.

"And what else happened?"

Well, what?

"I watched Dan Smythe secretly taking photos. Of something in the parking lot."

"Good. What else?"

Sarius thinks about it. What else should he talk about?

"Tell me about Eric Wu. Or Jamie Cox," the messenger prompts him.

He already knows everything, Sarius realizes. And he's testing me.

"They were talking to each other."

"What about?"

"No idea."

"That's a shame."

The messenger rises from his seat in a supple motion. He seems superhumanly tall in the tiny room. He turns back once more at the door, as if something has just occurred to him.

"I am worried," he says. "*Erebos* has enemies and they are growing stronger. You know some of them, don't you?"

Sarius's thoughts are whizzing around chaotically in his head. He won't talk about Emily and Jamie, no way. Maybe about Eric? No, better not. But he should say something, and fast; the messenger appears impatient.

"I think Mr. Watson doesn't approve of *Erebos*. Even though he certainly doesn't know much about it … He tries to question people."

"A valuable piece of information. Thank you."

The messenger's smile is almost warm.

"Now hurry. Whoever brings me a golden hawk's feather will be richly rewarded."

"What golden hawk?" Sarius enquires, but the messenger has turned his back on him and leaves the room without another word.

Sarius finds his way by asking. At the baker's he's informed that he should head south and be careful of the sheep. The first mistake in this world, Sarius thinks. Sheep!

A beggarwoman on whom he bestows a piece of gold reveals to him that he should keep an eye out for a pink-colored hedge. It's hard work, and slow, but after a bit more than an hour Sarius has finally collected enough information to take the—hopefully right—road.

He's promptly interrupted. As usual, it's the outside world that gets in the way.

His cell.

Jamie.

Sarius ignores it. He has stuff to do; he has to leave the city. Hopefully his sword is sturdy enough to stand up to a golden hawk. After another hour he knows better. He's been heading in the direction the gatekeeper at the city wall indicated to him. To the south. He's gone farther and farther without finding either sheep or a hawk. Instead, the hawk finds him. Unexpectedly, without any warning, an enormous, glistening golden bird swoops down from the sky, glowing like a meteorite. Sarius dives for cover, but he doesn't have a chance. He's standing in the middle of open country, and the hawk grabs him with its claws, lifts him a little way into the air, and then drops him. Most of his belt goes gray, then black.

Crawl away quickly, before it's too late. The shrill cries of the bird of prey and the excruciating screeching triggered by his injuries blend together. Sarius clenches his teeth—he still has healing potion, he just has to get to his inventory before the hawk strikes a second time.

But his adversary doesn't give him time; it has circled up into the air like a gleaming dragon and is readying itself for another nosedive. Sarius draws his sword; he sees the hawk swooping toward him, blindingly bright. He won't survive another serious injury.

The impact is hard and metallic; the injury tone becomes unbearable, but at least it's still there. That's good; it means life. Now, however, the hawk is preparing for the third attack, which will also be the last. A mosquito bite would be enough to kill him in his present condition.

No, please no. Frantically he tears open his inventory. There's the healing potion—quickly, the bird is still ascending, perhaps there's enough time, quickly ...

But the potion only works slowly. Bit by bit the color is restored, the tone is slowly, slowly becoming softer. In the meantime, the hawk has regained sufficient height and is getting itself into position. Even though there's no point, Sarius attempts to crawl to the nearest tree while the hawk rushes toward him, filling more and more of his vision.

"Should I hold it off?"

The messenger. He's appeared from nowhere, as always.

"Yes, please, quickly!"

Fantastic, Sarius is going to live. He knew he could rely on the messenger.

"But you must do something for me."

"Of course. Gladly."

Sarius has said yes, so why doesn't the messenger drive the creature off? It's already rushing down, and it's so fast ...

"Do you promise?"

"Yes! Yes! Yes!"

The messenger raises his arm in a casual gesture, and the hawk performs a sharp turn to the left, beats its wings several times, climbs higher, and gradually disappears from Sarius's view.

"Then come with me."

The healing potion has begun to take effect. Sarius's belt is almost completely restored; the tone is hardly more than a buzzing. The messenger leads him to the nearby tree and they stand in its shade.

"The higher you rise, the more challenging the tasks will be that I set you. That makes sense, does it not?"

"Yes."

"This time it is a task that Nick Dunmore is to fulfill. If he acquits himself well, you will become a Seven. That would put you in exalted company."

"Great."

"This is the task. Nick Dunmore is to ask Brynne Farnham on a date. He is to make sure she feels comfortable and see to it that she has a pleasant evening. He is to convince her that he likes her."

Brynne? But why? What does this have to do with *Erebos*? Sarius hesitates to answer. He doesn't understand the point of the task, and the thought of it fills him with repugnance. Everyone would find out. Emily would definitely find out, because Brynne would tell everyone about it.

"Well? Why aren't you answering?"

"I'm not sure I understand properly. Why Brynne? What's that supposed to achieve?"

It's as if a cloud has moved in front of the sun. The world becomes gray.

"Your behavior is ill-advised, Sarius. I detest curiosity."

"Fine, all right," Sarius hurries to say. "I will do it. Agreed."

"Do not return until your instructions have been carried out."

Just as before, when he was driving off hawk, the messenger raises his hand. This time darkness descends.

Brynne! Nick rubbed his face with both hands and groaned. Why couldn't it be Michelle at least? Or Gloria? Any of the nice normal girls. But, oh no, he had to cope with Brynne and her affected behavior.

If he did what was being asked of him, he would never get rid of her again—that much was obvious. Besides, she would spread it around—she always did—and Emily would turn her back on him. Although to do that she would have had to turn *to* him in the first place.

Nick stared helplessly at the black computer screen. What did the messenger gain from giving him such pointless, annoying instructions? Did he want to punish him? Or just test his obedience?

Assuming he went through with it, what sort of a date was it supposed to be? Sitting in a café and making small talk? Eating burgers at McDonald's? A walk along the Thames with hand-holding thrown in? Or—god forbid—the movies, where there was no possibility of escape and he would pass out in Brynne's cloud of perfume.

Okay, café plus small talk. At least then there'd be a table between them. He would let her ramble on, nod appropriately, and maybe even smile. "Make sure she feels comfortable and see to it that she has a pleasant evening."

One level was nowhere near enough reward for that, Nick felt. He rummaged for his cell and found to his astonishment that he actually had Brynne's number stored on it. He pressed Call but hung up again while the phone was still connecting. He didn't feel like it. Tomorrow was soon enough. Why should he ruin this evening?

Should he maybe return Jamie's call instead? Yeah, right, so he could go on at him again with his concerns about *Erebos*.

No.

The only thing he really wanted to do was play, and he could forget that—again.

Nick grabbed his iPod, plugged his ears, and thought of Emily. A date with her—now *that* would have been a task for him.

The thing with Brynne was occupying Nick's thoughts so much that the chemistry assignment had faded completely into the background. It was only after dinner that he remembered he had to hand it in tomorrow. He sat down at the computer, typed up the handwritten sentences, searched for the rest of the information and a few images on the Internet, and added them in somehow or other at the end. Then he printed the whole thing out and hoped against all reason that Mrs. Ganter would bestow an A on his scribblings. He hated chemistry.

And Brynne, not to forget Brynne. He hated her too. After chemistry the next day he intercepted her, taking care to ensure that Emily wasn't in sight.

"Hey," he said. His whole face hurt from the fake smile. "I wanted to ask you something."

Brynne's eyes were big blue headlights, full of anticipation. "Yes?" she breathed.

"Maybe we could ... meet after school today. What do you think? We go could to a café maybe?"

"Oh. Yes, sure. Amazing." Nick got the impression she'd spoken the last word more to herself than to him.

"Café Bianco, for example. We could go there straight after school," Nick suggested.

"Well, actually I'd like to go home and get changed and so on beforehand."

Oh hell. She'd spend two hours painting and polishing and squeezing herself into the tightest and shortest skirt she could find.

"You know what, Brynne," he said, deepening his smile till his bones hurt, "I really don't think you need to. Let's just go straight there. Once I get home"—he rolled his eyes—"I might be so dead tired that I just collapse into bed. I haven't been getting that much sleep recently."

Did that sound like an excuse to her? Evidently not.

She giggled and winked conspiratorially. "You think I have? I barely know the meaning of sleep anymore."

They agreed to meet at the Tube station after art class. Nick hoped that no one would see them together in the crush.

Three minutes later he spotted Brynne outside the physics classroom, gesturing as she babbled to Gloria and Sarah. What it was about would have been obvious—even if they hadn't constantly looked over in his direction.

Later—Nick was sitting by himself in the farthest corner of the lunchroom, stuffing a tuna sandwich into his mouth without much enthusiasm—Jamie came up to him. They hadn't talked to each other so far today, and if Nick was honest, it was mainly his fault. The chemistry assignment and the Date With Brynne had gotten under his skin so much that he wasn't particularly keen to have an argument with Jamie.

But who actually said there would be an argument? They were old friends—just because they didn't agree about one thing didn't mean it had to ruin their friendship. Exactly. Nick would make that clear to him.

Jamie's face was pale, and he looked serious. "It's a pity you didn't return my call yesterday," he said.

"I had a lot to do."

"Yes, of course."

"What else is up?" Nick tried to steer the conversation onto safe ground. "Did you talk to Darleen? You were going to."

"No. Nick, I'd like to show you something."

Show? That sounded fine. It didn't sound as if Jamie was going to try to talk him out of the game again.

"Okay. What is it?"

Jamie pulled a tightly folded piece of paper out of his trouser pocket and thrust it into Nick's hand. "I found that jammed into the luggage rack on my bike yesterday."

Nick unfolded the paper. For a moment he thought he was having déjà vu. There was a gravestone drawn on the piece of paper, not drawn well, but recognizable. The inscription read:

Jamie Gordon Cox
Died of curiosity and unwelcome interference.
May he rest in peace.

The artist had painted trails of blood next to the letters, thick drops that were running down the gravestone.

"That's a pretty stupid joke," Nick said. "Any idea who it's from?"

"No. I think you know that scene better than I do."

He wasn't going to let himself be provoked by Jamie's sideswipes. "The writing doesn't look familiar. I couldn't even say if it's from a girl or a—"

"Don't you get it? It's a threat," Jamie interrupted him. "A death threat, and quite an obvious one at that. I'm not supposed to interfere, and I'm to keep my nose out of your game, or—" He made a beheading gesture with the flat of his hand.

"You're not taking it seriously are you?" Nick asked. "It's a stupid joke! Tell me, who is supposed to kill you?"

Jamie shrugged his shoulders. He really did look upset.

"Who says it even has anything to do with ... well, you know what. You can't possibly be sure about that."

It was too bad that Nick himself was very sure. There was no doubt that the dubious artwork came from someone who had gone for a night walk in *Erebos's* graveyard.

"I'm not that stupid," Jamie snorted. "Tell me, what else could it possibly be about? What do you think is meant by 'unwelcome interference'? That I complained in the cafeteria because there's not enough salt in the spaghetti?"

"Okay, but you're not going to take it seriously, are you? It's nonsense, that's all. Someone wants to frighten you, and you're letting yourself be scared. You don't need to, honest."

Jamie looked at him for a long time before he spoke again.

"So what was up with Aisha? Why did she scream the other day? And that girl from sixth grade, Zoe? What about her?"

"No idea. Go ask her."

Jamie smiled bitterly. "That's exactly what I did. I talked to both of them and asked them what it was that frightened them so much. Guess what? They're saying nothing. Keeping completely mum."

"Probably they realized ages ago that someone was playing a stupid joke on them."

"No. They're scared. Yesterday I found two people who've been chucked out of the game. They don't want to talk about it either, at least not yet. But I think one of them is considering it. Maybe he'll go to Mr. Watson; at least that's what I suggested to him."

Don't tell me about it, Nick thought, please be quiet. Otherwise what am I supposed to do if the messenger asks me about you?

He looked around frantically—was anyone listening to them? No, none of the nearby tables was occupied, and the people who were sitting farther away were all caught up in their own conversations.

"See? You're completely paranoid yourself already!" Jamie cried. "Why? Explain it to me!"

"Not so loud!" Nick couldn't help hissing. "I'm not paranoid. You just don't get it. It's all very complex and very exciting, but it could easily be ruined, which would be a shame. That's why a few of the people might overreact when someone wants to spoil their fun."

"Fun?" Jamie whispered, and held the drawing under Nick's nose. "That's fun?" He folded the note back up and put it in his pants pocket. "I'm going to give it to Mr. Watson. He's been really worried since the incident with Aisha; he's already talked to a few students and he's going to contact the parents soon too. Perhaps this piece of drivel will help him. Perhaps he'll recognize the writing."

"Come on, stop exaggerating like that!"

Why didn't Jamie get the fact that it was all a game? The very fact that it kept spilling over into reality was what made it so fascinating—but that didn't mean by a long shot that any of the players would so much as touch a hair on Jamie's head.

"I'd like to know whether I can count on you if push comes to shove," Jamie said. "Are we still friends?"

"Of course we're friends. But this scaremongering because of one or two idiots who write pretend threatening letters is really ridiculous. Take my word for it. If you give the note to Mr. Watson he'll blow it out of proportion and there'll just be trouble."

Jamie put his hand on his pocket. "If the trouble finds the right people, that's okay," he said, and stood up. Before he went, he leaned down to Nick one more time. "Sure you don't just want to get out? Drop it. Nothing good will come of it—somehow I just know it."

Nick shook his head. "You're making a much bigger deal of ... this thing than you need to. I enjoy it, it's an adventure, you know?"

"You can't even just come straight out and say it's a game."

Nick stared at him angrily, but didn't say anything. What did Jamie know about the rules—being discreet was just what you did. If he'd accepted *Erebos* from him and taken a look at it, he would be just as enthusiastic!

"Emily would be glad too if you dropped it. She said so."

"Emily should just keep on looking after Eric," Nick blurted out, "and not interfere in my business."

Jamie exhaled noisily. "Shit, Nick," he said, turned, and left.

FIFTEEN

Only three tables were occupied in Café Bianco, and there were no familiar faces at any of them. Nick heaved a sigh of relief. The shared trip on the Tube had already been hard work, with Brynne rabbiting on endlessly. Now they'd have a drink together, Nick would pay for Brynne's soda, and then he'd be out of there, off home. For the next quest he'd be a Seven.

" ... was in a complete state yesterday. I think she got the worst of it in some fight."

Who was she talking about again? Nick inquired, and got a searing look.

"Weren't you listening to me? Zoe, the fat girl in Year Seven. She howled so much that snot was running down her face." Brynne pulled a disgusted face. "Then Colin whispered something in her ear and we got some peace."

Colin seemed to be sticking his nose into everything these days.

A waitress with three lip piercings took their order. To Nick's surprise Brynne ordered a beer.

"I really love beer, don't you?" she cooed.

"Hmm," Nick said, and looked away. How long did he have to sit here before the messenger would count it as a proper date? The five minutes he'd completed so far were presumably not enough. Damn.

"Colin is such a cool guy," Brynne said, feigning contemplation. "Almost as cool as you, Nick."

A pained sigh escaped Nick, which he tried to make up for immediately with a wide smile. He was to *make sure she felt comfortable*; that was the deal. *Let's see whether Brynne would feel comfortable even on thin ice.*

He checked again to see whether there were any familiar faces among the patrons. No. So it was worth a try.

"I'd really like to know," he said slowly, "what name Colin is playing under. Do you have any idea?"

"Come on, Nick," Brynne said, and put a hot, damp hand on his arm. "I'm not that stupid."

"What do you mean?"

"I'm not going to break the rules. It always comes out and then it gets ugly. You know that."

Nick resisted the impulse to pull his arm away.

"But no one can hear us here."

"You never know."

The drinks came, and Nick managed to discreetly shift his limbs out of reach.

"What do you mean, it gets ugly? You get chucked out. Of course that's a major pain, but—"

"Have you ever been there when they came to get a traitor?" Brynne interrupted him. "I have. They took him away and ... executed him. That happens to everyone who goes over to Ortolan's side."

She sipped her beer without taking her eyes off him. Nick lowered his gaze into the dark depths of his soda glass.

"Do you know who Ortolan is?" he asked. "We can talk about that, can't we?"

"Can you see a fire?"

She'd obviously completely lost it now. "Fire? What are you talking about?"

Instead of answering, Brynne pulled a scrunched up note out of her bag. "I mostly keep the rules with me; see, it's written here: During the game you can converse around the fires."

She got a lighter out, and made a little flame leap up. "Now all we have to do is play," she whispered, and drew her finger along the back of his hand. The feeling was pleasant as long as Nick ignored the fact that Brynne was causing it. He shut his eyes.

"I can imagine that Ortolan might be a magician," Brynne whispered close to his ear. "Or a dragon with three heads. He's certainly very strong. The players in the Inner Circle are getting special training so they'll have a chance against him later on."

If it weren't for Brynne's overpowering perfume, Nick could have imagined that it was Emily stroking his hand. Straightaway the thought caused him pain, because an image of Emily and Eric followed in its wake. Nick opened his eyes. The lighter was still burning and Brynne was looking at him expectantly. *No, I'm not going to kiss you.*

"Well, let's wait and see," he said aloud, and reached for his glass.

Brynne appeared unsure for a moment, but she quickly pulled herself together.

"What was up with Jamie today? Did you get a load of the look on his face?... I mean, his face is never a pretty sight, but today ..." She gave Nick an arch look. "Did he tell you what his problem is?"

"No."

"Ah. I thought you two were so close. But you're not, are you? I'm glad. He's really annoying." Make her feel comfortable, Nick repeated. Feel comfortable. The silly cow.

"And he's not a gamer either. Have you seen how he's always

hanging around with Eric? Colin always calls him Sushi. I already explained to him that Sushi is actually Japanese, but he thinks it's hysterical anyway. Now Eric has hooked up with Emily apparently, that boring frump. Honestly. Colin says he's never met anyone so lame. Never opens her mouth and always looks as though her guinea pig had just dropped dead." Brynne burst out laughing.

Feel comfortable ... you're supposed to make her feel comfortable.

"It's probably a matter of taste who you think is lame," he said, and forced a smile onto his face. "Colin and I mostly like completely different girls."

This time Brynne was the one who didn't answer. Nick suspected that the penny had finally dropped, but he wasn't going to worry about that right now. He was still chewing over the fact that Eric and Emily were supposedly together now. Was it true? And if so, how did Brynne know about it? Too bad he couldn't ask her. Too bad he'd tried to lure Emily into *Erebos*. He could kick himself.

"I wonder if we're missing something important?" he murmured when the silence got painful.

"There's always something important," Brynne said. "No matter when you enter or leave, you're always going to miss something. I get nervous about that too. I hope they're not announcing the date for the next Arena fights right now."

"Were you there for the last ones?"

She pursed her lips. "Are you sure that you're not trying to trick me and then rat me out afterward? You know what the rules are. If I were to tell you I was there, that I fought twice and won a level, then it would be really easy to figure out who I am. Or who I'm not. The messenger explained it to me. He takes all that really seriously."

"Yeah, okay, fine."

"Are you actually glad that I gave you *Erebos*?" she asked, without looking at him.

"Sure. Of course. It's incredible."

Brynne pushed a strand of hair behind her ear with exaggerated slowness. "Don't you sometimes think it's eerie?"

Damned eerie. "Oh, it's fine. I think it's meant to be like that."

"Yes." She twisted her glass between her hands, first one way, then the other, then the first again. "I only wish I could understand how it reads my mind."

Reads her mind—that was an exaggeration, Nick thought as he traveled home on the Tube. Brynne had gotten out at the previous station, but not without first giving him a hug and pressing a kiss right next to his mouth.

The game certainly couldn't read his mind. Or at least not all of it. If you ignored the inexplicable fact that it had given him a Hell Froze Over shirt for loyal service. And it had talked to him about Emily, even though he'd never mentioned her.

The train doors slid open with a hiss, and Nick got out. It was getting dark outside; hopefully dinner would be ready when he got home. He certainly couldn't afford to wait ages for it; he'd neglected *Erebos* for far too long already.

"A Seven, Sarius. You carried out my instructions. Here is your reward."

The messenger points a bony finger toward one corner of the dark vault they're standing in. It resembles the cellar of the Final Cut Tavern, but it's not as big, and it looks as if no one's been in here for years. Spiderwebs stretch between the vaulted walls, and small, greenish mushrooms are growing in the corners.

Sarius finds a new sword and high boots with metal toe caps in the spot the messenger indicated. The sword shimmers golden; Sarius almost gets the impression that light is radiating from it.

"Thank you."

"And thank you. Is there any news you would like to report to me?"

Sarius hesitates. He's not going to say anything about Jamie's plans concerning Mr. Watson—no way. Should he mention the threatening letter with the gravestone? Better not. He drags something out of his memory that both Jamie and Brynne have told him about.

"Apparently a girl named Zoe really went to pieces recently. I didn't hear much about it though."

"It would interest me more to know what Eric Wu is up to," the messenger says. "I would be pleased if you could devote more attention to his activities. According to everything I have learned, he is not well disposed to us. Now go."

Sarius makes his way outside with mixed feelings, through a tube-like passageway that leads out of the cellar. He has absolutely no desire to watch Eric sticking to Emily like glue. What will be next? He's been out with Brynne, and that was bad enough.

The dark passageway is getting wider; it finishes at a torch-lit wall with an open door that leads outside.

Finally, Sarius thinks, and stops that same instant, rooted to the spot.

The wall! He goes back a few steps in order to make sure. No, there's no mistake.

Someone has painted a picture on the wall that takes up almost its entire surface. It resembles an old mural of the type often found in churches—a fresco. The picture shows two people sitting at a table with their heads together. The girl has a burning cigarette lighter in one hand; the other is lying on the hand of the boy who is sitting opposite her. He is very tall and his long dark hair is tied back into a ponytail that hangs down his back ...

Someone must have taken a photo. There's no other way, Sarius thinks. And we look like lovers.

He turns away, stumbles through the door into the open. He feels strangely naked and threatened. Even though it's only a picture. Something in him is afraid that one day this life-sized picture could be hanging on the wall at school.

"LordNick found a wish crystal."

"Wicked! Did he say what he's going to do with it?"

"No, of course not. He's not stupid."

The bunch that's sitting around the fire is made up almost entirely of familiar faces: Drizzel, Feniel, Blackspell, Sapujapu, Nurax, and—like a guest of honor, somewhat separate from the others—BloodWork. The ruby-red ring is swinging conspicuously on a chain around his neck, identifying him as a member of the Inner Circle.

Twilight is moving across the horizon in blue and red streaks; it will be dark before long. Sarius sits down with the others at the fire, noting two new arrivals. Sharol is a dark she-elf, a One; Bracco is a lizard man and a Two. They are staying in the background while Drizzel and Blackspell conduct their vampirish conversation.

"I could really do with a wish crystal. The two I've found so far were worth their weight in gold," Blackspell is saying.

"Shut your mouth," BloodWork interrupts him. "There are beginners here; they need to experience things for themselves. Your drivel will just confuse them. Got it?"

"Sure. Since when have you been so considerate, Blood?"

"None of your business," the gigantic barbarian says. He's wearing a new helmet that covers his face right down to the nose; its slanted eye slits make him look more demonic than ever. "Just do as I tell you. There's too much talk as it is. The messenger is not pleased."

"Oh, the messenger is not pleased," Blackspell mocks. "I wouldn't be either if I were such a yellow-eyed skeleton."

BloodWork straightens up a bit and reaches for his ax, but then he seems to reconsider.

"I've known a few idiots who went around talking their heads off, and now I know another one."

"Oooh, I'm so scared," Blackspell says.

The conversation is getting on Sarius's nerves, just like the fact that everyone has obviously already found a wish crystal except him. "So have we got a task today? Or are we just hanging around here?"

"Finally, someone with the right attitude," says BloodWork. "We're waiting for a message. It can't take much longer."

But the message doesn't arrive; instead, orcs, armed to the teeth, jump out of the bushes. They are in the definite majority and they've got the advantage of surprise. Sarius leaps up and swings his golden sword. He massacres three of the orcs without getting so much as a scratch. BloodWork goes berserk and cuts his enemies into pieces. Drizzel's using fire spells these days. One of the newcomers, Bracco, has taken a lot of damage. He's got a head wound that's bleeding ferociously, and he's lying on the ground without moving.

Sarius's blade sings when he whirls it around. Fighting was never so good. He feels stronger, more skillful, lighter on his feet since he became a Seven. It's a real treat.

He kills six orcs before victory is announced, and he's taken less damage than ever before. The messenger also declares himself satisfied when he appears shortly afterward.

"Sarius, you have acquitted yourself well. I will reward you with fifty pieces of gold."

The others receive this and that. Bracco, the wounded lizard, drags himself over orc body parts and is pulled up by the messenger onto his horse.

"Those who are still strong enough should go off in search of escaped sheep," the messenger orders. "Four shepherds have already died."

With these words he spurs his horse and gallops away, with Bracco swaying on the saddle behind him.

"I'm going looking for sheep," Sarius announces.

"Me too."

"Me too."

Sapujapu and Nurax join him; they're both Sixes. They've each earned a level since the arena fight, but Sarius is still superior to them.

Drizzel strolls up as well without saying anything. His pale vampire body towers over Sarius by more than a head.

"BloodWork, are you coming too?" Sarius asks. The barbarian isn't moving, just sitting and staring mutely into the flames of the fire.

"Blood?"

"Leave him," Drizzel says. "He's probably nodded off."

They walk over heathland. It's already very late in the evening, and visibility is steadily getting worse, but there are barely any obstacles in their path and they make good progress. Sarius would like to chat with the others, to ask them, for example, what sort of a quest looking for sheep is supposed to be. But no fire means no conversation. In his memory he sees a lighter flickering. He shudders.

They are walking alongside a hedge full of pale pink blooms. The color is clearly visible despite the darkness, but before Sarius can feel suitably surprised, he spots something else, something that's hanging in the hedge, that makes the blooms fade completely into the background.

A dead body.

As if at an inaudible command, the whole group comes to a halt. Only now does Sarius notice that Feniel and Blackspell have followed them too. So at least there are six of them, which is comforting in view of the badly mauled corpse in the hedge.

The dead man is hanging there as if he had been pegged out to dry. Something has been eating away at him—no, it has almost eaten him up. There's hardly any flesh left on the bones. A crooked staff is lying on the ground below the corpse.

Here we have one of the dead shepherds, Sarius thinks, and at that moment he spots the first sheep. A powerful animal with dirty white wool, grazing under a barren tree.

Experience has taught Sarius that it's stupid to let other people go ahead. His sheep, his prey. He will capture it, as the messenger requested, but he doesn't see any fenced pasture he could return it to.

The sheep keeps grazing calmly while Sarius creeps up on it through the falling darkness; that's good, it makes the task easier. As he approaches he discovers something peculiar ... red and brown stains in the wool, like fresh and dried blood. Must be from the shepherd, he thinks, but he only really understands when the sheep notices him and raises its head.

A nightmarish head. The sheep's mouth is wide and protruding, and now the animal draws its lips back like a shark about to attack, exposing needle-sharp metallic teeth the length of steak knives.

Sarius, who wasn't expecting a fight, hasn't even drawn his sword. He makes up for that now while the sheep is running at him. Sarius spots a scrap of the shepherd's cloak in its teeth.

The first sword thrust misses its mark; the sheep has doubled back and is snapping at Sarius's left arm ... Damn, he's forgotten to get his shield from his shoulder; his whole left side is uncovered.

Behind him Sarius hears the noise of swords, and also whistling blows that could be coming from Sapujapu's ax. More sheep must have appeared, but there's no time to look; his own horror sheep demands Sarius's complete concentration. It's so hideously fast, and its teeth so frightening, that he can hardly tear his eyes away from it. Finally a sword thrust hits home, but it merely cuts through wool. The sheep is going for his unprotected left side again. Sarius parries and strikes at the animal. At least he hits one of its ears, which begins to bleed. But he's finding it hard to concentrate. The scorpions, the orcs and trolls … none of them threw him off balance as much as this bizarre, unnatural sheep. Now it's attacking again. Blood is running down from its injured ear into its mouth and glistening on the steel teeth.

Because Sarius doesn't want to look at it anymore, because he just wants it gone—in the hope that it won't follow him into his dreams—he throws strategy to the winds. He runs to meet the animal and bores his sword into its chest. The pointy teeth snap at him, only just missing his hip. He draws the sword back out, thrusting it into the sheep's body again and again. A soft singing in his ears tells him that he's injured, if only slightly.

The sheep staggers, but it doesn't die. Because it's not a sheep, Sarius realizes, but a monster, an infernal creature, a demon. He lifts his sword as high as he can and buries it in the animal's nape. It takes three strokes before the head rolls into the grass.

He feels sick. He wishes the carcass would just sink into the ground without leaving a trace. But there is blood all around him, trickling into the ground. It's sticking to the golden blade of his sword. Blood and sheep's wool. Another wave of revulsion rolls over him, and as if to dispel it, Sarius lays into the sheep's body again with all his strength, over and over.

As Sarius is about to turn away, he sees it. A green sparkle somewhere between his dead adversary's ribs. He overcomes his aversion and stoops down. Reaches into the body and fetches out a big stone that glows from inside. Finally.

Quick as a flash he looks around, not for more sheep, but to see whether one of the other fighters has noticed anything. No. They're all still engaged in their skirmishes. He whisks the stone away into his inventory. His elation at the find dispels the last remnants of his revulsion.

Drizzel has finished his fight too; he's systematically taking his slaughtered sheep to pieces. In vain, Sarius notes with great satisfaction.

Blackspell and Nurax are still fighting—they're sharing an opponent—while Sapujapu is fending off a pitch-black sheep alone, with his long ax.

Behind him a dark she-elf is lying on the ground, not stirring. Feniel. So you've finally bought it, Sarius thinks spitefully. That's what you get when you just can't help pushing yourself forward all the time.

A gossamer-fine streak of red remains on Feniel's sash, no more. The injury tone must be murderous.

Fleetingly Sarius thinks of his healing potion, which he certainly won't be administering to his fellow dark elf. Sapujapu he'd help. Maybe. But not this stupid cow.

He turns away, watches Drizzel and Nurax, who are finishing off their sheep. Finally. He can hardly wait for the messenger to appear. He'll redeem his wish crystal—who knows how many levels he'll get for it. Right on the dot, as the last sheep takes its last breath, he hears hoofbeats.

"I congratulate you. This was no easy task," the messenger says in greeting.

"It was trivial," Drizzel declares.

"Well, then something trivial should suffice as your reward. Three units of rat meat for Drizzel."

Sarius can't get over his malicious delight. First Feniel, then Drizzel—it doesn't get any better.

"Sapujapu, as a reward I will improve your equipment," the messenger continues, and presents the dwarf with some sort of Viking helmet in black metal with gleaming red horns. The thing apparently commands lightning spells.

One after another, they receive gold, potions, or weapons. The messenger considers Sarius second-last.

"I will strengthen your fire spell, Sarius. From now on you can not only light fire, you can also fight with it. But the greatest reward is the one you earned yourself, isn't it?"

Feeling uncomfortable, Sarius says nothing. Actually, he didn't want to let on about finding the wish crystal in front of the others, but the messenger doesn't seem to be bothered about that.

"Yes," Sarius says finally.

"Good. Then think about a wish for your crystal."

Finally the messenger turns to Feniel. "Do you want to die or follow me?"

She lifts her head hesitantly. "Follow you."

"I thought so. Then come."

Abruptly he lifts her up behind him on the horse and they gallop off, without looking back.

And my crystal? Sarius wants to ask, but it's already too late for that. Disappointed, he joins the others at the fire.

"Sari found a wish crystal and isn't saying a word. Must be shy," Drizzel snipes.

"I've never found one," Sapujapu complains. "What am I doing wrong?"

"You have to pretty much tear your dead opponents to pieces," Sarius explains. "I know it's not very appetizing. This is my first wish crystal too. I nearly had one once, but Lelant grabbed it from under my nose, the ass."

It wasn't quite like that, admittedly, but who cares. Lelant is an ass; that bit's true, anyway.

"What are you going to wish for?" Blackspell enquires.

"Don't know yet. And besides, why would I tell you?"

"Can you show it to me?" Nurax reaches out his werewolf paw, causing Sarius to take an involuntary step backward.

"Forget it."

The conversation peters out. They're standing around the fire and waiting.

"Maybe I'll just go to bed," Sapujapu says suddenly. "I'm dead tired."

Now that Sapujapu has mentioned it, Sarius notices his own tiredness, as if it were an animal that raised its head when called. But there's no way he's going to bed before he knows what he can use his wish crystal for.

"You're going to miss everything if you stop now," says Nurax. "The coolest quests are always at night!"

"That's not going to help if I nod off and they butcher me," Sapujapu retorts. "Honestly, people, I've had it for today."

Sapujapu has barely finished his sentence before two of the gnomes appear out of the bushes, frantic as ever.

"Alert! Ortolan is setting new monsters on us; they are attacking the smithy. We need reinforcements, follow us!"

Drizzel sets off immediately, with Nurax right behind. Blackspell isn't taking his eyes off Sarius—what is he waiting for? An opportune moment to nick the wish crystal? Just in case, Sarius draws his sword, whereupon the vampire turns away and follows the others.

"You really not coming, Sapujapu?"

Sarius and the dwarf are the last two standing at the fire.

"No, sorry. I can hardly see straight anymore, and I'm seriously worried that one of these monsters might do me in. Maybe we'll see each other in the morning, huh?"

Sapujapu shuffles off toward the rose hedge. Even at night its blooms are bright dots in the landscape. Sarius looks after him regretfully. It's a shame—Sapujapu's good value, unlike these other idiots he'll have to follow now, like it or not.

He sets off. The others are making heaps of noise; he's not going to lose their trail in a hurry. Maybe if he hurries a bit, he might even catch up with them.

A hoarse screech makes him flinch. He spots a patch of gold that's circling like a giant flying star in the night sky. When it screeches again he realizes that it's the golden hawk, and ducks instinctively.

"Don't worry, he's not hunting."

Sarius cries out in fright. The messenger is standing in front him and beckoning with his bony hand, beckoning him over.

"What is your most ardent wish, Sarius? You found one of the magic crystals. Use it wisely. What do you wish for?"

As much as I can get, Sarius thinks. He looks up at the messenger, looks directly into the yellow light of his eyes.

"What about a few levels, say? Or a place in the Inner Circle?"

The messenger smiles.

"A place in the Inner Circle is a thing one must achieve for oneself. Like a person's love, or a friend's trust. However, apart from that sort of wish, many things are possible—probably more than you can imagine."

Sarius's mind is at work. It's like a fairy tale—he has one wish. Except that the fairy turned out to be really ugly.

"Perhaps Nick Dunmore has a request?" the messenger suggests. "A special request?"

Nick Dunmore would like to mutate into a chemistry genius, Sarius thinks bitterly. He would like to get top marks in his exams without any effort. But presumably that counts as one of the things you have to earn for yourself.

If he's honest, that's not really his biggest wish. Because, more than anything ... there's Emily. Yeah, except it won't work. *Emily must fall in love with Nick.* Ha ha. The messenger has just ruled that out.

But ... perhaps it could work the other way around? You can't wish for love to develop, but what about wishing for it to end?

Should Sarius risk it? He hesitates. It's not right. But it won't work anyway. Perhaps it really would be better to choose something simple? No.

"Nick Dunmore wishes that Emily Carver would break up with Eric Wu. He wishes they weren't a couple anymore."

Silence. The messenger places his long finger on his chin in a reflective gesture.

So? ... So? Just say you can't do it!

The messenger doesn't move a muscle. Is he thinking about it? No, it's taking too long. Besides, everything is getting darker, even darker. Why? Has something stopped working? No, please, not right now! Sarius tries at least to move himself, but that's not easy either. As if he were wading through syrup.

When Sarius has already given up, the messenger finally answers.

"Emily Carver, you say. Good. I will ensure that Emily Carver and Eric Wu are no longer a couple."

The messenger's words unleash a veritable torrent of emotions in Nick. Incredulity, first of all, followed by triumphant joy, and— hidden in its shadow—his bad conscience.

"Really?"

"You will see, Sarius. Now go. The others are already far ahead of you."

SIXTEEN

"Nick? Nick! For god's sake, are you okay? Wake up!"

Opening his eyelids was hard enough, but nothing in comparison with the effort it cost him to drag himself upright. Something crashed down onto the desk—the keyboard, which had gotten stuck to Nick's cheek. He glanced hastily at the screen. Completely black—luckily.

"Did you sleep here? Sitting up?"

"Erm ... maybe. Probably."

His mouth felt dry and his temples were throbbing.

"Don't tell me you're turning into a computer junkie, are you? What in the world were you doing all that time?"

Chopping the legs off giant spiders.

"Chatting. It was fun and I forgot about the time. I'm really sorry, Mom. It won't happen again."

His mother pushed a lock of hair off his forehead.

"Can you even go to school in this state? You must be dead tired. Why would you do such a thing, hmm? I thought I could rely on you. You need your sleep. You know how tiring school is—"

"It's okay, I'm fine," Nick interrupted her. "I'll just go have a cold shower, then I'll be fighting fit."

The offer to skip school tacit in his mother's flood of words had a lot going for it, but unfortunately today was the wrong day for it. The spiders had inflicted so much damage on Sarius that in the end he had needed the messenger's help again, and had accepted some orders. So gaming instead of school wasn't an option. Apart from that, he was brimming with curiosity. He wanted to see Emily and Eric. He wanted to know what was happening. Whether anything was happening.

Nick gazed at the bathroom mirror, checking out the deep imprints the keyboard had left on his face. When had he fallen asleep? He could still remember his orders and how he'd searched with burning eyes for a scrap of paper to write the messenger's requirements down. He must have nodded off after that.

He showered hot, cold, and then hot again, making himself dizzy. The coffee aroma from the kitchen was mingling with the smell of shower gel; the combination nearly turned Nick's stomach. It could well be that staying home was the best option. But free days were precious. He folded up the scrap of paper on which he'd written down his orders and put it in his wallet. Then he stowed his camera in his school bag. He didn't understand the point of the instructions any better today than last night. But it didn't matter. Afterward, he would be an Eight.

The memory of his wish stayed with him the whole way to school. Although it was nonsense. In a few days the messenger would wave him over and ask him to wish for something different. Nick needed to be prepared for that—he was going to think up something good. Something sensible. Exactly. So there was no need for him to feel guilty.

On that thought he turned into the street leading to school, where it was unusually quiet. As if someone had gotten hold of a remote control and turned the volume down. As usual, there were students hanging around by themselves or in small groups in front of the building, but the noise level was minimal. Those who were talking to each other were doing so quietly. Nick spotted two younger girls who were pointedly standing next to the school gate and trying to make eye contact with everyone who entered. Their body language was unmistakable: We haven't got it yet.

Emily was standing under a chestnut tree with red autumn leaves. Eric was not with her. That fact made Nick's heart jump into his throat. *Don't make a fool of yourself. It has nothing to do with your wish. Nothing.*

But she wasn't alone either; she was speaking to Adrian. Young McVay had his arms wrapped around his body, and wasn't looking at Emily as he spoke. She listened, wiped her hand across her face in an abrupt gesture, and turned away.

The impulse to join them was hard to resist, but it was clear to Nick that they would immediately break off their conversation if he even came near.

In the meantime, one of the girls at the school gate had finally succeeded: a boy who played the saxophone in the school orchestra waved her over, whispered something in her ear. She nodded, he whispered a bit more, and after a little while pulled a flat object out of his bag ...

"Nick?"

The quiet boy, Greg, had snuck up from behind. Nick whipped around, his heart pounding like crazy yet again. Why had he gotten such a shock?

"You have to help me, Nick. Please."

Greg's bottom lip was shaking slightly, as were his hands, which were holding a blank DVD in its original packaging.

"I got kicked out last night. But it was a mistake, honest. I just have to talk to the messenger, and you have to copy your game for me. Please!"

Involuntarily Nick took a step backward, away from the DVD that Greg was holding out to him, but Greg immediately stepped closer again.

"I had gotten so far, I was a—"

"I don't want to hear!" Nick shouted.

A couple of students who were standing a few paces away turned their heads toward him. Nick marched toward the entrance without another word, but he'd hardly gotten inside the foyer when Greg grabbed him by the sleeve.

"I'm telling you it was a mistake! I did everything he wanted. I was only a tiny bit too late, and then he just ..." Greg bit his lip.

"At any rate, it's a mistake. Copy your game for me, please. Please!"

Died of unpunctuality, Nick thought uneasily.

"I can't; you must know that," he said. Was Colin back there? Was he looking over at him?

"The rules are clear. You can only play it once. I'm sorry about that."

"Yes. Yes! But in my case it was just a mistake. That's why it's a bit different. How about if I helped you next time too? We can study chemistry together. Or I'll pay for the copy, okay? I'll bring some money tomorrow. Would that be all right?"

Nick walked off and left him. Colin really was over there, leaning casually against the wall and observing the scene.

"You're an ass!" Greg screamed after Nick. Suddenly he wasn't so quiet anymore. "You stupid ass!"

Colin grinned as Nick walked past him.

"What did Greg want from you?"

"None of your business."

"Looks as if he didn't get it."

"You noticed."

I really should have stayed home, Nick thought as he stood in front of his locker and suddenly couldn't think what he needed for the first period. Was it the biology books? Or English? What day was it actually today?

He yawned and said hi to Aisha, who looked straight past him without saying anything back. It looked as though someone else had slept badly. She had to have several goes to get the key of her locker in the keyhole. When she'd finally gotten the door open and was reaching for her things, a whole pile of books fell out and landed all over the corridor. Someone giggled nastily.

Aisha let her arms hang down and made no move to pick up her stuff.

"Hey," Nick said. "Want me to help?"

She shook her head violently and bent down slowly for the first book, but then she didn't stand up again. She stayed cowering on the floor, with the book pressed into her chest. Her shoulders were shaking.

"Aren't you feeling well?" Nick asked quietly, but got no answer. He looked around for help. Where had the others gone? Jamie, for example, or Brynne. She was always hanging around.

Because he didn't know what else he should do, Nick collected the books and packed them back in the locker.

Rashid walked up, yawning, didn't even spare Aisha a glance, and walked away again with his biology books under his arm.

So it was biology. Nick tried to catch Aisha's gaze one last time, but she'd closed her eyes. Feeling bad, but relieved at the same time, he grabbed his stuff and ran after Rashid.

It was hard to stay awake, so hard. Nick rested his chin in his left hand and stared at the board until his eyes watered. Anything rather than look to the right, where Greg was sitting, looking daggers at him. Or to the left, where Emily and Jamie were sharing a desk and whispering urgently to each other. Aisha was there too; she seemed to have gotten a grip on herself again. There you go.

If he closed his eyes they didn't sting so badly. Just for a little while. That felt good. Really good. Really—

A painful punch in the ribs nearly pushed him off his chair.

"Don't doze off, you idiot," Colin hissed. "We're not supposed to be noticed. Or had you forgotten?"

"What? No ..."

"Whatever. Pull yourself together."

"Don't hit me again, got it?"

Colin raised his eyebrows in amusement. "Yes ma'am."

Nick struggled through that lesson and the next. In the recess that followed he went and stood in the line in front of the coffee-vending machine. Someone tapped him on the back. It was Brynne. He'd hardly turned around before she gave him a peck on the cheek.

"It was nice yesterday afternoon," she murmured.

"Yes. Nice." Nick made a show of yawning so she'd be more likely to take his lack of enthusiasm for tiredness. Nevertheless Brynne's smile cooled.

"Are you desperate for coffee too?" Nick asked, trying to find a harmless topic, but Brynne didn't get the chance to answer. A piercing scream silenced every conversation.

Aisha stood in the middle of the hall, surrounded by a growing cluster of people, and clung to Emily. Eric Wu stood in front of them both with a stunned expression.

"Don't touch me! Never again!" Aisha screeched.

Nick abandoned his place in the coffee lineup and pushed his way through the increasingly dense crowd of spectators, as if he were a doctor in a hurry to get to the scene of the accident. His mouth was dry.

Aisha had buried her face in Emily's shoulder and was sobbing.

"I'm sure you're mistaken," Emily said quietly. She stroked Aisha's head, accidentally pushing her headscarf back. "It must have been someone else."

"No. I'm positive. It was him. After Book Club he wanted to walk me to the Tube, and he said that the path through the little park was much nicer ..." Her sobs were getting louder.

Emily tried to pull the headscarf back to its original position with trembling fingers, but soon gave up.

"He ri ... pped ... my ... shirt and tou ... ched me all o ... ver." Only broken syllables were coming out of Aisha's mouth. She rolled up her sleeve and showed a bluish-red bruise on her elbow. "There!" she stammered.

Nick bit his lip until it really hurt. *This has nothing to do with me. Of course not. Not so soon. No.*

"But none of this is true," Eric cried out. He was pale and could hardly stop shaking his head. "It's just not true."

"I saw you both leaving together," Rashid said.

"I did too," Alex chimed in.

Emily stared at Freak Two with narrowed eyes. "Well, that's interesting. You're not in the Book Club, either of you."

"So? There are other things that can keep people back after school," Alex retorted.

Emily's gaze traveled back and forth between Alex, Eric, and the sobbing Aisha.

"She's lying," Eric said, louder this time.

Aisha whirled around. "That's what men always say afterward, isn't it?"

"What do men always say?" Mr. Watson pushed his way through the crowd of students, pressing a thermos and a half-eaten sandwich into Alex's hand as he passed. "Aisha? What happened?" He put his hand on her shoulder, but Aisha moved away from him and pressed even closer to Emily.

"Don't touch me."

"As you wish. Sorry. Everyone else, please go to your classes. The next period is about to start."

No one moved an inch; only Eric took a step forward.

"Aisha claims I ... groped her in the park yesterday. She has a blue bruise on her elbow that's supposed to be from me. But not a word of it is true."

Aisha howled louder. "He tried to ... rape ... me. He tore my skirt and pushed me onto the ground ..."

"I just can't see how that could be true," Emily whispered. Carefully but firmly she removed Aisha's cramped fingers from her shirt and moved away from the crying girl. Aisha, deprived of her human barricade, crouched down on the floor and threw her hands up in front of her face.

I didn't want this. Nick clenched his ice-cold hands into fists. *Not like this. I don't have anything to do with this, honest.*

But what if it was true? Eric could actually have molested Aisha, and the messenger could have found out about it last night. That would explain why he could make such grand promises so easily.

Mr. Watson, who'd been rendered speechless, was slowly regaining his composure. "That's a very serious accusation, Aisha."

"Not a word is true! I swear it!" Something akin to desperation could be heard in Eric's voice for the first time. "It's totally insane!"

"We certainly won't clear it up here in front of everyone," Mr. Watson said. "Aisha, Eric—come with me."

Both of them followed, each intent on keeping the greatest possible distance from the other.

They'd hardly left before loud discussion broke out in the hall.

"I think she's lying!"

"Why would she?"

"Eric is no angel, that's what I always thought."

"Wanted to get his hand up the Turkish chick's skirt."

"That's crazy, she's lost her mind."

"Hey, wicked scandal!"

"Will Watson get the cops? I mean, they haven't been here for a few days."

In the meantime, Nick hadn't taken his eyes off Emily. She was standing there, lost in thought, smoothing out the tear-stained patch on her shoulder.

I should go over to her now, Nick thought. Engage her in conversation. Comfort her.

But before he'd gathered enough courage to take the first step, he spotted Jamie going up to Emily and saying something to her. They exchanged a few sentences, then went up the stairs together.

The next period was math—that was all Nick needed. But at least it had occurred to him straight off, and he didn't feel tired anymore either. Aisha's performance had been more effective than a double espresso.

At lunch, Jamie waylaid him in front of the cafeteria. "How are you?"

Aha—the first normal sentence Jamie had directed at him in ages. It was sure to be a trap.

"Fine. How about you?"

"I'm really worried," Jamie said, and made a face to match. Brow well and truly furrowed. "That thing today with Eric ... What do you think made her do that to him? He's completely shattered; Mr. Watson sent him home."

Nick suppressed the impulse to just run away.

"What made her do that? Hmm, let me think. Maybe the fact that he put his hand up her skirt?"

"You don't believe that for a minute."

"Oh—but you believe Aisha would blacken his name, just like that? Did you see how she was bawling? And her bruise?"

"I think," said Jamie, "that someone is interested in putting Eric out of action. He's no fan of your game, remember?"

"What a load of bullshit!" Nick pushed past Jamie into the cafeteria. "Ever since that gravestone letter you've been completely paranoid."

He took a tray from the stack, and suddenly felt a hand on his shoulder. Jamie had followed him in, and he looked as if he was about to burst into tears.

"Do you know what else has happened? Somebody hid a gun and some ammunition in the schoolyard. Behind the garbage cans. The principal says it can't have been any of the students, but he just doesn't want any press around the place."

Nick asked for a serving of fish and chips. Both looked anaemic and soggy.

"But Jamie knows better, of course," he snapped. "Jamie knows that the evil computer gamers are behind it." He bit his lip and plonked a bottle of soda down on his tray. Enough of this conversation.

"Jamie thinks a few things are odd," Jamie answered, staying markedly calm. "I talked to Mr. Watson, and he says a professional would have been smarter. Hidden the pistols better and not just stuck them in an old cigar box behind the bins."

"Aha. Maybe Mr. Watson is in fact Dr. Watson. And you're trying to be Sherlock Holmes. Leave me in peace, Jamie. I've got nothing to do with any pistols, or any rapes either."

"And someone wrote some sort of code or message on the box as well," Jamie continued, as if he hadn't heard Nick. "That's just like that kind of game, isn't it? A few numbers and a weird word, not Galaxis, but something similar."

Crash!

Nick was just as shocked at the crash as the others in the dining room. He hadn't noticed that he'd let go of his tray.

Galaris.

It all fit. The cigar box, the word, the numbers that were his date of birth. No, please.

The box had been heavy and the object in it quite small ... Could it have been a gun? Yes. Yes, of course.

"Why can't you pay attention?" the cook behind the counter scolded. "You can clean that up yourself! Goodness me!"

"Sure," Nick whispered, and took the broom and pan. He felt Jamie's gaze sticking like cold porridge to the back of his head, but he wasn't going to turn round.

A gun? But why? Why would the messenger get him to hide a gun at the Dollis Brook Viaduct?

"You know something about it," Jamie declared behind his back.

"No. I don't."

Had someone taken a photo? Like the picture of him and Brynne in the café? He knelt and swept his fries into the pan, kept sweeping although there was nothing more there. He couldn't stand up. There were black spots dancing in front of his eyes.

"But I saw it, Nick. You were scared out of your wits just now. You know something."

"Just shut it, okay," Nick muttered, and struggled painfully to his feet. The black dots solidified to a swirling wall. He thrust the pan into the cook's hands and leaned heavily on the counter.

"Come with me to Mr. Watson. Shed some light on this whole thing; you'll feel better afterward. What's going on here is just shi—"

"Shut your face!" Nick screamed. Emily, Eric, a gun, Aisha, Galaris ... it was all too much. He couldn't cope anymore. The cafeteria smells were turning his stomach; any minute he'd be throwing up right there on the floor in front of everyone. If there was a photo and the school got hold of it, he'd be kicked out. As sure as the sky was blue.

He dashed out of the lunchroom, shoving into people right and left, found an open window, and stuck his head out. Fresh air, thank god.

He had to think about it. Maybe talk to the messenger. He was sure to be grateful if Nick told him. Perhaps the messenger would even explain what the business with the gun was about. But first he had to carry out his orders. His incredibly pointless orders.

SEVENTEEN

It was shortly before 5:00 p.m. when Nick got out at Blackfriars station and made his way along New Bridge Street. The parking garage was on Ludgate Hill—finding it wasn't a problem. Getting inside without being noticed might be, though. He made himself as tall as possible and jangled his bunch of keys, as if he was already looking for the car key. However, his fears proved unfounded. No one stopped him when he entered the lot; he wasn't even sure if the attendant, who was reading the newspaper in his cabin, had even noticed him.

He fished the note out of his pants pocket. LP60 HNR was the license plate of the car he was supposed to look for.

"If you don't find it," the messenger had said, "you will go back again. Over and over again, every day between 5:00 and 6:00 p.m., until you have carried out your orders."

Nick was on the second floor when he got lucky. He looked at the car and whistled through his teeth. LP60 HNR was the license plate of a silver-gray Jaguar. It stood out from all the other cars simply by the fact that it gleamed like the crown jewels. Not a splash of mud in sight.

Nick whipped out his camera and took a few pictures. They wouldn't be enough, obviously, but it was a start.

What he needed now was a place where he could lie in wait. So he could keep an eye on the car, but not be seen himself. The best he could find was the narrow gap between an old Ford and the parking garage wall. If he lay down on the ground there and no one took a close look, he would be as good as invisible. Nick turned off the camera flash and set the aperture to maximum to compensate. Then he made himself as comfortable as it was possible to be on the cold floor. It was 5:17 p.m. Okay, easy does it.

When his cell suddenly started ringing, loudly announcing that he'd gotten a text, Nick's heart nearly stopped. He hadn't turned off the ringtone—how dumb could you get?

From his uncomfortable lying position, sandwiched between the car and the wall, he could hardly reach his pants pocket. When he finally managed it and saw who the text was from, his heart began to pound. Emily.

Hi, Nick! I'd really like 2 meet with u & take the opportunity 2 introduce u 2 someone. His name's Victor & he may b able 2 help us all. Pls get back 2 me. Emily.

The name Victor didn't mean anything to Nick. He was happy for it to stay that way. What was that supposed to mean, anyway: he may be able to help "us all"? Presumably what Emily mainly wanted was to help Eric, who was up to his neck in trouble. But she wanted to meet with him. Emily. Didn't matter why—she wanted to meet with him.

Bang! A door closed. Steps coming closer.

Nick held his breath and tried to press himself into the concrete floor. He was pointing the camera at the Jaguar so he could take a picture immediately, if the owner appeared. A pair of legs in black pants came into sight, walked past the Jaguar, came closer. An attendant who'd seen him on the video camera? Please! No! And please not the driver of the Ford Nick was using for cover.

When the man walked past him without so much as a glance at his hiding place, Nick breathed a sigh of relief. Shortly afterward, a red Mazda drove off toward the exit. Silence descended again.

Only five minutes had passed. Nick shifted his weight around as best he could and put his camera down carefully. Steps were approaching once more, but they stopped long before they came level with Nick. A car door slammed and an engine started.

After another five minutes Nick's right leg began to go to sleep. He tried to ignore the pins and needles and focused on the noises in the parking garage. The whirring of the ventilation. The muffled street noise from outside. A heavy metal door opening and closing again. A woman laughing, and a man joining in. The clatter of high heels on concrete. The clunk of a car lock operated remotely, only a few meters away from Nick. The lights of the Jaguar went on.

Nick's heartbeat sped up. He raised the camera and pointed the viewfinder at the car. The man and the woman came closer. Came into view. The man radiated nervousness the way a furnace radiates heat.

Click!

The woman could have been a star in a daytime soap. Glittering earrings, fur jacket, blond hair piled up. The man was tall, with dark hair that was already graying at the temples. He was wearing a suit and tie. Maybe a doctor. Or a lawyer.

Click!

The man opened the car door and put a bag on the back seat.

Click! Click!

"Next time we'll go to Refettorio," the woman said. "Vivian tells me the lamb is superb there."

"As you wish, sweetheart."

Click!

The woman got into the car.

Click!

237

The man paused suddenly and looked around. Had he heard the camera? Nick tried to blend into his dark corner.

"What is it, darling?"

"Nothing." The man ran his hand over his hair. "Nothing. I must have been mistaken. Lately, you know ..."

Nick didn't hear the rest, because the man had gotten into the car and closed the door. He shook his head and shrugged in a gesture of helplessness, and then started the engine. Half a minute later, the Jaguar had left the garage.

That was a wrap. Nick hugged the camera to him. Now to get out of here, quickly. No, first he'd check whether the photos were any good.

Well, okay, they were a bit blurry and quite grainy, but you wouldn't do better without a flash. You could certainly make everything out. The woman, the man, the car's license plate. Twelve passable pictures.

Nick got out his cell in the crowded train and read Emily's text again. "Victor." "Help us all." That didn't sound like a date. It sounded as though she wanted to help Eric out of a tight spot. Nick began to type an answer, decided it was stupid and deleted it, and closed his eyes.

If it came out that he had had something to do with the Galaris box, Emily would find out too. No one would believe that he hadn't known what he was hiding. The papers would write about a planned school massacre that had only just been averted. Or something like that. His father would kill him.

Nick opened his eyes again and looked at the tired faces of the people around him. They'd all see his photo in the paper.

Emily would see his photo in the paper. He typed another text to her and then deleted it again immediately without sending it. What if this Victor was from the police?

Nick shut his eyes. He needed to make sure that *Erebos* remained well disposed to him.

"I received the pictures," the messenger says. He's sitting on a rock at the edge of the moor, stretching out his long legs and looking contented.

Sarius relaxes. Uploading the pictures onto the server as specified hadn't been entirely straightforward; the connection had crashed twice.

"Have you already eaten dinner?"

"Yes."

Since when has that interested the messenger?

"Did you chat with your parents? Did you make a cheerful, normal impression?"

"I think so." *I babbled like a brook so it wouldn't occur to them to ask about my homework.*

"Good. We must be careful. There is too much talk outside Erebos. Our enemies are positioning themselves. We must be careful not to leave ourselves open to attack. I would therefore like you to attend school every day and behave inconspicuously. Give no one any reason to find your behavior suspicious."

"Yes, all right."

"You are now an Eight. I will increase your life energy and your fire magic. Tell me before you go: has your wish crystal already started to take effect? Have you received what you wished for?"

I don't know, Sarius thinks. That didn't have anything to do with me. I don't believe that awful scene was my doing.

"Will you give me no answer?"

"I'm not sure. Perhaps. It's possible that it has. That it's begun to take effect."

The messenger nodded his satisfaction.

"You see? Just wait. That will continue; the rest is in your hands, Sarius."

He can't tell that I'm scared, can he? He can't possibly see it in my face.

He's waiting for the messenger to finally dismiss him, but he just keeps looking at him, and spreads out his bony fingers.

"It would not be a bad thing if Aisha had a witness," he says. "Someone who could confirm her accusations. Can you think of anyone, Sarius?"

He can't be serious, Sarius thinks. I'm not going to do it. Bloody hell, why is he asking that of me?

"I was with Brynne in the café at that time. That means I'm no good as a witness."

"I know. I asked you whether you could think of someone, not whether you would do it."

"Oh, I see. I'm sorry. I can't think of anyone either."

"Then go."

The messenger waves him away, and Sarius, who is glad to escape from the gaze of those yellow eyes, obeys his gesture. Neither of them has mentioned the Galaris box, but there's no doubt the messenger knows all about that too.

Sarius sees the glow of the enormous campfire even from a distance. The moor is to the right; to the left, a round structure reaches up into the night sky. A meadow stretches between them, on which nothing but thorny bushes and a few stunted trees are growing.

"Hi, Sarius!" Arwen's Child is the first to notice him. She's sitting next to LordNick by the fire, which reflects off her new breastplate. Both of them must still be above him—he can't see their levels. Lelant is sitting a bit farther away; he's recovered since their fight and is a Seven again.

"Have you registered for the next Arena fight yet? Over there!" Arwen's Child points over to the round building. "That's about all you can do at the moment. Nothing's happening right now. We've been sitting here for half an hour or so."

Sarius hadn't known anything about a new Arena fight, but of course he wants to take part. What he hasn't bargained with is big Goggle-Eyes himself accepting his registration in person. He's standing on the sand of the nighttime Arena with gnomes swarming all around him, and he seems gigantic, almost twice as big as Sarius. Once again Sarius is thrown by the giant's strange appearance—he doesn't resemble any of the others here. And he's almost naked.

"Register yourself here," he says, and points with his peculiar staff to the list hanging on the wall.

"In seven days, two hours before midnight, the fights will begin."

Sarius writes his name underneath Bracco's. Well, well, so he's still alive too. Blackspell is on the list, BloodWork, Lelant, LordNick, and Drizzel. Sarius can't read any more because the master of ceremonies shoos him off.

"Don't be curious, little elf. Run back to the others."

As he comes out of the Arena, Feniel walks toward him. She must have been playing day and night, because the last time Sarius saw her she was a badly injured Four. Now he can't see her level. So it's at least an Eight. All her armor is new, and she's carrying two swords. Something tells Sarius that he would lose if they were to face one another again.

It looks as though the regulars have settled in for a chat around the gigantic fire. Sapujapu is sitting in the middle of a mob of dwarves who are comparing their axes, but he greets Sarius straightaway.

"No quest today?"

"Doesn't look like it."

"Still, makes a nice change."

They chat about the Arena fight, which Sapujapu also plans to contest, then Sarius saunters on. He sees BloodWork sitting alone on a tree stump, staring into the flames. The ring he wears on a chain around his neck glows ruby-red in the firelight. Sarius hesitates at first, but then he addresses the barbarian.

"Do you know what else is happening today?"

"No."

"Okay. Sorry. Have a nice evening."

BloodWork raises his head.

"I'm dog-tired."

"No wonder. I think we've all been missing out on sleep recently."

"You have no idea."

Sarius could do without the self-importance right now.

"So call it quits for today and just crash on your barbarian skins," he says. But BloodWork can't take a joke.

"Screw off, elf fart," he says. He heaves his gigantic body up and shuffles over to another barbarian and a cat person who are standing a bit apart from the rest. They have red circles dangling around their necks too.

The cat guy wasn't one of those on the tablet at the last Arena fight, Sarius is certain of that.

"Don't get your hopes up."

Drizzel has turned up next to Sarius and jostles him roughly aside. "You'll never be one of the Inner Circle, you wimp. But I will, I bet you. Just watch out, and wait till the next Arena."

He bares his long fangs.

Sarius is about to draw his sword, just in case, but his attention is distracted.

A gnome with light-green skin has gotten himself up onto a rock near the fire.

"The warriors of the Inner Circle are expected at the secret meeting place. There is news."

BloodWork, both his companions, and the elf mage called Wyrdana stand up and head for the wooded area that lies to the left like a wall of shadow. There's no fifth chosen one to be seen, but then Blackspell emerges from the darkness next to the Arena and follows the other four. The red insignia sparkles on his black cape.

"Blackspell belongs to the Inner Circle?" Sarius asks in astonishment.

"Shit. I didn't know that either," Drizzel responds. "But so much the better. I'll make mincemeat of him in the Arena!"

Sarius is secretly looking forward to seeing that. Doesn't matter who makes mincemeat out of whom—he can't stand either of the vampires.

Blackspell disappears into the darkness of the forest as well, and Sarius really has to keep a grip on himself to remain by the fire. He would just love to know what's being discussed in the Inner Circle.

The green-skinned gnome, meanwhile, is still standing on his rock; he has further announcements to make.

"Warriors!" he begins. "The last battle is drawing near. The time has not yet come, but now more than ever it is important to separate the wheat from the chaff."

He leaves a significant pause.

"The camp here is none too distant from Ortolan's fortress. We are drawing closer to him, step by step. My master thinks that Ortolan can already sense us. But he will not attack. He *cannot* attack us, because he has no suspicion of who we are."

Another significant pause.

"Others are attempting to foil our mission, however. They are spying on us, defaming us, trying to harm us. If we do not close ranks, they will infiltrate us. They will destroy our world. More than ever it is imperative to stay silent. Keep calm. Guard your secrets. Treat your enemies as enemies."

With that, the gnome climbs down from his stone and makes his crooked-legged way back into the Arena.

The warriors sit together over the next hours. At first they're waiting for something to happen, but no one gives them orders, no one attacks them, none of Ortolan's monsters swoops down on them. So they occupy themselves peacefully. They throw dice for pieces of meat. The mood is relaxed; no one feels like turning on his neighbor. Sarius hardly notices time passing. When he takes his leave from the others it's two o'clock in the morning, and he's pleasantly tired. He has never felt more secure, more at home in Erebos.

EIGHTEEN

Nick, you have no idea how disappointed I am in you, in all of you, and the way you missed the last practice without even taking the trouble to inform me. Unfortunately you're not the only one. Last time I was left standing in the gym with four people. Feel free to find someone else to take for a fool. One more unexplained absence and you're off the team.

F. Bethune

"What on earth happened to you?"

"Have you been in hospital?"

"Looks impressive."

Brynne and a few of her friends were surrounding the quiet boy, Greg, who was trying, with obvious difficulty, to get his books out of the locker.

"I fell down the escalator." Greg forced a smile. Judging by his tone of voice, this wasn't the first time he'd told the story.

"Tripped and then went crashing down. But it's not half as bad as it looks." He touched the crusty scrape on his nose and grinned wryly.

Half as bad would still be bad enough, Nick thought. Greg's left wrist was bandaged, and he was limping slightly.

"Want me to carry your bag for you?" Nick offered, but Greg declined hastily.

"No. It's fine. No drama. See you."

Nick looked after him, and pushed aside the thought he hadn't been able to get out of his head since Greg had appeared.

It was nothing. Greg said himself that he'd tripped. As if that had never happened to Nick. After a collision at basketball, he'd gone around for two weeks with bandaged ribs. There you go. Things like that happened.

"Nick?"

It was Emily, and she was by herself. No Eric, no Jamie, not even Adrian was nearby.

"Hi, Emily. Sorry I didn't answer your text."

"Why didn't you? I've been waiting."

Nick stared at her for a moment before answering. Was that real disappointment in her voice, or just wishful thinking on his part? He shook his head and refocused.

"Who's this Victor you mentioned?"

"That's not so important either. Can I ask you something?"

"Sure."

"Let's go over there." She tilted her head toward the stairwell, where they could talk undisturbed.

Nick followed her. He could sense Brynne's gaze on his back, threw her a quick smile, and silently called himself a coward.

"What do you think?" Emily began straight off. "Do you think it's true, what Aisha said about Eric?"

She knows, Nick thought, and felt himself going red. She knows about my wish crystal.

246

But there wasn't the faintest reproach in Emily's eyes, only genuine interest in his opinion.

He made a gesture of puzzlement with his arms. "No idea. Maybe. I mean, I don't know him that well ... so ... I ..." He began to stutter under her steady gaze.

"Knowing is always relative, anyway," she rescued him. "You know, ever since yesterday I keep wondering whether there is something more behind Aisha's assertions. At first it all seemed totally absurd to me, but who knows."

Nick was stupefied. "You believe Aisha?"

"No. Maybe. I don't know. People do the most unbelievable things. Things one would never have thought them capable of."

Bull's-eye. Nick's face felt hot; he must be bright red by now. *She does know.*

If Emily noticed his embarrassment, she hid it well. She looked thoughtfully over to the coatracks, where Brynne was still standing and staring at them doggedly.

"I don't know Eric so well either. We both love English lit and that's what we mostly talk about. He's very smart, and I like that. I would have thought he was too smart for something like this, but now on top of everything a witness has turned up who claims to have seen—"

"Who?"

Emily shrugged her shoulders. "No idea. Mr. Watson told Jamie about it this morning. Jamie was absolutely livid. He thinks it's a setup."

It would not be a bad thing if Aisha had a witness. Nick closed his eyes.

"Why are you telling me all this?"

Emily lowered her eyes. "What did you want that time, on the Sunday morning, when you rang me?"

Nick couldn't help smiling. I wanted to give you a world, he thought. A cool, unbelievable, exciting world.

Thrilling. Mystical. Terrible. Nightmarish. All of those put together.

"You can probably guess, can't you? I didn't want Adrian's phone number, it was about ..."

"Got it." She nodded. "I was pretty dismissive, I know. It wasn't personal. I'd probably react differently today. You know, if *you* think the thing's good, there must be something to it." She smiled at him once more and walked away.

Nick looked after her, speechless. If that was the effect of the wish crystal, he was really getting scared. Things like that just didn't happen. Besides. Emily and *Erebos*? How come, all of a sudden? He ran his hand over his hair, astonished at how little the thought appealed to him. After all, that's what he'd wanted. A cat Emily or an elf Emily, maybe even a vampire Emily at his side. But he'd already copied the game for Henry Scott, so that was that. He wouldn't be able to offer it to Emily, even if she wanted it.

"It's so sensitive of you to flirt with Emily when I'm standing right there!" Brynne had planted herself behind him. Anger was making her voice unpleasantly high-pitched.

"Pardon?"

"Didn't our date mean anything to you?"

"But ... I ..." Damn it. He was stuttering yet again.

"Do you think you can mess around with a different girl every day? Do you think I don't have any feelings?"

"I did not mess around with Emily!" Nick said, outraged. "I just talked to her!"

"Yes, and ignored me! Do you think I haven't noticed how you gawk at her?" Brynne threw her hair over her shoulder in a theatrical gesture. "I'm so disappointed in you, Nick!"

She left him standing there. Nick rubbed his eyes and sighed.

He was an idiot. He had actually justified himself for talking to Emily.

It was a day of strange conversations. In one of the next free periods, Mr. Watson came up to Nick and asked if they could have a quick chat in one of the empty classrooms, which immediately caused Nick's heart to race.

The gun. He knows I have something to do with the gun.

"I want to talk to you because I think you're a smart person," Mr. Watson declared. He put his thermos down on the table and looked thoughtfully out the window. "But I think you've gotten caught up in something that's no good for you."

He's going to mention the weapon any minute.

"I know that heaps of students at our school are playing a computer game by the name of *Erebos*. I think you know me well enough to realize that I don't have anything against computer games. I've even given one of my classes an essay topic set in a World of Warcraft scenario. But this is different. It's dangerous, and I have to do something about it."

Nick looked at him silently. Colin, Rashid, and a few others were bound to have noticed that Watson had collared him. So he wasn't going to be able to keep any of this a secret from the messenger.

"I would really like you to help me, Nick. I'll be frank with you: I haven't been very successful in my campaign so far. A few of the students who have been eliminated have talked to me. But the game is no longer to be found on their computers. I think the police might have better luck with that, but I can only call in the police after something has happened." He sighed. "I'm really worried that something will happen. Aren't you?"

Nick made an indefinable noise, somewhere between a snort

and a cough. "So what do you think might happen?" he asked, since Mr. Watson was obviously expecting an answer.

"I don't know. You tell me."

"Well, I don't know either."

Mr. Watson gave him a sharp look. "I think what's happened to Eric is bad enough. Of course, you can say that it's his own fault if he molests Aisha. But Aisha doesn't want to go to the police. Not for anything. Don't you think that's strange?"

Nick shrugged his shoulders uneasily. "She's probably too embarrassed; that's understandable. It's her business, after all."

"Yes. Sure. Everybody around here is just minding their own business, right? Except your friend Jamie, who's resolved to do something about it. Or hadn't you noticed?"

"Can I go now? I really don't know how I can help you."

Mr. Watson nodded resignedly. "You can come to me any time if you need support, okay? You and the others."

Nick left the classroom. He was hurrying a bit too much to appear calm and cool, he knew. But he didn't care. Mr. Watson hadn't mentioned the gun. That was the main thing.

"Do you have any news to report?"

Sarius is standing facing the messenger in an utterly unfamiliar place. He's never been here before. It's a hill dominated by a decaying tower. The tower exercises a disturbing fascination on Sarius. It gives an idea of the grandeur of the castle it must once have been part of, but at the same time looks ready to collapse. To its left, yet another peculiar hedge runs through the barren landscape. It is divided in two lengthwise: half green, half yellow. The yellow comes from the funnel-shaped flowers that are growing on the left half of the hedge in unbelievable profusion, while leaving the right side completely bare.

Sarius can't help thinking of a deranged gardener giggling insanely as he planted his peculiar shrubs in the middle of this gray, stony land.

Sarius doesn't want to mention the conversation with Mr. Watson if he doesn't have to. He gives something else a try. Something he can't understand.

"I got the impression that Emily Carver is becoming interested in *Erebos*. She hasn't been so enthusiastic about it, but today she indicated that she's changing her mind."

"Aha. Good, Sarius. That's enough for today; you'd better go now. You must realize that we are drawing near to Ortolan's stronghold. You need to take the utmost care. If you follow the hedge westward, you will come upon a statue—a monument, no less."

He giggles, which sends shivers down Sarius's spine.

"There you will find friendly warriors—but possibly also a few enemies who must be defeated. Good luck."

The hedge glows in the dark—how very practical. It runs through the countryside, straight as a ruler. For a moment Sarius thinks he sees something else in it, as he might in a puzzle picture: a truth concealed behind the obvious. But the impression disappears as quickly as it came.

The journey to the statue seems like a long way to Sarius. But he must be headed in the right direction; the glowing hedge proves that beyond doubt.

Finally, he sees something gigantic in the far distance—probably the monument. Except that it's moving. As he approaches, Sarius can make out what it is—a well-known Greek sculpture of a man whose name escapes him, and his two sons, who are being strangled by massive sea snakes. The three stone people high atop their pedestal are fighting for their lives as the snakes wind their way around their bodies.

A whole crowd of warriors is standing around the base of the pedestal. Drizzel is there, and LordNick, Feniel, Sapujapu. Lelant, Beroxar, and Nurax are a bit farther back, waiting to see what happens.

Sarius goes and stands next to Sapujapu. Together with the others he watches the agonizing drama that's unfolding above their heads. He would like to ask Sapujapu what it's supposed to mean, but there's only a small fire burning, and it's too far away to make conversation possible. Nonetheless, it's sufficient to throw an eerie flickering light on the writhing statue.

Perhaps the task involves killing the snakes? But how is Sarius to get up the pedestal? The others aren't trying either, not anymore at least.

There's something hypnotic about the movements of the stone figures. Every time the snakes wrap their bodies tighter around the three men, Sarius gets the feeling he can't breathe.

A gnome with snow-white skin turns up. One of the messenger's messengers.

"A pretty sight, isn't it?" he says, and shows his teeth. "Do you understand what it means?"

No one speaks up. *Is it supposed to be a riddle? Is there a reward for solving it?*

"No, you understand nothing. That's exactly what my master expected. Then go, run into the forest, and slay orcs. He who brings me three heads will be rewarded."

Sarius sets off at a run, happy to escape the spine-chilling spectacle. As has happened so many times before, wonderful music starts to play, convincing him he is invincible.

Three heads are child's play.

NINETEEN

Wham! The ball bounced off the board a good foot from the basket. Bethune cursed, and Nick gave the wall a kick. Garbage, complete garbage. He didn't feel like all this pointless leaping around in the stinking gym anymore. He wanted to be home, seeing to it that things finally started looking up for Sarius.

The last four days had brought nothing but disappointment. A fight against a nine-headed dragon, another against poisonous giant woodlice, and yesterday a battle with very alive skeletons in a very dark tomb. Sarius had gotten through it all quite well, but he hadn't particularly distinguished himself. He was still an Eight. Nothing more had come of his efforts than a bit of gold, some healing potions, and some new gloves. No orders from the messenger. No chance to prove himself.

Nick ran after Jerome, poached the ball from him, and dribbled across the court. Aimed. Shot. *Wham!* Missed again.

"Should I hold you up to the basket, Dunmore, or do you need a stepladder?" Bethune bellowed.

No. He needed a new sword and an upgrade of his special abilities. The Arena fight was getting closer and closer, but whereas the others were getting stronger, Sarius was just marking time. If only the messenger would give him a chance, a task, so Sarius could show what he was worth.

Jerome got the ball back and ran past Nick with long strides. Almost automatically he ran through Jerome's possible gamer identities. Lelant? Nurax? Drizzel? Stronger than Sarius? Weaker?

"Having a nap, Dunmore? Would you like to do some sit-ups to wake yourself up?"

Nick was grateful when practice was over. He'd be off home. Of course he did have an English essay waiting to be written, but that was a piece of cake. What was the Internet for? Copy out two pages, and it's done. After that he'd turn the game around and finally end his run of bad luck. Tonight would be the night—he could feel it.

The darkness is pressing down on the land as if it had mass and weight. The warriors are running; they are in a hurry. They must capture a bridge: those were the gnomes' orders. The road they're running along is dark blue; the color resembles deep water.

Sarius is trying to be faster than the others; he overtakes three of his companions: Drizzel, Nurax, and Arwen's Child. LordNick is running level with him; Sapujapu, Gagnar, and Lelant are following a bit farther back. A couple of new arrivals are bringing up the rear; Sarius doesn't bother to remember their names. They're Ones and Twos; they won't be able to touch him in the Arena.

Now he can feel they're nearing their goal. He's tense, but it's an enjoyable tension, full of curiosity and blood lust. Will it be orcs, scorpions, or spiders they'll have to wrest the bridge from? Whatever it is, it's fine by him. This time he'll fight so well that the messenger will have to reward him. There are still three days till the Arena fight. He wants to be at least a Ten by then.

Running hasn't been a problem to him for ages now. He fleetingly recalls the time when he had to stop after every hill and take a rest. Now he can sprint uphill and downhill at full pelt without the slightest sign of exhaustion. It's great to be strong. It's great to be at a higher level.

A gentle, even, uphill stretch lies before him. Too even to be natural. Sarius takes a closer look and sees that the road rises from the ground and stretches right out across the darkness like a watery blue rainbow. The bridge.

In the darkness up ahead metal is striking metal. Has the fighting already started? Sarius draws his sword and sees that LordNick is following suit. If only they could see the enemy. But there are only a few gigantic silhouettes. *Dong!* A sound like a bell ringing. Something falls from the bridge. Something? Someone?

The sounds of fighting are getting louder; now gleaming outlines are silhouetted against the sky. Giant, silver-armored knights who are defending the bridge.

Sarius's enthusiasm evaporates. How is he ever supposed to defeat them? He throttles back his speed and sees Drizzel dodging the extremely long sword of one of the knights, dancing back and forth but unable to land a blow. Nurax is in the same boat.

There must be a trick, Sarius thinks. A vulnerable spot, something. *When I'm closer I'll see it.*

LordNick passes him, rushes at the next armored giant, thrusts his sword into the back of his knees. The knight doesn't even flinch, and now LordNick really has his work cut out to avoid being split in two with one blow.

I could try to get past them. The orders are to capture the bridge, not to defeat the knights.

Close up, their adversaries are as tall as towers. Their movements are enormously strong, but not very fast. Sarius runs past the first knight, and the second as well. The third one tries to stop him, lowering his sword. Sarius dodges him … that's the edge of the bridge there. He must be careful. *Dong!* The knight takes another step toward him, lunges with his weapon, and that's when it happens. The giant sword touches Sarius lightly, just very lightly. It doesn't injure him, but it throws him off balance. Sarius realizes he's not going to make it. There's nothing he can hold onto, no parapet, not even a curbstone.

He falls. Away from the knights, away from the blue bridge that's now arching over him. Away from his dream of becoming a Nine tonight. He can't even imagine what's below him. Water would be good, or at least soft grass. But in his mind's eye he sees sharp stones and thorns. The air whistles around him. Still no ground.

Died from stupidity.

It can't be happening, not now, not so soon. Not like this. Not just because of one false move.

When the impact comes, the injury tone sets in with an intensity that makes Sarius groan out loud. For a moment he wants nothing more than for it to stop, immediately. But the screeching is a sign of life; it means he has a chance. He has to wait. He must endure it.

So he waits, trying not to move at all. Soon his head starts to ache; the tone is sheer agony, drowning out everything, even the sounds of fighting from the bridge. Why is it taking so long? Are they even fighting on the bridge anymore? Probably. But except for him, no one has fallen.

"That was not exactly a masterly performance, Sarius."

Finally. He's never been happier to see the yellow eyes.

"I assume you need my help?"

"Yes. Please."

"You will appreciate that I am gradually becoming bored with the constant necessity of getting you out of trouble."

Sarius doesn't answer. What is he supposed to say? But the messenger seems to be waiting for an answer, and Sarius certainly doesn't want him to become even more bored.

"I'm sorry. I was clumsy."

"There I must concur. Clumsiness is pardonable in a Two; in an Eight it is a disgrace."

He's about to take a level from me, Sarius thinks unhappily. If not even more.

"You could always rely on me in the past, couldn't you?"

"Yes."

"Can I rely on you too, Sarius? Even when things get difficult?"

"Of course."

"Good. Then I will help you once more. But you must carry out some orders for me, and this time you must not be clumsy."

The injury tone recedes, and Sarius sits up slowly. That was close. He'll control himself next time; this will never happen again. The Arena fight is in two days; he wants to be fit by then.

"I will carry out your orders. I don't mind if it's difficult. It's not a problem."

The messenger nods deliberately.

"I am glad to hear it. Allow me to ask you a question first. Mr. Watson is your English teacher?"

"Yes."

"They say he often carries a thermos around with him. Is that true?"

Sarius has to think for a moment.

"Yes. I think it has tea in it."

"Good. Tomorrow morning, five minutes after the beginning of the third period, you will go to the bathroom on the first floor. The one where the mirror over the washbasin is cracked. You will find a small bottle in the garbage can. You are to tip its contents into Mr. Watson's thermos. The nature of these contents need not concern you. However, your ingenuity will be put to the test. No one must observe you doing this."

Sarius has followed the messenger's instructions with growing disbelief. He briefly considers running away and pretending he hasn't heard a word. Or he could lie there and wait for the messenger to take it all back and pronounce it a bad joke. But his companion simply crosses his arms in front of his bony chest.

"Well? Did you understand everything?"

Sarius gives himself a shake. "Yes."

"Will you do it? Since the task is difficult, the reward will be ample. A new magical power and three levels. Then you will be an Eleven, Sarius. As an Eleven you would be a contender for a place in the Inner Circle, and I could tell you the name of its weakest link."

Sarius takes a deep breath. It is a game, isn't it? Probably the messenger is just demanding a test of courage, and there's milk in the little bottle. Or sugar water.

"I'll do it."

"Excellent. I will expect your report in the morning."

This time the darkness comes quickly. It leaves Sarius feeling more at a loss than ever before.

Create. Sustain. Destroy.

For each of these tasks the Hindus have a different god. I master all on my own.

I created what no one before me has created, but the world is not my witness and never will be.

Next I tried to sustain what I had created—with all my strength, with all my will. Painfully, sometimes also tearfully, and always at considerable sacrifice.

Now I will destroy. Who will hold it against me? If there is justice, then at least this final act will succeed.

I would rather have remained a creator and taken pleasure in my creation, sustained it, shared it with others. But destruction can also be of some interest. Its appeal lies in its finality.

TWENTY

Nick couldn't remember the last time he'd slept so badly. He'd turned the orders over and over in his mind, calming himself down one minute, and panicking the next. Attempted hundreds of times to imagine the scenario for the next day. He'd tried hard to come up with a plan, but he'd never gotten any further than the bit where he was supposed to unscrew the thermos lid and tip the unknown substance in.

But now the time had come. Two minutes ago the bell had rung for the third lesson. Nick climbed up the stairs to the first floor, his heart hammering.

He had a free period. One of the many advantages of finally being a senior student. The others who didn't have a class now were in the library or the common room. Nick didn't think anyone was following him, but he kept looking around. Secretly waiting for Dan or Alex or someone or other to ambush him with a camera.

Nick stopped in front of the bathroom door. He wanted to be somewhere else, anywhere else. But that didn't change anything.

All right. Open the door. A quick look in the cracked mirror at his pale face, the dark circles under his eyes.

There, to the left of the washbasins, was the garbage can. Half full, with used tissues, empty drink cans, a banana peel, a half-eaten sandwich, and a few scrunched up pages from a notebook.

Nick separated the bits of paper gingerly. Nothing there. There wasn't anything under the first drink can either.

He didn't really have a choice; he kept burrowing. There was even more crumpled up paper. A clumsy drawing of a naked girl. Nick shoved his hand a bit deeper. If there was still nothing there, he'd take the garbage can and upend it, and root through the trash like a pig at a trough. Or explain to the messenger that there hadn't been any little bottle in the garbage can—now there was an idea. The hope had barely begun to blossom in Nick before he saw it—a small carton, blue and white. "Digotan®, 50 Tbl, 0.2 mg," Nick read. He lifted the carton out, felt something in it. Bloody hell.

He shut himself in the last cubicle and opened the packaging. A small brown bottle was revealed, about two-thirds full of white tablets.

Nick opened the bottle, smelled its contents, didn't notice anything obvious. The tablets looked harmless; they were white and chalky, with a score line in the middle.

He could still hear the messenger's words—that he needn't concern himself with what was in the bottle. But there was no way Nick could ignore the instruction leaflet.

The active substance in the small white pills was called ß-Acetyldigoxin and was used, according to the instructions, to treat heart disease.

> Digotan® improves the heart's performance; it pumps more slowly and strongly. Blood circulation throughout the body is also improved.

It sounded trustworthy so far. Nick turned the note over and looked for the side effects.

Warning: Medications containing cardioactive glycosides can easily become toxic in the presence of electrolyte imbalance or by interaction with other medications. Danger: An overdose can be fatal. You should therefore seek immediate medical attention if you experience any of the following symptoms: nausea, vomiting, visual impairment, hallucinations, or abnormal heartbeat.

"Can be fatal." Nick saw the instruction leaflet trembling in his hand. The stuff could easily become toxic, it said—what would happen if he emptied the whole contents of the bottle into Watson's thermos? Would just one sip of tea be enough to poison his teacher?

Nick leaned against the cubicle wall with his eyes closed. There was no way he could do that. He couldn't kill anyone. He would ask the messenger for new orders—taking photos, maybe. This was just insane. It was probably a programming mistake anyway, and the messenger would be glad if Nick pointed it out to him.

Yeah right, sure.

He remembered what the green-skinned gnome had said by the campfire several days ago: that they had to treat their enemies as enemies. Those who sought to destroy the world of *Erebos*. Had he really meant they should kill them?

Nick weighed the little bottle in his hand. Briefly he considered tipping the contents into the toilet, but he couldn't bring himself to do it. Perhaps he'd still need the pills. He had to think of something.

For the rest of the period he roamed around the school, restless as a ghost. He needed an idea—and not just any idea, a good one. One that would allow both Watson and Sarius to stay alive.

Next recess Watson was on yard duty. Nick watched him closely; he couldn't take his eyes off the shiny chrome thermos the teacher carried around, tucked casually under his arm.

261

At this rate Nick was never going to get at it. It was completely out of the question. The only possibility was to wait until Watson put it down somewhere. And he would presumably only do that in the staff room, where there were always loads of people. He couldn't simply march in there and chuck pills into someone's tea.

It would never work! Nick felt for the bottle in his pants pocket. It wasn't fair. The orders couldn't be carried out even if Nick threw his conscience out the window, even if he—

"Nick?"

He stifled a yelp.

"Adrian! Must you sneak up on me like that, damn it?"

"I'm sorry."

But Adrian didn't look sorry. He appeared resolute, even though he was pale and wetting his lips constantly.

"What do you want?"

"Is it true that those DVDs of yours have a game on them? A computer game?"

Adrian looked at him pleadingly, but Nick didn't answer. Mr. Watson was just putting his thermos on the windowsill in order to sort out a quarrel between two younger girls.

Unfortunately the yard was full of people; he couldn't just go over there ... And besides, he wasn't going to do it! He had to stop even thinking about it!

"Nick! Is it true?"

Nick whipped around, saw Adrian biting his thumbnail, and suddenly felt unbelievably angry.

"Why don't you leave me in peace? Why don't you try it out for yourself? I can't tell you anything about it, and I don't even want to! Screw off!"

Colin was standing quite close to him, and Jerome was a bit

farther away. Both of them turned their heads to look. A thin smile stole across Colin's face, and Nick regretted his outburst. He didn't want Adrian to be the next to go tumbling down the escalators.

"Just drop it, okay?" he said quietly. "If you're interested, get hold of one for yourself. It's not difficult. Otherwise, just forget about it."

"If it's a game," Adrian whispered, "then stop it. Seriously. Please stop it."

Nick looked at Adrian blankly. "Can you tell me why?"

"No. Just take my word for it, please. I'm afraid the others won't—even the ones in my class."

"And why should they?" Nick watched Mr. Watson walk back to the windowsill and retrieve his thermos. Damn. He turned back to Adrian.

"Tell me! Why should they listen to you? You don't even know what it's about. Why do you want to spoil other people's fun?"

Fun. He'd said fun.

"That's not what I want. But I've got a feeling that—"

"A feeling," Nick interrupted him. "Well, let me give you some good advice. Stop bugging people about a feeling. All it will get you is trouble. The painful kind."

Oh terrific, now he'd warned Adrian about the other gamers. If word got around, the messenger definitely wouldn't be amused, that much was certain. And then there was the business with the pills. He still hadn't had any bright ideas.

He walked away from Adrian without another word.

An hour later Nick was on the way to the cafeteria. He had zero appetite, but he had to find something to do. Just sitting around waiting for lunchtime to be over would drive him crazy.

Eric was back—Nick saw him standing in a corner with three people from the Book Club, having an animated discussion. As he approached they turned the volume down, but Nick had distinctly heard Aisha's name. Emily was nowhere to be seen.

But he did spot Mr. Watson, who was standing with Jamie and a heavy girl by the wall of windows outside the biology classroom. Nick studied the teacher closely. No thermos, not even on the windowsill.

Without stopping to think what he was actually doing, Nick headed for the staff room. He wasn't going to carry out the orders—of course he wasn't—but he needed to know whether it was possible in theory. So he'd be able to tell the messenger why it wasn't possible. If it actually wasn't.

The door to the staff room was open. Nick stuck his head in. There were only two teachers sitting at the long tables set up in a U shape. They didn't even raise their heads when he took a step into the room. One was correcting papers, the other was reading the paper and chewing on a sandwich. There was no sign of Mr. Watson's thermos.

Half disappointed and half relieved, Nick turned on his heel. What now? He had to at least act as though he was going to carry out the orders—someone was bound to be watching him and reporting in. There. Dan was just crossing the corridor, and although he didn't even look in his direction, Nick was convinced he was only there because of him.

Nick slowly walked back the way he had come, but after only a few steps, an idea made him pause. Where else did the teachers keep their things, apart from the staff room? In the cloakroom! He was right in front of the little room, and the conviction was pounding in his brain before he'd turned the doorknob. His gaze flew to the flask immediately, as if magnetized by it. It was peeping out of a leather shoulder bag that hung on a hook between jackets and coats.

Quick as a flash Nick slipped into the room and closed the door behind him. Even just doing this could get him into serious difficulties; students had no business being in here. But no one could watch him here: not Dan, nor Colin, nor Jerome.

Nick lifted the flask partway out of the bag. It sloshed a bit; it must be about half full. He could feel his pulse throbbing right up to his scalp as he unscrewed it. Peppermint tea. The bottle of pills weighed heavily in his pants pocket, as if trying to get his attention.

I could do it, Nick thought. Now. Quickly.

No. He wasn't crazy! What the hell was he doing here at all?

Even more hurriedly than he had opened it, Nick screwed the thermos closed, wiped the fingerprints off the chrome surface with his shirt, and stuck the bottle back in the leather bag.

But he had been here. Someone was bound to have seen him going in. That was the main thing.

It took nerve to walk out of the staff cloakroom—what if he walked straight into the arms of Mr. Watson? But nobody took any notice of him as he left the room and closed the door quickly behind him. Except that Helen was just going past; she skewered him with an unfathomable look.

He disposed of the pill bottle after class in a garbage can at the Tube station and suddenly felt surprisingly lighthearted. He'd gone about it the right way; he'd thought of every detail. He could have done anything in the cloakroom; nobody would be able to prove otherwise. Mr. Watson would live, and Sarius too. He was practically an Eleven already.

TWENTY-ONE

A cathedral of darkness, Sarius thinks as he stands facing the messenger. They are in a gigantic space with Gothic windows that admit no light, although the stained glass seems to be glowing palely. Stone statues, twice as tall as Sarius, with demons' faces and angels' wings, stand between the windows, staring at nothing.

The messenger is sitting on an elaborately carved wooden chair, a sort of throne. Something gapes behind it, even darker than the rest of the surroundings: a fissure or an abyss. Sarius can't see it clearly from where he's standing.

The messenger has folded his long fingers under his chin and is studying Sarius silently. All around, hundreds of gray candles are flickering in their holders.

"You had orders," says the messenger.

"Yes."

"Did you carry them out?"

"Yes."

The messenger leans back and crosses his legs.

"Tell me about it."

Sarius keeps it brief, although he doesn't omit any important details. He reports on finding the pills and on his search for the thermos, and finally describes how he tipped the pills into the tea.

"All of them?" the messenger inquires.

"Yes."

"Good. What did you do with the empty bottle?"

"Threw it away. In a garbage can at the Tube station."

"Good."

Silence reigns again. A candle flame goes out with a hiss; a thin plume of smoke rises up and assumes the shape of a skull. The messenger leans forward and his yellow eyes take on a reddish cast.

"Explain something to me."

I was dumb—he knows, he knows everything.

"One of my scouts found the bottle. It was full."

Sarius goes hot with panic. An explanation, quick ...

"Perhaps the scout found the wrong bottle."

"You're lying. Other scouts report that Mr. Watson is in the best of health. They say he's still at school."

"Maybe Mr. Watson hasn't drunk any of his tea," Sarius puts in hastily. "Or he tipped it out because the pills made it bitter."

"You're lying. I no longer have any use for you."

"No, wait! That's just not right!"

Sarius searches desperately for arguments that will convince the messenger. He's been clever; nobody can prove that he didn't go through with it.

"I did everything as agreed. If Mr. Watson didn't drink his tea, it's not my fault. I did—"

"There is no place for the indecisive or the frightened, or those who hesitate or moralize, in my master's service. They are not fit to destroy Ortolan. Farewell."

Farewell?

At a gesture from the messenger, two of the stone demons break away from their places between the windows and spread their wings.

"No, stop, it's a mistake!" Sarius cries out. "That's unfair! I did everything right!"

The two demons reach for his shoulders with their clawed feet and lift him up.

Sarius struggles with all his might, writhes in the grip of the stone giants. How can the messenger do this to him? He's always helped him before ... And now, just because of this one time, this one order ...

"Just wait a minute! It's all a misunderstanding. I'll try again," Sarius cries. "This time I'll do it better; it will work this time, I promise!"

The messenger pulls his hood down over his face.

"You will not repeat anything about *Erebos*. You will not turn against us. You will leave the remaining warriors in peace. You will not throw in your lot with our enemies, or you will regret it."

"Please stop! I will do it, this time I'll do it right!"

They carry him to the fissure that yawns behind the messenger's throne. It's clear to Sarius that the fissure is his death. He struggles with all his strength against the grip of the stone demons. In vain.

"Nick Dunmore. Nick Dunmore. Nick. Dunmore," echoes softly through the cathedral.

Then they drop him. The air around him sings; again and again he thinks he can hear his name. He falls down, down, down. There's still a tiny bit of light; he can see the silhouette of his hands, which he has stretched out in terror.

Then the impact. A short sharp screech—the injury tone, louder than ever before.

Then silence. Blackness. The end.

Nick hammered at the keyboard, thumped the mouse, struck out at the monitor, the computer, the desk. Sarius wasn't dead, couldn't be dead.

Okay, calm down, take it slowly. Turn off the computer first. Then turn it back on again. Watch it booting, don't get impatient. Think about it.

Who had betrayed him? Who had gotten the damned bottle of tablets out of the garbage? Nick hadn't seen anyone, but then he hadn't paid attention to whether someone had followed him once he was out of the school.

What an idiot. Some gamer must have crept after him. Probably got loads of gold or another level as a reward.

But still. The messenger couldn't prove that Nick had refused to carry out the orders. He couldn't just kick him out without proof! It hadn't even been a day since he'd said that Nick was a candidate for the Inner Circle.

The thought was painful. And the Arena fight was tomorrow! He wanted to be there; he *had* to be there. He would make it, he just had to find an opportunity to speak to the messenger and clear up the misunderstanding.

He thought of Greg. Another misunderstanding. *Except that it wasn't one at all, in my case.*

But he wasn't Greg. He wasn't going to just let himself be kicked out. There was a way back in, he knew it. For certain. Nick just needed a second chance. He had to get back into the game.

He rapped impatiently on the desk with his knuckles. How come the computer was taking so long to boot?

Assuming the messenger gave him the same orders again, would he do it this time? Would he poison Mr. Watson? Did he regret not using the opportunity he'd had?

Yes, damn it all! Yes. What was Mr. Watson, after all, compared to Sarius?

Nick shut his eyes. Probably nothing would have happened. He would have sipped at his tea, thought it was disgusting, and spat it out. So? No big deal. That had probably even been at the back of the messenger's mind. If all the pills had dissolved in the tea, it would have been completely undrinkable. Not remotely dangerous. But no, Nick had to have scruples about it.

The computer had finally managed it; there it was, the usual desktop display. Nick automatically moved the cursor over to the spot where the *Erebos* icon was. Or where it had been. The red E had disappeared.

Shit. Frantically Nick fished the *Erebos* DVD out of the case and put it in the drive. The Install window appeared. There you go. Perfect. Install.

It took ages, like the first time. But that didn't matter; he could be patient.

So. Right. Where was the icon?

He couldn't find it, any more than he could find the re-installed program. He searched the whole hard drive, twice, three times. Nothing. He'd install it again.

Hang on. Maybe you had to copy the DVD first? After all, that was how it was when you passed the game on.

He copied it, installed it, twice, three times. Thumped his computer desperately in between. Tried it a total of seven times, in every conceivable variation. It just didn't work. And he knew that it wouldn't work, but he couldn't make himself stop. If he stopped it was final. Then it would really be over. He kept back the rising tears. Sarius was a part of him; no one was allowed to simply take a piece of his own self away from him. He'd install it again. And again.

After more than three hours Nick gave up. He'd screwed it up. He'd sacrificed Sarius for his stupid English teacher—for someone who just had to go snooping around in other people's business. Would have served him right, getting a bit of a wake-up call. But Nick had been too much of a coward.

Died from cowardice?

The thought of his gravestone finally brought the tears to his eyes. Would cowardice really be engraved on it? Or disobedience? Indecision?

He wouldn't even be able to find out.

"Lasagna, Nicky?" Mom was balancing a foil container in one oven-mitted hand. It smelled of cheese and Italian herbs, but Nick didn't feel hungry.

"Yes, please. But not too much," he said nevertheless. They were supposed to behave inconspicuously, messenger's orders. Hang on. That didn't apply to him anymore. He rested his head in his hands. His eyes were burning.

"Are you okay?"

"Sure. I'm just feeling a bit tired."

"Must be the weather. Karen Bricker nearly fell asleep on me during her perm ..."

He let Mom talk. Occasionally he smiled; twice he joined in when she laughed, even though he'd lost the thread long ago.

After he'd stopped blubbering just now, he'd had a new idea. Surely he could install the game again on another computer. He could make a new login—just not as Sarius, unfortunately. Did he want to do that? Would it still be better than nothing?

Oh hell, he'd completely forgotten that you had to give your real name at the start. Last time the game hadn't let him lie to it. It didn't matter—he had to try, at least. The messenger would see that Nick Dunmore was taking the matter seriously. He would re-admit him.

Sarius is standing in the middle of the Arena, there's a red ring dangling around his neck. But it's not made out of rubies; it's made of fire.

The crowd around him is cheering—this time it's made up entirely of spider men, with twitching legs growing out of their heads. Sarius turns away. LordNick is standing next to him with a spear sticking into his body.

"So what?" he says, and shrugs his shoulders.

Then the spear turns into a snake, which retreats back through the stab wound in LordNick's body as if into a cave. The injury heals. Magic.

Sarius is looking for Sapujapu, but there's no sign of him. Lelant is there instead, pulling a stupid face and giving him the finger. There's a thermos tucked into his belt.

"Fight," bellows big Goggle-Eyes. He hammers on the ground with his staff, and a fissure opens in the earth.

Not again, Sarius thinks, I've only just managed to get back. He looks up—the golden hawk is circling there, with the two stone demons alongside him. They mustn't see him.

The fissure grows wider and wider. Some are jumping in of their own accord, but Sarius isn't going to—he's not crazy. He retreats farther and farther, but soon the hole fills the whole Arena. He has to climb over the barricade, into the stands, but the spider people are there, stretching out their arms as if he were a welcome feed ...

He's falling again, falling endlessly. Doesn't matter, he thinks, at least I know how I can get back now.

The alarm tore Nick out of his fall. At first he was perfectly happy, because *Erebos* was open to him once again. The next moment reality had asserted its rightful control of his head, and Nick buried his face in his pillow and tried to crawl back into his dream.

Did his face show it? Nick got the impression he was being stared at as soon as he entered the school. Colin studied him mockingly, he thought; Rashid, on the other hand, looked right through him as if he were thin air.

Neither of them would help him, that was obvious to Nick. What he needed was someone like Greg. Someone who'd already been through the plunge into the abyss and was searching for the way back into the world of *Erebos*.

The minute he wasn't being watched he tried Greg, which meant he practically had to follow him into the bathroom.

"Can I ask you something quickly?"

Greg shrugged his shoulders uneasily. The scrapes on his face had gotten darker, and he still had a bandage around his left arm.

"If you have to."

"Have you found a ... solution to your problem?"

Greg frowned, then began to grin. Obviously Nick was really easy to see through.

"Don't tell me they've kicked you out now too? Oh well, tough luck, Dunmore. Considering how helpful you were, I wouldn't tell you how you get back in even if I knew myself."

He slammed the bathroom door in Nick's face.

Okay, so that hadn't been very clever. Turning to Greg, of all people. But who else did he know about who'd definitely gotten chucked out? No one. Did anybody look particularly depressed and withdrawn? He thought of Helen. All Helen did these days was stare into space, and she spoke even less than before. He would ask Helen, even though she didn't particularly like him. Actually, she didn't particularly like anyone.

But so what? At worst she'd rub his face in his own stupidity and give him a verbal kick in the butt. He'd survive. He didn't have any time to be picky. The longer Sarius was dead, the more difficult it would be to bring him back to life. It was still possible now, Nick sensed. Perhaps Sarius wasn't even in the graveyard yet, and he could be brought back and allowed to continue. He just needed to convince the messenger. Somehow.

He found Helen in the next free period. She was sitting in the schoolyard, under a linden tree, and twirling a heart-shaped yellow leaf between her fingers. She looked unusually peaceful, and Nick hesitated to disturb her. Oh well, he was going to be nice.

He sat down next to her on the bench. "Helen?"

She didn't move, just turned down one corner of her mouth as if an irritating thought had crossed her mind.

"I'd like to ask you something. You ... played too, didn't you?"

"Get lost."

"It's just ..." He looked for the right words. "I've got a problem. I can't get in anymore and I was wondering if you would be able to help me."

She ran her finger over the jagged edges of the linden leaf.

"I had the feeling," Nick went on cautiously, "that you were already in the same situation. That's why ..."

She turned to face him. There were shadows under her eyes, and the eyes themselves were bloodshot. She's played all night, Nick thought. She's in. But—still, or again?

"What's past is past," Helen said, and threw the leaf away. "You'd better leave me in peace."

"But I need help."

She seemed to find that entertaining. "What gave you the idea that I would help you?"

Because I was always a bit nicer to you than the others.

"Just because. But that's okay," he answered. It wasn't okay at all. In a few hours the Arena fight was going to start, and he wanted to be there; he wanted to be there more than anything else.

274

During English class he stared hypnotically at the thermos on the teacher's desk. Mr. Watson had it with him today in class, as if he wanted to mock Nick. Now and then Watson poured himself some tea and took a sip. The fact that he'd done that on previous occasions too was just beginning to dawn on Nick.

Emily was sitting diagonally in front of him. She was wearing her hair loose today, but although part of Nick found her beautiful—as always—a different thought was demanding his attention. She could still accept the game from him. She hadn't mucked it up yet. The big adventure still lay ahead of her.

She must have felt his gaze, because she turned her head and smiled. He gave a strained smile back. Did she already know about his expulsion? Jamie had given him an unusually friendly look today too; did they know about it? Could they know about it?

During the lunch break he rang his brother, but Finn only answered after the tenth ring.

"Sorry, little bro, but I've got a customer right now. What's up?"

"Finn, can you lend me your old laptop? For a couple of weeks?"

"Why—isn't your computer working?"

"Yes, but ... I need a second one just now. Please."

"Well, Becca won't be very pleased, she uses it sometimes for her designs. But fine. You can have it."

"Thanks," Nick said with relief. "Can I pick it up this afternoon?"

"Oh. That could be tricky," Finn said. "We're closing the shop at three and going out to Greenwich to visit friends. Maybe tomorrow?"

No, the Arena is today, Nick thought desperately.

"Okay. Tomorrow. See you then."

He spent the rest of school brooding and feeling that time was running away from him. He had to do something. He had to find a solution.

As he was setting off for home, Jamie pulled up next to him on his bike and got off.

"Something's happened, hasn't it? You look completely exhausted. Is it serious, or does it have something to do with *Erebos*?"

Nick suppressed the desire to slug Jamie.

"I thought you took *Erebos* so seriously that you'd declared war on it," he said. If Jamie wanted an argument, he could have one. Gladly. Nick was in dire need of someone to let all his frustration out on.

"That's true. But I'm taking the consequences seriously, rather than the game." Jamie pushed his bike along next to Nick, like old times. As if there wasn't a whole world between them.

"How are things going with Eric?" Nick asked, hoping the answer would be "bad."

"He's okay. He's trying to get Aisha to talk to him, but she's blocking everything. She doesn't want to talk to a female counselor, she doesn't want to do anything. But she's sticking to her allegation. It's not easy for Eric." Jamie threw Nick a sideways glance.

"Luckily he's got a really fantastic girlfriend; she's standing by him 100 percent. I met her recently; she's studying economics. She's really nice. You'd like her."

A girlfriend. A university student.

He felt as if he had hot rocks in his stomach. Nick swallowed hard, but the rocks stayed put. So it had been easy for the messenger to make big promises.

But—why the thing with Aisha then? Was it just a bonus? To convince Nick? Or was Aisha the pill in Eric's tea?

At this last thought he gave a short laugh, which Jamie immediately misunderstood.

"I knew you'd be glad to hear that. Her name is Dana, and she's helping us with our campaign against the game. Getting information materials together for parents and so on. I could have told you that ages ago if you'd only listened to me for a few minutes like a normal person."

Criticism was the last thing Nick could take right now. "Normal, huh? Who's the paranoid one here? And you talk about normal!"

They'd reached the entry to the Tube station. Nick ran down the steps without saying good-bye, without turning around again.

Handouts for the parents! Jamie was lucky he'd only talked to Nick about it. An active gamer would've immediately fed the information to the messenger.

Ten o'clock at night. Nick was lying on his bed, his arms folded behind his head. He'd wasted another two hours trying to get access to the game; he'd copied the DVD twice and re-installed it three times. It hadn't made the slightest difference.

He shut his eyes. Now they'd all be inside the Arena, each species in its own room: the barbarians, the vampires, the cat people, the dark elves ...

Any minute now they'd be allowed up top; the crowd would cheer them, the master of ceremonies would call out the first name. And Sarius wouldn't be there.

Would Drizzel challenge Blackspell? Who would win? Would someone die again, like Xohoo? He would never find out, and that really sucked.

It was a shame Nick didn't know who Xohoo had been. He would have liked to talk to him. He had never felt so alone.

He slept badly that night. He longed for the ability to be Sarius again, at least in his dreams, but the more doggedly he pursued it, the farther sleep retreated.

TWENTY-TWO

The next day began shining and golden, as if the real world wanted to tempt Nick with all the charms autumn had to offer. But Nick just felt provoked. Clouds and rain would have suited his mood much better, not to mention darkness. But this afternoon he would borrow Finn's laptop, re-install the game, and take it from there. If necessary he would just have to start right from the beginning. Maybe as a vampire this time. Or a barbarian.

He spent the whole school day in a daze. Thank goodness it was Friday. On the weekend he'd be able to set up his new character and send him racing through the levels. He should be able to manage at least four; he was experienced now, after all.

Finally, the last period was over. He packed his things up in a hurry; Finn's shop was on the other side of town, and it would take forever to get there. On Fridays the Tube was even more crowded than normal.

But of course Jamie had to hold him up again, almost the instant Nick came out of the school building.

"They're saying you're out of the game. Is that true?"

"Who says that?"

"It doesn't matter."

"Does to me."

Jamie's delight was plain to see, and Nick felt like punching him in the face. Of course that wasn't fair, but then no one was being fair to Nick either. And if Jamie was so delighted about something that was making Nick totally miserable, then ... then ...

"I promised not to say who told me. But I'd be so happy if it was true, Nick! You just don't know how much you've changed in the last few weeks. I mean, we are best friends after all."

Nick literally saw red.

"We're what? What? You're always trying to interfere in my life—and now you're practically throwing a party, you're so happy something went wrong for me. Provided, of course, that someone wasn't telling you complete and utter bullshit!"

Jamie looked stunned.

"You're taking it the wrong way—"

"Am I? I don't think so! You're offended because I'm spending time on something that doesn't interest you! As if I ever stopped you from joining in."

All the color had drained out of Jamie's face. "You're talking such drivel, Nick. I'm just happy that you've gotten out of something really nasty and dangerous."

"Oh yes, of course. Jamie knows all about it. Jamie is oh so clever. Jamie is above it all, huh? And Nick is too stupid to realize. You can screw yourself, honest. Just get lost!"

Without another word Jamie turned around and walked over to his bike.

Nick watched him, furious that he couldn't continue his outburst, and at the same time wounded because ... because—he didn't exactly know. Because Jamie wasn't on his side?

He exhaled deeply and made his way to the Tube station, watching Jamie out of the corner of his eye. He was obviously pretty mad too; he was pedaling flat out, at any rate, and he whizzed down the street past Nick.

Nick kept going in the opposite direction, not sparing Jamie another glance. He'd soon be at Finn's place. He'd borrow the laptop and sort things out. He didn't even register the thud at first, or the blaring of horns. It was only when cars drew to a standstill next to him and one of the drivers got out that he realized something was wrong. He turned around.

The traffic jam stretched from the intersection in front of the school, right up to the Tube station Nick had nearly reached.

"There must have been an accident," the man next to the car said.

Nick didn't know how he knew. All at once everything in him became as cold as ice. He had started to run without noticing. His bag fell off his shoulder onto the pavement. He dashed over, blind to everything but the road, the intersection, and all the people standing there.

"... didn't brake at all."

"But there was a red light!"

"... don't understand it."

"Oh, how terrible ..."

"Don't look, Debbie ..."

He ran past the bus stop, shoving a few of the waiting people out of the way. He struck his shoulder on a lamppost, raced on, heard the shocked voices as if through cotton wool; his own breath drowned out everything else, was louder than the approaching ambulance siren.

There was the intersection. There was the bike. And there was, dear God, there was ...

"Jamie!"

He punched his way through the crowd, he had to get through, had to reach Jamie, had to twist his leg round the right way ...

"Jamie!"

So much blood. Nick's body suddenly gave way, he sank to his knees next to his friend. Jamie.

"Keep away, young man. The ambulance is almost here."

"But ..." Nick's breaths were coming in jerky sobs. "But ..."

"You can't do anything now. Don't touch! Someone take the boy away!"

Hands on his shoulders. Shake them off. Hands dragging him up. Lash out. Thrash. Yell.

The ambulance. Blue flashing light, fluorescent yellow jackets.

"Shallow breathing."

A stretcher.

"Please ... please, he can't die!"

"I think this one needs attention too, he's suffering from shock."

"Please."

Howling. From the ambulance, inside Nick. Please.

Hands on his shoulders. Shake them off.

Stroking his hair. Look up. Emily.

They gave him something to drink and he swallowed. Emily sat by him; her hands shook slightly when she took the bottle. Several times he opened his mouth to ask her something, but all that came out of his throat was dry sobbing.

He curled up, heard himself whimper, felt Emily's arm around his shoulders. She didn't say anything, just gently held him close.

She wouldn't do that if she knew the truth.

When Nick became aware of his surroundings again, the onlookers had already dispersed. Emily was still sitting next to him. It took every ounce of his strength to smile at her.

All he felt was guilt. He'd made Jamie mad; that's why he hadn't braked at the intersection. Nick hated himself.

He didn't want to go home. The thought of sitting around and waiting was ghastly. But he couldn't stay here either. Bashing his head against a wall seemed pretty attractive in comparison.

"I've got your things here. I hope that's all of them."

Where had Adrian suddenly appeared from? He held Nick's filthy bag out to him. Nick looked at it blankly. He didn't want his bag; he didn't want anything else to drink either. He just wanted one thing: to turn back time and have the conversation with Jamie over again. Not to let him get on his bike. Not to be such a complete ass.

"Thanks," Emily said instead of Nick and took the bag from Adrian.

"Do you know how Jamie is?" he whispered. "Did anyone say anything?"

Nick couldn't get a word out. He could feel Emily shaking her head by his side.

"The police are over there interviewing witnesses. If one of you saw how it happened, I'm sure they'd be glad if you talked to them."

"I didn't see it," Nick whispered. "I only heard it, and then ..." He didn't say any more, because the tears were already starting again.

Adrian nodded. His gaze was hard to interpret; it was understanding, and at the same time professional, like a psychologist's.

"I didn't see anything either," Emily said quietly. "But I think Brynne was standing quite nearby. They couldn't interview her. She was given a sedative and she's barely responding."

I am so afraid. So afraid. Nick threw his hands up to his face, dug his fingernails into his scalp. The pain helped. It was much better than the other pain, which Nick could hardly bear. The good pain gave him an idea.

"Does anyone know where they took Jamie?"

"To Whittington Hospital, I think," Emily said. "Someone mentioned the Whittington. But that might not be right."

Nick jumped up without another word, swayed a bit because things went black, felt Emily's arm supporting him.

"I'm going to Jamie." His voice was hardly more than a croak. "I have to know how he is."

Emily went with him. They got off the Tube at Archway. Nick was freezing; the trip to the hospital seemed to be taking forever. He was glad that Emily didn't say anything or ask anything; he needed all his strength to put one foot in front of the other. His fear grew with every step. They'd arrive at the hospital and someone would tell them that unfortunately it hadn't been possible to save Jamie's life. That he'd died in the ambulance. Nick suddenly felt as though he couldn't breathe. He stopped in front of the wall of glass at the entrance and rested his hands on his knees. He felt dizzy.

"They will have taken him to the Emergency Department," Emily said. "It's farther around the back."

"But Reception must be here. I'll go ask."

Nick walked into the foyer. The walk to the inquiries counter was like the walk to the scaffold. The thin blond woman who gave out information there would decide Nick's future. The thought turned his stomach.

"Good afternoon. Has a Jamie Cox been admitted here?"

She studied him through narrow glasses.

"Are you a relative?"

"Jamie Cox. It was a traffic accident. I have to know how he is. Please."

The woman gave a tight smile. "We are only allowed to give information to relatives. Are you related to Mr. Cox?"

"We're friends." Best friends.

"In that case I'm sorry."

Nick didn't so much walk out of the hospital as drag himself out. His sentence had been postponed. But how was he going to endure it? How could anyone expect him to endure it?

Emily led him to a small patch of green that lay a little distance from the hospital. The ground was cold and slightly damp; Nick took off his jacket so they had something to sit on.

"I can't go home," he said. "Not till I know how Jamie is."

They were silent for a while, watching the cars as they drove past.

"We could ring the school," Emily suggested. "They might know the latest."

"No, not the school." Nick's stomach tensed again. "I wonder if his parents already know."

"They must. They would have rung them. If he's still alive." Emily plucked a blade of grass and stared hard at the bus stop opposite. "They only come in person if someone is dead. Two of them come; it's probably too hard to do that sort of thing on your own. They ask for your name, and then they tell you how sorry they are ..."

Nick looked at her sideways but said nothing. She smiled painfully.

"My brother. It was a long time ago though."

"Was it an accident as well?"

Emily's face hardened. "Yes. An accident. Even though the police said at the time that it was suicide, but that's complete and utter drivel."

Another clump of grass fell victim to Emily's fingers. Nick bit his lip. He didn't know if he should ask anything else or just leave it. Probably neither was right.

"He was such a good swimmer," Emily whispered. "He wouldn't have jumped into the water to kill himself."

Nick put an arm around her shoulders without fearing that she would push him away. Neither of them would push the other away.

They embraced, not like lovers, but like two people who need to hold on to something.

It was Emily who saw Jamie's father coming out of the hospital. He looked so frantic that Nick didn't want to approach him, but Emily saw it differently. She sprinted after Mr. Cox and stopped him. Nick saw them talking to each other, but he couldn't hear what they were saying. Mr. Cox wiped his hands over his eyes, and spread his arms out in a helpless gesture that made Nick's heart sink. Emily nodded several times, and squeezed Jamie's father's hand tightly for a long time before she returned to Nick.

"He's alive. He suffered a cardiac arrest in the ambulance and they had to resuscitate him, but now he's fairly stable, his father says."

The words cardiac arrest made Nick's own heart trip. "Stable, you say. That's good."

"Not really good. They've put him in an induced coma, he's so badly injured. His left leg is broken in several places, and his hip too. And he has brain trauma." She looked away, past Nick. "It's possible there will be some lasting effects. If he survives."

"What lasting effects? What do you mean lasting effects?"

She pushed her hair off her brow. "He could be disabled."

The wave of relief that had borne Nick for a few seconds ebbed away. Disabled. No. No way. He pushed the thought right away. That wasn't going to happen, because it wasn't allowed to happen.

"Can we visit him?"

"Unfortunately not. He's in Intensive Care. He's not even conscious, he wouldn't know that we were there. We just have to wait."

That's what Nick did for the next two days, and it felt like hell. Incessantly. It didn't matter what else he was doing—eating, studying, talking to people—in reality he was waiting for the news that Jamie was awake and that he would make a complete recovery. Only occasionally did his thoughts wander, and pictures flash up—the Arena, big Goggle-Eyes, BloodWork with his giant ax. Most often it was the messenger as he'd looked that last time, when his yellow eyes turned red. It was torture. He couldn't think of *Erebos* while Jamie was lying in a coma. But the pictures returned, over and over.

It was the weekend; he didn't even have school to distract him. Every time the phone rang Nick jumped, torn between panic and hope. "Get lost"—those were the last words he'd hurled at Jamie; every time he thought of that he cringed inwardly. *Don't get lost, Jamie, please don't get lost.*

On Monday Jamie was the number-one topic at school. Everyone had seen something or heard something and wanted to talk about it. Only those who had actually been nearby at the time maintained a gloomy silence. Brynne especially, who was almost unrecognizable without makeup. On the day of the accident she'd been taken to the hospital too; there was a rumor that she had needed counseling.

No one was talking about Eric and Aisha anymore. Nick had the impression that Aisha was more relieved about it than Eric.

To all appearances, the afternoon outside the hospital hadn't changed anything between Nick and Emily. They didn't sit next to each other in class, or at the same table at lunch. But something was different. It was small glances, a smile that lasted a bit longer, or an encouraging nod. Emily had never made those kinds of gesture to Nick before. For Nick, they were the only bright spots in a grim, seemingly never-ending ocean of waiting.

Finally, on Tuesday, there was news. Mr. Watson announced it in English class. "Jamie's parents rang. He's out of danger. But he is still being kept in an induced coma. The doctors don't know for how long at the moment. This is great news nevertheless. I can't tell you how glad I am."

The relief in the room was tangible, like a breath of fresh air. Some people clapped, Colin jumped up and did a little dance. Nick felt like flinging his arms around Emily's neck, but restricted himself to exchanging a long look with her. Joyful, but with an element of uncertainty remaining. Mr. Watson hadn't said anything about whether the risk of brain damage had been averted.

TWENTY-THREE

It was in the next free period. Nick was sitting by himself in one of the study rooms, trying to memorize chemical formulas. The door to the corridor was open, and he happened to look up just as Colin was walking past. Very quietly, very carefully. So carefully that Nick's curiosity was instantly aroused. He pushed his chair back and stood up, almost without making a sound. He saw Colin sneaking along the corridor. Now he turned left. Nick followed. Was there a secret meeting somewhere?

Colin walked down the stairs. It looked as if he was heading for the coatracks. Not a bad place for a meeting at this time of day. Nick stayed behind him, at a generous distance, nearly lost track of him, and then spotted him again—by the staircase leading to the student coatracks, just as he'd thought. Nick could see that he was going along the rows of coats and jackets, searching. Finally he stopped. Nick couldn't exactly see what Colin was doing among all the clothing, and he couldn't go any closer without being noticed. He squinted and thought he saw something bright orange, moving. Just very briefly. Seconds later Colin headed back and Nick beat a hasty retreat, hid in the nearest bathroom, and counted to fifty. Colin had to be gone by now.

Nick found the splash of color among the school clothing almost immediately. The fluorescent orange badge adorned a smallish jacket probably belonging to a girl. What had Colin been doing with it?

Nick had a good look around before he stuck his hand in the jacket pocket. He could feel a neatly folded piece of paper. A love letter? Then it wouldn't be any of Nick's business. But maybe it was a message. Whatever, he was far too curious to back down now. He pulled out the piece of paper and unfolded it.

A gravestone:

> *Darleen Pember*
> *Died from lack of insight.*
> *May she rest in peace.*

Something clicked in Nick's brain. Jamie had received a letter like this too. Perhaps ... Nick shoved the thought away immediately, but it came back. Like a balloon that you try to push under water.

Perhaps Jamie hadn't ridden across the intersection without braking because he was angry and careless. Perhaps he had braked, or at least tried to. He had shown Nick the letter with the gravestone. A threat he hadn't taken seriously. Jamie had, though. And now ...

Cutting the brakes on someone's bike or mixing an overdose of Digotan in someone's tea—they weren't such very different things.

Colin. Colin was handing out death notes. Was he carrying them out too?

Without stopping to think, Nick stormed up the stairs and raced across the corridor that led to the cafeteria—Colin was strolling along up ahead, as if nothing had happened.

"You ass!" Nick leaped on him from behind and he staggered. They both went down.

"Nick? Nick, are you crazy?"

Instead of answering, Nick shoved the letter in Colin's face, rubbed it into his cheeks, his nose, his eyes.

"Recognize that? Do you? Ever seen that before?"

"Get off me, you idiot! What is that?"

"You bastard!"

They were making too much of a racket; people were already coming out of the cafeteria. Nick let go of Colin, and they both scrambled to their feet.

"Darleen Pember, huh? Is she about to have an accident too?"

Colin stared at the letter—clearly the penny had dropped. "Give that to me now!"

"I wouldn't dream of it."

"You can't just take it away ... I have to—"

He rushed at Nick, but he'd been expecting it, and dodged him. He ripped the letter down the middle with enormous relish, ripped it into tiny pieces and shoved them into Colin's hand. "There. You can put that in Darleen's jacket pocket. I'll tell her who it came from."

Colin's face reflected a mixture of hatred and helplessness. "You can't do that."

"So now you're getting scared, huh? Your friend with the yellow eyes won't be at all happy."

"Be quiet!"

"There's a couple of levels gone straightaway." Out of the corner of his eye Nick saw the the Freaks approaching, attracted by the argument like vultures to carrion. Dan was grinning from ear to ear, but Alex appeared unsure.

"It was you who did that to Jamie. Admit it. You've got him on your conscience. I saw your letter to him. Was it at least worth it? Did you get a wicked little pair of boots?"

Colin's nostrils were quivering. He took a step toward Nick. His fists were clenched so hard that Nick could see the veins in his arms standing out.

"You're going to regret this," he said, turned around, and left.

It was only that afternoon, after Nick had gotten home, that the magnitude of his mistake dawned on him. He'd allowed himself to get carried away and officially declare himself an enemy of *Erebos*. Even though he couldn't prove that Jamie's accident had anything to do with the game.

Take the pliers that you will find under the park bench next to the school gate and use them to cut through the brake cable of the dark blue bike. The one with the Manchester United sticker on the crossbar.

He could virtually see it. Snip, snip—job done. One more level. It was quite possible that it hadn't been Colin himself. It was equally possible that the saboteur hadn't even known whose bike it was.

That evening Nick sat down at the computer, checked his e-mail, and thought about what he should say to Darleen Pember. Whether he should even approach her.

Pensively he ran the cursor over the spot where the red E had been. Would he like to be in one of the caves now, around one of the fires? Yes. No. Yes. He would like to talk to the others. But above all, what he would dearly like to do was to chop the messenger up into little bony pieces.

In their free period on Wednesday Emily intercepted Nick in front of the library. They were as good as alone, since most people were lounging around outside, making the best of the last nice autumn days.

"I've got some news," Emily said.

"About Jamie?"

"No."

The Freaks walked past some distance away. They weren't talking to each other; it looked more as though they were on patrol. When Alex spotted Nick, he smiled and raised his hand in greeting, while Dan twisted his piggy face into a grimace.

Nick dragged Emily into the library, where they retreated to the farthest corner. Emily was practically vibrating with energy.

"Go on, tell me."

She smiled, opened her bag, and pulled out a DVD case, on which someone had written "Erebos" in rounded handwriting.

Contradictory feelings were fighting a pitched battle inside Nick. Disapproval. Concern. Greed. "You really want to get into it?"

"Yes. I think it's the right time for me."

Nick looked at the DVD, which he'd only recently been desperate to get. Emily would explore *Erebos*, travel through all those bizarre, awful, beautiful landscapes, go on adventures. The yearning in his gut was spreading. He shook his head disapprovingly.

"Jamie was right. You're not in it anymore, are you?"

He just nodded. "Kicked out," he said hoarsely.

"Well, it's a shame. Then we can't play it together."

"No." Nick bit his lip. It was just as well. He knew it was just as well. All the excitement, the tension, the thrills ... He didn't need it anymore.

"How come ... What's the reason for changing your mind? You didn't want to have anything to do with the game."

"That's right. But I want to understand what fascinates you all so much." She looked away thoughtfully. "Jamie was convinced that this game is not simply a game. He had his own theory about it." She turned the case over in her hands. "Jamie thought there must be more behind a game like this. Some sort of goal. All these things that are happening in the real world, they must benefit someone, don't you think? But the only way I can find that out is if I take a look at *Erebos* myself. That's why I've dropped remarks here and there about how I'd be interested in a copy now."

Nick remembered. He himself had passed the message on to the messenger, and a few other gamers were bound to have done so too.

"Well, the only objective of the game that I know anything about is that a villain by the name of Ortolan is supposed to be destroyed," Nick said. "What happens in real life is only designed to protect the game against people who have something against it."

"Like Jamie? Then we should try to stop it."

Stop it. Nick thought of the accident and the pool of blood, and knew Emily was right. Even if Nick wouldn't ever be able to run around the White City again, or take part in the Arena fights. He sighed. "I don't know how exactly, but we can try."

The door to the library opened and closed again quietly. Nick signaled Emily to be quiet—but it was only Mr. Bolton, the religious education teacher.

"We'll really have to watch out," Nick whispered. "If they notice, it's possible that ... well, it could really get dangerous. The game is incredibly smart. I'm still not entirely sure that it wanted to get rid of Jamie, but I know what it had in mind for Mr. Watson."

Emily raised her eyebrows inquiringly.

"I'll tell you another time," Nick said. "You have no idea how difficult it will be to outwit it. And as soon as you look suspicious or you fail, you're out quicker than you can count to five." In his head a stone demon spread its wings. Nick chased it away.

Emily smiled cheekily—an expression Nick had never seen her wear before.

"Oh, I'll be careful. And I wonder"—this time she looked around surreptitiously and lowered her voice to a whisper—"whether maybe you could help me. I don't really know much about computer games; I always just play solitaire."

Rule number two flashed through Nick's mind. When you play, make sure that you are alone.

What would happen if there were two of them? Would the game notice? Nick took a deep breath. He would just have to give it a try.

"Of course I'll help you, gladly in fact. You'll make much faster progress if I give you tips."

"Perfect." She beamed. "Come round to my place after tea, okay? Half past five would be good."

Nick arrived early. Ten minutes before the agreed time he was standing in front of Emily's house in Heathfield Gardens, wondering which window was hers.

He had been careful. After the incident with Colin yesterday he had expected that someone would follow him, but that hadn't happened. Nick looked around—the street was almost deserted. No one knew where he was.

He didn't want to ring the bell; that would have looked too keen. So he went for a walk around the surrounding streets, which were attractive and well kept.

It occurred to him that he hadn't brought anything; a well-chosen gift would have shown that he was an original guy with hidden depths. It was too late for that now. But if he didn't behave too idiotically, maybe there would be a next time.

On the dot of half past five he pressed the doorbell, and Emily opened the door. As it turned out, hers was the attic room. It wasn't one of those frilly pink dolly rooms with soft toys on the bed and film star posters on the wall—it was a very grown-up space, Nick thought. Two bookshelves, a futon bed, and seating in the corner with a coffee table, also piled high with books. Under the sloping roof there was an extremely tidy desk, on which an open laptop was waiting. If Emily ever felt inclined to pay him a return visit, Nick would have to carry out a large-scale cleaning and tidying campaign.

"We need to be quiet; my mother went to lie down half an hour ago. She may not even come out of her room again today."

Nick didn't ask questions, even though it seemed odd to him that a grown-up woman had already gone to bed in the afternoon. In any case it was ideal for their joint project.

"We won't make a racket. The game is quiet at the beginning. You should use headphones later on. For·various reasons. I saw someone die because they didn't hear something."

"Headphones." Emily nodded. "Okay. Can we start?"

She fetched the DVD out of her bag and pushed it into the drive. "I'll just install the game in my program folder normally, right? Anything I should pay attention to?"

"No. Not yet."

The Install window opened. There it all was. The ruined tower, the scorched countryside. The sword with the red cloth tied to its handle was stuck in the dry earth. "Erebos" was written in red lettering across the sky.

Nick felt his stomach pulsing with nervousness. He wiped his damp hands on his pants legs.

"Should I do it?" Emily asked.

"Sure."

She clicked on "Install." The blue bar began to edge forward, sluggish as ever.

"It'll take ages," Nick said, without taking his eyes off the progress bar. How did it start again? In the forest. Yes, exactly, and he was about to see it. Every lurch of the bar brought him closer to Erebos. As if he were sitting in a train heading toward home.

Emily gave him a sideways glance. "Is something worrying you?"

"What? No! I just can't ... I can't wait to see what you think."

"So far, mainly slow," Emily said, and rested her chin in her hands.

They waited for a while without saying anything. Nick divided his gaze between the pen holder on the desk, the screen of the laptop, and Emily's profile. He couldn't see a single one of her drawings anywhere in the room. Too bad—then they would have been able to talk about them.

"Does your mother always go to bed so early?" he asked, when he thought the silence had lasted too long. He felt right away that he'd been rude, and wished he could take the question back.

"She's going through a bad patch at the moment. Sleeping a lot, not eating much, and talking even less." Emily stared at the progress bar even more intently than before. "That's how it's been ever since Jack died. It goes up and down—I've gotten used to it, like the seasons."

"And your father?"

"Married again, two children, Derek and Rosie. Second time lucky." She moved the mouse as if she hoped it would speed up the installation. "Don't get me wrong, I'm not mad at him. It was impossible to take anymore—and he didn't. I'm incredibly glad that the two little ones came along. I just wish I could have run away like him."

Nick needed a moment to digest what he'd just heard. "You never talked about it at school."

"Not with you, that's true."

But with Eric, I bet. For a moment the old jealousy flared up. But now Emily was sitting here with him. Talking to him.

"How about you? Do you have brothers and sisters?" she asked.

"Yes. A brother. He's five years older than me, and he's already moved out."

"Do you get on well?"

"Yes, really well." Nick thought of Finn, tried to imagine what it would be like to lose him, but straightaway abandoned the attempt. He didn't know how Emily could bear it.

"Unfortunately he's fallen out with my parents. Well, with my father, to be precise. They're not talking to each other anymore."

"Why not?"

Nick took a deep breath. "Well, my father always wanted to be a doctor, but his parents couldn't afford for him to go to university. Now he's a nurse at the Princess Grace Hospital. I don't know if he'll ever come to terms with it. At any rate, it was always understood that Finn would become a doctor."

"But Finn didn't want to."

"At first he did, he crammed like crazy and his marks would probably even have been good enough. But then he changed his mind. He met Becca, and wham, that was the end of medicine."

Emily looked at Nick out of the corner of her eye. "Why was that?"

"Becca had just taken over a tattoo studio. Finn was hooked straightaway. He did a few courses, and now he's tattooing and piercing like a champion. My father said he'd never talk to him again."

A tiny smile appeared on Emily's face, but disappeared again immediately.

"Do you have to become a doctor now?"

She'd seen through Dad without even knowing him.

"Oh, well, it would please him, and I'm interested in it."

Finally she turned right around, and looked at him as if she wanted to check that he was telling the truth.

"So you're not mad at your brother because you're responsible for your father's wishes now?"

Nick turned around and pushed his ponytail off the nape of his neck. "No. I'm not mad at him at all."

Even though he hardly ever got to see them, Nick knew exactly what the two flying ravens that Finn had tattooed just under his hairline looked like. He felt Emily's fingers like a breath of air on the tattoo. He swallowed.

"Why ravens?"

"At first it was because we both have such dark hair that Mom always used to call us the raven brothers. But Finn says they're good luck. And besides they're a bit like a ... seal, a sign that we belong together."

Emily gently took her hand away, much to Nick's regret. His ponytail slipped back into its normal place.

"He has a knack, your brother. It looks really good."

The install was slowly nearing completion. Emily went to the kitchen to get a bottle of ginger ale and two glasses. When she came back, the screen was going dark.

"Is that how it's supposed to be?"

"Yes. I thought at first something was wrong too. Just wait a moment."

Black. Black. Black. Then the letters appeared, red and throbbing.

Enter

Or turn back.

This is Erebos.

"Well, then," Emily said, and clicked on Enter.

Dark forest, moonlight. Her figure was huddled in the middle of the clearing. He looked just like Nick's game character before he became Sarius. Nick fought a renewed surge of melancholy as he watched Emily get familiar with how to control her own Nameless.

"It's easy to get him to run around," she said. "Can he do anything else?"

"Yes! Climb, fight ... everything! There'll be keyboard shortcuts for special abilities later on, but there's no hurry."

Emily made her Nameless walk up and down the clearing. She

had a really good look at everything before she decided on her line of approach.

"I think I'll go where the forest is not as dense; I don't have to make things harder than necessary for myself."

Branches snapped, the wind rustled in the treetops. If Nick had had his way, Emily would have raced her game character through this first sequence much faster, but he was trying hard to conceal his impatience. She was handling it really well, considering she was a newbie. Contrary to what Nick had done, she didn't make Nameless rush around pushing his stamina meter to the limit; instead she was pacing him. It was only after about twenty minutes of wandering that she turned back to Nick. "Is there a goal? Or is it a test of patience?"

"There is a goal. Somewhere around here there's a fire, and someone you can talk to."

What the tree had been to Nick, back when he'd used it to get an overview, a tall rock was to Emily. Nameless climbed up, and for the first time the stamina meter went down a bit. But the view was compensation enough. A sea of treetops all around, and, on the right, a hill with dots of light hinting at the existence of a settlement.

"There!" Nick cried, and pointed with his finger at a weak golden-yellow glow between the trees. "That's where you have to go!"

It was only Emily's look of surprised amusement that made him realize how agitated he must have appeared.

"Well ... that's where you go, over there. If you're interested."

On the way to the small fire pit Emily, too, encountered an obstacle. It wasn't a crevice, like Nick's, but a rampart that she couldn't scale. Every time her Nameless took hold of it in order to pull himself up, stones and earth crumbled off.

"And now?" Emily asked after the fifth failed attempt.

"You need to learn how to solve problems like this. It's something you'll have to do quite often. Imagine that it's real. What would you do then?" Nick felt like some idiotic teacher, but he wanted Emily to grasp how fantastic and lifelike this all was.

And Emily grasped it quickly. She made Nameless drag some small boulders over, all the time keeping an eye on his stamina meter and giving him little rests. In the end he scaled the rampart without any trouble.

From the other side they could already see the campfire flickering. Nick also recognized the dark shadow that was silhouetted beside it. His heartbeat sped up. He wouldn't give Emily any more tips now. She needed to see for herself what *Erebos* could do.

The man by the fire didn't move when Nameless slowly approached. But the shimmering silvery words appeared at the edge of the screen.

"Greetings, Nameless One. I have been expecting you."

He hadn't said that to Nick. He'd praised him for his speed. And for his ingenuity.

Emily took her game character closer to the man and tried to peep under the black hood. But he lifted his head of his own accord. Nick had nearly forgotten the narrow face with its small mouth; the man hadn't ever turned up again.

"You are curious. That can help you or destroy you. It's something you need to be aware of."

Emily threw Nick an uncertain look.

"Would you like to proceed?" the man asked. "Only if you ally yourself with Erebos will you be any match for this game. You need to know that."

Emily was still looking back and forth between Nick and the screen, at a loss.

"He's waiting for an answer," Nick said, and pointed to the keyboard.

"Seriously?"

"Yes. Try it out, you'll see."

Emily placed her fingers on the keys, hesitated at first, and then typed.

"What does that mean, ally myself with Erebos?"

The man poked around in the fire with his staff. Sparks flew, rose up into the air, burnt out.

"It means overstepping limits, overcoming limits. What it really means in the end will depend on you."

Emily took her fingers off the keyboard and looked at Nick in astonishment. "He just gave me an answer. How does that work?"

"No idea," Nick said. "That's one of the special things about this game." He suppressed a smile, because he could literally see how Emily was getting fired up.

A delicate melody started to play now, something with flutes and violins, very soft, very seductive. It was a melody Nick had never heard during his time in Erebos. Not one single time.

"Would you advise me to ally myself with Erebos?" Emily typed in. "Would you advise me to proceed?"

The man fixed his gaze on Emily's Nameless for a long time.

"No."

"Why not?"

"Because the darkness is full of pitfalls and abysses. Some of them you will not emerge from unscathed. Some of them swallow a person forever."

It seemed to Nick that Emily had forgotten his presence completely. She stared at the man's words, her hands floated over the keyboard, and finally she asked the same question that Nick had asked before her.

"Who are you?"

The man put his head to one side thoughtfully, without taking his eyes off Emily.

"I am a dead person. Nothing more."

Nick heard Emily draw breath.

"If you are dead, what are you doing here?"

"I am waiting and keeping watch. Do you want to proceed now? Or will you turn back?"

His eyes were green, Nick noticed, and so lifelike he could almost swear he had seen them before. In a flesh-and-blood face.

"I will proceed," Emily wrote. "That is what you were expecting, isn't it?"

"Everyone proceeds," the dead man said. "Turn to the left and follow the stream, until you come to a ravine. Walk through it. After that ... you'll take it from there."

He said that to me too, Nick recalled. *But that wasn't all.*

"And watch out for the messenger with the yellow eyes."

Nick warned Emily about the hostile toads that had given him such a hard time, but when she reached the ravine the attack came from above. Small but extremely vicious bats swirled all around her Nameless, snapping at him with sharp teeth. The red bar on the life meter was sinking steadily.

"You have to use your stick! Press the left mouse button!" Nick had to restrain himself to avoid taking the mouse out of Emily's hand and killing the bats himself. "Shake them off with Escape. Jump with Space."

It took awhile and cost Nameless a lot of blood, but finally Emily killed all the bats.

"You can take the meat with you," Nick explained. "It can be sold in the city later on."

With a shrug of her shoulders Emily stowed the remains away. "And now?"

But her words already mingled with the sound of approaching hoofbeats. Nick couldn't help ducking. What would the messenger say if he saw him there? The next minute he shook his head. *He can't see me. He can only see Nameless. I'm a complete idiot.*

Emily sent her game character farther along the ravine. There, up ahead, was the rock face with the cave yawning in the middle, and on the ledge right in front of it the familiar figure of the messenger, waiting on his armored horse.

"Wow, is he creepy," Emily whispered.

The messenger looked toward Nameless without moving. The horse seemed restless; it pawed the ground and snorted.

"Greetings, Nameless One. You have made a good start."

"I'm glad," Emily typed.

"However, you should continue to practice your fighting skills, otherwise you will not be destined for a long life."

"All right."

The messenger turned away from Nameless and looked at Emily, who couldn't help sliding her chair back.

"It is time you are given a name. Time for the first rite."

"What must I do?"

The messenger pointed with his bony fingers to the cave behind him.

"Enter. All else will follow. I wish you luck and the right decisions. We will meet again."

He pulled his horse around and galloped away along a small, barely visible path high above Nameless's head.

"I assume I have to go up these stairs, right?" Emily asked.

"Yes. Up the stairs and into the cave."

Nameless disappeared into the darkness of the mountain and the computer screen darkened.

"This will take quite a while again," Nick said. "You mustn't get nervous."

Emily jerked the mouse back and forth, but the cursor was nowhere to be seen.

"It's amazingly real," she said after a little while. "I felt as though that messenger was really looking at me. As if he wanted to show me he's perfectly aware that it's not the game character that matters, but the person controlling it."

"You'll find that happens a lot."

They looked at their reflections in the monitor.

"Is this first rite difficult? As difficult as the thing with the bats?"

"No, quite different. You'll see in a minute."

Tap tap! Tap tap!

"Sounds like a heartbeat. What is it?"

"It just means it's about to continue. Press Enter."

The black screen created red letters.

"This is Erebos. Who are you?"

Would Emily lie? Would she enter a false name?

"I am Emily."

"Tell me your whole name."

"Emily Carver."

Ghostly whispering. "Emily Carver. Emily. Emily. Carver. Emily Carver."

They do that to welcome you, and before they throw you into the abyss, Nick thought wistfully. Emily sought his gaze, and he smiled at her: all quite normal.

"Welcome, Emily. Welcome to the world of *Erebos*. Before you start playing, acquaint yourself with the rules. If you don't like them, you can end the game at any time. All right?"

"I wouldn't have expected that," Emily murmured, while she typed "Okay." "Any time. It actually sounds fair."

"Good. Here is the first rule. You have only one chance to play *Erebos*. If you squander it, it's over. If your character dies, it's over. If you break the rules, it's over. Okay?"

"Yes."

"The second rule. When you play, make sure that you are alone. Never mention your real name in the game. Never mention the name of your game character outside the game."

Emily took her fingers off the keyboard and looked at Nick.

"That means I need to chuck you out now, doesn't it?"

"Just type 'yes,'" Nick said. "You could still do with a bit of help at the moment." Was she really going to throw him out? He didn't want to go. He wanted to be there for the first rite. Maybe even for her first fight.

A small smile tugged at her lips as she wrote "Okay."

"Good. The third rule. The content of the game is secret. Do not speak to anyone about it. Especially not to people who are not registered. During the game you can converse with players around the fires. Don't pass any information on to your friends or your family. Don't post any information on the Internet."

"A few things are becoming clear to me," said Emily.

"The fourth rule. Keep the DVD somewhere safe. You need it to start the game. Don't copy it under any circumstances, unless the messenger asks that you do so."

"Okay."

Light streamed across the screen, almost out of the screen. Nameless sat in the sunny clearing. The ruined tower, in which the first rite would take place, was waiting behind him.

Emily had scarcely touched her game character with the cursor before he stood up, peeled the face off his head, and walked toward the tower.

"These are important decisions now," Nick said. "You mustn't rush them. I'll help you."

Emily's Nameless stood before the first copper tablet. "Choose your gender."

"It's not so important what you choose here, although the men are a bit stro—"

Emily had already clicked on "Woman." Nameless's body changed, became narrower overall; the chest and hips swelled.

"Sorry, Nick, but this is going to be *my* character," said Emily.

"Choose a race."

"Fine, I won't interfere, but barbarians are ace," Nick said. "They are really strong and have fantastic endurance. If I had the choice again, I would choose a barbar—"

But Emily had already made her choice.

Human? Disappointed, Nick gave her a sideways glance. How come she chose a human?

"I do know my own species best, you know," she said in answer to his unasked question. "I like being a human."

"Choose your appearance."

Emily gave her human woman short tousled red hair that stood up on her head, and dressed her entirely in black. Boots, pants, shirt, and jacket. Only the belt was red, but then, so was everyone's.

She spent more time on her facial features, made them soft and friendly, with a sense of humor, brown eyes, and high arched eyebrows.

"Choose a vocation."

"There's not really anything much that appeals," Emily declared. "If I decide on a bard, does that mean I have to sing?"

Nick didn't know. He'd been a knight, but he'd never had to solve any special knightly tasks during the game.

"I don't think the vocation is all that important," he pronounced, and Emily decided on bard.

At that moment a gnome entered the tower. Nick had forgotten all about him—the disagreeable visitor during the first rite.

"A human. How original. And ridiculous, don't you think?" he said.

"No, not at all."

"Oh, oh, oh. And a bard to boot. Don't think much of battles, hmm? Rather warble the day away?"

Emily ignored the gnome and looked for the next copper sign.

"Choose your abilities."

"Healing is useless," Nick said at once. "That comes off your own life energy. I chose it; it was a big mistake."

The cursor hovered over the words: strength, stamina, death curse, sneaking, lighting fires, ironskin, climbing ...

"Healing seems the best of them to me," Emily said after a time, during which the gnome had been hopping from right to left and left to right, pulling wild grimaces. "After all, you play with other people, don't you? I heal someone one time, and the next time he heals me. I think it will be quite convenient."

"But that's not how it works!" Nick yelled. "You have to make sure that you make progress yourself. It's no good if you make yourself weaker."

The gnome turned his head. "Are you alone, human woman? Are you following the second rule? Answer!"

"Of course I'm alone. Why wouldn't I be?" Emily typed.

All at once she was pale, and Nick suddenly felt chilled too. What had made the gnome ask such a question? After all, he couldn't see them or hear them; it wasn't possible. The messenger hadn't been able to either.

"I'm taking too long," Emily murmured. "If I were alone I would decide faster. That's why he's asking, I think."

Now she hurried. Chose healing, speed, lighting fires, ironskin, jumping power. After a short pause she added far sight, stamina, water walking, climbing, and sneaking.

"Not bad choices," the gnome declared. "For a human. It's a shame you won't live for long."

"That's life," Emily answered, and concentrated on choosing weapons. She selected a slim, curved sabre with emeralds on the handle. And then a small bronze shield.

"Very pretty, but unfortunately just playthings," the gnome sniped.

The last tablet. "Choose your name."

"It's going to be a really ugly human name," the gnome bawled. "Petronilla, Bathilda, Aldusa, or Berthegund? Well? I'm waiting! We're waiting! You must know a name!"

Emily hesitated for a moment. "I did actually think about one. Let's see what he says about it."

"Hemera," she typed.

Nick was a bit disappointed. Hemera didn't exactly sound illustrious. It reminded Nick of the name of a kitchen appliance. The gnome, on the other hand, was obviously impressed.

"O-ho! Someone's been doing some research, have they? This could be interesting. Hemera! Don't fall out with my master, little human!"

He hopped and limped toward the tower's exit. Nick almost expected him to stick out his incredibly long green tongue as a parting gesture, but the gnome wasn't in the right mood this time, apparently. Wordlessly he slammed the door shut behind him. Plaster trickled down from the tower walls.

"What did he mean by 'doing some research'?"

"Find out for yourself." Emily was obviously having fun. "And

I'd like to find everything else here out for myself too. I'll see you in the morning, okay? I'll carry on alone."

But it's just getting exciting! Disappointment settled like a lead weight in the pit of Nick's stomach.

"Listen, you're underestimating this. You'll get ahead much faster if I help you, and you won't get so many injuries. Just take my word for it, hmm?"

Emily took the headphones off her iPod and plugged them into her computer. "That was one of your tips, wasn't it? If I've got these in my ears I won't be able to hear what you're saying anymore."

"But ..."

"It's fine, Nick. You saw how suspicious the gnome got just now. I'll manage, okay? For now I'll just stick to the rules like everyone else and play alone."

Nick conceded defeat. "If you're about to go berry picking, be careful," he said. One last cryptic comment couldn't hurt. "And if you get stuck or need help—I'll be glad to. Honest."

"Good to know," Emily said, smiling. "Thank you, Nick."

At home he consulted Wikipedia. It turned out that Hemera was the daughter of Erebos, and, what was more, the complete opposite of her father. Hemera was the goddess of day, of morning, of light.

Some say one must be born to victory. The longer I think about it, the more I am inclined to agree. I put my disappointment at not being one of those chosen few behind me a long time ago. Nonetheless, I do not feel equal to a further defeat. If I should triumph in the end, I will not be present. That is deliberate. My presence at the finale is not required. Others will be the actors. They will pursue my goal with all their strength.

The time has nearly come. Then my part will be done and I can go. At the end there will be winners and losers. Who the winners will be is irrelevant. What is crucial is who the losers are. I pray that they are the right ones.

TWENTY-FOUR

The goddess of the morning was the first thing Nick thought of when the alarm clock rang the next day. Hemera. He could hardly wait to hear Emily's report. What things she'd seen, how she'd gone, whether she'd received any orders. He would help her, and he'd soon be able to watch her play again. Perhaps it would be easier to recognize motivations when he wasn't in the thick of it. Patterns. He whistled in the shower, and sang as he got dressed. It was going to be a good day.

Mostly Emily was at school before him, standing around with her friends—or with Eric. Today, however, he couldn't spot her anywhere. He did see Eric chatting with a few girls from Year Ten. He looked more relaxed than in recent days, and seemed to have gotten over the shock Aisha had given him. Would he ever take action against *Erebos* again? Nick doubted it. He was presumably glad not to be the center of attention anymore.

Then Emily arrived. She was walking quickly, as if she was in a big hurry. Eric waved an invitation to her, but she barely nodded back, and kept walking. Nick caught her just before the school gate.

"Hi, Emily!"

"Hi."

It was obvious that she couldn't talk about *Erebos* right there in front of everyone, but a wink, a conspiratorial smile ... surely something would be forthcoming? Nick searched her face for a sign, but it was as expressionless as a blank page.

"Fourth period? Library?" Nick whispered uncomfortably.

Emily shrugged her shoulders. "We'll see." She left him standing there without another word.

Rashid was standing farther on with Alex; Emily headed in that direction. What did she want with them? Nick didn't get it at all. Incredulously he watched Emily hanging on Alex's every word as he began talking about something or other with extravagant gestures and a mysterious expression. What could it be, though? He could hardly be broadcasting details from the game.

All day long he kept an eye on Emily, but she avoided him, looked past him, or through him—not once did he manage to catch her on her own.

Probably it was because he was so focused on Emily, but for whatever reason, Nick didn't notice till the afternoon that Colin was trailing him. It didn't matter where Nick was, Colin was nearby. He couldn't tell whether Colin was actually watching him; he was just there like a dark shadow. Nick considered talking to him, sorting out yesterday's argument. After all, they'd been friends not all that long ago. But just the thought that Colin had planted the threatening letter on Jamie, and maybe even sabotaged his bike, kept him from doing it. If Colin made one wrong remark, Nick would break his nose.

With every passing minute of the day he'd been so looking forward to, Nick felt more lost. His best friend was lying in a coma, he and Colin didn't trust each other an inch, and Emily was pretending he didn't exist. Even people he'd been reasonably friendly with, like Jerome, were looking at him warily. The people Nick knew had been kicked out of the game, like Greg, were trying to make themselves invisible and had no wish to talk.

At some stage during the afternoon Nick encountered the jacket with the fluorescent orange badge in the schoolyard. The girl wearing it must be Darleen Pember. He only knew her by sight, but he remembered that she'd caught Jamie's eye. There was a lot he had to make up to Jamie for.

Nick looked around, tried to spot Colin. There was no way he would talk to Darleen if his pursuer was anywhere around. But Nick couldn't see any sign of him. Right then, quickly.

He drew her away from the two girls she'd just been talking to. "Tell me, Darleen, did you find a note in your jacket pocket yesterday? Or somewhere else, say in one of your books?"

She looked at him with a mixture of fear and curiosity. "No. Why?"

"No reason. If you happen to find one, keep it. Give it to Mr. Watson, but don't let any of the others find out about it."

She chewed on her bottom lip. "A note like the one Mohamed got? Or Jeremy?"

Who were Mohamed and Jeremy?

"What sort of notes were they?"

She shrugged. "I couldn't see properly. They certainly weren't handwritten though; they were printed out on a computer. Mohamed called in sick after that; he's been away for two days. Do you know what's on it?"

Nick shook his head. "Not exactly. Can I ask you something?"

She smiled expectantly; Nick hoped the expectation wasn't anything to do with him. He looked around.

"In? Or out?"

She didn't get it immediately. Nick mimed a few fencing moves.

"Oh! Out, unfortunately. But if they think I'm putting up with it, they've got another think coming. I've already tried to get a new copy, I've been to a few shops and I even—"

"Just drop it," Nick said. "The whole thing. Pretend the game never existed."

"But ..."

"I know. But still."

She looked at him with wide eyes. Nick tried to imagine her and Jamie together on a park bench, at the movies, in a field of flowers. A nice image. He hoped she'd maybe ask him how Jamie was. But she didn't.

That evening he sat in his room, not knowing what to do. The one thing he did know was that he couldn't bear the uncertainty. When he thought about it, Nick realized Emily had behaved logically when she'd ignored him. Completely. Unless ... unless the game had somehow made him look bad to her. There was an image in his head that had been haunting him the whole day: the messenger telling Emily that Nick had spied on her online. That he'd helped to bring a gun into the school grounds. And to top it all off, the photo of him and Brynne would turn up, and then she'd be through with him forever.

But that was all nonsense. Emily had been cool toward him because she was taking her cover seriously. He'd ring her and clear things up. Now.

But Emily wasn't answering her cell; her voice mail wouldn't even pick up. Nick tried once more after ten minutes, and again after half an hour. The result was the same.

Oh well, she was probably playing. He hadn't ever answered the phone then either.

Should he go over to her place? *Yes, good idea, keep ringing the doorbell and wake up her depressive mother—since Emily's headphones will certainly stop her from hearing.* Maybe that applied to the cell as well.

He sat down in front of the computer and thought about it.

Surfed over to deviantART and looked through Emily's page for new entries. But nothing had been added since "Night," the poem he already knew.

He spent the rest of the evening with Mom and Dad in front of the TV. He couldn't remember the last time he'd done that, and Dad was pleased, Nick could tell. "Studying all the time isn't so good either," he said, and patted Nick on the back of the head.

That night Nick dreamed his way into the graveyard in *Erebos*, and searched desperately for Sarius's gravestone, but suddenly all the inscriptions were convoluted symbols that he didn't know.

The next day Emily didn't come to school at all. Nick sat in chemistry class and stared at her empty seat; he felt like howling. He knew the pattern: the game had gained control of her, just like all the others. *I shouldn't have left her alone with it. How would Emily, of all people, happen to be immune?* But now it was too late. There was nothing he could do—she wasn't going to speak to him anymore, wasn't going to let him near her. From now on she would only care about carrying out her orders. He should have told her more about the game—instead, he'd allowed her to run straight into a trap, unprotected.

He rang her at recess, but of course she didn't answer. Fine. Then he would just go to her place after school.

After he'd made the decision, he immediately felt better. He would talk to Emily and remind her of their joint plan: to stop *Erebos*. After all, it had been her idea.

The feeling of elation lasted till English class, when Nick opened his book and found a note he certainly hadn't put there himself.

His heartbeat accelerated. He unfolded the note.

"There's an empty bed next to Jamie," the note said in clumsy block letters.

Nick took a deep breath. He hoped no one could tell he'd gotten a fright. He checked out of the corner of his eye for someone who might be watching him, waiting for his reaction, but no one looked conspicuous. Helen was yawning and scratching the back of her neck absently. Colin? Reading. Dan and Alex were whispering to each other; perhaps it had been them? Alex was always grinning at Nick with such overt friendliness; perhaps that was his idea of a disguise.

He folded the note up again and stuck it in his pants pocket. So there was an empty bed next to Jamie. Those rotten bastards. That was practically an admission. The accident *had* been planned; someone had sabotaged Jamie's brakes. Because of a stinking lousy game.

Suddenly, he hated them all so passionately that he felt like jumping up and bashing them over their heads with his chair. So they would have some idea of how much fun it was to have a brain trauma. He looked over at Colin again; the urge to go for his throat was overpowering. Nick jumped up.

"Yes?" Mr. Watson asked. "What is it, Nick?"

I'm about to go crazy.

"I'm not feeling very well. I'm afraid something has upset my stomach."

He was sure that Mr. Watson had caught the ambiguity in his words. It was clear from his expression, but he didn't inquire further.

"Then perhaps you should go home."

"Yes. Thank you."

Nick didn't care that someone was bound to think the threatening letter had scared him away from school. That didn't matter. What was important was Emily. He had to talk to her. She couldn't be so caught up in it already that arguments would have no influence. He had to tell her about his Jamie theory and show her the letter. Now. Quickly.

He got his cell out of his bag—he'd have one more try at ringing her.

The display immediately caught his attention. *1 new message*, the display said. He pressed Read.

Whatever u do don't send me emails & don't try 2 reach me via MSN or Skype. If u have time, come to 32 Cromer St, Bloomsbury @ 4pm. Don't say a word 2 anyone & make sure u r not being followed. Emily.

He swallowed, looked around frantically. Looked at the display again. No e-mails, no MSN—why? Had Emily found out something? He took a deep breath and tried to get things clear in his head. At least the text sounded as though Emily still had all her wits about her. And she wanted to see him! But there were still three hours to go before four o'clock. Nick had no idea how he was supposed to control his impatience for so long.

In the end, he used the time to make sure—really really sure— that no one was following him. No one had ever gone to Cromer Street a longer way around, or used more Tube lines to get there.

TWENTY-FIVE

There was a very odd fellow standing in front of the house numbered thirty-two. A fiery-red beard, long fiery-red hair. Both braided. He must have been waiting for Nick, because he went straight up to him as soon as he laid eyes on him.

"You're Nick, right? The lady described you well. I'm Speedy. Come with me."

He dragged Nick up a narrow staircase to the first floor, where he opened a green wood-panel door. "Come on in. Do you want soda, beer, or Ginseng Oolong? Victor claims the stuff's good for the brain. It works for him."

Nick, who hadn't said anything at all yet, apart from a brief greeting, asked for a glass of water. Why had Emily asked him to come here? Was she here too?

He followed Speedy through an amazingly jam-packed kitchen into a big room filled with a chorus of humming sounds. Nick counted twelve computers, not including Emily's laptop. She was sitting in a corner by the window with her headphones on, staring at her screen with intense concentration.

"Better not interrupt her," Speedy said. "It's all happening right now. Come on, I'll take you to Victor."

He led Nick around a giant structure made of various bits of technology, behind which a plump man, all in black, was sitting, completely hidden. Nick only noticed him in passing; his gaze was immediately drawn to the screen, which measured at least 22 inches. On it, a shimmering purple lizard man was just felling a worm-like monster. He was incredibly adept with his sword, and lightning-fast in his movements. The gamer's chubby fingers flew over the keyboard and controlled the mouse as precisely as a scalpel. The giant worm didn't have a chance, despite its needle-sharp teeth. One chop and it was cut in two. The front bit, the bit with the teeth, kept fighting until the lizard severed its head.

Speedy pulled one of the earphones on the man's headset from his ear. "Nick is here!"

"Ah, perfect timing! Take over for me?"

"Sure. By the way, Nick only drinks water."

"We can't have that!"

The man stood up and stretched. He just about reached up to Nick's chin. "You have to at least try my tea. I'm Victor."

"Pleased to meet you."

"We'll go next door. We can talk in peace in there."

He put his headset on Speedy, who was already looking out for more enemies, and gestured toward a graffiti-covered door. Nick already had hold of the doorknob when something occurred to him.

"Dissect the worm," he called to Speedy. "Chop it up as small as you can; perhaps you'll find something!"

Speedy held up a thumb and began to slice up his fallen adversary.

"Not so fast," said Victor. "Otherwise it will notice the difference. You need to keep the same pace as me."

A deep sigh escaped Speedy. The lizard man was chopping more slowly now, although still as quickly and skillfully as a Japanese sushi chef.

"You go ahead," said Victor. "I'll get us some tea."

Behind the graffiti door were three giant sofas and the same number of coffee tables. Not one piece matched another. Nick wasn't all that sensitive, but the color combination alone gave him a slight headache. He sat down on the most hideous of the sofas—olive-green with yellow roses and blue sailing boats. That way, he wouldn't have to see as much of it. Seconds later Victor entered the room with a tray that made it clear to Nick that there was method behind the mixture of styles.

"Victorian bone china with violets, or the Simpsons?"

"Since you're Victor, I'll leave you the Victorian one," Nick said, and took a mug that featured Homer over the words "Trying is the first step toward failure."

While Victor sat sipping from his bulbous cup, his eyes blissfully closed, Nick took the opportunity to study him more closely. He guessed he was about twenty-two or twenty-three. At first glance he seemed older, but that was probably the beard. A beard like a musketeer's, long and curling up above his lips, and a pointy triangle on his chin. Victor looked like Porthos. A Gothic Porthos—he wore skull studs the size of pound coins in his ears, and at least one silver ring on each finger. There were enough skulls present to form a parliamentary majority, with the snakes close behind. A lone angel dangled from a chain round his neck to compensate.

"Drink your tea," Victor said.

Nick sampled it dutifully and was astonished at how good it tasted.

"What Emily's brought us is really pretty unusual," Victor announced after another sip of tea. "I know a bit about computer games, let me tell you. But I've never gotten my hands on something like *Erebos* before."

"Did she give it to you just like that?"

"Not at all. It was all very proper, as part of the third rite. I'm her novice." He twirled his mustache between his fingers and grinned. "I'm still very new; I've only been playing since this morning." He sketched a bow. "Squamato, lizard man. Actually, I wanted to call myself Broccoli, but the charming gnome in the tower probably would have thumped me with my bronze shield. He explained that *Erebos* must not be mocked. Humor is not this game's strong point." He put his cup down. "But the interactivity! My goodness!"

"It talks to you, I know," Nick said. "You ask questions and it gives logical, correct answers. Do you have any idea how that works?"

"None at all. At first I actually thought someone was sitting at a central terminal and playing the role of the messenger or that dead bloke. But that could never work. Emily says heaps of people are playing. How many, do you reckon?"

Nick thought of the Arena fight. And not everyone had even taken part. "About three or four hundred. Perhaps even more."

"Exactly. You'd need a whole army of messengers, and then they'd still have to have the relevant orders and interconnections in their heads. Computers can master these memory tasks thousands of times better than any human, but complex conversations are not usually their thing."

Victor's teacup was empty; he gave himself a refill, and topped up Nick's too.

"Tell me a bit about the orders. Yesterday Emily had to do surveillance on a thirteen-year-old who went to buy pepper spray. She didn't know the girl and vice versa. She was probably from another school. But this messenger provided Emily with the girl's name and a photo, and with the time of the purchase and the address of the shop as well. Totally insane. Were your orders like that too? Was there anything to suggest a pattern?"

Nick thought hard. "Unfortunately not. Once I had to take a wooden box from Totteridge to Dollis Brook Viaduct. The box turned up at our school later with a gun in it. Apart from that, I once took pictures of a man and his car, and ... asked someone out to a café."

Victor snorted in amusement. "Doesn't really sound very threatening. Do you have any idea why you were supposed to do all that?"

"No. Except the last orders—I'm pretty sure about them. I was supposed to slip Digotan into our English teacher's tea. He thinks *Erebos* is ... well, that it's dangerous, and he's trying to get people off it. One of the gnomes said at one stage that we should treat our enemies as enemies, and I think that's what the game means by that."

Victor looked distraught. "In his tea?" he asked, as if that was the most reprehensible thing about the order.

"Yes. But I got cold feet, and that's why I got kicked out." Nick was astonished at how good it felt to talk about it. All of a sudden everything seemed less threatening.

"Have you ever thought about why the game demands what it does?"

No, he hadn't. Not seriously. Well, maybe a similar question had flashed through his mind a couple of times, especially when it had come to the date with Brynne and the photo assignment. Who had benefited from that?

But the thought had always faded into the background. They were just tasks. Obstacles that had to be overcome in order to move on.

"I thought it was just about making the game interesting and thrilling," he said, and realized, as he said it out loud, how unlikely that was.

"If I'm not very much mistaken, the game makes its players work together like a well-oiled machine," Victor said. "One person hides something, the next one gets it and takes it to another place.

321

One person buys something, the next one watches him doing it and reports in, so the game can plan its future moves. Based on what Emily has told me, I believe you're all working on something that no one can understand, because each of you only knows about a tiny little part. One or two pieces in the big puzzle." Victor chuckled. "And now I'm part of it too, but I want to see the whole picture, damn it!"

The whole picture. For a fraction of a second an image flickered in Nick's head, a colorful, familiar image, but it was gone before he figured out what it was.

"Know what would help? If I could hear more stories like yours. If we knew what other orders the game has been handing out. We could put all the pieces together and, who knows?" Victor rubbed his hands together. "Maybe it will turn out that we're looking for the Holy Grail or something!" Victor's good mood was infectious.

"If you want, I can try asking a few of the former gamers," Nick suggested. "But it's possible that no one will tell me anything. When you get chucked out you're instructed to say nothing."

"It's worth a try, at least. In the meantime, we'll set up our own little research lab here. I'm hoping it's about time for the next level. My shimmering Squamato is still only a One; it's pathetic."

"You have to get him into difficulties. When he's about to kick the bucket the messenger comes and rescues you, and saddles you with a task, and when you complete it, you get into the next level."

Victor slapped himself on the forehead. "You mean I'm playing too well to make progress? That's just wrong. Wait a sec, I have to tell Speedy to mess some things up ..."

Victor darted out and came back a minute later chuckling. "Speedy's just having a boxing match with an overgrown skeleton. Do you want to watch?"

322

The old excitement stirred in Nick's stomach. Yes, he wanted to see it, to be part of it—of course he did.

They positioned themselves a short distance behind Speedy, who was just making Squamato dash forward recklessly, straight at the strongest bone warrior, whose head was adorned with a crown. They couldn't hear what was happening—the headset meant the sounds were reserved for Speedy—but they saw Squamato's belt getting grayer and grayer. The skeleton king lunged and the lizard parried badly, another blow ... and there he lay with just a tiny, barely visible remnant of life, while the battle kept raging around him.

Nick dug his fingernails into his palms. A lot of these warriors were unknown to him, or he knew them only from the Arena. Hang on! That was Sapujapu! So he was still alive—good. And Lelant was fighting back there—not so good. Nick kept scanning the screen and caught himself looking for Sarius. How foolish. And it was foolish to still miss his other self so badly.

Minutes later the battle was over and the messenger turned up. Nick couldn't help taking a step back, then chided himself and resumed his spot behind Speedy. The messenger's words appeared in the familiar silver on a black background.

"Lelant fought like a hero; he deserves the greatest reward."

He handed the dark elf a sack of gold and a shield that shone like a star. Sapujapu, who was slightly injured, received three bottles of healing potion—that was heaps. Nick was happy for him. The others were fobbed off with mediocre stuff. Finally, the messenger turned to Squamato.

"You were exceptionally adept at first, and then suddenly very weak. That does not please me."

"O-ho," Victor said.

"I'm sorry, I was interrupted. But it won't happen again," Speedy typed hurriedly.

"I hope so—for your sake. You are as good as dead. If you remain here, you will die. If you follow me, I will save you. What is your decision?"

"I will come with you."

"Good."

The messenger lifted Squamato onto the horse and they rode off. Nick was very sorry that he couldn't hear the music that must be accompanying them on their ride.

What happened next was what always happened. In a cave the messenger laid his cards on the table: Squamato would live and become a Two if he carried out some orders.

"Go to the Cavalry Memorial in Hyde Park tonight at 7:00 p.m. Behind the memorial there are white benches. Underneath the third from the right, you will find an envelope with an address and a few words. Go to the address and graffiti the words onto the garage wall. Photograph your work afterward, and *Erebos* will welcome you back as a Two."

"That's not so easy," Nick murmured.

Speedy's reaction was spot on: he acted surprised.

"I don't think I understand. I mean, that doesn't have anything to do with the game."

"Yes, it does, Squamato. More than you think."

"So you mean the real Hyde Park and the real Cavalry Memorial?"

"That's right."

"And if I don't find anything under the bench there? If there's nothing there?"

"Then you will return and report that to me. But don't lie to me. I would notice."

Speedy exchanged a look with Victor, who seemed embarrassed.

"The orders are not exactly legal either," Speedy typed. "What happens if someone catches me?"

The messenger pulled his hood down over his face; his yellow eyes shone out in the dark.

"They've only caught you once so far. Make a good job of it—and don't give me any sob stories. We will meet again when your orders have been carried out."

And darkness fell over Erebos.

"Well, that's a pain," Victor declared. He waved Nick and Speedy into the next room, since it seemed Emily had just gotten to a tricky phase of the game. They could hear her frantic clicking.

"What does he mean by 'caught you once so far'?" Nick was truly astonished. "Caught you doing what?"

"I had a short career as a graffiti artist years ago," Victor said. "But how Yellow Eyes knows about that ... I have no idea. It's too bad. I'd prefer to be transporting wooden boxes around London compared to risking a charge of property damage."

"But did you notice?" Speedy put in. "He didn't realize that I was playing in Victor's place. He was just annoyed because I did such a bad job at the end."

"Yes, yes, that worked all right. But we won't take that risk again, even so. The game is hideously clever. Until we know a bit more, we'll play it safe. Anyway, soon you're going to be my novice. You do know that, right?"

Speedy ran his hand through his red hair. "I should hope so. Call me when it's time; I'm off now. Kate's going to be waiting for me."

After Speedy had gone, Victor began rummaging around in his cupboards—looking for old stocks of spray cans, Nick guessed. Emily was still sitting in her corner, completely focused on her game.

Should he go? Should he stay and wait for Emily? Undecided,

Nick leafed through one of the computer magazines that were piled up on the tables everywhere. He hadn't quite figured Victor out yet. Was this his flat? His office? Both? What was his job anyway?

It wasn't a good time to question him; Victor was battling mountains of paper that were trying to force their way out of the cupboard.

What was Emily battling?

Nick went closer, very quietly so he didn't disturb her, and took a look over her shoulder. Hemera was running through some sort of tunnel. For a Three she was already equipped with a pretty good breastplate and a decent sword.

The figures running in front of and beside her were familiar: Drizzel was there, Feniel, and Nurax. Hemera had ended up moving in the same circles as Sarius had earlier.

Crash! A couple of files detonated on the floor. Victor had disturbed the delicate balance of his overflowing cupboard, and now the contents were coming straight for him. Empty printer cartridges were raining on his head out of a broken shoe box.

Emily looked up briefly, but focused back on her game again immediately. She'd gotten out of the tunnel into the light and was now standing under an enormous tree that bore a golden crown in its leaves. Beneath its branches a campfire was burning. A conversation was slowly starting up.

Was there any news? No, the discussion just revolved around the difficulty of finding wish crystals.

A look at the clock told Nick that it was nearly six. He should go now; Victor would also have to set out soon if he was to be at Cavalry Memorial on time.

The last of the daylight gleamed in Emily's hair. They hadn't exchanged a single word since Nick had gotten there, but that was okay; she couldn't let herself be distracted. But she was so beautiful—Nick couldn't just leave, he had to take a memory with him. If not words, then a picture. He took his cell out of his pants pocket and took a photo of Emily at her laptop. She didn't even notice. Nick stowed his cell away carefully, like a treasure. From now on he would carry her with him.

Victor had finally found his spray cans. "I hope they're not completely gummed up," he muttered, and shook one with a green label.

"I'll be off now," Nick said.

"All right. Bear in mind that you mustn't send me or Emily compromising e-mails. I'm not entirely sure, but it wouldn't surprise me if the game can access your messages too. And don't forget that it understands what we write."

Nick promised to bear that in mind. Damn it all, he couldn't stop thinking about it. Did the messenger read his e-mail?

On the way home in the Tube, he looked at the photo he'd taken of Emily, over and over again. He felt like kissing the screen right there and then, but decided to wait until he was alone.

TWENTY-SIX

"No way. Forget it," Greg said. Even though almost two weeks had passed since his fall, the scrapes were still clearly visible.

"Just the orders," Nick pleaded for the second time. "I don't need to know who or what you were. It's what the messenger ordered you to do that's important."

"What for? You're out anyway. You won't be getting back in, no matter what you try, believe me."

It was enough to make you scream. Since the beginning of the week, Nick had been trying to find former gamers and squeeze them for info—so far with precious little success. And now Greg wanted to take off again, but Nick was holding him by the sleeve.

"Please! No one can see us. I'll tell you stuff about me too. Come on, talk to me."

"Why should I? There are some things I'm not incredibly proud of—no way am I going to tell you about them, Dunmore. Now let go." He freed his sleeve and disappeared into one of the classrooms.

Nick cursed loudly, turned around—and saw Adrian dart off. The picture of a guilty conscience. He sprinted after him.

"Hey! Stop! Were you eavesdropping on us, by any chance?"

Adrian turned his pale face toward him. "I didn't hear anything. So what was it that Greg didn't want to tell you?"

It was unfair of Nick to take his frustration out on Adrian, sure, but there was no one else around.

"Stop spying on people! Just wait—one of these days someone will thump you so hard you won't know which way is up."

"Leave the kid in peace," a deep voice behind Nick said.

Helen. Now he was really confused.

"What's it got to do with you, anyway?" he snapped at her.

"I said, leave him in peace. If I find out that you're threatening him again, you won't recognize your own face in the mirror the next day."

Nick looked back and forth between Adrian and Helen, bewildered.

"I didn't threaten him," he blurted out. "I told him something. You're the one threatening someone, namely me!"

"Well spotted. Now get lost."

You could tell by looking at Adrian that he was just as taken aback by Helen's intervention as Nick himself. "It's okay, Helen, he didn't do anything to me."

"Well," Nick said. "You know that, and I know that, but Helen obviously thinks you need a nanny." He left them both standing there.

The next class was English again. Nick studied Mr. Watson, without really listening, while he talked about Elizabethan theater. There hadn't been any news about Jamie for days now—that was better than bad news, at least. But would they even be told bad news?

At the end of the lesson Nick went over and pointedly stood next to Mr. Watson's desk. He didn't want anyone to think he had something to hide.

"Do you know how Jamie is?" Nick's mouth was dry. "I wanted to ring his parents, but I can't bring myself to do it. That's why I thought maybe you could tell me ..."

"He's still in an induced coma," Mr Watson said. "But things aren't looking too bad. His hip is healing well. The head injury is the main concern; something like that can have a lasting effect, but I'm sure you're aware of that."

So there was nothing new. Nick said thanks and walked out of the classroom, throwing Emily a quick glance that she didn't return. She was chatting to Gloria; she waved at Colin and ignored Nick. They hadn't spoken a word to each other for days, and Victor hadn't contacted him. Nick checked his cell constantly, hoping for a text inviting him to Cromer Street. But no luck.

He had a free period again straight afterward. The very thing he'd been so pleased about at the beginning of this year—having lots of free time between lessons—was now making him uncomfortable. There was no one he could spend them with.

On the other hand, maybe that wasn't true. There were thousands of things apart from *Erebos* he could talk to the others about, gamers or not. Jerome, for example, who was sitting a bit farther on, clutching his can of Red Bull.

"Hey, Jerome. How's it going?"

"Mmph."

"Were you at basketball last time? I missed it, but this time I sent Bethune an e-mail so he wouldn't go ballistic."

"Smart of you." Jerome shut his eyes and sipped his drink.

"So were you there?"

"Yep."

"And?"

"It was okay."

Nick gave up. Attempting to have a conversation with Jerome, of all people, hadn't been a good idea anyway; he never said a great deal. As if he was paying by the word.

"Well, see you then," Nick said, and left him to it. He would find some way to kill the rest of the time.

On the way to the library Eric stopped him. "Have you got a minute?"

Nick couldn't help himself—just the sight of Eric awakened his jealousy. His whole manner was so sensible and mature ...

"Yes?" Nick asked.

"I'm worried about Emily. Is it possible that she's playing your game now too?"

Nick smiled. She hadn't confided in Eric.

"No idea. I'm not part of it anymore, you know."

"Oh?" Eric raised his eyebrows. "Good for you."

There was a snippy answer on the tip of his tongue. *How would you know?* He swallowed it; Eric might be able to help him.

"Yes, that's how I feel now too. The problem is that I'd like to talk to a few of those who were ... affected. I know I'm not the only ex-gamer here, but I can't seem to get the others to listen."

Eric pursed his lips. "Does that surprise you? Why should they trust you? You can't even prove that you're out of *Erebos*."

There was some truth in that. But ...

"If you told them they could trust me, then they certainly would."

"It's possible. But the thing is, Nick—I hardly know you. I know from Jamie that you've changed a lot. I can't vouch for you just like that."

Unbelievable. Eric was likeable even when he was snubbing you. Nick had one last go.

"I want to do something to combat *Erebos*. I was part of it, I know the mechanisms. Most of them, anyway. But there's more to this than a game. I have to find out what it is, and that's why I need more information."

Eric shrugged regretfully. "I can understand that. But I promised the people who've spoken to me that I wouldn't pass anything on. I have to keep my word; I'm sure you can appreciate that."

Everyone has clammed up like an oyster, no matter what side they're on, Nick thought. "Okay," he said. "Then it will be every man for himself."

The idea of having to turn up empty-handed at Victor's place was getting Nick down. Who else could he turn to? To Darleen. She was out of *Erebos*. Besides, she had mentioned a Mohamed and a Jeremy who had received threatening letters—but that still didn't prove anything. Aisha had gotten one as well, and she was probably still playing. Greg was definitely out, but wouldn't talk.

Nick would stick with Darleen. She hadn't seemed to be intimidated or withdrawn. After a bit of a search he found her in the cafeteria. Amid loud giggles from her girlfriends he towed her outside to the corridor, where it was more peaceful and he had a better view of what was happening. No Colin, no Dan, no Jerome.

"You again," she said, and grinned. "Kelly and Tereza are getting jealous."

She and Jamie would really suit each other, Nick thought.

"Tell me, Darleen." He approached the subject cautiously. "You said that you're not playing anymore. Do me a favor: tell me a few things you did when you were still part of it."

She seemed a bit unnerved. "But you said yourself that I should act as though the game never existed."

Nick took another look around. "I only want you to talk about it just this once. To me." He heard people coming, took Darleen by the hand, and led her into an empty classroom. He closed the door behind them and leaned against it.

"What do you want to know?"

"What orders you carried out, for example. Was there anything special about them?"

She thought about it, studying Nick out of the corner of her eye as if she wasn't sure it was safe to tell him such things.

"Do you still remember the stolen laptops?"

"Yes, of course."

"I was in on that. I kept a look out. If someone came, I was supposed to raise the alarm on my cell. But don't tell anyone about it, I'll deny it anyway."

Nick tried hard to see where this information fit in. "Do you know what happened to the laptops?"

"No. But I can imagine. They were meant for the people who couldn't start playing the game because they didn't have their own computer. I think Aisha got one of them."

That made sense, but it was a piece of the puzzle that wouldn't actually help Victor.

"Anything else?"

"God, you're nosy." She sighed. "Yes, I copied some documents that I fished out of a garbage can in Kensington Gardens. But don't ask me what it was exactly. Legal stuff, a whole stack of paper. I didn't understand a word of it."

Nick would have given a lot to get a look at the "legal stuff."

"Anything else? Did you threaten anyone at any time, or ... break anything?"

Now her gaze slid away. "No. But I know what you mean. No, I didn't. The rest of my orders were harmless. Writing an assignment for someone, buying a SIM card and leaving it somewhere, that sort of thing."

"And why did you get kicked out?"

"Because my idiotic mother blocked my Internet access for three days. After that, the messenger said I was of no further value to him. Seriously? I could still howl with rage. As if that was my fault!"

"Okay. Thanks," said Nick. "You've been a big help, but I think you'd better go before one of the watchdogs finds us here."

She nodded. "Pretty crazy stuff, huh? Do you think we ever met each other in the game?"

Nick smiled. "I don't know. What was your name?"

At first she hesitated, then shrugged her shoulders. "Samira."

"Hey, then we really do know each other! You were a cat woman, right? And you were there when I first started."

"Honest? So who were you?"

Some distant part of him still ached when he thought of his other self in the past tense.

"Sarius," he answered. "I was Sarius."

TWENTY-SEVEN

The weekend had finally arrived—along with an invitation from Victor. They were all going to stay the night in his studio, as he called it. "Gaming, chatting, drinking tea," he said on the phone. "You just have to come. I've found out a few amazing things!"

"It's nice that you're getting out again," Mom said when he told her about his plans. "You've hardly moved from your desk lately."

Nick set off with his sleeping bag and pillow and an enormous supply of snacks. He must have made a strange sight, looking around several times at each corner, each crossroad, to check that no one was following him. He went an incredibly roundabout way again on the Tube to shake off any unseen pursuers.

"Welcome, my friend!" Victor opened the door and relieved him of his things. "I haven't had a pyjama party in ages! You'll say yes to a cup of tea, I hope, and hi to Emily?"

Emily was sitting in the same spot as last time. She looked up briefly as Nick came in, pointed apologetically to her laptop, and turned back to the game. A red hiking pack was leaning against the wall behind her. Was she going to stay the night too?

Next door, Speedy was already sprawled on one of the garish sofas with a girl whose hair was died jet black and shaved on one side.

"Kate," Speedy introduced her. "My woman."

"Nice to meet you."

Kate smiled, revealing eyeteeth embellished with diamantes.

"Your turn, Speedy," Victor said. "And try not to flaunt your skills, okay?"

"I'm not stupid, you know," Speedy grumbled, and wandered off. He sat down at a different computer than last time.

"It's necessary," Victor explained, probably noticing Nick's look. "The first thing the program will definitely check is the IP address. If it recognizes that, it won't even show you the teensiest fir tree from the opening sequence."

So Nick's idea of borrowing Finn's laptop hadn't been so silly. "How did the graffiti operation go?"

"Oh. Good, if you can call it that." The mug Victor put on the table for Nick was shaped like a kraken, obligingly clasping two of its tentacles to form a handle. "I found the note, went to the address, sprayed, and didn't get caught."

Victor cleared a few computer magazines out of the way and unearthed a photo: the wall of a building with the words "He who steals our dreams puts us to death" written in expert blue-black letters.

"A quote from Confucius," Victor explained. "The person who programmed *Erebos* is very fond of quotes."

Nick must have looked confused, because Victor grinned. "Get used to the idea that *Erebos* didn't invent itself. Somebody out there wrote a source code, just like with any other program. Except this one is a programming masterpiece. An incredibly brilliant thing."

Nick could have sworn that Victor's eyes were damp.

"Do you know how many years people have been trying to write a program that speaks and thinks like a person? Can you imagine what this development is worth? Millions, Nick! Billions. But the game is being served up to us gratis, like something you find in a box of cornflakes. Why?"

336

Nick had never looked at it from this angle before. From the beginning, the game had always made him feel as if he was relating to a living being; he'd never thought about its financial value.

"Because ... it's trying to accomplish a goal?" He grasped Victor's question, and was rewarded with a radiant look.

"Exactly! It's a tool—the most expensive, ingenious tool in the world. I metaphorically bow down before its creator in humility and worship." He took a sip of tea. "Someone who can bring off something like this doesn't make random allusions. So what is he saying to us—or rather to the unknown garage owner?"

He who steals our dreams puts us to death.

"That he wants to kill him? Or that the other person is threatening him with death?"

"Exactly. It sounds like a warning to me. At any rate, it's not just some random quote, and neither was it just some random address." Victor was crumbling a biscuit, while Nick was almost bursting with impatience.

"And? Who lives there?"

"Well, that's not at all thrilling, unfortunately. An accountant, divorced, no children, middle management in a company that exports food. It's hard to imagine anything more run-of-the-mill. But of course he could be a complete monster in private."

An accountant. That really wasn't exciting.

"Did you find any pieces of the puzzle?" Victor asked.

"I'm afraid not. I only found one ex-gamer who was willing to talk." Nick reported on Darleen's orders—the computer theft, the copied documents, and the SIM card.

Victor made a note of it all. "Who knows—one day things may fall into place," he said. "Let's turn our attention to the allusions that are hidden in the game. Maybe they will tell us more. How good are you in art history?"

Uh-oh. Nick shook his head. "Sorry, you've got the wrong guy."

"Okay, fine. So we'll start with ornithology. What does Ortolan mean to you?"

"That's the enemy the *Erebos* players are fighting," Nick said, happy that he finally knew an answer.

"Very true." Victor twirled his mustache between his fingers; now he looked like a magician who was about to conjure a rabbit out of his hat. "May I show you a picture of Ortolan?"

There was a picture?

"Sure, I'd like to see it," Nick said.

Victor fetched another laptop from next door. "This one is completely *Erebos*-free. That means we can use it to move around on the Internet without the program noticing and giving us a rap on the knuckles." He opened the lid. "Okay, now search for Ortolan," he said.

Nick entered the word in Google. The first hit took him to Wikipedia, and he clicked on the link.

"Well, that's pretty stupid," he declared.

Ortolan was nothing but a different name for the garden bunting, a songbird long considered a delicacy in France and Italy.

"It's extremely confusing, hmm?" Victor chuckled. "And unfortunately I haven't found out what our Mr. Programmer is trying to tell us. But I haven't the slightest doubt that he wants to tell us something. I've discovered something else, too; I'm positive that you'll like it." Victor clapped his hands like a child in front of his birthday cake, put his skull-ringed fingers on the keyboard, and then changed his mind. "No, first I want to ask you something. Were you at any of these sinister Arena fights? There's one on again tomorrow night, and all the heroes are practically wetting their chain mail pants with excitement."

Nick grinned. "Yeah, I took part in one. Unfortunately I wasn't around for the second. It's pretty exciting. You'll see."

"Excellent. And I suppose you have to register for them, hmm? With whom, pray tell?"

There was no question about it—Victor loved little puzzles.

"The second time it was right in the Arena, with the master of ceremonies. The first time it was with some soldier in Atropos's tavern."

Victor's grin gave way to an expression of comic disbelief. "Did you say Atropos?"

"Yes. So?"

"Where will it all end?" Victor cried in feigned despair. "Do children learn nothing at all in school these days? At least tell me whether you noticed anything unusual about this master of ceremonies."

"He didn't go with the game. He didn't look like the other figures; he was ... wrong, somehow. I always called him 'big Goggle-Eyes.'"

Victor was most amused. "Terrific—very appropriate. But didn't Goggle-Eyes remind you of anything?" He opened his own eyes wide and tried to imitate the facial expression.

"No. Sorry."

"Then have a look at this."

Victor typed an address in the browser, and the home page of the Vatican Museum opened. Two more clicks, then he turned the laptop around so Nick could see the screen better.

"There's your Goggle-Eyes. Painted by Michelangelo himself."

It was a few moments before Nick could make head or tail of it. What Victor was showing him was a gigantic painting teeming with hundreds of figures. Jesus and Mary were in the middle, and all around them half-naked people were sitting and standing on various clouds. Farther down, a couple of angels were blowing their trumpets, and other angels were pulling people from the ground toward heaven. At the bottom edge there were figures writhing in the mud, and then, a bit to the right of the center ... there he was. The master of ceremonies, exactly as Nick knew him from *Erebos*. Naked except for the loincloth, with the strange tufts of hair on his head and his long stick, which he was swinging as if he wanted to hit the people who sat in his boat.

"Yes, that's him," Nick yelled excitedly.

"And do you know his name?"

"No."

Victor sat up straight and put on a solemn face.

"That's Charon. The ferryman, who, in Greek mythology, carries the dead in his boat over the river Styx to the realm of death."

Nick took a closer look at the picture and couldn't help shivering. Here Charon seemed to be *beating* the dead across the river.

"Your Goggle-Eyes' parents probably also deserve a mention: Charon is the son of Nyx, the goddess of the night ... and of Erebos."

Nick's head was spinning. "And what does it all mean?"

"Hard to say. But perhaps we'll get warmer if we study the title of Michelangelo's masterpiece. Take a look!" He pointed the cursor at the words underneath the photo.

Michelangelo Buonarotti
The Last Judgement
Sistine Chapel

"At the Last Judgement God separates the righteous from the damned," said Victor. "It's not a very pretty sight. And I wonder whether the game isn't doing something similar. Making a selection. Why else would it be so ruthless about eliminating everyone who fails at their tasks?"

340

"Isn't that a bit crazy?"

With a few clicks Victor enlarged the picture to the point where they could see Charon's facial features in detail. "Crazy maybe. But above all it's meticulous, planned down to the last detail. What was it you said before? The shop where you registered for the big fight in the Arena was called Atropos's tavern?"

"Actually, it was called 'The Final Cut,'" Nick explained.

"Oh, my boy, my poor blind boy!" Victor cried theatrically and typed something in once again. "Look at this: Atropos is one of the three Moiræ, the Greek goddesses of fate. She is the oldest and the least agreeable; in fact, it's her task to cut through humans' life threads. The final cut." Victor closed the laptop with a sigh. "The game gives us very broad hints. The programmer has a particular weakness for Greek mythology. That's the first thing. Each of the symbols he uses is connected with disaster and death. That's the second. Combine it with the brilliance of the program and its addictiveness—and ... oh my. I'd be less worried if I were sitting on a barrel of dynamite."

Victor didn't actually look worried though; he looked extremely satisfied. He topped up his cup again and leaned back.

"That's all very well," said Nick, after they'd both remained silent for a time. "But what do we do with our knowledge?"

"We enjoy being so clever. And keep our eyes out for more hints. Sooner or later there'll be one we can make use of."

Nick spent the next half an hour watching Speedy become Quox the barbarian in the tower. Victor had supplied him with a pad and a pencil and Nick was making note of the details he spotted in the tower. The tablets were made of copper; was that significant? He jotted down every sentence the gnome uttered, and looked for hidden messages. Kate helped him; she pointed at scratches in the wall of the tower. Nick sketched a copy. Was there an image concealed in them, a plan, a name—anything?

Victor was back sitting at his computer, driving Squamato across barren heathland with much brandishing of his sword. Every few steps, vipers as tall as a man shot up out of the ground beside him, snapped at him, and then disappeared back under the earth. But Victor seemed to have a sixth sense—he always dodged and didn't get bitten a single time.

Meanwhile, Hemera was standing by a fire with four other warriors, Nurax among them, chatting about the coming Arena fight. Nurax declared that he was aiming for at least two more levels, and that if everything went as planned he might even attempt to win a place in the Inner Circle.

Emily was shifting restlessly on her chair. Nick suspected that it made her nervous to have him looking over her shoulder. He retreated back to the next room with his notes, sat on the roses-and-sailing-ships sofa, and opened the laptop that Victor had said was clean. The thought that his own computer at home might not be worried him. Was that why Emily had insisted he shouldn't e-mail her under any circumstances?

If this computer wasn't being monitored by *Erebos*, what would happen if he searched for the game on Google?

He entered "Erebos" and found the "Erebos—the game" link that had issued him a personalized warning on the previous occasion. He clicked on it again now, and the text that was displayed was completely different.

> Joy, thou beauteous spark divine,
> Daughter of Elysium,
> We are entering, drunk with fire,
> Heav'nly one, thy holy shrine!
> Thy enchantments bind together

What stern custom did divide.
All mankind will be as brothers
Where thy gentle wings abide.

Shaking his head, Nick closed the page. That was familiar to him from a Beethoven symphony. But it didn't make any sense here. Presumably it was just intended as dummy text for non-gamers who happened to pass by. Whatever. On with the research.

Nick entered "copper tablet" and found loads of suppliers of copper tablets. In addition, copper tablets obviously had something to do with the printing of illustrations in old books. That was presumably a false lead.

Next he tried a combination of "snakes" and "Greek mythology." There was Hydra with her nine heads—but Victor's snakes had only had one. He found a snake that wound itself around the staff of Asclepius and one that guarded the oracle of Delphi. None that sprang out of the ground. So far so bad.

What now? Nick cast a glance through the half-open door to the next room. Everyone was absorbed in the game; only Kate was clattering around in the kitchen. He went to check if he could help her; but the two trays of pizza had already disappeared into the oven.

"Tell me, what's Victor's surname?" he asked.

"Lansky." Kate turned the thermostat up a smidge, sighed, and turned it back down. "Other people's ovens are terrible; my pizzas either turn out soggy or black. I just hope you like prosciutto and heaps of onion."

"Oh, absolutely. Thanks." Nick retreated to his sofa and entered "Victor Lansky" into Google. He found a Victor Lansky in Canada, and one in London. Bingo. Victor was anything but a dark horse on the computer scene. He even published a small gaming magazine, which only came out sporadically but had a good reputation. Ah, and here was something else. One Zobbolino wrote on his home page that he was a good friend of the infamous Victor Lansky.

> Victor and I share fond memories of the time when not a single wall or railway car was safe from our art. To spray or not to spray—that was never the question. We were the bright gods of graffiti, and if we hadn't been caught that once we'd still be painting the town red (and every other color ...)

Nick read the text through a few times. It clearly stated that Victor had been involved in graffiti and that he'd been caught. *Erebos* could read, and it made everyone register under his or her own name. It probably conducted research on every novice. Wow.

Erebos *draws on information from the Internet,* Nick wrote down. *We hadn't considered that before. The whole Internet? It certainly scans the hard drive and it maybe even tracks which sites you visit on the net. That makes it practically omniscient.*

If that was true, it had probably read the instant message transcript on Nick's computer and made use of his dialogue with Finn. That's how it knew about the Hell Froze Over shirt.

Nick would have liked to discuss his observations with Victor, but Squamato was fully occupied at the moment, climbing a gigantic wall while trying not to fall off. Impatiently Nick gulped down two cups of stone-cold tea. He knocked over the third one as he reached for his writing pad again in order to check his notes.

"Shit!" He evacuated the pad, about a ton of computer magazines, and his notes—the latter had come off worst.

"Oh. Problems here as well?" Emily was standing in the doorway wearing a tired smile; her eyes were red.

"Yes, I'm all thumbs. Wait, I'll just get a cloth." Nick sprinted into the kitchen, located a roll of paper towel, and ran back. Emily was trying to stop the tea from dripping on the floor using tissues.

"How's Hemera?" Nick asked, wiping up frantically.

"She's wounded in the stomach and leg. The screeching from the headphones was almost unbearable." Emily collapsed onto the second-ugliest sofa and yawned. "I desperately need a coffee, but Victor doesn't have any in the house. And I've still got orders to carry out today. Nothing difficult, fortunately. But still something I really don't want to do." She yawned again.

"I'll go round to Starbucks and get you a coffee," Nick offered.

"It's too far," Emily said, and in the same breath, "I'll come with you. I need fresh air anyway. And a phone booth."

"For your orders?"

She nodded. "Any phone booth. That means I don't have to go right across London, at least."

Nick had already taken a look out of the window—to be on the safe side—but hadn't seen anything in the darkness that looked suspicious. He had another thorough look around from the front door. "If there's someone lying in wait for us, they're certainly well hidden."

They walked along Cromer Road and turned onto Gray's Inn Road, which was almost deserted at this time of day. Emily looked over her shoulder several times when groups of young people crossed their path. Their uneasiness made them quicken their pace. As they reached King's Cross station, the first phone booths came into view, and Emily stopped just short. "I can't do it," she said soberly.

"What can't you do?"

"Make a threatening phone call." She looked up at Nick pleadingly, as if she were hoping he would have a solution to her dilemma. "I can't even try to make it sound nice, because I've been told what words I have to say."

"Oh. Yes, that's not pleasant," Nick said, fully conscious of how lame that sounded. "But look at it this way: it's for study purposes. You don't really mean it. You're doing it so we can find out about *Erebos*."

"Except my victim won't know that," Emily murmured.

"Think of Victor and his Confucius quote."

"Unfortunately, my message isn't a Confucius quote. That's for sure." Grim-faced, Emily steered toward the first booth. "I'll get it over with now," she murmured, and fetched some change, her iPod, and a note out of her shoulder bag.

"What's with the iPod?"

"I have to record the conversation. And upload it. As if it wasn't bad enough already."

Nick watched her while she dialed, turned on the iPod, and held it to the receiver. She closed her eyes almost as soon as the ring tone started. Nick heard someone answer at the other end.

"It is not over," Emily said in a graveyard voice. "You will never find any peace. He has not forgotten. He has not forgiven. You will not get away with it."

"Who is this?" Nick heard a man at the other end of the line bellow. "I'll set the police onto you all, you damned criminals!" Then there was nothing except a quiet "Damn" and the busy signal. Emily placed the receiver back in its cradle.

"I think I feel sick," she said dully. "What twisted garbage. I'll never do something like that again. And now I need coffee."

They found a quiet corner in the Starbucks on Pentonville Road. Emily ordered herself a large cappuccino with an extra shot of espresso. Nick followed suit, added two chocolate chip muffins, and was ecstatic when she allowed him to pay.

"Where do you know Victor from?" he asked, after they'd eaten half their muffins and were blowing in their cups because the coffee was still boiling hot.

"He was a friend of Jack's." She smiled pensively. "Of course, Victor says he *is* a friend of Jack's and what does a little bit of drowning matter between friends."

Even before he realized what he was doing, Nick had put his hand over Emily's. She didn't pull it away; on the contrary, she linked her fingers with his.

"Victor helped me a lot. He adopted me as his little sister."

"He's fantastic," Nick said fervently. He didn't get any other words out; he had the feeling that he was about to take off and float. To cover his embarrassment, he sipped at his coffee, which had finally reached a drinkable temperature.

"We'll be in trouble with Kate," he declared. "We're stuffing ourselves with muffins and she's just making pizza."

"I can handle muffins mixed with pizza," Emily said. "And so can Victor, by the way. Don't worry. But we should be making our way back soon anyway. Firstly, this isn't really a very safe area at this time of night, and secondly, I want to Google the telephone number of my victim."

Outside, Emily took Nick's hand as if it was the most natural thing in the world. The area really wasn't suited to a romantic stroll, but as far as Nick was concerned, it could have lasted the whole night long.

There was hardly any pizza left when they got back to Victor's flat.

Kate raised her arms in apology. "Victor. He says a genius needs food. Lots of food. There's half a pizza left. I could make you some pasta if you like."

They declined, took the leftover pizza, and opened a can of peanuts. The sofa with the roses and ships was suddenly the nicest place in the world. Nick opened the laptop and typed the number Emily dictated to him into the search engine.

"No hits. Unfortunately."

"That's sort of what I expected," said Emily. "It's probably a private number. Too bad he didn't say his name."

The word "private" struck a chord in Nick—there was something he had to tell Emily. Now.

Hopefully the smile on her face wouldn't evaporate immediately. "I need to confess something to you. I've been reading your blogs on deviantART for a few months. And your poems. They're brilliant, and so are your drawings."

She caught her breath. "How do you know that it's my account?"

"Someone let on once. Please don't get mad. You really don't need to be embarrassed."

She looked away. "It's a pity."

"Why?"

"Because I would have liked to show you those things myself. Some time or other." She leaned her head on his shoulder and yawned. Nick, who was inwardly cavorting with relief, only now noticed that Victor was standing in the doorway.

"It's group hug time around the campfire," he said. "So I thought I'd come and see how you're doing. But it's hugging time here too, hmm?" He plopped himself down on the sofa opposite.

Emily reported on her orders. "I threatened a total stranger. Who knows what he's thinking now. He probably has no idea what I was talking about."

"What did you have to say, exactly? Do you remember?"

348

Emily passed the note to Victor.

"It is not over. You will never find any peace. He has not forgotten. He has not forgiven. You will not get away with it." Victor was almost vibrating with excitement. "Far out! Okay, let me summarize: A certain *he* is very angry with the person you talked to, Emily. I'd bet he'd like to see him take a trip in Charon's boat or arrange for Atropos to snip away at his life thread."

Emily looked confused, which gave Victor another opportunity to show off his general knowledge.

"Unfortunately, this telephone number probably doesn't belong to my garage owner, otherwise we could have sent him a friendly warning." Victor checked for tea in the teapot, but didn't find any, and let his mustache droop. "If you ask me," he went on, "*Erebos* has only one goal: to take revenge on someone. On Ortolan, our songbird."

"Yeah, but ... graffiti-ed garages and dubious phone calls? Somehow that's not my idea of revenge," Nick put in.

"I would be very surprised if that's where it ends," Victor said. "I think I remember you telling me something about a gun in a cigar box."

Nick felt himself going cold, and hot, and then cold again. "You mean *Erebos* wants us to shoot someone?"

"It's very possible. If I'm not mistaken, the game is in the process of forming an elite troop for special operations." Victor smiled, but this time it didn't look happy. "It would be good to know who the members of the Inner Circle are."

The Inner Circle went around in Nick's head for the next half hour like a burning wheel. An elite troop. A revenge squad. But what were its orders?

After Victor had returned to the game, Nick and Emily went

into the kitchen to boil water for a fresh pot of tea. "You'll be going straight back in, won't you?" he asked. "Now that your orders have been carried out?"

"Tomorrow is soon enough. I want to be there for the Arena fight; perhaps I can come to some conclusions. Too bad we don't know who's behind the player names."

She poured boiling water on Victor's precious tea leaves. "By the way, there's someone running around in the game who looks like you."

"I know. It bugged me the whole time, but what can I do?"

Emily smiled. "The sight of him cheers me up."

Back in the sofa room, he told Emily about Sarius.

"He was cool, you know? Amazingly quick with his sword and a fantastic runner. After Level Five I left them all for dead."

"How come you got kicked out?"

"Because of Mr. Watson and his thermos." Nick told her about his orders and how he'd nearly carried them out. "It was a really close thing; I was seriously tempted."

Emily shivered as though she was freezing. "The game defends itself really well against its opponents. Do you think that's how the business with Aisha and Eric started too?"

Nick looked at her sideways, but couldn't spot anything other than genuine interest.

"It's quite possible. Probable, even."

"We have to watch out, Nick. Especially you. Colin made an odd remark recently. 'Time to bring Nick down'—that was just after you had that fight outside the cafeteria. Don't underestimate it."

Yes, Nick thought, but then Colin has a big mouth.

He poured tea into Victor's cup and took it to him at the computer. Squamato was just chatting with Beroxar about the advantages of axes in comparison with swords.

Beroxar. Nick grabbed a pen and a piece of paper. *Beroxar was in the Inner Circle before he was ousted by BloodWork,* he wrote.

Victor gave him the thumbs-up.

Evening turned into night. Emily unpacked her knapsack and wrapped herself in her sleeping bag. They talked about the people from school and tried to come to some agreement about which student was behind which game character. But mostly they had differing opinions.

Shortly after midnight Victor staggered in. "That's enough for today. I'm worn out. Has anyone got anything to eat?"

Emily got a chocolate bar out of her pack and Victor broke off half with an apologetic look. "Something's up," he said, chewing. "Nonstop gnomes, everyone's nattering on about a great battle and how the proving time is approaching."

"I think there'll be a fierce battle tomorrow for the places in the Inner Circle," Nick said. "I would have attempted it at the last Arena if I hadn't gotten chucked out. The messenger said he would be able to tell me the weakest fighter in the Inner Circle. He probably would have done it if I'd ... carried out his orders." He wondered if his sacrifice really had saved Mr. Watson's life, or if his task had just been given to someone else.

Victor nodded with his mouth full and lifted a finger. "Very true. He would have given you tips in order to have you there. The question is: why would he want you? The answer: because you would have proved you were prepared to walk over dead bodies for *Erebos.* Or go to prison."

Nick and Emily exchanged a look. Someone had almost walked over Jamie's dead body. Was that person's name going to be on the golden shield tomorrow?

"Of course, walking over a teacher's dead body is no big deal,"

Victor muttered and pilfered the rest of the chocolate. "In my day I felt like doing that quite a few times without needing a messenger to encourage me."

At some stage Victor retreated to his bedroom. At some stage Speedy stopped playing and camped out on a giant air mattress in the computer room with Kate.

At some stage Nick and Emily pushed two of the sofas together so there was a big area to lie on and the arms shielded them from the rest of the world.

"Good night," Emily whispered, and pressed an incredibly soft, gentle kiss on his mouth. Her fingers tousled his nape. "Good night, raven."

Then she leaned her head against his shoulder and closed her eyes. Nick felt her hair tickling his neck and heard her breathing become deeper. He wanted everything to stay like this, exactly like this. He wanted to keep lying here forever. He wanted to stop the world.

TWENTY-EIGHT

Toast with jam and tea. Victor brought them breakfast in bed the next morning. "Something to fortify you before the big battle."

Emily thanked him, yawning, while Nick tried to figure out whether it was his numb arm or the sight of Victor's Snoopy dressing gown that was immobilizing him.

Nick watched the Arena fight as if in a trance. He kept changing his vantage point, flitting between Emily, Victor, and Speedy, who were each housed with their respective species. It was still quite empty in the humans' area—although LordNick and Hemera were waiting together in the same anteroom. Emily winked at Nick meaningfully.

The barbarians by contrast were quite a large crowd; Quox seemed to be the weakest among them. He was still a One, but given Speedy's abilities Nick wasn't too worried.

The same was true of Victor and Squamato. Even if the lizard man entered the Arena as a Three, he would presumably leave it with a few extra levels.

Big Goggle-Eyes turned up. Now that Nick knew his origins, he found the master of ceremonies even more sinister. An emissary from the underworld.

It was the arrival of the Inner Circle, though, that Nick was awaiting most eagerly; he held his breath as the golden platform was carried in.

BloodWork was still there, and seemed more gigantic than ever. Also Wyrdana, the dark she-elf, whom Nick knew from the last Arena fight. Another barbarian by the name of Harkul, a werewolf named Telkorick—and Drizzel. Drizzel had made it into the Inner Circle! Stunned, but not surprised, Nick saw the round red symbol dangling on a chain around his neck.

Before things got started, the master of ceremonies walked into the center of the Arena.

"Take a look at the warriors of the Inner Circle. You still have the opportunity to take their places if you prove yourselves and wish finally to be initiated into the deepest mysteries of *Erebos*. Some will triumph today; others will eat dirt. Let the fights begin."

Nick hadn't remembered it being so quick. One after the other, the fighters chose their opponents. Soon it was Quox's turn; he was challenged by another barbarian who was also a One. Speedy worked quickly and precisely, and defeated his opponent almost in passing. Hemera defeated a werewolf, but was wounded; Emily was suffering visibly from the noise emanating from her headphones.

Squamato had to wait a long time to be called, and the fight, when it finally came, was exceedingly hard. He'd challenged an overly strong opponent and only just managed to win.

However much Nick tried, he couldn't read anything into the events—the fights, Goggle-Eyes' words, the faces in the crowd. Neither did he discover any other unusual figures to search for in the Michelangelo painting. The Arena fight was a completely run-of-the-mill bloodbath, nothing more or less. It wasn't going to provide any further insights.

Late in the afternoon, after all the fights had been decided, Nick and Emily packed their bags and prepared to set off toward home. Hemera had got to Level Six, Victor to Seven, Speedy had improved by three levels and was already a Four—and he hadn't even carried out any orders yet.

"We're stuck," Victor declared as he accompanied Emily and Nick to the door. "True, we're doing pretty well in the game, but we still don't understand the bigger picture. If I had a bit longer I'd try to make it into the Inner Circle. But I fear that this final battle everyone's talking about won't be long in coming. We're running out of time."

Standing in the Tube on the way home, Nick didn't take his eyes off Emily. "How will it be, from tomorrow?" he asked. "Can we ... so, will we see each other when we're at school? Will we have lunch together? Or will we keep acting as if we don't have anything to do with each other?"

Emily took his hand. "The latter, I'm afraid. But just until it's all finished. Just for camouflage, okay?"

"All right. Will you text me with what's going on? I think we're safe with the cells as long as we make sure that no one else gets their hands on them."

"Yes, I will. And we'll meet at Victor's again on Wednesday afternoon."

Even though they'd discussed it, and even though Nick was expecting it, Emily's pointed show of indifference hurt. Particularly since she was acting unusually cheerful with other people—Colin, Alex, Dan, Aisha, even Helen. She flung herself at Colin and spent recesses with Aisha. Nick nearly died from longing. Once, he saw Eric go up to Emily. She walked off after two sentences, leaving him standing there. It seemed he wasn't any better off than Nick—that was something.

In the free period after math Brynne broke in on his gloomy thoughts. "Can I speak to you for a second?" He saw her pale, expectant face and sighed inwardly.

"Okay."

"I've stopped," she whispered.

That actually was a surprise. "Why?"

"Because it's ... evil. I think. And ... it's haunting me, day and night."
She looked away. "You're not part of it anymore either, are you?"

He hated talking to Brynne about it. "What difference does that
make?"

"A huge one. Both of us could go to Mr. Watson and tell him
about our experiences. I know he'd be really keen. We could form a
countermovement."

Oh no. Brynne and Nick against the world—that was not going
to happen.

"Go find someone else to do that. There are enough ex-gamers,
after all." Out of the corner of his eye he saw Dan, who was slowing
down the closer he got. They were attracting attention.

"What do you want to say to Mr. Watson?" Nick whispered. "He's
known for ages that *Erebos* is responsible for the incidents at school.
He needs the names of people who've been up to something. If you've
got them, go to him. Just leave me out of this, whatever you do."

Brynne looked forlorn. "I can't stand it anymore."

"Can't stand what? You're out, end of story."

Now Dan was very discreetly standing not three steps away,
apparently absorbed in the ballet notice board. Nick had to get away;
he didn't want to become even more of a target. The less attention he
attracted, the better it was for their little reconnaissance team.

Brynne wasn't going to accept his refusal just like that. "Is Nicky
a coward?" she said, so loudly that Dan must have heard. Not to
mention a few other students at the end of the corridor.

"Screw off," he said, and walked off.

"Fine!" she called after him. "Then I'll do it by myself. I'll
manage! I'll take you all on!"

Even though he didn't want to, Nick turned around and walked back to her. "Quiet! Do you really want to get yourself into trouble?"

She laughed. It was a horrible laugh, as though she was crazy, or about to become so. "Trouble? Nicky, you have no idea. Totally no idea. It can't get worse, no way."

For the rest of the day Nick had the feeling he was walking around with his head ducked, constantly waiting for some disaster that was about to strike. But nothing happened. In fact, it was quieter than usual. Exhaustion lay over the school like a gray veil.

Mr. Watson came into English class with some news. "Jamie's condition has improved to the point where the doctors are going to wake him up within the next few days. They don't know what state he will be in when he's conscious again, so you should still leave it a while before you visit."

For a short time this news lifted the mood of the class. Nick himself remained strangely unmoved. The unspoken words—brain damage—were too much of a barb in his flesh for him to feel glad.

They wake Jamie up and his speech is slurred. Doesn't recognize me. Doesn't talk anymore. Never cracks another joke.

Nick rubbed his face with both his hands until it felt hot. That just wasn't going to happen. Full stop.

In the afternoon he sat at home and stared at his cell. Victor had said he would send a text, Emily too. Why hadn't he heard from anyone? Too bad that they weren't meeting this afternoon. It was an eternity till Wednesday.

Tuesday was as gray and joyless as Monday. Nick couldn't rid himself of the feeling that time had stopped flowing; it just stuck together and crumbled into small pieces. That changed abruptly when a text arrived shortly before noon.

SOS! Need ur advice. Come over as quickly as u can. Victor.

As far as Nick was concerned, that was the end of school for the day. Quickly—that meant as soon as possible. He would leave before lunch. Should he let Emily know? He located her in the schoolyard, where she was pressing buttons on her cell. She was alone for once. Nick risked a lightning-fast exchange of information.

"Get a text from Victor too?"

"Yes."

"Do you know what's happened?"

"No."

"I'm going over there. Right now."

"Okay."

"Are you coming later?"

"Don't know yet. Maybe."

Victor opened the door. There was no trace of the customary cheeriness in his face; he didn't even offer Nick tea.

"I'm going to show you something right away and I hope you won't freak out. It's possible that it's a lie, but Speedy and I are at a complete loss."

The three of them sat down in the sofa room, where Nick was immediately overcome by wonderful memories of the weekend. "So what happened?"

"Speedy got some orders. He's supposed to put up posters at your school tonight. At least ten, and they're supposed to be as big as possible."

So far it didn't sound very dramatic. "And?"

"The problem is the words. It's ... well, I don't know. At best it's defamatory. At worst it's a matter for the police."

Speedy handed Nick a folded piece of paper. "That's what I'm supposed to put on the posters. At least I don't have to spray it," he added with a forced smile.

Nick unfolded the note. Read, without understanding. Read again.

"Do you think it's true?" Victor asked.

No. Or was it? Probably. It added up. Nick stared at the paper, full of helpless rage.

Brynne Farnham tampered with the brakes on Jamie Cox's bike.

"If that's put up around your school, this Brynne Farnham is history, whether she did it or not," Victor said. "Speedy and I have spent hours discussing what we should do. If the posters don't appear, he's definitely going to get kicked out of the game, right?"

Nick felt numb; his lips were numb too, and barely capable of forming a "yes." Brynne. That's why she'd been so distraught. That's why she had bailed out. He wished he hadn't found out. He wished Emily were here, and that he didn't have to decide this by himself.

"I'll get in touch with Brynne. It's just that she's still in school." Nick got his cell out and typed a text: *Ring me, it's urgent.*

"She'll contact me as soon as she can, I'd say. Can I have some tea in the meantime?"

Victor darted into the kitchen.

"By the way, I've already signed Kate on as a novice," Speedy told him. "She's doing well. She's a dark elf, like you used to be."

Nick just smiled, and even that was an effort. He wasn't capable of conversation right now. The thoughts were turning over in his head so fast he could hardly follow them. If it had been Brynne, then she deserved the poster campaign, most definitely. Except she already looked as though she was about to crack. The school was seven stories high, and suddenly Nick could imagine Brynne jumping ...

If Speedy didn't carry out his orders, he was done. There were huge numbers of witnesses in Nick's school, and not a single one would report seeing any posters. Quox or Brynne. Brynne or Quox. Nick propped his head in his hands. Why wasn't Emily there? He didn't want to take sole responsibility for what would happen to Brynne. He felt sorry for her—and yet he hated her the instant he thought of Jamie. So how could he make a good decision?

Victor came back with a tray full of assorted cups and a steaming teapot. "Yesterday was a most instructive day. We were camped in the shade of a temple, and heaps of gnomes were harping on about how we should be on our guard because we were right near Ortolan's fortress. Then suddenly every creature imaginable leapt out of the bushes and pounced on us—orcs, zombies, giants, the whole deal. Some of us took a lot of damage." He poured tea into the cups; the fragrance spread around the room. "I get the impression that things are drawing to a close. But I still can't make sense of them. It's enough to make you weep. Tomorrow I'll try—"

Nick's cell rang. He took a deep breath. It was Brynne.

"Hi, Nick! Have you changed your mind?"

"No." How come he had so much saliva in his mouth all of a sudden? "Where are you now?"

"In the park opposite the school."

"Alone?"

"Yes."

"I've found out something that I have to talk to you about."

"Ah. Okay." Could she hear the impending disaster in his voice? Or was she really completely oblivious?

"It's about Jamie. I know now that his accident was not an accident. Someone tampered with his bike. Tell me, Brynne, was it you?"

There was a long pause. Nick could hear Brynne breathing. "What?" she finally whispered. "Why ... why would it be me?"

"Just answer yes or no."

"No! Where did you get that idea from? I ... no." Her voice faltered, and Nick could feel the rage rising in him, hot and unstoppable.

"You're lying. I can hear that you're lying!"

"No! How would you know that anyway? You just want to destroy me, and I haven't even done anything to you!"

Nick exchanged a look with Victor, who looked like a troubled teddy bear. "On the contrary. I want to warn you. It's quite possible that tomorrow morning there'll be posters all over the school for everybody to read, saying that you were the one who sabotaged Jamie's brakes. And that his accident was caused by that."

"What?" Now she was sobbing, although Nick could hear how much she was trying to get herself under control. "B-u-u-t that isn't tr-rue."

"Yes, it is," he said, and was himself astonished at how sure of it he suddenly was. "Go on. Say it. Everyone will know by the morning anyway."

"No! It wasn't me! Where ... why would you say such a thing?" The panic in her voice was as thick as syrup.

"The game says it, and who could possibly know better? It wants everyone to find out." So much for the triumph, Nick thought. The satisfaction of having collared the person responsible for Jamie's condition. He didn't feel anything of the sort—just pity and a bit of disgust.

"But I didn't mean that to happen!" Now she was screaming. "I only meant him to fall flat on his face, sprain a wrist at the most— nothing more! Not ..."

Nick suspected that she was seeing the same image in her head as he was: Jamie lying in a sea of blood, limbs twisted.

"He went down the road at such a rate—I even shouted after him, but he didn't hear me, he just kept speeding up ..."

That's my part in the catastrophe, Nick thought.

"Why did you do it?" he asked hoarsely.

"Why do you think? Because the messenger wanted me to. He described the bike and how to disconnect the brakes. He even had instructions with pictures." She gave a short laugh. "You can't imagine how often I've wished that I could make it all undone. I'm afraid all the time, day and night. I always dream that he dies. And then he comes to visit me." She laughed again, a high, uncontrollable little-girl laugh that gave Nick goose bumps.

He looked at Speedy and Victor. "Listen," he said. "Perhaps I can stop the business with the posters."

Speedy nodded. "Sure," he whispered. "Quox can have a nice spot in the graveyard. A real hero will gladly sacrifice himself for a lady."

"So." Nick rubbed his forehead. "Pay close attention to me, okay? You're going to come clean about this. To the police, or to Mr. Watson, whoever you like. But above all to Jamie, as soon as he's awake again. I think things won't be so bad for you then."

Brynne said nothing for a long time, and when her answer came it was barely audible. "I don't know if I can do that. I have to think about it."

"One thing's for sure—I'm going to tell Jamie what happened." *If his brain is sufficiently intact to understand me.*

"Yes. Of course." Now she almost sounded sensible again. "I can see some people coming, Rashid and Alex, I think. I'd better stop talking now. Nick?"

"Yes?"

"I didn't want any of this to happen. When I gave you the game, I just wanted to make you happy."

"I know."

"Can you just tell me who you were? As a player, that is?"

"What for?"

"Just because. I've often wondered."

"Sarius."

"Really? I wouldn't have thought of him." She gave another short sob. "I was Arwen's Child."

Two hours later Emily arrived. She looked tired, but smiled when Nick put his arm around her. He told her all the news about Brynne and was glad she approved of how he'd handled it.

"Of course, it's possible that someone else will be given the poster job," she observed. "But at least she's gained some time. Perhaps she really will be smart and go to the police. Why does the game want to get back at her anyway?"

"She decided to fight *Erebos* and went around telling everyone about it at school yesterday."

"Oh dear. Bad timing. It looks as though something's brewing. A few people are constantly going on about the great goal, and how it's close. Alex for example. Whereas Colin is acting extra secretive. I'm finding life quite stressful at the moment."

Nick, on the other hand, was finding it much nicer again since Emily was there. They spent another hour watching Victor play before they said their good-byes.

"Say farewell to Quox," Speedy sighed. "He is destined to meet an early death. A terrible shame—he was such a good boy."

"Are we here again tomorrow?" Nick checked on the way out the door.

"As soon as you have completed your school work. Uncle Victor doesn't want to be responsible for you ending up cleaning toilets."

TWENTY-NINE

No posters the next day, and no Brynne either. It wasn't hard to understand why she preferred to stay home. She wouldn't do anything stupid, would she? Nick thought about ringing her, but decided to saddle Mr. Watson with the job instead. He spoke to him at recess.

"Brynne Farnham has been having some difficulties recently. I just wanted to let you know—perhaps you could talk to her."

"You don't say." Watson's face was serious, with a hint of reproach, as if he knew that Nick had told only part of the truth. "Brynne's mother rang this morning and excused her for this week and the whole of next week. She's in a very fragile state mentally. Apparently she's thinking of changing schools."

That's another option of course, Nick thought. Running away. He wondered whether she'd told her mother the real reason.

Emily seemed to be a bit chaotic today, and even more tired than yesterday. She avoided Nick's questioning looks, but a bit later he found a text on his cell. *Played till 3 am, received unbearable orders. I'll b kicked out soon, I'm afraid. Looking forward 2 seeing u! Bye. Emily.*

Nick read those five words at least twenty times. She was looking forward to seeing him.

He tried hard not to run around with a blissful smile for the rest of the day, but he felt lighthearted, so lighthearted. Soon it would be the afternoon, which meant the prospect of tea at Victor's, maybe with a few new theories, and definitely with Emily. Sometimes life was just perfect.

The last class was hardly over before Nick was running to the Tube station. He would shorten his detour a little today, maybe go two stations in the wrong direction, three at the most, then change and somehow return via the city to King's Cross.

Everything went like clockwork and no one was behind him—he made very sure of that. He was lucky with the connections too—hardly had to wait when he changed trains.

Soon, he thought, as he stood in the crush on the platform at Oxford Circus and heard the train approaching. I'll be there soon. Only three stations away from Emily and from Victor's collection of teacu—

The shove was violent, and came from behind. For a moment Nick didn't understand what was happening; he just saw the round Underground logo on the opposite wall coming toward him, heard the screams of people around him, felt the ground vanish from under his feet. Then, in slow motion, he saw his foot miss the edge of the platform, saw the tracks. Realized that he was going to fall onto the rails. Heard the train, tried to regain his balance, clutched at thin air. Lights were shining out of the dark of the tunnel. People were screaming.

Soon. Nick's earlier thought echoed in his head with a dreadful new meaning.

Then something tore at him. The train? No, a hand. Pulled him backward, flung him onto the ground while the train thundered into the station.

People all around him, lots and lots of voices.

"He was pushed!"

"No, I would've seen it."

"That's what comes of everyone shoving."

"No, it was on purpose! The bloke ran away."

Nick struggled to his feet. A tall man in blue overalls helped him.

"My god, that was close," the man gasped. "I could already see you going under the train."

Nick didn't get a word out. He swayed, and the man propped him up. Nick held onto his sleeve with both hands, took in splashes of white paint on blue fabric.

The train left again; most of the people had gotten in. Then a policeman in a yellow safety vest turned up and asked questions. Nick struggled to regain his voice. Yes, he thought he'd been pushed. No, he hadn't seen who'd done it. Yes, the man in the work clothes had saved him. No, he didn't need any medical attention.

The policeman noted everything down, including the name and address of the witnesses—one of whom claimed to have seen a youth with a hood pulled down over his face running away—and promised to get in touch if the surveillance cameras on the platform yielded any useful pictures.

Nick got into the train after the next. He could barely feel his legs, put one foot carefully in front of the other. *Just don't think about it. Think about it later. For now, just breathe in and out.* Nick fixed his eyes on the route map that was hanging on the wall of the car, diagonally opposite. He was grateful for any distraction. The familiar picture was comforting; it reminded him of the guessing game he used to play on every train trip with his dad. Central Line? Red. Circle Line? Yellow. Piccadilly Line? Dark blue. Victoria Line? Light blue. Hammersmith & City? Pink.

He could feel his heartbeat calming and his breathing getting deeper. He wasn't dead. He wasn't lying in a coma. He'd think about the rest later on.

※ ※ ※

"Someone tried to *what?*" Victor had dragged Nick into the sofa room. His mustache was quivering, and Nick almost had to laugh.

"Nothing serious happened." He looked at Emily's chalk-white face. "But I still feel a bit dizzy. Can I have something to drink? Something cold?"

Victor ran into the kitchen, where he dropped something that shattered with a loud crash. Then came sounds of cursing, banging around, and sweeping.

"We should have traveled here together," Emily said. She sat down right next to Nick and put her arms around him.

"No. Then your cover would have been blown. I'm glad they haven't got you in their sights."

"My cover is going to be blown soon enough anyway. I'm certainly not going to carry out my next orders."

"What are they?"

"I don't want to talk about it right now; I'm still too shocked about what you told me."

Victor came back with a giant glass of iced tea.

"Did you see who it was?" he asked.

"No. And I don't see how I can possibly know him. I was on my guard the whole time and looking around for our people."

They sat there for a time without speaking. Nick saw how agitated Victor was, and would have liked to reassure him. *It's okay, nothing's going to happen to me.* But could he still make that statement with a clear conscience?

To take everyone's minds off things he asked after the absent Speedy.

"He's fine. He's just waiting for Kate to need a novice, and then he'll be in again. With a false name, of course." Victor pointed toward the computer room with a beringed index finger. "I've got six false Internet identities; Speedy can have one of them. That should work; my virtual selves even have official addresses." He raised his eyebrows. "And by the way, Nick, you can have one of them too if you want to. You could play again; you just need to wait until Speedy II signs someone up ..."

Did he want to do that? Nick asked his inner voice. The answer was a clear "no." It didn't appeal to him anymore. The opposite, in fact. He was glad he was only an outside observer now. "It's okay, thanks Victor. Maybe not. But I would like to know whether there's any news. How's the game going at the moment?"

"Hectic. I've got the feeling that things are coming to a head. Last night there was a battle against earth monsters that were shooting heads out of cannons; loads of people came off really badly. That always means heaps of new orders."

"Like mine," Emily added. "But I wasn't there for the cannon business; I was defending an embankment against river spirits."

Earth monsters, river spirits. Heads coming out of cannons. Cannons. Nick felt a pressure in his temples, a tickle in his head. There was something, some niggling thing he kept on overlooking. Just recently he'd been so close to getting it, he was sure, and today as well somehow, in a different way.

"Could you keep playing for a little while?" he asked Victor. "I'd like to watch."

"There's no such thing as a little while with *Erebos*," Victor snorted. "If I get started, I'll be stuck for a couple of hours, you know that. And it'll be good-bye cosy chat with tea and biscuits." He started to beam. "Of course, you could always feed me! That would be heaven on earth: playing and being fed at the same time!"

They decided to give Victor a taste of heaven, and laid on

peanuts, biscuits, gummi bears, and the big teapot, while Victor "woke" Squamato, as he put it.

The lizard man was alone, standing in the middle of a flat meadow where the grass looked withered. There wasn't another fighter to be seen.

Quiet music was coming out of Victor's headphones. Nick listened intently; the melody was not the same one he knew from his time as Sarius. Odd.

Now Squamato was heading toward a hedge; that was definitely a good idea. If you found a hedge and followed it, it always led into interesting territory—a similar thing happened with rivers. This hedge seemed familiar to Nick—Sarius had walked alongside it too, not all that long ago. At night. The funnel-shaped yellow flowers had glowed, and they'd only grown on one side of the hedge. Just like here. Nick frowned.

"Gummi bears, please!" Victor interrupted his thoughts, opening his mouth wide so Emily could stuff a bunch of them in.

Squamato continued on. Up ahead there was something big and white that was moving, writhing ...

"I've been here too," Nick cried out. "It's a statue—three men being strangled by snakes. Pretty famous."

That earned him a narrow-eyed look from Victor. "The Laocoön group, my friend. Also from ancient Greece. Very apt, by the way."

There were warriors standing all around the statue this time. Nick recognized BloodWork with his glowing red circle around his neck, and Nurax was not far off.

"I suspect that this is a warning," Victor said. "Laocoön was the one who didn't want to let the wooden horse into Troy. You do know the story, I hope," he added, giving Nick a sideways glance. "Poseidon subsequently sent sea snakes, which not only finished off

Laocoön, but his sons as well. The game has a lot in common with a Trojan horse, I feel."

Nick pulled a face, and Emily passed Victor a handful of nuts to interrupt his flow of words.

The messenger had said something to Nick before he sent him to this location. He'd been amused; his yellow eyes had glowed more brightly than usual—was it the allusion to Troy that he had found so entertaining?

Nick scrutinized the Laocoön group once more. The men's contorted faces, their desperate attempts to shake off the snakes ... the hedge behind, green and yellow, the flowers planted straighter than any real gardener could ever manage. Nick pictured the chuckling messenger again.

"If you follow the hedge westward, you will come upon a statue, a monument no less."

For a moment everything went black before Nick's eyes. Was it ... was it possible ... Monument ...

"I've got it!" Nick shouted. His voice wobbled, and, as he leapt up, so did his chair. "I've got it now. I've got it."

Victor looked at him wide-eyed and took the headset off. "What? What do you know?"

"The code! I know where we are! It's ... take a look ... yellow and green and the Monument!"

Emily and Victor exchanged looks of incomprehension.

"What do you mean, exactly?" Emily asked gently.

"I know where we are. I've figured out the code. Green and yellow and red and blue."

They still didn't get it.

"The colors represent the lines on the London Underground. This is Monument station here, where the Circle and District line trains run. Yellow and green. Like the hedge. Got it?"

Victor's stunned gaze swung back and forth between the screen and Nick's face. "Yes indeed," he whispered. "Of course. Damn it all." He reached his hand out to Nick in a solemn gesture. "I take back all those things I said about your intellectual capacity. You're a true genius!"

Victor suffered like a dog in the minutes that followed, because while Emily and Nick were searching every drawer for a map of the Underground, he still had to take care of Squamato.

"Ooh, not a battle now, please! Do you think I could just get out quickly? Nothing's going on at the moment, absolutely nothing. But if a gnome goes and sends me into the next battle, I'll be caught for two hours. Oh, what the heck. The messenger can go jump." He clicked a couple of times and leapt up.

Emily had struck gold in the meantime. She spread the map out on one of the little tables in the sofa room. "You're right," she said breathlessly, and reached for Nick's hand. "The first battle I ever had was on a red river with ruined windmills around it. At first I thought of Don Quixote. But that was nonsense. It's Holland Park, on the Central line." She placed her finger on the corresponding spot on the map and kept on searching.

The red river. Nick recalled his underground odyssey, and the fact that the river had finally led him to the White City.

"White City," he said. "After that I followed the pink hedge—in other words the Hammersmith & City line. There, the first station: Shepherd's Bush Market." He looked up. "You've never seen such revolting-looking sheep. There wasn't much left of the shepherds." He traced further with his finger. "Goldhawk Road. The golden hawk nearly did me in."

"The pink hedge," Emily yelled. "I was there too! That's where there was the giant tree with the crown in it." She tapped the map. "Royal Oak. This is just crazy."

Victor hadn't said anything yet, but he was literally vibrating with nervous tension. "Yesterday," he began, "and the previous days as well, they kept announcing to us that we were near Ortolan's fortress—where the deciding battle is going to take place." His index finger traced around the Circle and District lines. "Temple," he said. "The gnome was most agitated near the temple. Today we started at Monument—ah yes, just look at that. Cannon Street is right next to it. But why on earth they shot heads out of the cannons I don't understand."

The three of them studied the multicolored route map.

Knightsbridge, Nick thought. It was my downfall, literally. Giant knights who push you off the bridge—why didn't that occur to me?

"So Ortolan's fortress is located somewhere near Temple," he said, thinking out loud. "In the middle of the City of London."

"It's obviously not a fortress in the usual sense," Emily said. "Anybody got an idea how we're supposed to find it?"

The problem occupied Nick throughout the following night. There were three of them—how were they supposed to check the neighborhoods around four or five Tube stations? What were they even supposed to look for? And if Victor was right, they were nearly out of time.

THIRTY

Early the next morning, a helpful text arrived from Victor: *The gnomes r babbling about Ortolan & his dark brothers. Maybe we weren't so wrong about Blackfriars station.*

He'd also informed Emily. "What is there in Blackfriars that's so special?" she wrote to Nick.

But there wasn't anything, apart from the Blackfriars Bridge, the theater, and the big station—would that pass for a fortress? Apart from that—office buildings, restaurants and ... that parking garage where Nick had taken photos! That had been near Blackfriars station. Maybe it was a coincidence—but maybe not.

Nick quickly ran through the available options in his head. The parking garage and the Jaguar were his only clues. It was only half past seven. If he kept watch in front of the garage for the whole day ...

You're out of your mind.

The stupid thing was that he couldn't think of anything better. He sent Emily a text saying he wasn't coming to school today, and put his things in his backpack.

When he arrived at the parking garage it was quarter past eight. The place was totally unsuited to waiting around. Not a corner or a recess in sight where Nick could hide. So he walked up and down, trying to look as inconspicuous as possible while keeping an eye on the cars. The garage was obviously popular with the office workers nearby.

Car after car passed through the yellow-and-black striped barrier. But there was no Jaguar among them.

It's no wonder, Dunmore, Nick berated himself. It was a really dumb idea. Just because the man parked here once doesn't mean he's going to do it again.

And yet, at the time the messenger had said that Nick was to come here as often as necessary until he had the photos—and the messenger knew what he was talking about.

Back to walking up and down the street. A Ford, a Toyota, a Suzuki, another Toyota. A VW Golf. Nick noticed that his attention was drifting. He pulled himself together. *Don't let your thoughts wander.* A Mercedes was coming. A Honda, another Honda.

Half an hour later, Nick was getting worn down. His intention of sticking it out for the whole day no longer seemed achievable. Besides, he was getting cold; he cursed himself for not taking a thicker jacket. He'd stick it out for an hour, he owed this business that much ...

A silver-gray Jaguar stopped at the barrier. Was it the right one? Nick screwed up his eyes. LP60 HNR. That was the number. The barrier opened, and the Jaguar swept forward.

Victor is right—I'm a genius, a genius!

Now he just had to be careful not to miss the Jaguar's owner when he came out of the garage. Where was the pedestrian exit? He could find the car exit, but ...

Nick began to run. People were coming out over there, was that the right spot? Was there more than one exit?

He stopped, turned around once more, and then saw him. It was undoubtedly the man he'd photographed, and he was walking in the direction of New Bridge Street. Good, now Nick just had to make sure he didn't get shaken off. He followed him at a bit of a distance, hardly daring to blink for fear of losing sight of him.

They walked down New Bridge Street. Had the man noticed he was being followed? He appeared to be nervous; every few steps he looked back over his shoulder or hurriedly to the side. Like someone who was afraid. Nick increased the distance between them, although it made his gut hurt. He couldn't allow anything to hold him up, not even the Japanese tourist couple who smilingly asked him the way to St. Paul's Cathedral. Nick pointed wordlessly in the direction he thought was correct and kept walking.

They reached Bridewell Place, where the man entered an office building that was being renovated. Scaffolding was blocking most of the front windows and the white facade from view. Nick stopped, undecided. His first instinct was to go in as well, but he didn't want to attract attention, not for anything, so he just watched his target greeting the doorman and walking over to one of the gleaming brass elevators.

That meant his office must be in one of the upper floors. Of course—expensive car, expensive suit, expensive office. Nick immediately rejected the idea of questioning the doorman. But there were company nameplates mounted in front of the entrance; perhaps they'd be helpful.

Management consultants, an estate agency. Judging by the man's appearance, either was possible. A pharmaceutical company, and also a ... Nick caught his breath. He'd hit the jackpot with the fourth company:

Soft Suspense
Games for PCs, cells, and consoles.
Never outdone on the fun.

Just to be sure Nick took a picture of the nameplate with his phone. Should he let Emily know? No, she was still in school. Victor! He would tell Victor about it. But Victor wasn't answering. Damn. Well, then Nick would just go over there.

He set off for the Tube station, and it was probably only thanks to the fact that his senses had been sharpened by the preceding chase that he immediately noticed Rashid on the other side of the street.

Had he noticed Nick too? Didn't look like it; Rashid was shuffling along the street with his head down, as always, looking neither right nor left. He was carrying some sort of gray-green pouch close to his chest; Nick was dying to know what it contained.

Naturally Rashid was heading for the office building. Nick ducked into the shadow of an entrance. Rashid stopped, looked up at the facade, and got a camera out of his pants pocket. He was taking photos of the building—from close up, from farther away, from different angles.

Nick had photographed the man's car, and now Rashid was photographing his office. Presumably he wanted to get some shots from the side as well, because he turned left, with the camera still at the ready.

Nick waited for him to appear again, but nothing happened. Nick peered uneasily out of his entrance. If he followed Rashid he might possibly run straight into him. He didn't want to risk it. He waited another five minutes, told himself he was an idiot, and left. Even if Rashid had got away from him, his results from this morning were quite respectable.

"I hope you've got a good reason for dragging me out of bed in the middle of the night." Victor was standing at the door in his Snoopy dressing gown, yawning, with eyes that were only half open.

"I'll make you some tea," Nick said, "and then we'll talk."

376

"You sound like my ex-girlfriend." Victor wandered blearily into the kitchen and leaned against the fridge. "Incidentally, I fought until half past four this morning, around the temple. I've got golden armor now, which goes really nicely with my violet lizard skin."

Nick turned on the electric kettle and put tea leaves in a strainer. "Does the name Soft Suspense mean anything to you?"

"Sure," Victor yawned. "Never outdone on the fun. They did *The Damned of the Night, First Shot,* and *Peregrine,* among other things. Quite good games, all of them."

"They have their offices near Blackfriars. In Bridewell Place."

"Aha." Victor frowned. "Sorry, but I'm not sure what you're getting at."

Nick told him about his photography assignment, about the Jaguar and the man it belonged to. "That was the only thing during my whole time as a player that had anything to do with Blackfriars. That's why I went there this morning and waited in front of the parking garage. The man turned up, I followed him, and you can guess where he was headed."

"The Soft Suspense office." Victor's frown deepened. "The penny still hasn't dropped for me. I'm certain that Soft Suspense didn't develop *Erebos.* I would have heard about it; there would have been reports in the media ages ago. The gaming world would have been licking their lips waiting for it."

"What else do you know about the company?"

"Nothing, really. I just know their games. And I know that they swallowed a few smaller software development companies, which is pretty typical in the industry. Their business is doing well. That's all."

Nick poured the boiling water over the tea leaves thoughtfully, breathing in the aroma that wafted up.

"There must be some connection between the company and

Erebos. One of my classmates was at Bridewell Place as well, taking photos of the building."

"Really? Was he following the Jaguar guy too?" Victor gave his head a good hard shake. "It's really got me stumped. My brain isn't working yet. It needs more sleep."

"But now we've finally got a lead. I have to find out who the man is."

"Yes, that would be good," Victor murmured and closed his eyes.

For the time being Nick abandoned the idea of teasing sensible statements out of him. He carted him to one of the sofas, poured tea into him, and scraped together his last remaining coins to go buy breakfast for them both.

While he was waiting in the lineup at the bakery he couldn't resist sending Emily a text. *Got amazing news. @ Cromer St, wish u were here.*

When he got back a pale but very alert Victor was waiting for him. "I can't eat anything right now."

"Why?"

"While you were at the shops I was Googling. You're not going to believe this."

He waited until Nick had put down his croissants and dragged him to the laptop. "There. Take a look at that."

The Soft Suspense website was open; a new game called *Blood of Gods* was advertised on their home page. The gods didn't look Greek, though; they looked more metallic. Nothing about the graphics resembled *Erebos.*

"And?"

Victor put a hand on Nick's shoulder. "That's only the home page. You need to go to the news items."

Nick clicked on "News" and read:

Soft Suspense is delighted with its record sales for *Peregrine*. The game sold over 600,000 copies in the first month after its release.

Below that was a photo of the Jaguar driver posing in a leather office chair and smiling into the camera. Yesss! Nick thought. My lead was right. Then he saw the photo caption. He exchanged a look with Victor.

"No, can't be."

"Yes, it is. You've struck gold. Aladdin's treasure. Damn it, Nick, we have to warn him."

"Yes. You're right." Nick studied the smiling face in the photo, but his eyes kept returning to the words underneath the picture.

"We have put all our resources and creativity into *Peregrine* and are delighted that our game has been so well received," said the managing director of Soft Suspense, Andrew Ortolan.

A bird. Yeah, right. "We should have done more research," Nick muttered. "Then we would have found him a lot earlier."

"Or maybe not. There are loads of people with that name. Well, okay, not loads, but a few."

Andrew Ortolan smiled impassively out of his photo.

Had *Erebos* really only been created in order to ... destroy him, as the messenger had said? Why? How should they warn him? And above all, about what, exactly?

"I'll do it," Victor said, and dialed the number that he'd found on the company's home page.

"Yes? Hello? I'd like to speak to Mr. Ortolan please. Yes, please put me through."

Pause.

"My name is Victor Lansky," Victor said, obviously to somebody else. "No, he's not expecting my call."

Nick didn't catch what the secretary said, but he heard her high, disapproving voice.

"As you wish," Victor persevered. "I'm from the press, and there is something important I need to tell Mr. Ortolan."

Another shrill, rapid, secretary-type answer.

"Please listen to me," Victor said with deliberate patience. "I'm sure your boss will want to hear what I have to say. No, there's no message. Sorry? Lansky. L-A-N-S-K-Y. Yes, he can ring me back. And he should hurry up about it!"

He hung up and snorted. "Of course he won't ring. The cow in reception didn't even ask my number."

"Perhaps she saw it on the display?"

"Hardly." Victor fished a chocolate croissant out of the bag. "Private number. Nothing shows up."

Nick thought for a moment and pressed the redial button.

"Good morning, I would like to speak to Mr. Ortolan."

"I'll put you through to his executive secretary."

There was the sound of saxophone music until someone answered again at the other end.

"Andrew Ortolan's office, Anne Wisbourn speaking." It was the unpleasant voice from a moment ago.

"Er, hello. My name is Nick Dunmore and I need to speak to Mr. Ortolan. Urgently. It's a matter of life and death."

"Pardon?"

"Life and death! I'm serious!" Nick's mouth was dry with nerves. How was he going to be able to explain the situation to Ortolan without him deciding he was loony?

Rustling was coming from the receiver, Nick heard muffled voices—the secretary presumably had her hand over the receiver. Then there was a noise as if something had snapped, the noises became clear again, and a man bellowed into the phone:

"I'll get these calls traced! This is telephone terrorism! I'll find out what you criminals are up to, and then they'll put you behind bars! That was my last warning, understand?" Crash. The receiver was hung up.

Nick's heart was hammering as if he'd run a hundred-meter dash.

"He thought I was threatening him."

"So I heard. He was certainly loud enough."

It wasn't hard to add two and two together. "I bet he's had a few scary phone calls of late."

"Yes, from Emily, for example," Victor said.

Not much was said during their shared breakfast. Each of them dwelled on his own thoughts. Nick's revolved around the options that were left to him. He could go to Blackfriars again and hammer on Ortolan's office door until he listened to him.

But you don't know why Erebos *hates him so much. There must be a reason.*

"Victor? You know the computer scene well, huh?"

"Absolutely."

"Can you explain it? In some way that would make sense?"

"Not at all. I'm completely in the dark. I think we need to find out more about Mr. Ortolan."

When Emily arrived, earlier than expected, they still hadn't got any further. They knew that Ortolan was a member of the Wimbledon Park Golf Club, that he sometimes organized charity dinners for UNICEF, and rarely gave interviews.

Emily, who was still completely fired up by the discovery of Ortolan's true identity, approached the search with fresh vigor. "Perhaps it's not personal. Perhaps it doesn't have anything to do with the man, but with the company instead." She turned the laptop around to face her and entered "Soft Suspense" in Google.

"It will be a wild goose chase," Victor prophesied. "By the time you've churned through all the game reviews and eBay auctions, it'll be Christmas."

"You're right." Emily narrowed her eyes to slits. She submitted "Ortolan enemies" and found a whole lot of information about Peregrine falcons that ate songbirds. "Damn … Okay then, we'll try something else."

The search terms "Soft Suspense" and "victim" mainly got game descriptions for *Peregrine*, the company name together with "competition" got various bits of economic data about the computer game industry.

Emily swore in an unladylike fashion. "It's all double Dutch to me. If it's a competitor who's doing this to get rid of Soft Suspense, we'll never figure it out." She brooded over the list of different games companies. "Perhaps the company did something wrong," she said, and did a new search: "Crime Soft Suspense."

This time the list of results wasn't long—only four pages. The first links were about the fact that bootleg copies were a crime and that Soft Suspense had recently improved copy protection on its games. Emily kept on scrolling and clicking. She paused at a court report that was two years old.

> … was found guilty of fraud and theft and sentenced to six years' imprisonment. The game, which apparently incorporates revolutionary new technology, is produced by the company Soft Suspense, which …

Emily clicked on the link. It was an archived story from the *Independent*. Nick and Emily only had to read the first lines to know that they needn't look any further. It was right here on the screen in black and white, and worse than Nick could ever have imagined.

Games developer sentenced

After two years the court case over copyright ownership of the *Elysium* computer game has finally ended in a judgment. Larry McVay, owner and managing director of London software development company Vay too far, was found guilty of fraud and theft and sentenced to six years' imprisonment. The game, which apparently incorporates revolutionary new technology, is produced by the company Soft Suspense, whose managing director Andrew Ortolan welcomed the judgment. "The game represents years of work and millions of pounds," said Ortolan. "That's not something you can simply allow someone to steal from you."

McVay had maintained since the beginning of the case that it was he who had programmed *Elysium*, and that it had been stolen from him by Soft Suspense. However, he was never able to produce the appropriate evidence to support his claim. He explained this with allegations of theft, bribery, and tampering by Soft Suspense. Managing Director Ortolan denied all allegations. "We are an utterly respectable company, not a criminal organization, and are happy that this has been recognized. This is simply someone trying to turn the tables on us without having a scrap of proof." McVay announced that he intended to exhaust all legal avenues, and that he "was not going to give up."

Nick opened his mouth, but not a single word came out. He looked at Emily, who was pale, her lips pressed tightly together.

Victor, on the other hand, clapped his hands. "Well, well! Emily, you have an excellent nose—like Sherlock Holmes and Philip Marlowe rolled into one. Fantastic."

Nick's thoughts were in chaos. Could he be sure Larry McVay was Adrian's father? The surname wasn't common. He simply couldn't believe it was a coincidence.

"What is it?" Victor asked in astonishment. "You're not saying anything. And we've made a giant step forward. This Larry McVay could be a piece of the puzzle. At any rate, he lost a court case against Ortolan. He's bound to be mad at him. Perhaps he knows something about *Erebos*. We should talk to him."

Nick struggled to regain his voice. "That's not going to be possible. He killed himself."

They filled in Victor, telling him about Adrian and his strange behavior over the last few weeks.

"He was constantly asking what the story was with the DVDs, and then, later, when he knew that it was a game, he practically begged me to stop." Nick still didn't understand why. The game at the center of the court case hadn't been called *Erebos*, it had been called *Elysium*. "Joy, Thou beauteous spark divine, Daughter of Elysium," Nick recalled grimly.

Victor grabbed the laptop and read the article through again. "I think I remember the case now. The interesting thing about it was that neither party wanted to explain exactly what was so extraordinary about the game. They both just held their ground, like dogs fighting over a bone. But the game still hasn't been released."

While Victor immersed himself further in his reading, Nick and Emily discussed what else they could do.

"We have to talk to Adrian." Emily gave a deep sigh. "He's an unbelievably nice guy. We had quite a long talk recently; he's really mature for his age, and he made a few very intelligent remarks."

"Let's talk to him," Nick agreed. He was just remembering what Adrian had said to him a while ago: that he wasn't allowed to take the DVD but needed to know what was on it. In some remote corner of Nick's brain that suddenly made sense, but he couldn't say how. He would be completely open with Adrian. Tell him everything he wanted to know, and in return ...

"No!" Victor's shout made Nick and Emily both turn around. "Shit, people. This is just getting creepy."

"What is?"

"Programmer commits suicide," Victor read out. "On the evening of September 13, L. McVay, the proprietor of a software company, was found hanged in the attic of his house in north London. According to preliminary investigations, the police are ruling out outside involvement. All indications are that McVay took his own life. The reason attributed is the judgment in a fraud trial three weeks previously, in which McVay was sentenced to serve a six-year prison term. He had been released on bail, and had announced that he would lodge an appeal."

"We know that already," Nick said.

Victor threw him a dark look. "And did you know Larry McVay? Did you ever meet him in person?"

"No. Adrian only came to our school after his death."

"I thought so. Then get ready for a surprise." Victor turned the laptop around.

A soft cry escaped Emily and she reached for Nick's hand. "That's ... isn't that ..."

"Yes," Nick whispered. He looked into McVay's face, recognized the eyes, the narrow face, the small mouth. Larry McVay was the dead man.

THIRTY-ONE

Victor turned the laptop off. "Who programmed the guy into the game?" he asked in a faint voice. "Whose macabre idea was that?"

No one answered.

Nick glanced quickly at the clock; it was just after one. Adrian was probably having lunch. After that he would have two or three more classes; there was no point going to school right now.

"We have to talk to him today," Emily said, as if she'd read Nick's thoughts.

"Yes. Let's go to school, maybe we'll catch him between classes. No, that's no good. We can't let anyone notice that we want something from him."

"Why?" Emily put in. "No one's going to become suspicious of me. I'm officially addicted to *Erebos*."

That was true. Now they just needed a place to meet where they could be sure no one would see them together.

"Here!" Victor yelled out.

"Too dangerous. If someone follows us here, your cover is blown, and you're our last connection with the game. You're the only one who can tell us what's going on in *Erebos*," Emily pointed out.

"Hang on. You're still in too!"

"But only theoretically." She smiled and looked at her watch. "In seventeen minutes I'm supposed to go to see Mr. Watson and put him in a compromising situation. But I'm not even remotely considering it, so—good-bye, Hemera."

"Very well," Victor growled. "But it's pretty inconsiderate to rely only on me. What happens if the game asks *me* to seduce this Mr. Watson now? Then I'll have to do it, I suppose, so we don't lose our access?"

They laughed, and it broke the tension.

"Then there's still Kate, but she's not as brilliant as you," Nick said. "You should be back playing right now, by the way. Your lot are so close to Blackfriars that the battle could start any minute. And then we need to know about it, okay?"

Victor stuck out his bottom lip and took himself off to the computer room. "So I don't get to find out what Adrian McVay has to say?"

"Yes, you do. We'll send you a bug-proof carrier pigeon," Emily said with a completely straight face. "Nick, where are we meeting? A café is too dangerous—what about a park? A spot in Hyde Park where we can see the surroundings?"

"No. We could still be seen there." A thought flashed into Nick's head. He wrote an address on a piece of paper for Emily. "We'll be safe there, 100 percent. I'll wait for you both there."

First Becca flung her arms round his neck, then Finn. "Hey kid! What a nice surprise! Do you want a coffee? Are you here about the laptop?"

Nick answered both questions in the negative. "I need a quiet place for a sort of ... meeting. I've asked two friends here. They'll be coming in the next hour. Is that okay?"

Finn put his arm around his shoulders, which wasn't all that easy given that Nick was half a head taller.

"You're so nervous—are you in trouble? Could it be that your meeting is about something not entirely legal?"

"What? No!" Nick shook his head violently. "No. If anything, it's the opposite. It's very complicated, but certainly not illegal."

"Well, in that case ..." Finn took him to one of the three studios. The walls were covered with photos of freshly inked tattoos on every imaginable body part. "Is this okay? I need the bigger studio today, and a few people are booked in with Becca for piercings."

"It's perfect."

"Good. Everything okay with Mom and Dad?"

"Yes, it's all fine."

Finn raised his eyebrows—each of them now sporting six piercings, Nick noted—probably in amazement at his brother's unusually monosyllabic replies. He left, but came back three minutes later with orange juice and cookies. "We don't want anyone accusing the Dunmores of being bad hosts."

"Thank you."

The minutes dragged. Nick tried to distract himself by studying Finn's gallery. A back covered in climbing roses, biceps with an alpine panorama, and a knuckle with dolphins kissing.

Would Emily manage to get Adrian to come along? On the other hand, why wouldn't he want to? He'd been so curious to find out something about the game.

There! The little bells Becca had put over the shop door were ringing now. Customers? Or Emily?

"Hello, we're supposed to meet Nick Dunmore here." Emily.

Finn led her and Adrian in.

Nick couldn't help noticing that Emily studied his brother with great interest. The slightly shorter version.

"Hello." She pressed a kiss on Nick's lips that made him float for a moment. Adrian was standing behind her, smiling. His blond hair was standing up on one side of his head, giving him a puckish appearance.

"The pictures are fantastic," he said, and pointed to the walls. "Perhaps I'll get one done too someday."

Finn beamed. "Then come and see me, and I'll give you a special price. And now I'll leave you to your secret meeting. If anyone needs anything, the kitchen is the second door on the left, and the bathroom's just opposite." With that he left.

Adrian sat down on what Nick called "the treatment chair" and looked at him expectantly. "Emily says you need to discuss something with me? It's about *Erebos*?"

Adrian certainly couldn't be accused of beating around the bush.

"Yes," Nick answered. "First of all, Emily and I aren't part of it anymore. So you don't have anything to fear from us."

"Okay."

Nick was finding it hard to know where to begin. He was about to open an old wound in Adrian and then poke around in it. He pushed a nonexistent strand of hair out of his eyes.

"*Erebos* is somehow connected to your father." He saw Adrian's eyes widen, and mentally slapped himself. *Very sensitive, idiot.*

"How do you know that?" Adrian whispered. "Not from me. I didn't let on to anyone."

Nick and Emily exchanged a look.

"I'm a bit surprised that *you* know," Emily said.

"Of course I know. I just didn't know for ages what it was." He smiled as if he wanted to apologize. "Of course, I thought it was a game. My father programmed virtually nothing else. But I wasn't sure."

Nick didn't understand a word. He needed to start again, from the beginning. "You said to me recently that you weren't allowed to accept any of the DVDs, but that you needed to know what was on them. Why?"

"I wasn't allowed to accept one because Dad had forbidden me."

Again Nick and Emily exchanged a quick look.

"I don't understand," Emily said. "Your father is dead, after all."

"Of course." Now he looked away, studied the toes of his shoes. "Dad wrote to me about it. He wrote down all the details for me."

"What? What did he write down for you?"

Without looking up, Adrian shook his head. "No, you first. I want to know what sort of game *Erebos* is."

Nick heard himself sigh. "It's a fantastic, exciting game. Once you've started, it's almost impossible to stop."

Adrian beamed at the floor. "All Dad's games were like that."

"But are you sure that your father programmed it?" Emily put in.

Now Adrian looked up, and there was mild indignation in his eyes. "Oh, definitely. Otherwise he would never have said that it's his legacy."

"He said that?"

"Wrote it. In the letter. That it's his legacy, and that I should pass it on." Adrian looked from Nick to Emily and back again, and seemed to realize that they couldn't make heads or tails of his explanation.

"Dad died two years ago," he said. "On the second anniversary of his death his solicitor rang me and said he had a letter for me. There was a letter from my father in the envelope, and two DVDs."

Nick's jaw dropped. "You distributed the game at our school?"

"Distributed? Well, I gave one DVD to someone from my class. I gave the other one to a boy I know from earlier who goes to another school. Dad didn't want both DVDs to end up in the same place. And he also wanted me to think carefully about who I gave them to.

Give it to someone whose life seems empty, was what he wrote. And promise me that you won't look at the DVDs. They are a part of my legacy, but it's a part that is not meant for you."

Something inside Nick throbbed painfully. "And you kept to that?"

"Of course," Adrian whispered. "After all, it was the last thing I heard from my father. I hadn't expected to see or read anything more from him ... I was so happy!" He blinked tears away.

And he used you.

"Now it's your turn again. What is the game about?"

To Nick's relief Emily took over the explaining. "At a superficial level it's about a dark world where you need to complete all sorts of tasks and survive threats. But the tasks you need to complete are not limited to the world of the game; they overlap with the real world. For example you have to ... take photos of someone or write an assignment for someone."

Adrian looked ecstatic. "That's *Elysium*, Dad's favorite project. He wanted the players to give each other presents or give each other a hand in other ways—in real life. So they're not just sitting in front of the computer, so friendships can develop. He talked to me about it so often, before ..." Adrian's gaze slid away. "Well, before someone tried to steal it from him. Have you noticed that it's a bit different for every player? For example, the music depends on what sort of mp3 files you've got on your hard drive, or what songs you listen to on YouTube. Once the game's gotten to know you a bit, it knows what sort of quests you enjoy the most, and sends you on them. Dad integrated psychological software that customizes the game just for you." Adrian was really reveling in his memories.

Nick was so furious with Larry McVay that he felt like smashing the furniture to pieces.

"Could it be … so, do you think it's possible that your dad reprogrammed the game? That he added some neat new details? I mean, it's not called *Elysium* anymore. It's called *Erebos*."

"What? Yes, possibly." The glow faded from Adrian's face. "The thing is, someone tried to steal *Elysium* from him. Then there was a court case that dragged on forever … Dad was … well, different the last two years. He didn't talk to me much anymore, so I don't know if he changed something. He worked like crazy, at any rate. In fact, that's all he did; he barricaded himself in his basement, hardly ate, didn't even take the time to wash." He looked at Emily and Nick apologetically. "Mom says he wasn't himself anymore, even at the beginning of the trial. He couldn't cope with the fact that they accused him of theft and fraud. And what's more, we were the ones being burgled. Four times. At the office, at our home—even the cars were broken into."

Adrian's story was starting to add up to Nick, and the answer wasn't pretty. It went like this: Soft Suspense had gotten wind of McVay's new development and tried to get hold of the program. That hadn't worked, or at least not to their satisfaction, so they'd taken McVay to court. And won. Was that possible?

"Listen," he said. "I'm going to explain what the objective is in *Erebos*, is that okay?" Even though he felt Emily's gaze resting on him, he couldn't stop now. "A monster must be killed, and the best, strongest, and most ruthless warriors are sought for the task. They must prevail over anyone who wants to stop *Erebos*, and they must make preparations for the last battle. This last battle is going to take place very soon—and do you know the name of the monster who is to be destroyed in the battle?"

He saw from Adrian's eyes that he suspected, at least.

"Exactly," Nick said. "Its name is Ortolan."

Adrian exhaled audibly. Gave one short laugh. Became serious again. "Really?"

"I swear."

Adrian's face showed a number of emotions at once—satisfaction, grief, and hatred.

"You mean," he said in a raw voice, "that someone is going to kill Ortolan?"

"Possibly. I believe something of the sort will happen."

"I considered doing that myself a couple of times. After Dad changed so much, and ... definitely later." He smiled at the ground again. "After I distributed the DVDs and so many people suddenly changed—I got worried that Dad had made a mistake. A game that destroys the players, you know? At the end he was ... oh, whatever. He'd completely changed. Just like all of you. That's why I was so scared." He looked up now. "But he didn't want to hurt you at all. Only Ortolan."

When Emily spoke, it was very quietly and carefully. "That's not how it's working out, Adrian. The game has made the players do dreadful things. Someone sabotaged the brakes on Jamie's bike."

Adrian's head jerked up. "What?"

"Yes. It wasn't an accident. A whole lot of bad things have happened just so your father's revenge plan won't be jeopardized. Yesterday someone tried to push Nick in front of a Tube train."

Adrian shook his head, his face pale and incredulous.

"If one of the players kills Ortolan, he'll destroy his own life as well," Emily went on. "You must see that. And your father must have seen it too."

Adrian avoided her eyes. "Did the game talk to you? You asked questions and it answered? Or the other way around?"

"Yes," Emily said.

"That was what Ortolan was desperate for. The AI that Dad had developed. Artificial intelligence," he explained in response to Nick's questioning look. "He'd developed a program that could learn like a person. Languages too. Dad said that when it was fully developed and complete he'd get the Nobel Prize for it. He was incredibly proud of it, and he went to great lengths to keep his invention secret."

There it was again, that vulnerable, sensitive quality that Nick had noticed so often about Adrian.

"But one of the accountants in Dad's company accepted a bribe. Ortolan always had his radar tuned to what other people were developing, and from the moment he found out Dad had taken a big step toward creating artificial intelligence, there was no more peace."

Nick was pretty sure that the above-mentioned accountant was now the proud owner of a graffiti-sprayed garage.

"At first Ortolan wanted to buy the idea from Dad, but he said no. He had his own company, and he wanted to release his program himself. That's when the terror tactics started."

Emily stood up from her chair, and sat down next to Adrian. "That's all horrible. So unfair it makes you want to scream. But it doesn't mean someone should be turned into a murderer because of it, does it?"

"No," Adrian whispered. "You're right."

"That's why we're going to try to stop it."

"Okay. Do you need my help?" That sounded pleading, and Nick could understand how Adrian felt. He didn't want to be reduced to being a spectator again.

"Of course," he said. "After all, you're almost the key to this mystery."

While he was waiting for his train, Nick called Victor, who answered after the first ring.

"Finally! What does young McVay say?"

"That Ortolan is a bastard."

"Really? Well, there are a few of them in the industry."

"Apparently. He also said that his father had developed a sort of artificial intelligence and incorporated it into his game. Something completely new that Ortolan wanted to get hold of at any price."

"Oh. That doesn't surprise me. My goodness, that would have made him a gruesomely wealthy man."

Artificial intelligence. When he got home Nick connected Finn's laptop and tried to find out more about it. It seemed that legions of specialists were all busily trying to find a way to teach computers human thinking in all its complexity. Adrian's father had managed it. His software learned, it could read, and it could make use of what it had read. It analyzed the computer user and gave him what he really wanted, deep down inside. Amazing. No wonder none of them had been able to drag themselves away from *Erebos*. The game was a weapon that had developed a life of its own.

Nick read on, found out about the Turing Test, the Loebner Prize, neural and symbolic AI. After two hours his head was aching and he gave up. He wouldn't even be able to understand the basics of what Larry McVay had achieved.

THIRTY-TWO

Victor's text came in the middle of the night. The "alert" tone jolted Nick out of a deep sleep. The screen on his cell was a stark white patch in the pitch-dark room.

He leapt out of bed so quickly that he felt dizzy and had to prop himself up with his hands on the desk.

1 new message.

He pressed Read.

Looks as if Ortolan's in 4 it. They're getting the Inner Circle ready 4 the battle. Torches, oaths, white robes, the whole thing. I think 2day's the day. We r besieging the fortress in the meantime. PS Found a wish crystal just be4 (yellow). If it's all going to b over soon, guess I might as well just stick it on my hat.

Victor had sent the message at 3:48 a.m.; it was now 3:50. Nick crawled back into bed clutching his cell and rang him. "What does that mean, you're besieging the fortress?"

"Hi! Oh, well, we're sort of lounging around in front of it. It's a hulking big white thing that glows in the night, with blood running down it. Yuck."

Nick couldn't answer because of an enormous yawn.

"I woke you up, hmm? Sorry, but I really wanted to keep you up to date. Just in case you ... oops, now they're shooting heads again!"

Nick heard frantic clicking.

"All sorted. As I was saying, you might have wanted to do something right away."

"I don't know—what sort of thing? Has anyone said what the Inner Circle is supposed to do? Got any clues for us?"

"They're supposed to overthrow Ortolan. When they've succeeded, his tower will collapse, and we're all going to be awesomely rewarded, according to the messenger. There are heaps of people here now, sitting around, waiting for the thing to topple, even though the Inner Circle has only just left."

"What I'd really like to do is go to Blackfriars straightaway."

"The Tube's not running yet, and you can forget the night buses. Besides—what are you going to do there? Sorry. I shouldn't have woken you. You'd be better off going back to bed, Nick."

That had to be a joke. But Victor was right; they at least needed the suggestion of a plan. "I'll take the first train and come over to your place and then we can consider what to do."

"All right. I'm already feeling a bit queasy. I think it's really getting serious now."

"If something important happens, let me know."

"Of course. I'll do the night watch, all lonesome and forlorn. Apart from the other three hundred weary souls here, that is."

Nick sat on his bed and stared hypnotically at the hand on his watch. There was still over an hour to go before the first train ran. What happened if the tower collapsed in the meantime?

He couldn't bear sitting down anymore, and began to pace up and down, which made a ridiculously loud noise in the nighttime quiet of the apartment. He mustn't wake anyone up. He was better off going into the kitchen and writing a note saying he'd gone for a run with Colin before school. That was the best he could think of. With any luck his parents would believe it when they got up in two and a half hours.

When he crept out of the flat it was quarter to five. He took his knapsack with him so it wouldn't happen to catch Mom's eye, but he dumped it downstairs near the bikes straightaway. He could do without unnecessary baggage.

The streets were dark and empty, and the gates outside the station were still locked. Nick wrapped his jacket tighter around himself and counted the minutes. What would he do? He could intercept Ortolan and force him to listen. Or he could go to the police: *You see, Constable, it's like this. There's this computer game which clearly tells us that a nasty executive is going to be murdered today.* Oh yes. Terrific idea.

In the middle of these thoughts his phone rang to announce a new message.

Completely certain now. It will happen 2day. Got the appropriate orders. Contact me!

He rang Victor immediately.

"If someone asks me, I'm supposed to say I was having breakfast with a certain Colin Harris. Today, between eight and ten."

Nick didn't get it straightaway. "Why should you have breakfast with Colin?"

"Because I'm supposed to be giving him an alibi. Provided, of course, that they don't catch him in the act. Do you know this Colin Harris?"

"I certainly do."

"Okay, whatever. Listen Nick, all this is making me pretty bloody nervous."

"I'm already on my way to your place. What does the tower look like? Is it still standing?"

"Yep. Still standing, still shining and bleeding."

When the gate to the station finally opened, Nick ran down the steps as if the messenger himself was chasing him.

No detour this time, straight to King's Cross. In less than twenty minutes he was ringing Victor's doorbell.

"Here, you have a look," Victor said.

There was the tower, gigantic and pallid white in the darkness. Blood was running and dripping out of the windows, the embrasures, the cracks in the walls. In the darkness around it hundreds of warriors of all races and levels were standing around. They were waiting. Nick could imagine how curious they were. How curious he would have been himself, if he hadn't known what was behind it. As it was, the sight just made him feel slightly sick.

"I'll go to Ortolan and warn him personally. Even if he is an ass. If he doesn't take me seriously, at least I've tried," he said.

"Or," Victor put in, "we go to the office building and lie in wait. As soon as one of the players turns up, we stop him. And notify the police."

That sounded good. That would work. "Okay," Nick said. "Who's in the Inner Circle at the moment?"

Victor counted them off on his fingers. "Wyrdana, BloodWork, Telkorick, Drizzel, and ... hang on ... Ubangato, a barbarian. Got in at the last tournament. Do you have any idea who they might be in real life?"

"No," said Nick. "But more and more I'm thinking that Colin might be BloodWork."

They set out shortly after six o'clock. Nick sent Adrian a text. Reluctantly, but he had promised him, after all, that he'd keep him up to date. Victor typed a text to Emily, whereupon Nick tried to rip the cell out of his hands.

"Are you crazy? What happens if it's dangerous?"

"I had to promise her. She'll throttle me if I don't notify her now." He pressed Send. "Besides, she has just as much right to be there as you and I. And Adrian."

Blackfriars. They got out of the Underground and set off on their way to Bridewell Place. Emily and Adrian were going to join them there.

It was drizzling, and Nick marched along silently next to Victor, constantly on the lookout for familiar faces. At the same time his thoughts were going in circles. What happened if no one turned up? If it was a false alarm? If the tower wasn't the building in Bridewell Place at all?

They walked up New Bridge Street. At least he'd been smart enough to put on a jacket with a hood so he could hide his ponytail, if not his height. He certainly didn't want to be discovered ahead of time by the gamers.

That's why they wouldn't be able to just stand around in Bridewell Place either. There was a pub farther back, but it only opened at eleven.

"Listen," said Victor when they came within sight of the office building. "You stay here for the moment and wait. Unobtrusively, of course. I'll take a walk and have a look around, since no one knows me."

Victor set off, and Nick didn't take his eyes off the building. The scaffolding obscured his view of the windows—that was a pain. Nick took a closer look. Was something moving up there? Someone? No, he'd just imagined it. And if there actually was someone up there, it would just be a construction worker.

A glance at his watch. Shortly after half past seven. Damn, it could still be forever. He looked up at the scaffolding again—the next minute he nearly jumped out of his skin when a hand landed on his shoulder.

"I said unobtrusive, Mr. Dunmore. You're about as discreet as a lighthouse." Victor stood behind him grinning from ear to ear.

"Did you have to give me such a fright?"

"Oh, come on, don't begrudge a lonely freak a little happiness in his life. Let's go, we need to get a bit closer."

They both watched the entrance for some time without anyone familiar showing up. Then Nick's cell rang, giving him such a shock that he nearly leapt in front of a car.

"Hi, it's me, Emily. Adrian and I are nearby; we're just buying sandwiches. Do you want any?"

"Sandwiches? Now? No thanks."

"I always eat when I'm nervous," she said. "Where are you?"

"Right outside the Soft Suspense building. Victor's here already too. But there's nothing doing yet."

"Perhaps you're too obvious, standing there. See you soon!"

Nick dragged Victor behind a parked delivery van—Emily was right, of course. They just couldn't mess this up.

Emily and Adrian joined them ten minutes later, but still nothing had happened. People were entering the office building all the time, but there weren't any school students among them.

"It's definitely today," Victor insisted. "The Inner Circle has been dispatched, and Nick and I both saw how the tower was bleeding."

Ten more minutes passed. Nothing. Nick's back was beginning to hurt because he had to crouch down behind the delivery van so as not to stick out. Had the Inner Circle suddenly chickened out, now that it was crunch time?

"Here comes Ortolan," Adrian said. He said it quite calmly, but Nick saw his jaw muscle tense and his hands curl into fists.

The warriors of the Inner Circle would have to appear now. Surely it was now or never. But no one was turning up. No one was standing around in one spot for ages. With every minute that passed Nick became more convinced that something wasn't right. Had their approach been too simplistic? Was the location wrong after all? Was someone planting a car bomb on Ortolan's Jag right at this moment?

The thought was just taking shape in his mind when he heard the sound of something breaking. It came from the office building, high up. A windowpane?

Nick stared upward, but he couldn't see anything because of the damned scaffolding ... But there was another breaking sound, no, a banging ...

"We are such idiots," he muttered. "They're in already."

Clang! Not very loud, just enough to be heard above the traffic noise.

They looked at each other, and started running as if someone had issued a command.

They ran across the street, across the forecourt, reached the foyer.

"Slow down now," said Victor. "Otherwise they won't let us past. And take the stairs, not the elevator."

There was gray marble, columns, lots of glass, and a reception desk with a woman who smiled at them. And there was Rashid, in a concealed corner of the foyer, almost invisible as he lurked on a black leather chair.

"Soft Suspense?" Victor asked, and whipped out his press pass.

"Fifth floor. One moment, I'll let them know you're here."

Rashid looked uncertainly at Nick; he obviously hadn't been expecting someone to turn up and cause problems. Then he seemed to come to a decision, jumped up, and ran toward them.

"Kind of you, but you needn't bother," Victor said.

The steps were just over there, and they raced toward them.

Nick didn't hear what the receptionist called after them; the real question was whether Rashid had a gun.

First floor. Nothing unusual so far: no panicky people, no noise. But these were only the offices of the real estate company.

Second floor. Where was Rashid? Nick took a look over his shoulder—there was nothing behind him except a deserted stairwell. But that still didn't reassure him.

They passed the third and fourth floors—business as usual everywhere, and for a moment Nick hoped against all reason that they might really be mistaken, that nothing was going to happen today. He clung to this hope as he ran up the stairs to the fifth floor. They'd hardly gotten there before Rashid blocked their way.

"Stop. This doesn't concern you."

At least he wasn't holding a gun. It was a spray can that he was holding out toward them. Pepper spray.

Rashid's hand was shaking, as was his voice. "Stop, I said. I don't want to hurt you. Stop ... or better still, go back, then no one will get hurt."

When Emily answered, her voice was completely calm. "You don't have to do this, Rashid. Look, you can just go down these stairs and out onto the street. No one will do anything to you. Not us, not the messenger, not any of the other players. I promise you."

Rashid's face twitched. "Be quiet. You've got no idea. Now clear off."

Emily tried a new approach. "If you hurry, you'll be gone before the police arrive. They'll be here soon, I'm afraid, and then you could be in serious trouble."

Rashid's finger moved on the spray nozzle. Nick pulled Emily back.

"We're not threatening you," Nick said quickly. "Exactly the opposite. We're helping you. Run away!"

"But ... then ..."

"But then you'll be kicked out of the game? To be honest, I don't think the game will exist after today."

The hand with the pepper spray sank slightly. "The messenger would kill me."

"Do you see a messenger anywhere here? An orc? A troll? This is the real world, Rashid, and you will really go to prison for really aiding and abetting a real murder!"

Now Rashid let his arm drop limply to his side. Nick thought about jumping Rashid and grabbing the pepper spray from him— but it probably wasn't necessary anymore.

"You're not going to turn me in?" he asked quietly.

"No. Absolutely not."

He threw them one last frightened look and began to go down the stairs, slowly at first, and then faster and faster.

"Rashid!" Nick called after him. "How many are left?"

"Don't know," Rashid called back. "The two guards outside may be gone already. The five from the Inner Circle are definitely in there."

After that they heard only the sound of heavy steps, as though he was taking the stairs two at a time.

"Five people and a few guns," Victor groaned. "We should at least have taken the pepper spray away from that fellow."

Privately Nick agreed, but it was too late now. They pushed open the heavy glass door that separated the stairwell from the offices. There was some sort of reception there, but no receptionist. There was no one walking around in the corridors, and all the office doors were closed.

"How come there's no one here?"

They snuck along the first corridor and cautiously opened a

door. There were two work spaces in there, but no people. The next room? No one either. Nick opened one door after the other, terrified each time that he'd find a pile of bodies behind it.

"Have they all got the day off?" Victor asked.

"I hear something down there," Adrian said. He pointed to the end of the corridor, at a wooden door with brass fittings that was quite different from the modern style of the rest of the offices.

They listened carefully, and there was actually something: a dull thud and a muffled voice shouting something.

"Okay, now we know where they are, at least," Victor observed. "Do we go in? Or do we get the cops?"

Nick made a quick decision. "Adrian, you go into one of the offices and call the police. We'll hold our position here."

After a moment's hesitation Adrian did what Nick had said. Emily, Victor, and Nick grouped themselves around the wooden door.

"Or we could go in and rely on the element of surprise," Victor suggested.

Nick shook his head. "I don't think I want to surprise anyone with a gun in their hand." He pressed an ear against the door; now he heard voices, but couldn't understand what they were saying.

"I wish we had asked Rashid who the people in the Inner Circle are," Emily said, "then we could get a better idea—"

In the middle of Emily's sentence the door flew open and a figure dressed in black burst out. He was wearing a mask over his face—the contorted white face with a gaping mouth from the film *Scream*.

"I'll get water," the mask-wearer called, and stopped abruptly when he spotted Nick, Emily, and Victor. "There are ... people here! Oh shit, where have they suddenly come from?" He turned on his heel and ran back through the still-open door.

"Stay calm," Nick called frantically. Oh god, this was going seriously wrong. There were one ... two ... no, three masked figures with pistols. He was looking straight into the muzzles of two of them. A fourth guy with a devil's mask was doubled up on the floor, groaning. That was Colin, no doubt about it. There was a baseball bat next to him, and it looked very much as though he'd been on the receiving end of a few blows. There must have been a fight; two of the windowpanes were cracked. The fifth person, the one who'd just been going to fetch water, didn't seem to have a weapon, but that was somewhat cold comfort.

"Dunmore," a dark voice behind a skull mask said. "You frigging ass."

Nick fell back a step. He knew the voice, just as he knew her whole massive appearance. Helen. She had her weapon pointed directly at Andrew Ortolan, who was sitting, pale-faced, on his swivel chair, his bound wrists resting on the desk. There were two women and three men lying on the floor with their hands bound behind their backs. One woman was crying softly.

Now Ortolan also looked over to the door. "So who have we here? Reinforcements?" It sounded contemptuous. Nick noted a bloody scrape on his forehead.

"Shut your mouth," Helen barked at him. "And just do what I tell you, or I'll shoot you in the leg!"

The leg was currently located behind the desk, making it a less than ideal target. Ortolan smiled tolerantly.

Don't underestimate her, Nick thought. She will shoot. She's crazy.

"Perhaps you should do what she asks," he said cautiously.

"You shut your mouth too!" Helen bellowed. "And will someone kindly fetch some water now!"

The *Scream* bloke ran off again, pushed past Nick through the door and down the corridor. Hopefully Adrian was smart enough to hide.

Apart from the woman's sobbing everything was quiet. Nick felt the sweat running down the back of his neck. Behind his devil's mask Colin was groaning. The person kneeling next to him was a girl; her Gollum face couldn't conceal that fact. "I think he's a bit better now," she said.

The last of the gang was a youth, very tall and stocky, with fat fingers. He was wearing an alien mask, and didn't look familiar to Nick. What he was holding in his hands looked like a sawed-off shotgun. Despite that, it was Helen who seemed to be pulling the strings. She, more than any other, was the one they had to get along with.

It was only now that Nick noticed she was wearing something around her neck: the symbol of the Inner Circle, red with the tip pointing into the center. She was the only one wearing it; Nick suspected she had made it herself out of thick wire.

Scream came back with the water. He passed the glass to the girl kneeling on the floor without saying a word. So he hadn't seen Adrian.

Colin turned away from Nick, Emily, and Victor when he lifted up the devil's mask. He half sat up, took a few sips of water, and coughed.

"You okay?"

"Yes. Better."

"Good. So, let's continue. Stand up, Ortolan."

He really didn't want to, you could see that. Nick was finding it hard to figure out whether he was scared or not. On both the occasions Nick had watched him, he had seemed more afraid. *He must have sensed that some trouble was brewing around him. But it wasn't tangible. Now it's happened, and he's relaxed.*

"You will pay for your deeds," Helen said. That was obviously her supplied text. "For your greed, for your ruthlessness, your lies."

At a gesture from Helen the thickset alien jumped forward and flung one of the windows open. Straight in front of them was Bridewell Place. And the top plank of the scaffolding.

Ortolan got the message. "I would say I have already paid," he said hastily, "even though I'm neither greedy nor ruthless nor a liar. You know full well all the things you've done to me. It's enough, do you hear?"

Presumably Ortolan, like Nick, would have given a lot to be able to see the reactions on the faces of the masked figures.

"Get out of the window," Helen said. Her gun was pointed at Ortolan. Her voice wasn't shaking, neither was her hand.

"Listen," Victor put in. "We don't know each other, and what I'm going to say now will sound hackneyed, but you're all making a big mistake. What good will it do you if the man falls out the window? You'll go to prison! Leave him in peace, go home!"

The Gollum girl spoke for the first time. "Are you a friend of his? An accomplice?"

"That's crap, I don't even know the guy," Victor yelled. "But I know *Erebos*. And I swear to you that *Erebos* has taken you all for a ride. Whatever the messenger promised you for ... this, you won't get it. Forget it. Leave."

"We've got everything so far," the *Scream* mask said. "Every single time. So don't talk about things you don't understand."

"Exactly," the fat alien added. "You're all nothings. We are the Inner Circle. So get yourself out of that window, Ortolan."

Now the fear in the man's eyes was unmistakable.

"I can't."

"Then I'll have to shoot," said Helen. She lifted the gun and fired; the bullet narrowly missed him and went into the wall.

"All right!" Ortolan bellowed. "I'll do it. I'll do it, okay? Don't shoot again."

The woman on the floor was crying more loudly now; hopefully she wouldn't make any of the Inner Circle nervous. Nick himself was dizzy with nerves. Somebody was bound to have heard the shot and would turn up soon to find out what was going on—and that could make everything even worse.

Andrew Ortolan climbed onto the windowsill. The window was tall, but he was taller, and had to duck down in order to fit through. With his hands bound he was finding it hard to hold on. He looked back pleadingly into the office.

"Farther," said Helen.

"No, please."

She lifted her gun again, and the alien followed suit.

"It wouldn't have to be a perfect shot; just a graze would do for takeoff," the alien bawled.

Now Ortolan was standing on the windowsill; he climbed up, left leg first, onto the somewhat higher plank of the scaffold.

Climb across it and then down, Nick thought. That would have to work. You'll reach the street in one piece if you keep your nerve.

But Ortolan's legs were shaking. He was clinging to the window frame with his hands; you could tell he knew exactly what he needed to do. Change his grip, grab hold of the metal scaffolding pole. But it seemed he couldn't bring himself to do it.

"No calling for help, otherwise something will go bang," the alien said.

Ortolan's bound hands scrabbled for the pole like a crab's pincers. It was torture to watch him crawling across onto the scaffold with a chalk-white face and cramped limbs.

Just at the moment when he'd made it and was kneeling

somewhat less precariously on his plank, Nick heard a sound behind him. Adrian had rejoined them.

The sight of him triggered a series of reactions.

"You?" Ortolan panted, and nearly lost his hold.

Helen, obviously equally surprised, lowered her weapon briefly. "What are you doing here?" she barked at him. "Get lost."

"You're going to let him run off?" Colin asked behind his devil's mask. "Have you gone crazy?"

The gun swung around to him. "Quiet. He's off limits."

"Who says that?"

"The messenger. Who do you think?"

If they started to fight, Nick would take the chance, and run for it with Emily, Adrian, and Victor.

"Did you call the police?" he whispered in Adrian's direction. He didn't get an answer. Adrian's attention was entirely focused on the man on the scaffolding.

"Good morning, Mr. Ortolan."

At the sight of Adrian, Ortolan had clutched the pole even tighter. "Are you behind all this?" he asked.

"No." Adrian walked up to the window and looked down. "It's a long way down."

"You're kidding." For a moment Ortolan's rage won the upper hand. "Tell these masked losers that they should let me back in."

"Why should they listen to me?"

"Because you've got something to do with it. Don't treat me like an idiot. I only have to look at what the girl has around her neck, and it's obvious!"

Adrian turned to Helen, saw what Ortolan meant, and walked up to her without hesitation. He reached for the symbol of the Inner Circle and studied it. "Why are you wearing this?"

410

"Back off, you don't understand!" Adrian's proximity was making it difficult for her to keep Ortolan in her sights.

"You made that yourself, didn't you? But why?"

"Because I'm in the Inner Circle and that's its symbol." She pushed Adrian aside; it was a gesture that looked almost apologetic, but at the same time had enough force to send him reeling backward through the room. Emily caught him before he fell.

"Actually," he said, "it's the logo of Vay too far. My father's company."

"Exactly," Ortolan said. The word ended in a shout, because a gust of wind was buffeting the scaffolding and making the brackets rattle.

The wind also carried a sound. Sirens. Was it police cars? Quite possibly, and they were coming closer. Ortolan's face showed relief.

"Jump," said Helen.

"Pardon?"

"I said, jump."

She walked closer to the window, lifted the gun, and pointed the muzzle at Ortolan's chest. "Jump or I'll shoot you off."

The sirens came closer; the alien and the Gollum girl exchanged frantic looks.

"We should get out of here," the girl said. "Someone's called the police. Let's go, people, quick!"

"Jump now, you ass," said Helen behind her skull mask.

The image burned itself indelibly into Nick's memory. As if death itself had spoken.

"Your friends are right; the police are on the way." Fear was forcing Ortolan's voice higher. "They're going to catch you committing a murder, do you understand? If you shoot, you're a murderer. You'll go to prison for the rest of your life." He couldn't take his eyes off the gun. Helen was standing so close that if she squeezed the trigger she'd certainly hit him and he would certainly fall—dead or alive. He was talking for his life.

The effect of his words on one of the five mask-wearers was already obvious. *Scream* had edged closer and closer to the door, and now he raced off. The alien and Gollum looked as though they'd really like to follow him. They only had the two groups—those standing and those lying on the floor—covered half-heartedly now.

Victor must have noticed that. "Just go," he encouraged both of them. "And know what? I'll tell you a secret: The game is over. It won't matter in the slightest what you do now; the messenger won't reward you. But some court will punish you. *Erebos* is all over, it's—"

"Shut your mouth, you don't even know what you're talking about!" Helen screamed. Her gun was pointed at Victor for a few seconds, until she remembered her actual orders and got Ortolan back in her sights. "Jump!" she bellowed, and took another step toward him.

For a moment it looked as though he was going to obey. He took a look down, as if he was trying to estimate the height, or his chances of reaching solid ground by climbing. Then Adrian put himself between Helen and the window.

Victor and Nick jumped forward at the same time, and checked themselves at almost the same time too. Helen had to remain calm; she simply mustn't shoot now.

"Move away, Adrian," Nick said.

Adrian didn't budge. Nick saw that Helen was getting nervous; she was leaning from one side to the other so she could get a better aim at Ortolan again. But she didn't lower her gun.

"You're not going to shoot at Adrian, are you?" Nick asked. "None of this insanity is his fault." A siren interrupted him.

Now Gollum and the alien were making off. Nick only saw it out of the corner of his eye; they bolted as if they'd only just realized how serious the situation was.

"No," Colin screamed after them. "Don't leave me here! Take me with you, you cowardly bastards!" He tried to stand up, screamed with pain, and collapsed back onto the floor. The devil's mask slipped a bit, revealing his dark skin.

"Mr. Ortolan," Adrian said. "Tell everyone here how you tried to steal *Elysium* from my father. If you don't, I will step aside."

"Why doesn't someone finally take the gun away from the nutter?" Ortolan shouted. "It just can't be that difficult!"

Tires squealed in front of the building. Blue lights flickered on the wall of the building opposite.

"I'm up here!" screeched Ortolan. "Here! Get me down!"

He turned back to the open window. "That's enough, I'm coming back in. Enough of this madness!"

Adrian stepped aside just as he'd said he would; Helen's muzzle was now aimed directly at Ortolan's head.

"No! Please!" He ducked down on the scaffolding, started to sway, cried out, and steadied himself again.

"Say it," Adrian repeated.

"What for? No court in the world would allow it. I'm being threatened!"

"That's not what matters to me. Say it. We both know that it's true."

There was a commotion in front of the building. Someone called out something in a commanding tone, car doors slammed. The tied-up office workers moved around restlessly. Nick prayed that none of them would lose their nerve; Helen's patience seemed to be exhausted. Sweat was dripping out from under her skull mask and down her neck. Nick could feel her mounting rage as if it were his own.

Adrian had put himself in front of Ortolan again, and looked at him.

"Your father was a bloody genius," Ortolan cried, "with no idea about business. We could have set the industry on fire, but he just had to do everything by himself."

"Did you steal his program?"

"Yes! Yes, I damned well did! And I did the right thing, you hear me?"

"You blackmailed him? Robbed him? Terrorized him?"

"Yes, if you want to put it like that. But it didn't work, okay? I never found a complete version of *Elysium* anywhere. Nothing I could do anything with. So get a grip on yourself."

Adrian turned around. "Helen, let him go."

"No, I'll let him fall, nothing else. Out of the way."

Adrian didn't budge. Helen put her death's head to one side. "I'm really sorry," she said, and gave him a punch that sent him right across the room to the opposite wall.

Nick and Victor reacted at the same time—they jumped on Helen from behind—Victor pushed her to the floor with his weight, while Nick tried to get at the hand that held the gun.

Helen fought them off with all her strength. "Let go of me! I'm the last warrior who can win the battle!"

"There's no battle," Nick gasped. "There's no messenger, and no more orders. Stop it, Helen! Please!"

"Traitor!" she screamed.

Then something went bang right next to Nick, so loud that at first he thought he must now be dead. Shot dead. The next second he realized that Helen's bullet had only hit the wall, but the shock had made him loosen his grip. Helen twisted around and shot at Ortolan, who was in the process of clambering back through the window into the office.

414

She hit him in the side. For a moment he stood there, as if frozen in position, half inside, half outside, then he slowly collapsed backward.

Nick saw a leaping black shadow rush toward Ortolan and grab his arm. Victor. He dragged the man over the windowsill into the office, and laid him on the floor. Blood was coloring Ortolan's shirt red.

"Did it," Helen panted behind the mask. "I knew it would work."

The shock that had paralyzed Nick's brain was dispersing, but it still took a few heartbeats before he had his body under control again. He ripped the gun out of Helen's hand and gave it to Victor.

"What do we do now? Look how he's bleeding ... We need an ambulance."

One of the two tied-up men held his hands up. "Cut the tape, and I'll see to his injury. Quickly!"

Nick did what the man said. He felt peculiar, a bit dizzy. As if he was about to keel over. "We need an ambulance," he repeated.

Sitting down was suddenly a good idea. Black and white dots were dancing in front of Nick's eyes; the black ones were multiplying. He groped his way to the next available chair, bent over, and waited for the faintness to pass.

When he looked up again, Helen was sitting next to him. She was studying her hands. Someone should hold her down, Nick thought. But she wasn't running away.

Footsteps on the stairs. One of the elevators was humming too. Help was on the way, for some of them at least. For others ...

"Helen?" he asked, and took her skull mask off, revealing her broad, sweat-soaked but contented face.

"Don't call me Helen," she said. "I am BloodWork."

Police, doctors, paramedics. The office was full of people who were all talking at once. First of all, they carried the injured Ortolan out and attended to Colin, who had suspected broken ribs and possibly a ruptured spleen. Ortolan had snatched the baseball bat away from him and dealt him several blows to the stomach, one of the employees told them. Nick was amazed that Helen hadn't shot Ortolan dead straightaway because of it—perhaps it was because she had never been able to stand Colin.

Before they carried him away, Colin called out to Nick, who leaned down to him. Colin grabbed his hand.

"Will you testify for me, Nick? They're going to prosecute me and lump me in with Helen. But I would never have fired; I'd chosen the bat specially. Please."

Nick found it hard not to pull his hand away. "It's ... too soon now. Maybe. Yes. Please let go."

"It wasn't me with Jamie either. I swear."

"I know," Nick said.

They carried Colin to the ambulance and Nick accompanied the policeman to the station for questioning.

It's easy to let go, once you have made the decision to do it. I look around and I feel like laughing. All this will soon be in the past, and I myself will only be a memory—painful for some, awkward for others.

My work is finished. I won't ever find out what happens now. How fortunate. That way I will not be tempted to intervene, to change the course of events.

Countless possibilities exist in the future, waiting to happen. I feel no curiosity. If curiosity were present, would I stay? I don't know. I'm tired. That, too, makes it easy to let go.

416

THIRTY-THREE

Through the sheeting rain the Whittington Hospital looked like a massive gray-brown hulk. Nick had pulled his hood down over his forehead, but he was getting wet anyway. He'd stowed the small package with Jamie's favorite chocolate safely in the inside pocket of his rain jacket.

The room was on the third floor. As he stood outside the door, Nick felt the overwhelming desire to turn tail and leave.

"He's awake," Mr. Watson had said. "But he's not really well yet." No one had asked for details.

Nick knocked. Knocked again. No answer. He opened the door, full of foreboding.

Two beds: one was empty; Jamie lay in the other. He looked small. Fragile. Nick took a deep breath.

"Hi, Jamie. It's me, Nick. I heard you're a bit better, so I thought I'd drop in."

Jamie didn't move. His head was turned toward the wall. One half was shaved, similar to Kate's, except that in Jamie's case there was a scar across the bare patch.

"I brought you something." Nick pulled the package out of his jacket and slowly approached. Now he could see Jamie's face as well. He was lying there with his mouth half open, staring at the wall.

So it was true. Something was choking Nick right above his vocal cords. He looked away quickly.

"Emily says hello. She's going to come and visit you soon too. A lot's happened in the last few weeks."

Jamie's rigid stare was still fixed on the wall, although Nick thought he had seen a muscle twitch in his face. Perhaps it had just been his imagination.

"Jamie, I'd really like to know how you're doing. I'm incredibly sorry I was such a shit to you that day. I've wished thousands of times that I'd behaved differently. But the game is over; perhaps that will please you. Not just for me—it's completely over."

Was Jamie smiling? No.

"If you can hear me, if you can understand just one word of what I'm saying, then do something. Please! Blink, or wiggle your toes—anything."

Was he responding? Was he actually responding? Nick bit his lip as he watched Jamie push his right hand infinitely slowly over the bedcovers, raise it a bit, and stretch his fingers up.

"Well done, Jamie, that's great," Nick stammered. "You'll get better, I know you will."

Jamie's hand hung in the air. His fingers twitched. Then he bent them over, one by one, except the middle finger. Turned his head, looked at Nick, and grinned.

"Cox, you silly bugger, you scared me to death!" Nick yelled, and had to restrain himself from punching Jamie in the ribs, or at least flinging his arms around his neck. "You're better, huh? Boy, am I glad. I really thought you were ... gone."

"Me, better? Are you daft? I've got a headache like nothing on earth, and you have no idea how brilliant a broken hip feels." Jamie laughed, but at the same time screwed his eyes up in pain. "But I'm getting amazing pills for it. It was almost worth it just for that."

"Idiot. I saw you lying on the road and thought you were dead. I'll never get the picture out of my head."

418

Jamie was grinning shamelessly again. "Send me a print of it."

It turned out he remembered everything, apart from the two days before the accident. His anger over the game was unabated.

"It's not running anymore," Nick said. "None of the gamers can log in. After the battle was lost, it turned dark on everyone at the same time. It's over. Full stop. End of story. A few people are still totally messed up because of it."

"How can that be? Did someone turn off the server?"

"No." Nick had to remind himself that Jamie had no idea what *Erebos* had been, and all the things it had been capable of. "It was a really remarkable game. It could read, and it could understand what it read. My theory is that it was searching the Internet the whole time the battle was on and waiting for the announcement that—how can I put it—its enemy was dead. The announcement didn't come. There was a different one instead. At which point it turned itself off."

Jamie looked impressed. "Far out!"

"Yes."

Jamie's pale face became thoughtful. Was it too early to tell him the whole truth? No, Nick thought. The sooner it's behind us the better.

"Listen," he said. "Your accident actually wasn't one. Someone disconnected your brakes. That's why you tore into the intersection like a bat out of hell." He took a breath. "I know who did it. If you want, I'll tell you."

There was disbelief written all over Jamie's face. He opened his mouth, closed it again, and turned his face to the wall.

"I can't remember the accident. Or the days before it. I'd really like to know what went on." He felt for the scar on his head. "Did this game have anything to do with it?"

"Yes."

"Got it. I'll think about it. Perhaps I'll want to know a bit later on." He gave a crooked grin. "But I would like to know whether it's likely that I'll bump into that person in the schoolyard and give them half my sandwich out of the goodness of my heart?"

Nick shook his head. "No."

Brynne really had changed schools. She hadn't gone to the police, as far as Nick knew.

"How long do you have to stay here?" he asked.

"It could still be a while. After that I have to go into rehab to join all the other old ladies who've broken their hips. Can't wait to see how they like my hairdo."

Jamie's brain, joke center included, was unscathed. Nick felt like bursting into song.

"When you're back on your feet, I must introduce you to someone. You'll get along well."

"A girl?"

"Not exactly. But someone with a similar sense of humor who drinks even more tea than you."

Nick had another appointment in his calendar in two days' time. Emily had organized it because she thought it would be good to bring some resolution to things. "It's hard for lots of people," she said. "The game broke off so abruptly that it left a gaping hole."

Nick, who still remembered the gaping hole in his own life, agreed. Besides, there was an entirely practical consideration: a plan he could only carry out jointly with the other ex-gamers.

With Mr. Watson's help they'd booked the meeting room in a youth center, and put up notices at all the schools where they knew, or at least suspected, that there were gamers.

But he still hadn't expected such a crowd. When he walked into the meeting room, all the chairs had long since been taken, and lots of people were sitting on the floor. He tried to count how many were present, but gave up before he got to half. At any rate it was more than 150. They were going to have to open the windows soon, despite the cold November evening, if they wanted to get enough air.

Nick went and stood up at the front and waited till most of the conversations had subsided.

"Hi," he said. "I'm Nick Dunmore. Lots of you know me from school. I played *Erebos*, like you, and I loved it, honest. But it's a good thing that the game is over, all the same—you'll just have to take my word on that for now. Before I explain to you what was really behind it, I think I should introduce myself properly. The rules don't apply anymore. So, in the game I was Sarius, a dark elf, and I was thrown out as an Eight."

A few people laughed. "Sarius, hey, really? You were Sarius?"

Straightaway there were people wanting to kick off with their own stories, experiences, and anecdotes—Nick had difficulty applying the brakes.

"Hang on! First we need to discuss something important. Listen, you've probably all read about what happened in the paper. Ortolan wasn't a monster; he was an actual person. Not a nice person, but still a person. He's going to be released from the hospital in a few days, and he'll probably just carry on exactly as before." They were listening to him—excellent. "The sole aim of *Erebos* was to get back at Mr. Ortolan for one of his dirty tricks. It didn't work. On the one hand that's a good thing; but on the other hand he shouldn't be allowed to just get off scot-free."

A few people nodded; most just looked as if it were all double Dutch to them.

"So here's what needs to happen," Nick continued. "I know you've all carried out 'real' orders. I'd like to collate them, especially those that don't have anything to do with people at your school. Think of all the ones where you wondered why you were doing them and who was going to benefit from them, and write them down. If you took pictures, scans, or copies that you've still got, give them to me."

Now they were looking at him suspiciously.

"No one is going to use them against you, promise. But we're going to try to use them against Ortolan if it turns out he's got skeletons in his closet. Which I'm pretty sure he has. We'll meet again here in a week's time, okay? And now I'd really like to know who you all were."

It was as if the floodgates had opened. Nick tried to insist on people speaking in order, but soon everyone was talking at once. Everybody wanted to tell his story and find out who was behind the warriors they'd had dealings with during the game. Nick gave up trying to play the moderator, and mingled with the others.

Little groups quickly formed, but some people were left standing alone, like Rashid. Unlike the members of the Inner Circle, he hadn't been caught, but Nick could see how uneasy he was. He was still afraid that someone would talk.

Nick walked up to him and smiled. "I've been wondering for ages who you were. Blackspell?"

Rashid gave an embarrassed shrug. "I still think it's weird when we talk about our player characters. It just doesn't feel right."

"Oh, stop it. Come on, tell me. Blackspell?"

A tiny smile stole across Rashid's lips. "Missed! I was Nurax."

"The werewolf! I wouldn't have guessed that. How was it playing as a werewolf? Cool?"

They chatted about the advantages of the different species, about the adventures they'd shared, and the ones they'd had by themselves. Others joined them, talked about their player characters and experiences—the meeting room buzzed like a beehive.

Nick was working his way through the crowd, looking for the players he'd met most often. He wanted to know who Sapujapu and Xohoo were, or Galaris, whose name had been written on the wooden box. At some point, Aisha tapped him on the shoulder from behind.

"Hi, Sarius. You know you totally surprised me? I thought you were LordNick. That's what most people thought."

"I know," he sighed. "I'd really like to meet him and ask him what he was thinking. Let me know if you find him, huh?"

She gave him an offended look. "And you're not interested in who I was?"

I'd be more interested in finding out whether you're going to clear up that harassment business. "Yes, of course I am," he said. "Do we know each other?"

"Oh yes," she said, and smiled. "But we couldn't stand each other. You did me out of two levels in the Arena."

"Feniel?"

"Exactly."

After two hours Nick had gathered an impressive list of equations, and this time all of them were correct. Jerome had been behind Blackspell, and the quiet boy, Greg, had been disguised as LaCor, another vampire. Xohoo turned out to be Martin Garibaldi, whom Nick had seen pleading with a friend on the day after his elimination. Nick swallowed his disappointment. He'd hoped that Xohoo might become a friend in real life.

A bit later on he also found Sapujapu, who didn't bear the slightest resemblance to a dwarf. He was a tall, lanky guy named Eliott, who was just doing his last year at school and wanted to study English Lit after that. They exchanged cell numbers, talked about films and music, and it turned out that Eliott was also a fan of Hell Froze Over.

"I haven't got my fan shirt anymore, unfortunately," he sighed. "I sacrificed it for an *Erebos* level. No idea what for."

Nick could hardly breathe, he was laughing so hard. It took a while to enlighten Eliott.

"Hey, good excuse to go out for a drink soon and do some ax-grinding together," Eliott joked, and added that Nick bore an astonishing resemblance to LordNick.

"I know," Nick said, fed up. "I'd like to know myself who borrowed my face."

Someone behind him cleared his throat. "I think I may be able to help there."

He turned around. Dan, Freak One.

"Aha. And who was it?"

Dan looked at the ground, embarrassed. "Don't spread it around, okay? I'm pretty sure it was Alex. He ... admires you. Has done for the last couple of years. For a while he was trying to imitate you, did you notice? No? Well, anyway, I did." Dan scratched his rear. "When a Nick Dunmore clone turned up just after I gave Alex the game, I thought of him at once."

Who says it wasn't actually you? "Why are you telling me this?"

Dan scratched himself harder. "Well, Alex is my best friend. And it really upsets him, the way you always call him a freak. I thought if I told you he was a fan of yours then you'd be nicer to him. He didn't want to come himself. He was too embarrassed, which also supports my theory."

Nick found Dan's account oddly moving. He'd imagined all sorts of motives for LordNick's existence, but admiration hadn't been one of them.

"And you?" he asked Dan. "Who were you?"

"Uh-oh." Dan grinned. "This isn't exactly going to win me

bonus points. I was Lelant, and I'm really sorry, but I can't give your wish crystal back to you anymore."

Lots of things were cleared up, but not all. Nick didn't find out who Aurora was, the cat woman who'd died in the labyrinth in the fight with the scorpion. But a thin, pale girl with glasses in the Upper Sixth was the player behind Galaris. She hadn't had any more idea about the contents of the box than Nick; she'd just taken it from one place to another. Tyrania, the barbarian with the extra-short skirt, had been the shy girl, Michelle. She'd also supplied the pills with which Nick was supposed to poison Mr. Watson. Michelle had stolen them out of her grandfather's medicine cupboard. Without being caught, because Grandpa always hoarded two lots at home. Just in case. Henry Scott, Nick's own novice, had transformed himself into Bracco, the lizard man.

"Who were the people in the Inner Circle?" a plump Asian girl asked Nick later in the evening, when most people were getting ready to leave.

"Helen was BloodWork," Nick said. "She's having a really tough time of it at the moment. Mr. Watson says she's having psychiatric treatment."

"What about Wyrdana and Drizzel?"

Nick didn't know Wyrdana's real name. He always just thought of her as Gollum. She was from another school, as were *Scream* and the alien. One of the two must have been the person who tried to throw Nick in front of the train—but it didn't matter anymore which one. He felt the same way as Jamie did about the person who sabotaged his brakes.

"Drizzel was probably Colin," Nick said. "Do you know him? Tall, dark, plays basketball."

And was once a friend of mine.

THIRTY-FOUR

It was the first weekend in ages when Nick just wanted to relax. In peace and quiet. Sleep. Go to a movie with Emily.

Unfortunately, Victor didn't think much of that plan at all. He'd had an idea he just couldn't be talked out of. They argued for almost half an hour on the phone.

"That's just stupid."

"Absolutely not. It's the right thing to do."

"You'll really mess Adrian up."

"I don't think so."

Nick struggled for words. "Besides, it won't work."

"Yes, it will. I've tested it out already."

"Well, go right ahead then. But I don't want to be part of it."

Victor obviously hadn't expected that. "Oh, come on. We should all be there; I think we owe it to Adrian. Emily says she's coming."

In the end Nick gave in. Mainly because of Emily, if he was honest. But he didn't have a good feeling about it at all.

Victor had outdone himself. Three sorts of tea in three different teapots, cookies, and slices of pizza. They lounged around in the sofa room, talking and eating. Emily had visited Colin in hospital. He was going to have to face charges, as were Helen and the other members of the Inner Circle.

"We may be summoned as witnesses," Emily said. "The problem

is the game's not running anymore. It will be hard for the judge to figure out what really happened."

"On the other hand," Nick said, "hundreds of people can tell him. They all saw it and experienced it."

"Except for me," Adrian said quietly.

Victor couldn't have asked for a better cue. "That's true. The whole multi-player bit is over. I'm really sorry about that, but I don't actually think you would have liked a lot of things about it. However, there's something else you should see."

He pulled Adrian up from the sofa and led him into the computer room. He'd placed the best office chair in front of the biggest screen.

"Have a seat."

Adrian's face was a big question mark.

"The beginning still works fine," Victor said, pulling up a stool and sitting down next to Adrian.

Nick and Emily followed suit; they made a little semicircle around Adrian, as if to protect him.

Victor turned on the screen.

The forest clearing. Pale moonlight. The nameless figure in the middle, huddled on the ground.

As if in a trance, Adrian took the mouse and rotated the viewpoint.

"I know that place. It's near the Wye Valley," he said. "Look, behind there, the tree with the fork near the ground. We always wedged the backpack in there when we went for picnics."

He led his nameless figure over to the tree, stopped him. Made him bend down and pick up something that looked like a blue-painted piece of wood. Nick saw a single tear run down Adrian's face.

"What's that?"

"My pocket knife. I lost it up there when I was seven, and I howled for the rest of the day."

Nick and Emily exchanged a look. This could be tougher than they had imagined. Emily laid her hand on Adrian's shoulder.

Nameless located a path that led away from the clearing—more like a track that kept petering out between the trees. But Adrian knew where he was going, Nick realized. He stopped only occasionally to orient himself, but was conserving his stamina intuitively. After a short time he came to a small stream, where he made Nameless pause again.

"This is where we once ... There it is," Adrian whispered. At first Nick didn't know what he meant, then he spotted two glowing dots in the dark, and shortly thereafter the whole animal.

"You saw a fox here?"

Adrian nodded. It wasn't long before the fox slipped away, disappearing between the bushes.

Nameless continued on, along the stream. At a point where three stones formed something like a small bridge, he crossed it. The path led downhill there, and Nick felt the strong urge to drag Adrian away from the computer—he could already see the flickering of the fire.

The dead man was not sitting down this time, and he wasn't staring into the flames. He was standing upright and looking expectantly at Adrian's Nameless.

"Adrian?"

"Dad," Adrian whispered.

Nick saw how Adrian's hand clenched the mouse. Nameless swayed and stood still.

"You took our path. Tell me whether you are Adrian."

Adrian put his hands on the keyboard.

"Yes. I am."

The dead man smiled. "That's good. I hoped you would come when everything was over."

"Should we leave the room?" Nick asked.

Adrian shook his head. Several times he made as if to type, but seemed not to know how he should begin.

"How are you?" he typed finally.

"My plan has failed. If I were still around to see it, I would probably be very angry."

A sound between a snort and a laugh came out of Adrian's mouth.

"I'm angry too. At you. Why did you do it?"

"Do what?"

Adrian's fingers were almost flying over the keys.

"Well, what do you think? You just deserted us! Do you know how awful it was? Mom was under sedation for days—she found you. You didn't even leave us a letter. Nothing. Why?"

For the first time it seemed that the dead man hesitated.

"I wouldn't have known what to write. *Erebos* was finished, and everything was perfect. I'd created something unique. You can see how good it is, can't you? All that could possibly follow was battles, court cases, probably prison, a life in ruins. *Erebos* was perfect, but I wasn't. I was disgusted by everything on the outside."

"You didn't even know what was on the outside anymore," Adrian wrote. Tears streamed down his face, and he let them fall, as if he didn't notice. "You didn't go out for almost two years."

"Yes. I couldn't bear the world anymore. All that coincidence and unpredictability. That is why I withdrew from it, but I left *Erebos* behind. The best thing I ever created."

"The most brutal thing you ever created. A friend of mine is lying in hospital, and nearly died. A few of my classmates may have to go to prison because they tried to kill Ortolan. Dad? You knew something like that would happen, didn't you?"

"I left things open."

"How could you do that? They're not much older than I am, and they've got nothing to do with your revenge plans."

The dead man sat down on a rock by the fire.

"*Erebos* was the coin I tossed. By the time it was spinning in the air I was already gone. The players always had a choice; they could stop at any time. They all had to pass by me at the start, and I warned them. Every single one."

The spark flew up and reflected in Larry McVay's green eyes, the eyes that were so similar to his son's.

"Those who had scruples were saved. Those who were left I used. But they had a fair chance, like everyone else."

Nick remembered how close he had been to poisoning Mr. Watson. Then he thought of Helen's contented, sweaty face, and felt like howling.

"Nothing about it was fair, Dad. You influenced them, you changed them and exploited them for a revenge that you weren't even going to witness."

The dead man shook his head slowly.

"I warned them all."

"You didn't really warn them, Dad. Not in a way they would believe, did you?"

"I warned them."

Adrian's fingers slipped from the keyboard.

A gust of wind pushed back the dead man's hood and tousled his sparse blond hair. There was a pause. Adrian didn't take his eyes off his father's face for a second. It was as though a wordless dialogue was taking place between the two that the others couldn't follow. Then a shudder ran through Adrian's body.

"Let's get one thing straight. You didn't do this for me. I don't agree with it, and I don't understand how you could ask me to circulate the game."

A smile played on Larry McVay's lips.

"No blame is attached to you. Don't reproach yourself."

"I'm not! I'm reproaching you. You thought of me like a character in one of your games."

The dead man averted his gaze, looked into the fire.

"I protected you."

Adrian gave a laugh.

"If you had wanted to protect me you wouldn't have killed yourself. That was cowardly, Dad. So cowardly!"

"I'm sorry. But I can't change that now."

"No. Or make up for it."

"No."

Adrian lifted a hand from the keyboard, and for a moment Nick thought he was going to stroke the screen where the dead man's brow was. But Adrian checked his movement and let his arm fall.

"Dad?"

"Yes?"

"You actually prepared everything that you're saying to me now specially, in case I came. You thought about how you would answer my questions, depending on how the game turned out. Is that true?"

"Yes."

"When?"

"Do you mean which day?"

"Yes."

"It was the 12th of September, at 1:46 a.m."

Emily drew Adrian close as he gave a loud sob and hid his face in his hands. She held him for more than a minute while the dead man kept looking at them from the screen with the same friendly smile.

McVay had hanged himself on September 13, Nick recalled. Very shortly afterward.

"He could still have changed it then. Everything, he could have changed everything," Adrian whispered.

He took the tissue Victor offered him and blew his nose without averting his gaze from his father's face. His hands found their way back to the keyboard.

"The game was more important to you than we were, wasn't it? Ortolan was more important to you."

"I'm sorry."

"You didn't say good-bye, Dad. That was almost the worst thing for me. That you didn't leave a message."

"I'm sorry."

"I missed you so much. The two years before as well."

"I'm sorry."

It seemed that the dead man had come to the central theme of his message. Adrian nodded mutely. Again they looked at each other for a long time. It took a little while for Nick to realize that only one of them was really looking, but that didn't make it any more bearable. The fire crackled and the wind rustled in the treetops of the forest where Larry McVay and his son Adrian had long ago encountered a fox.

"Farewell, Dad."

"Are you going now?"

"I think so. Yes."

"Farewell, Adrian. Look after yourself."

The dead man smiled, lifted his hand, and waved. Adrian waved back. Then he turned the computer off, collapsed against Emily's shoulder, and cried himself to sleep.

The festive season had London firmly in its glittering grasp. Illuminated Christmas trees, snowflakes, candles, and stars lit up the shopping streets; in each and every store, customers were blasted with "Jingle Bells" and "Last Christmas."

Nick and Emily had arranged to meet in Muffinski's in Covent Garden. When he arrived, she was already there.

Her greeting was wordless and tender. Nick would never get used to the fact that he and Emily were together; every time they kissed he almost drowned in a wave of happiness.

"I've got good news," he said, and pushed the hair off her forehead. "Yesterday I got a whole new stack of material the exes have collected. There are notes on a conversation between Ortolan and a certain Tom Garsh, in which Garsh is being given clear instructions by Ortolan about burgling the offices of a competitor."

"Sounds good."

"Apart from that, we've got photos showing Ortolan and Garsh together. Victor checked it out: Garsh has been in jail three times already for burglary."

"Okay, but it's still not proof."

"No. But things are stacking up."

They ordered coffee and muffins. Judy Garland was singing "Have Yourself a Merry Little Christmas."

"Do you know what your photo assignment that time in the parking garage was about?" Emily asked.

"I think it was just the fact that the lady at Ortolan's side wasn't his wife. But we can't do anything much with the photos now; his wife has already left him. I think *Erebos*'s revenge plan has come true, at least in part."

"Yes," Emily said. "But he's still alive, at least."

"Yes, he is."

When they set off, it was just starting to snow lightly. They wandered through the streets arm in arm, stopped occasionally, kissed, laughed, walked on.

"I still haven't gotten a Christmas present for Victor," Emily declared as they were looking at the window of a comic book shop, where coffee mugs were displayed alongside the magazines and figures. "Did you see the one back there?" She pointed to a yellow mug with round indentations in it that looked as though someone had fashioned it from Swiss cheese.

"Bingo," said Nick. "He'll love it."

Emily invested five pounds in the yellow monstrosity. "Do you want one too?" she asked, grinning. "Or would you prefer a gift certificate for a haircut?"

Nick took her by the shoulders and pretended to shake her. "I've already got my present," he said, when they were outside again.

"No, you haven't."

He placed his hand under Emily's braid and left it there. He couldn't feel it, of course—how would he? "To me, it was a present," he said. "The nicest one you could give me. Better than a ring."

She smiled at him. "Yes, and much harder to lose."

"Exactly." He bent his head to her, pushed her hair to one side, and kissed the raven on her nape.

Acknowledgments

I would like to thank ...

... first of all, Ruth Löbner. She is the official godmother of this book, a true friend, and quite simply a gift from heaven. Without her, *Erebos* wouldn't be what it is (and quite possibly wouldn't be finished). She supported me through the writing, motivated me, and always said, "Stop!" at the right moment. In actual fact, she deserves her own Loebner Prize—not for artificial intelligence, but for every other type.

... Wulf Dorn, another godsend in my life, for the years spent sailing together on the same wavelength, for repeated encouragement, and for manuscript comments that were as perceptive as they were merciless. In short, for his friendship.

... my agents Roman Hocke and Dr. Uwe Neumahr of AVA International for their great support and dedication.

... my editors Susanne Bertels and Ruth Nikolay for their keen eyes and for the enthusiasm they brought to *Erebos*.

... the members of the Montségur Authors' Forum for a virtual writing home, and for countless suggestions and tips.

... and last but not least my parents, for many things, but above all a childhood full of books.

–U.P.

URSULA POZNANSKI started writing when she was seven or eight years old. She was fortunate in that she had teachers who encouraged her, and loving relatives who would read her essays to everybody who hadn't managed to escape in time. She found it quite embarrassing, but it did not deter her from writing.

Ursula's interests include photography, music (although she doesn't play an instrument, she has not given up hope that she may still do so one day), talking to interesting people, and traveling. She lives in Vienna, Austria, with her partner and daughter.

JUDITH PATTINSON was born in Melbourne and at an early age her reading transported her (in spirit) to the other side of the world—to chalets with flower boxes and hay-filled attics, and hikes through the Swiss Alps. As a consequence she couldn't wait to study European languages, which she did in Australia and on the shores of Lake Constance in Germany. She has remained in love with German and reading ever since.

Judith has worked as a translator, production editor, web designer, and bookseller; her early working life included stints in a shoebox factory, as a London barmaid, and as a checkout girl in her grandparents' grocery stores.

Lowell School
1640 Kalmia Road, NW
Washington, DC 20012